SONS

OF

LIBERTY

A Novel by

MATTHEW SPEISER

Black Rose Writing | Texas

ISBN: 978-1-68513-108-1
PUBLISHED BY BLACK ROSE WRITING
www.blackrosewriting.com

Printed in the United States of America
Suggested Retail Price (SRP) $23.95

Sons of Liberty is printed in Bookman Old Style

*As a planet-friendly publisher, Black Rose Writing does its best to eliminate unnecessary waste to reduce paper usage and energy costs, while never compromising the reading experience. As a result, the final word count vs. page count may not meet common expectations.

To Nate and Teddy, for their love of a good story.
And to Phoebe, for making our life together
the best story that it ever could be.

SONS
OF
LIBERTY

PROLOGUE

Prince William County, Virginia – November

1805

Patience, Ulysses thought.

Patience.

He was crouched at the roadside, tucked behind the winter chickweed – waiting, watching. Until there it was: straight from the west, where the wheat fields reigned. It was one of the new buckboards, locked in place by frozen grooves, yellow paint on all sides, a frontward axle for steering. The driver was slouched, reins draped lazily over his wrist, while his partner chewed violently on tobacco, spilling it over his chin in fits, brown and gold and mixed with phlegm.

Ulysses thumbed his pistol.

Cato was right there at his side, balanced on his heels, hands cupped to his face. His oval eyes were alert, lips taut, fists clenched tight against the chill. Above them, the forest was spruce, brown and dead, icicles sashaying from the branches. Past that, a lone wisp of a cloud.

Ulysses gave his nod, and Cato began the ruse, conjuring a fine flock of quail from nothing, flickering his hands, upping the volume. The sounds were well-practiced, all *chicks* and *kaws*, and sure enough, the wagon slowed, as the duo hopped down together, cocking their guns and ready for a meal, while Cato darted up the hillside, guiding them on.

Ulysses saw them clearly now. The older one was slower, cheeks browned, flat gray hair under a black cap. It was the other fellow who looked the more dangerous, bow-legged, eager for a fight, in that way of young men the whole world over. Silently, Ulysses skidded over behind them, into the road's muck.

The wagon's canvas flapped in the wind, and in an instant, he'd yanked out the rough-hewn nails at its edges, bristling at the noise. Staying careful, he eyed the cash box that was waiting, twin locks on either side, then lifted it slowly by the iron base, tucking it awkwardly beneath his arm, looping now to the wagon's front. The draft horse was sixteen hands at least, muscles tight as coils. Its eyes flitted to his face, breath misting, and he murmured in its ear, coaxing it by the reins, spooking the poor beast with a clap on its flank, sending it galloping.

Cato kept up the birdsong all the while. Ulysses had provided his friend a pass just in case, but he knew it wouldn't be needed. Cato was shrewd; he'd soon be home, back among the baying whips of Boxwood Grove – where God willing, he'd never even have been missed. And Ulysses sprung away in turn, fast as he could manage, his book of maps firm in his pocket.

1901

Drenched but defiant, Samuel Billings rejected the horse-and-buggies with a swift shake of his head. There was no depot building here, just a stone curb hemmed in by the old hitching posts, and drivers holding out their caps like beggars – *"welcome, stranger!" "wouldn't mind a day's occupation!"* – grasping for business.

Sam, however, had opted for the future.

Riding out of Manassas Junction, his was the only horseless carriage in working order, the only one he'd spotted at all: an Oldsmobile, and already its icy blue doors were spattered with Virginia mud. The drizzle was nasty, drenching the buckram seat, filling the floorboard with puddles, hijacking his memories of southern sun. The road was no better. Ruts as deep as sewers. Sinkholes gurgling, so that the carburetor belched smoke and the whole contraption lurched whenever it shifted gear. At least the driver was calm, chuckling beneath his mustache every time the vehicle jumped.

Sam clutched his bowler hat to his chest, and watched the terrain roll slowly by. Placard cottages and slanted barns. Sopping wet horses with manes like rangy blankets. Even the mountaintops seemed cut short, encircled entirely by cloud.

"It's not much for admirin', I'll admit."

He glanced front, and saw the driver eyeing him.

The fellow shrugged as if by way of apology, then nodded toward a building ahead. *"Liberty Inn,"* said the sign. *"Travelers Welcome."* Its windows glowed amber amid the dusk. Shutters flapped. Wicker chairs sat idle on the porch.

Without another word, Sam handed over a silver dollar, and carried his handbag inside. The door hung loosely from its hinge, and squeaked loudly. A cramped room awaited, lit by a candle not a lamp; inside, a wiry host rose from a butler's desk, his chin as narrow as a blade. "Mr. Billings?" He spoke in a quiet drawl.

"Evening." The temperature was even cooler than out on the road. A torn sofa sat jammed against the wall, its rosewood legs carved into paws, the ones in the rear replaced with stacks of yellowed newsprint.

"Here to pay tribute at the battlefield?"

"Something like that."

"You'll find it's no trouble. Jaunt of a ride to any spot you'd need."

"Glad to know it." Sam already had his directions, tucked carefully away. "You require anything from me?"

The clerk shook his head. "Your firm wired payment. I'll show you in."

"I'd be obliged," and Sam followed down a floral-papered hall. The next room was smaller: a dresser by the window, a bed of white sheets and a green pieced quilt, slender posts at the corners.

"It'll do?"

Sam nodded. And exhausted from his time on the train – it had left before sunrise – he lay down as soon as the door was shut, before even removing his shoes.

He slept soundly.

When he next blinked, a morning light was trickling in.

Sam pulled his pocket watch from his coat. Half past seven already! The sky had cleared overnight, though mist still caressed the Blue Ridge, and he retrieved his book of maps from his pocket and walked to the window. The book's leather was in need of re-binding, the ink inside gone smudged; he squinted at the page he'd creased for the trip, comparing its sketches to the vista that greeted him now. The horizon, at least, was the same, every dip and valley properly situated, and rubbing his eyes, he stepped into the hall and back outside.

Alas, where there ought to have been a stone wall, winding its way among spruce and streams, he saw only more meadow, waving in the morning chill. Had he been daft to come? The war had engulfed the place, to be sure. But he'd held onto faith that somehow the map would still function, that the treasure might have survived. Soon, he was high-stepping through a briar patch, using his compass, batting away stinging flies, until finally he'd reached flat ground, and he blew the dark hair from his eyes.

Then – just there.

A collapsed pile of stones. Disguised by moss – loose, lonely; and Sam scurried over, kneeling in the turf, ready to dig. The uppermost rock fell with a thump: a stream of brown bugs squirreled from their home, and he tugged at the rest, mud and moss ripping silently away. Scraping at the soil with his hands, he could feel his heart quicken, as his nails became torn. A slice of pain darted through his back, and his breaths grew labored. Maybe some lucky soldier had found it first, he thought, crouched right here in terror. Perhaps it'd simply been the shells plastering these fields, blowing men younger than him to bits, shattering this old cattle wall and anything else nearby.

Until at last, he shut his eyes, and paused. "It's here," he heard himself murmur. The walls were surprisingly firm, cool and smooth against his fingers – intact after all: an old iron chest, the very one he'd been seeking.

1981

Amid the muted orange, which the South called foliage, Alvin Starkman found relief. The drive had taken him past neon-lit strip malls and endless Levittown-lite: synthetic hardboard as far as the eye could see, milky white homes that looked like toys. Now at last he was on foot, breathing in the country breeze, moving briskly, doing his best to reject middle age.

The Visitor's Center looked tired, a gray-shingled farmhouse, hardly helped by new paint and an addition on the side. Out front, workers in denim overalls were stenciling plaques, their stone dust billowing like ash. Past them, a bronze statue beckoned: a bearded general calm atop his horse, as if what had happened here had been staid and civil, no more than a chess board come to life.

Alvin paused when he reached the payphones. Entering the number, he lifted the black receiver, dropped his dime in the slot, and waited while the connection clicked into place. It rang four times.

"Metropolitan Museum," the receptionist finally droned. "Department?"

"Faye Williams, please."

"You again sir?"

"Apologies."

"Alright. Please hold."

He leaned his head against the aluminum partition.

The voice came back on. "Faye's away from her desk, sir. You sure I can't pass along a message?"

"It's not urgent."

"In that case, have a good day."

He lingered another moment, cradling the receiver against his shoulder, listening to the purr of the dial tone roll back into place.

Faye was ignoring his calls.

She hadn't wanted him to leave, of course. She never did. But of late, she'd grown more urgent about it. "You know how it is," he'd tried that morning. "Unless a case goes cold, I can't drop it."

"So make it cold then," she'd snapped. "Turn it to ice."

Alvin sighed, and turned back to the fields, watching the wind etch its designs into the soft Virginia grass. He'd avoided the place until now, doubting it had much to offer: federally protected pasture, mowed daily, sculptures dotting the horizon like trees – what shred of treasure could possibly have survived here?

A tour group was approaching, gliding through dandelions abandoned by summer: fathers bounding like puppies, binoculars bouncing against their bellies, children and wives lollygagging behind, a pimple-faced guide with a bright orange flag keeping them all together.

Alvin trailed along behind. "Excuse me," he called when they were close, and the kid, heading toward the Visitor's Center, turned his head. "You happen to know what was here before? In these fields, I mean – before they were famous – before the battle?"

"Now there's a query we don't often get." The young guide grinned. "Plantations east and west. Not a whole lot here in the middle, so they say. Good spot for warring – lack of civilians."

Alvin nodded, and reached into his briefcase, pulling out his photocopies. The spot he needed was just yards off, and he studied the coordinates that Ulysses Brooke had once so carefully laid out – the scribble, too, added by Samuel Billings.

"Can I help with something in particular, sir?"

But Alvin shook his head. A stone wall had allegedly stood near. A dirt road had wound somewhere close. And now, here he was in turn, every bit as blind as the men he'd come to follow.

CHAPTER 1

New York City
November 1971

The bureau's chairs were frayed. The fluorescent bulbs buzzed like a fly caught against a screen. The secretaries raced by, folders squeezed tight against their starched blazers. All the while, more agents were filing through, their snippets of conversation like stations passing on a tuner: jokes about hippies, complaints it wasn't just the Freedom Riders anymore, that everyone born since Truman ought to have their phone tapped. Alvin watched them go, sporting their hair a touch shaggier than when he'd first arrived, backgrounds just the same: boarding school, Ivys, Nixonians.

"What about it, Starkman?" one of them called over. "You ready to crack some commie heads?"

Alvin forced a chuckle. Until at last, a receptionist called his name, and he stepped into the office behind him.

Claire Calloway had been brought in from DC amid much fanfare, the first female deputy in the New York command. She'd been transferred over from Justice, before there were even women agents in the field, a proper blueblood: lock-jawed, recalling case details as if she had playback in her ear, a pale blue gaze that darted like a bird's.

She wasn't wearing make-up. Her clothes were drab too – black blouse, flat shoes, tired yellow hair to match. Her desk was smooth and uncluttered, bearing only the standard issue lamp and phone. Even the paneled sideboard had been cleared, nothing but wood where decanters used to dominate. Her predecessor would be horrified: a rail-thin member of the old guard, forced out by lung cancer, growling to the last.

"Your files tell me you've had a good year," she said as Alvin entered, closing the door behind him, circling round to the desk. It was true: in the last six months alone, he'd tracked down an escaped convict, closed down a drug ring in the South Bronx, revealed a Scarsdale kidnapping to be a hoax.

"That's good to hear, ma'am. Glad to do the work."

"Let's get to it then." She sat, and he followed suit. "You've read the report on Jack and Betty Downing?"

"They really say they've got proof of stolen billions?"

"Honest-to-Christ. A book of treasure maps." She rolled her eyes. "Still, we did a little digging. Turns out they're more connected than you'd think. And they asked for you by name."

"Why?"

"Your reputation's grown, Agent Starkman. You're meticulous." She clasped her hands. "You can be trusted."

He shifted in his chair. It didn't quite click – since when were civilians the ones making requests? – but he supposed he should be pleased. "You think it's just a money grab?"

"That doesn't mean they can't also be right. They're insisting Billings Trust was founded on a lie, that every cent of its seed money was dirty."

"C'mon."

"I know. But that's what they claim – that the cash belongs to their family instead."

"Who are the backers?"

"Relatives. Richer ones. No doubt they studied up on you, probably figured you for a bleeding heart. Assumed you'd respond better to a couple of down-and-outers, so they offered up a few from their clan." Calloway met his eye. "Were they wrong?"

"Justice is blind, ma'am."

"Good." She looked to the door. "Follow me."

***

They arrived down the hall, where the Downings were waiting.

The husband's face was doughy, with oily sideburns straight down his jaw. His shirt was blue flannel, his Christmas tree tie clipped on, and he stood with his hands over his belt and his legs spread wide, like an actor imitating a cowboy. It was his wife who appeared the colder of the two – wavy orange hair past her shoulders, a chin that sank into her neck. No hint of a smile. Blue dotted sweater, black slacks.

Alvin reached to shake their hands. "I'm Starkman."

"Pleasure's ours," Jack Downing replied, and they all took their seats.

Betty was eyeing Alvin up and down, lingering on his curls, as if she could detect the bristle brush he'd used to force them down. "You're the FBI agent?"

"We don't all look like James Bond, ma'am." He cleared his throat, aware of Calloway watching him in turn. "So you two believe you're owed some cash?"

"My inheritance," Jack remarked. "Yes sir."

"Just to get this on the record: you're positing that a philanthropy that's paved the path for millions was based in fraud."

A nod.

"It's the most admired institution in our city."

"Maybe the problem is your city."

Alvin kept steady. "Charles Billings just won 'Man of the Year.' His third go-round."

This time, it was Betty who leaned forward. "Really, Mister. Surely you know something about his daddy's fortune."

"Cigarettes." Alvin shrugged. "Investments. He saw the future quicker than most." Like everyone else, he'd learned about the man back in grade school, and hadn't really considered him since. "You mentioned a treasure map on the phone?"

Now Jack Downing smiled. His teeth were the color of an oil stain – except for the ones that were missing, which were half of them. Slowly, theatrically even, he lifted his briefcase and unlatched the knob. From within, he unfurled what appeared to be the prize: a small book, not much bigger than his palm. The pages were brittle, and mottled brown. The black leather binding was filled with cracks. A chipped gold border traced its edge; a flap on the end was clasped like a belt. "Behold," Jack declared – a priest presenting his Scripture.

Alvin squinted back. He glanced at Calloway, then again to their guests. "May I?" he asked. Downing had flipped the book open, showing sheets cluttered with a bygone cursive, boxed inserts, figures scribbled in haste. And carefully, Alvin lifted it for himself, finding each page just as crammed as the next: stacks of hand-drawn maps, numbered captions, sketches of pastures and streets and barns, all laid over with some kind of grid. "What am I looking at here, folks?"

"Just what it seems," Jack answered. "Directions. Same ones that the Billings family never mentioned, all while the world cheered them on. Every bit tucked away ever since, at everyone's favorite charity."

"Until you came along."

"We won our lawsuit for a reason, Agent Starkman."

He nodded. Calloway had briefed him on the walk down the hall, how toward the close of his life, the legendary Sam Billings had gone off the deep end, abruptly declaring all his money the product of luck, not skill, sharing this book with the public, insisting the maps were real. He'd told the press he'd thieved them from ghosts – no matter that by then, the nation had written him off as a relic. Billings had responded by writing the book into the Trust's bylaws, codifying its protection, placing it at their midtown headquarters for storage.

By the time the Downings had arrived and claimed the book for themselves, the Trust's lawyers had painted its very existence as evidence not of their founder's guilt, but of his humanity, arguing the whole mess had stunk of dementia, demanding the court spare Sam Billings any posthumous embarrassment. It hadn't been enough. The Downings had won indeed, taking possession of the book at last, persuading the court it was their own ancestor who had drawn it up in the first place, not Billings – that he really had stolen it instead – citing handwriting experts, university consultants, antique bookbinding photographs as proof of its vintage.

"You actually believe this thing is real?" Alvin wanted to know.

"We know it is, Agent Starkman. It was my forbear, Ulysses Brooke, who buried its treasures. And Sam

Billings who dug 'em up." His voice rose. "I'm rightful heir to this book, and the jury agreed."

Alvin was tapping his pencil as before. He peered around the room. The taint of stale cigarettes was baked into the walls. Pale light reflected from the street. The wall clock echoed. From the far side, it felt like Nixon was right there, watching them, and no doubt that was the intended effect. After all, the same portrait hovered over every table in every room, across the entire building, lips contorted into a grimace of a smile, one eyebrow cocked as if the man were trying desperately to wink. "Tell me. Why would your ancestor bury all his cash in the first place?"

"Didn't trust the banks, I reckon." Jack laughed. "You go ahead, Starkman. You check it out."

"Maybe I will. Though if you got this all figured, what do you need me for?"

"Once your bureau verifies this whole thing's real, we won't just be suing for a book anymore. We'll be going after the Trust's gold itself." He leaned forward, jabbing his finger stiffly. "Folks will believe it if you say it, Agent Starkman. A judge would surrender to the truth."

CHAPTER 2

New York City
September 1875

The veterans liked to meet up on 23rd Street, in the cellar of a packing warehouse. The room spanned the entire block, filled with course-grained benches that only increased the noise – and when he entered, Samuel cupped his ears with his hands, but still couldn't keep out the racket.

His mother had been sending him here ever since the reunions had begun, insisting they'd provide him a sense of his father – honor him at least – perhaps offer some contacts along the way. After all, these men weren't just louts from Five Points and the East Docks: some had proper professions of their own, lawyering and accounting mostly, others had worn stripes during the war and still lived off their bounty, founding clubs and playing cards to pass the time. If nothing else, it got Sam out of the flat, and for that alone, he didn't put up a fight.

The school day had passed slowly as ever. The morning had started well enough: retrieving his slate, he'd sidled to his spot alongside his pals, then made his way through the brawling, bloody lyrics of the Star-Spangled Banner, while Schoolmaster Jacobs had raised the flag in front, and held aloft his prized pocket watch for the thirty-seven-second-count, one moment of silence for every state in the Union.

It was when they reached twenty-eight or twenty-nine that Sam had brought his palms to his lips, and blown as hard as he could: the loudest replica of a fart he could manage. The other boys had slid into a fit – even some of the girls, despite their blushing – and Jacobs had glared. He was a stocky fellow, with a pink face, and a scar down his cheek he swore had come from Antietam. "Don't have time for the republic, Billings?" He'd stepped closer. "Your old man got himself kilt at Petersburg, if I'm not mistaken?"

Sam had spent the rest of his day in the dunce cap.

Now, glad to be free, he caught one of the waiters wandering his way. The man's skin was dark – a 'bonafide African' the vets would call him – his bald pate shimmering.

"What can I fix, fella? Mug of wine?"

"Beer," Sam answered. "Dark."

With a nod, the waiter handed one over.

It was less bitter than Sam expected, and he gulped it gratefully. He was still lean, scarcely any whiskers atop his lip, and the beer would help him fit in. Up ahead, the ex-soldiers were mostly drunk themselves, toasting raucously, saluting beneath their old slouch caps, shooting their tobacco juice into the rotting spittoons below. Sam watched as a gaggle in the corner yanked up their sleeves to compare stumps.

Oil lamps in bronze castings made it all feel like an old royal hall. Along the back, the regimental flags hung in faded blues, captioned by the names of battles and the fallen. *"Grand Army of the Republic,"* pronounced the biggest one of all, framed with white embroidery.

Someone tussled his hair, and he turned.

It was his friend Bart Maynard's father. Sam offered a quick bow, and Mr. Maynard winked back. He was a beefy, barrel-chested man, with a square chin and black sideburns. His whalebone cane reflected the lamps' flames, his cravat was scarlet silk, the same shade as his face. "My boy tells me you've been mouthing off at the schoolhouse, Billings," he chortled now. "And why not? One day you'll be bathing in gold!"

At that, some of the other men howled, and Sam knew it wasn't his torn stockings or the hole in his britches that had caught their attention, but the rumors about his lunatic pa.

"Now, Billings, don't take it too hard. Your father was a fine man." Maynard leaned in closer, no doubt taking note of his flush. "You've heard tell yet of Ulysses Brooke?"

"We learned of him in school, I'd wager." Sam tried to recall the lectures from Jacobs. "Some sort of loon."

Maynard shrugged. "If he'd been born but a half-century later, they'd have called him a hero." He snapped a waiter over for more drinks. "Pilfering those slavers' riches. Telling the law he buried them!" The new stouts were handed over. "Fancied the Negroes would actually dig them up one day – fund their own rebellion – fund whole new lives." He took a long gulp. "I suppose we ended up doing that for them. And all the while, your poor father, yammering on about Brooke's old treasure map, crowing over how he'd go and claim his birthright soon as the war was done. Brain rot from too much hard tack, the officers said. God rest him." At last, Maynard's voice quieted, and the surrounding chuckles did too. "We all needed something, mind you. A place for putting our thoughts. Whisky and cards can only get a fellow so far."

Together then, they toasted, and Sam raised his own drink high, blocking his face with the mug, afraid that if he didn't hide it, the men would see the wet in his eyes.

***

That evening, he awaited his mother in the flat, knowing she'd been earning wages at the laundry since dawn. It was all they had now, without father's furniture shop – the army's pension offering scarcely enough for food. From the room's lone table, jammed between the icebox and wood stove, Sam watched a stream of ants along the sill, the same ones that arrived every fall, and listened to the drips from the corner pipes. Overhead, the warped ceiling hovered close, a water stain dead to center. Beneath that, the wallpaper was brown, peeling up from the floor, seams frayed, rusted nails at the edges.

Out in the hall, someone tripped on the laundry over the stairs, and an argument erupted, immigrant shouts cascading – Irish mostly, Sicilian too – every sentence a prelude to a brawl. Fellows of primitive tongues and papal faith, Sam thought with a rush of anger: when it was his father, not theirs, who'd laid down his life for this nation they called their own.

At last, the door creaked open. "These were just in at market," his mother announced, carrying a crate of artichokes, latching the bolt. "But then – " she caught his eye – "what is it's troubling you?"

Sam paused. His ma seemed older than ever, shoulders like blades beneath her calico apron, a gaze growing ever more crowded in with folds, as if she'd donned a new layer of armor to ward off life's slights. He took a breath. "It's time you told me, mother, what those boys in blue are always going on about."

"Still call themselves 'boys,' do they?"

"Don't dodge me, I beg of you."

She lowered the crate, and began removing the artichokes, dipping each one in a water pail by the window.

"The treasures," Sam pressed. "The ones they tease me for."

But his mother kept up her work.

"They say father had a map from Ulysses Brooke." Sam shifted forward on his chair. "Tell me it's true. Tell me some bit of it is real."

She only frowned. "How can I know, Samuel? I learnt only what your pa chose to share."

"Then share it with me in turn."

One of the artichokes rested in her palm; she paused in her motion. For a moment, she lifted her gaze. "He swore to me your grandfather knew Brooke personally," she sighed at last, letting Sam absorb the words. "That they stole from the plantations together. Not much older than you are now." She returned to her work. "To think – they actually put their faith in a race war."

Sam tried to picture it. He'd only ever seen daguerreotypes of his grandfather, dusty and scratched in their frames – his name, Thaddeus Billings, always scribbled and faded across the edges. Tad, they used to call him. He was handsome even in black-and-white, fine eyes glinting, a shock of thick hair, shadows of creases where smiles must have ruled. Sam rubbed his forehead. "Our primers at school never mentioned grandfather. If ever they speak of Brooke's scheme, they mention him alone."

"Yes, I gather Brooke wanted it that way, saving face for your grandfather – ensuring the law never came knocking here with questions." She'd started peeling back the artichokes, digging out their middles for worms. "He fell in with your grandmother, after all, the two of them hauling off as far north as this – surrendering his inheritance the instant he moved, opening that two-bit furniture store instead."

"And the treasures?"

She snorted. "Don't go sounding like your pa, Samuel," and her eyes grew distant. "A letter arrived one day. Postmarked from a Virginia jail. Penned by Ulysses Brooke himself, requesting a visit from your grandpa'ap of all things." She folded her arms. "By then, old Thaddeus was withered, wheezing, on his deathbed. Yet even at the end, he was joyous upon hearing from Ulysses – his oldest friend, he said, still a celebrity in those days, in radical circles anyhow – before he turned despondent all the same. Telling us it was too late, a journey to Virginia far too ambitious." Her voice lowered. "How he pored over that letter, Sam – tracing every word with his finger, reading it aloud to whomever would listen, calling in your father to hear. It must've been a thousand times, right up to his last breath."

"By God." Sam was chewing his thumbnail as he took it in. "It really was father, then. Father who went in his stead."

"Against my counsel."

"But he got there."

"If his boasts were to be believed."

"I'll be damned!"

"Mind your tongue."

"Mother." And now Sam was deadly serious. "He must eventually have gotten hold of the book. He must've given mention to you about where he left the thing."

"Come now Samuel. If it ever even existed at all! I never once saw it myself. The war was upon us. All other talk ceased for good."

"Tell me where."

She gazed towards the window, out upon the intersection: vendors haggling, mothers tugging little ones from market, men at the corner bars for hot water and eggs. "A school archive is all I remember him saying – somewhere down in Dixie. I didn't take it seriously. A place to stash the maps for the war's duration, was how he put it. I didn't question him beyond that. Not when he was marching off to battle." Suddenly, her voice thickened, and she turned back. "I beg of you, Samuel. It was wishful thinking then. It's no better now. It's nothing but a way to sink real thoughts, real plans, a chance at a real life."

"And what of real money, mother?" Sam couldn't just drop it, he was certain. All this while, he'd simmered at pa abandoning their tiny family with nothing. Now, for the first time, he felt a new notion stirring in his soul.

"For Heaven's sake, Sam, it's the South that got him kilt! It was the land of his forefathers, and it betrayed him. He rots there still."

"The war did that. Not the South." Sam knew, of course, that for her generation, they were one and the same. But he needn't press the point. "I'm not my father," he offered instead. "I'll forge a proper path."

Until at long last, something in her expression wavered. Her brow crinkled, and when she spoke again, the veil between them had slipped. "I told you. The clouds of war were brewing," she managed. "By the time your pa finished his visit, he couldn't trust the borders near the capital. He was panicked he'd be taken in, convinced he wasn't safe carrying that book, not on the open road. Your father was no coward, Samuel – only you must understand what it was like: rumors like snakes, talk of armies invading, New York itself breaking off next. Troops were taking over the turnpikes, men questioned simply for walking."

"It's alright, mother."

"He nearly missed you being born, you know. All so he could be down there, running after his dream."

"Down where, mother? Richmond? Farther south?"

"Along the coast, he said. Free from the armies massing." A squab had landed on the sill outside, and she clapped her hands and shooed it. "He bribed some smugglers with what little cash was left. He got himself home."

"So he must've stashed the book before that."

"Who knows that I even properly remember what he said?"

"But you must have considered it, mother! Didn't you at least try and see for yourself?"

"I was rearing you, Samuel. We'd scarcely enough for scraps. How possibly could I have made the journey?"

But Sam had already stood, and stopped listening.

CHAPTER 3

Williamsburg, Virginia
September 1880

A mere two weeks in, and everybody seemed to know him.

It had been that way back home too, it was true – Sam gaining more and more of a knack for saying the right thing, flashing a smile when it was needed – but here, it seemed, it was even easier. He was the rare Yank, the rare guttersnipe too, and the other lads had taken an interest.

"Howdy there, Billings!" one of them bellowed now, part of a roving crowd. They were all planters' boys, some from deep in the Delta, all flowing locks and toothy grins, never seeming to bother with how he'd found his way among them – how he'd hounded Mr. Maynard at the bank, right up until he had his letter of introduction, not to mention a loan.

"Glad to see you boys upright," he replied with a grin. There'd been a waltz the evening before.

"Aristotle awaits," the lead one drawled – their nickname for Professor Richard Atkins, lecturer in history and the college's librarian. They liked to joke he'd been on grounds since the Algonquian had fled.

The hall was more cathedral than schoolhouse: chestnut paneling, matching trusses at the sides. The only unvarnished item was Atkins himself, who seemed more shriveled by the day, scratching his white sideburns as be entered, silencing them with his gaze.

It would be a lecture about the war, of course, and Sam had to keep from rolling his eyes as it began. But he bided his time, looking as dutiful as the rest, until eventually the morning had gone and the sun was boiling through the windows. Finally, Atkins paused, stepping from the rostrum, fastening the clasps on his handbag; and while the other lads skipped off, Sam waited and watched. In time, the old man actually took notice, and gestured for him to follow.

They walked through a small door, past the blackboard, down a few more steps below. From there, it was into a small study, stained with tobacco, where Atkins pulled out his calabash pipe, striking a long match against the sole of his gaiter as he sat. Sam's eyes ran past the gilded bindings, and the rolling ladders at the ready. There were treatises on the Constitution, court cases going back to Marshall, photographic collections from the war. "Well, Mr. Billings?"

He cleared his throat. "I'd fancy a word, sir."

"Alas. I'd wager that was five."

"Do you charge by the tally?"

A smile.

Sam shifted on his feet. "The thing of it is, sir – my mother once told me of an archive on grounds." He paused once more. Finally, he was here. He'd set his mind to it not long after she'd first spoken to him of all this. In short order, he'd learned that his own grandfather had studied at William and Mary, had concluded in turn that father might've felt some connection to the place as a result. It had sat on pa's pathway home, after all – near enough the sea, away from the armies massing – offering just the kind of safe harbor that would've been needed, just the kind of place for storing something so small and precious as a set of maps. Still, this would be the first time Sam had uttered his true aims aloud. "A wing of the library, sir, where I might find the rarest of books."

"Why yes, Billings, and it's a fine wing at that." Atkins rested the pipe on his lip. "Congressional accounts, mostly. Though there are some scattered gems."

"My mother heard talk of it from my father, sir." He hesitated. "Felled at Petersburg, sir. In '64."

"A Union man, I gather."

"That's right."

"Chosen by destiny, then." He took a puff. "And by Lincoln." Atkins was leaning back now, squinting, all but shutting his eyes. "Remarkable. But one generation removed, and here you stand. I dare say I'm glad."

"I appreciate that, sir."

The pipe had lowered. Atkins let loose a chuckle, which threatened to turn to a cough. He shook his head. "My heavens, boy. It must be some special record you're after." He'd re-lit his tobacco. "I do hope you find it."

***

The archive was in the next building over, tucked behind a set of oak doors. It was guarded by one of Atkins' sycophants, steel-wired spectacles sliding down his narrow nose, clothbound novel upon his frock. "'Afternoon," the fellow offered without looking up.

Sam explained he was after a book without a listing – that it had been stashed here in a hurry just before the war – and he waited while the fellow stood slowly and led the way in: down a candle-lit corridor, into a reading room beyond, their boot-soles echoing against the paneled floor. There were squirrels scuffling in the rafters, overtop tall racks laid out at sharp angles, and when Sam's sleeve brushed one of the bindings, a moth the size of a hummingbird fluttered angrily away. Finally, they reached a stairwell. "Holler if you get lost," the librarian directed, but already he was on his way back out.

Sam fetched a lantern from the wall. The shelves were crowded, the aisles deserted, and though he wasn't a man of God, he wondered if this was what it meant to allow for faith. He tried to picture his father upon this very spot, no older than he was now – wracked by nerves after his visit with Ulysses Brooke – a book of maps in tow, requiring some place for hiding a fortune, free from questions about a trespassing Yank.

Sam focused his attention, gaping at the endless rows, each one named for some towering local figure: presidents of the college, legislators of Virginia, generals too. He took in the mounted plaques with the names upon them, all faded engravings, until at last he stopped, reading the last one over several times.

In honor of Senator Samuel Price.

Might this merely be chance?

Or might his father have taken this particular placard as some sort of beacon? Taking note that it shared a name with the son he was about to welcome?

Following the faintest of hopes, Sam crouched, heart pumping, and began sifting through – ignoring ancient census records, graduation rolls, blueprints – sneezing at the dust, his lantern burning low. He pushed aside a layer of lint as thick as cotton, feeling to the back of the lowest rack on the shelf, coming upon something else: a book lodged in the corner, jammed against the brick behind it.

It was small and square, and gently, Sam traced its edges. Cautiously now, as if it were made of glass, he drew it out, studying the twine undone at the spine, a sheath of stiff black leather in front, a chipped gilded border encircling its top. It was an old stationary, the sort that men used for settling accounts. And holding his breath, Sam loosened the twine.

His throat caught.

The writing inside was cramped but tidy, and studying it again, he felt a whisper of triumph, as though the world were absorbing the truth of what he'd just done. There was a rush straight through his soul like thunder. *Property of Ulysses Brooke*, the front page declared.

He flipped ahead.

There were graphs, and columns, drawings too; sketches of hilltops, shaded portraits of ponds and streams, tracings of fences and village streets.

Peering closer, Sam could make out captions – hamlets, cities, states – and it dawned on him that there was real order here: grids he recognized from cartography class, the same system his lecturers had always cited in their military histories, going all the way back to grammar school. These were Cartesian coordinates, he realized – Eastings and Northings – numbered by axis, horizontal and vertical. Maps indeed.

He flicked through more quickly then, forgetting the book's age, finding spots inside labeled all along the coast, as far up as his hometown New York, as far down as the Gulf. Could any of it be real? Could such a treasure be so vast?

Sam glanced about. Still, there was no one near, and quickly, quietly, he tucked the old thing inside his vest. Its binding was sharp against his midriff, and when he straightened, it didn't budge. He moved purposefully then, determined that it wasn't really theft, not if no one even knew the book was here – that this was America, besides, and how else to get ahead? The librarian was fully asleep now, and Sam sailed past gratefully, smoothing his tails, trying to slow. He'd done it, he realized. He'd trusted his instincts against all odds. There was a lesson in that – there had to be. For it couldn't just be a miracle of luck if it had come from a plan! Rather it was resolve, he thought – self-reliance. He was moving faster again, but no matter. In minutes, he was back outside, turning to the winding dirt path. It glowed red beneath the late sun, the smell of Virginia clay full of welcome, the crackle of possibility blowing through the poplars overhead.

CHAPTER 4

New York City
February 1972

Big Dip Records: cracked windows in front, and a neon sign that no longer worked, west of the park and crowded with pickpockets. The ceiling was fiber, the aisles barely wide enough for turning. Yet somehow it reminded Alvin of the filing rooms at the bureau – crowded with information, and thus with purpose. He liked coming in on Saturday mornings.

Besides, he needed the break; it'd been too long since he'd stopped in. Calloway had made him stick with the case, even if it was bound to turn up nothing. The powers-that-be were desperate to avoid this thing going to press, paranoid it would look bad if it were dropped, making them all look like they were in the Trust's pockets. For weeks then, Alvin had been reading what he could, growing tired of files that glossed over Sam Billings' early days, none of them ever explaining how he'd actually started investing, scrounging his fortune from nothing – let alone if any of his cash had truly been tied to old Ulysses Brooke in the first place: an old fanatic, infamous once upon a time for aiming to uproot the entire South, now known mostly as a kook who'd been caught.

The case was simply reaching its dead end.

Alvin glanced around. The patrons here were harmless: all flared pants and flowered vests, occasionally spitting out their venom about Nixon and Vietnam, mostly just perusing the stacks. They were young, hair down their backs, cigarettes behind their ears, a few scattered squares mixed in too – no doubt they'd call him the same.

But today, someone else.

A woman across the way. He'd seen her before. He'd even tried saying hello a few times, back before he'd had the case.

Her skin was rich as chocolate, her hair rising into an Afro. When she looked up, her gaze was sharp.

"What?" she mouthed.

"Apologies," he mouthed back. But he didn't turn away. He noticed her pupils now – narrow, interested – a shade lighter than her hair, and took in the nape of her neck. It was smooth as silk.

"Why you staring, fella?" Her smile floored him even more than her eyes.

He swallowed. Gold earrings, smoky eyeliner, a suede jacket that billowed at the sides. Her jeans clung to her thighs, her brown boots were scuffed. More than that, she was carrying records – half a dozen, at least – letting the world know it was the music that mattered, not just the hot air.

Suddenly, desperately, Alvin realized he wanted to tell her he thought so too, that beyond all the kids still pretending to be revolutionaries, he recognized real meaning: here, amid the beer and sewage in the crosscurrents, there was something worth looking for.

He took in a long breath instead. "You like them?" he asked dumbly, gesturing to the albums at her fingertips. "Sly and the Family Stone?"

"You didn't think a sister would?"

Now he felt even dumber. It was true he never really talked to black folks – a couple of the fellows from the mail room maybe – that was about it.

She was smirking ever more widely. "Nice buzz," she said. Alvin touched his hair. An FBI-regulation cut. "I suppose I ought to be the one who's surprised."

"I like music," he shrugged.

"What about progress?"

"That's what music is, no?" He wondered how to explain: that for him progress was why he believed in the bureau, and its drive toward justice.

She extended her hand. "Faye Williams."

"Alvin." He offered his right back. "Starkman."

"So, Starkman." Her eyes ran down his face. "You finally came over here to ask me out?"

He paused. "Why? Were you hoping I would?"

Her laugh was loud. But she started shifting away. "Duty calls."

"Where to?"

"I'm over at the Met." She was halfway gone. "Maybe next time you're expanding your horizons, you'll end up there."

Alvin blinked.

For a long moment, he remained stuck to the carpet. Then he reminded himself: at the bureau, he'd never let a case slip away. Another moment more, and he'd stepped back outside, looking both ways, fearing he'd already lost her. Until without allowing himself time to think his way out of it, he started east: past the dive bars on Broadway, the mystery-smells, straight into the treasured spine of

Central Park. It wasn't long before the museum came into view.

Flat-fronted buses were growling in place out front, cabs with broken tail lights, generators for the food stalls belching out black exhaust. The vendors were shouting, still sporting their fatigues from Saigon, hawking bananas, cigarettes, dirty magazines. At the lights, clunky VWs honked for no reason but self-expression, darting between the American-made monstrosities, angling for position. Sirens screamed.

At the head of it all, the museum's steps awaited, and Alvin skipped right up. The lobby was all gleaming windows and stately stone – a vestige of another city altogether – the tourists swirling, like schools of fish rushing blindly upstream.

He purchased admission; finally, he hesitated.

The receptionist was watching him. "Is there something else, sir?"

"I've got a friend working here," he offered, reverting to an amiable tone he'd learned from the bureau. "Faye Williams is her name," and suddenly he was grateful for his haircut and suit.

"One flight up," the woman directed after another second, marking a map, and he thanked her.

Hurrying now, he found a door marked *Staff*, and a narrow hall beyond it – blue carpet and dim light, like any office anywhere – and then, sure enough, there she was: a loose cardigan in place of the jacket from the record shop, sitting at her desk. When she spotted him, she smiled, more gently than before.

"Hi," he began.

"That was quick, Starkman."

"Hey, I'm FBI."

"You're serious?" The smile was gone.

"It was meant to impress."

But she'd leaned back, crossing her arms. "You any better at reading criminals than women?"

"I have a lot more practice with one than the other," and he was glad when the grin came back. "So what is it you do here?"

"Someone's got to log all the art that comes in. I do it over the phone – so they can't see my skin." She stood. "Come on. I'll give you a tour."

Together they walked now, dodging lone old men in fedoras, mothers hauling toddlers, tourist couples speaking French and Italian. In time, they were two floors up. It grew warmer, as if no one was minding the radiators; the artwork turned smaller and uncrowded. "It's my favorite spot," Faye announced.

And Alvin nodded, doing his best to ignore the looks from the guards. He followed her around another corner, and for a moment at least, they had the place to themselves. Overhead, a wooden mask hung from the ceiling. Beneath that, a set of kettle drums had been sculpted from gourd.

"No one bothers with African art," she explained.

"Maybe one day," he replied. The carpet was rumpled, the glass cases dusty and unpolished.

She faced him. "In the meantime, secret treasures."

Alvin met her eye. She was right: the sculptures were stunning – supple, elegant – hidden in plain sight. Yet all he could do now was hold her gaze.

"It's not a good idea," she all but whispered, inching nearer.

"Why not?"

"You know."

"Yes."

But it was then their lips touched, and hers were lovely and soft and warm.

Faye lifted her hand to his chin and pulled him even closer. His throat narrowed as he clasped her in turn, delighted by how her shoulders curved, and how she let out a murmur of a sigh.

At last, they pulled apart, and in the dim light, he saw her blink.

"What?" he wanted to know. "Tell me."

"It's just – it can't undo everything else. There's a whole world out there."

He worked to catch her eye like before.

"Besides," she went on. "This is where I work."

One of the museum guards had entered, a white man with dyed yellow hair. Reflexively, sheepishly, Alvin stepped back.

The guard glared.

"Let's go," Faye said.

And they did.

CHAPTER 5

It was hard to deny Cato was quieter these days. Ulysses had noticed how his eyes welled up at the sound of the whippings, and his jaw clenched at the yeomen overseers patrolling the fields, his voice turned to nothing whenever they were near. He'd always been earnest, it was true, devouring the books Ulysses had stolen for him from the schoolhouse, ready for debates about the events of the day – he knew more about Jefferson than any of the lads in the village – yet of late, there'd been something more: as if he were chewing on words begging to come out, unable to spit them quite loose.

"Go on then," Ulysses demanded now.

Cato simply nibbled at his drumstick. He was sitting on his bunk's edge – his mother and sisters hanging laundry out front, his father sold off the year before – snacking on the peppered goose that Ulysses had wrapped in broadsheets and brought down from the main house.

"Look here," Ulysses pressed. "It's not so easy my repairing to the slave quarters, you know."

"So put a halt to it."

"Beg pardon?"

"You heard right." Cato smacked the bird's juice from his fingers. "Why's this make you feel better, little Brooke?" He was the taller of the two now, scraping the doorframe whenever he stood.

Ulysses paused. Cato had never dogged him like this. "Am I wrong to think you're my friend?"

But it was then Cato began to laugh. He shook just the way he had when they'd been smaller – so that it took over his whole face, and heaved his wide shoulders – and despite himself, despite sensing he was somehow the butt of the joke, Ulysses joined in too, glad at least that Cato wasn't angry.

Alas, if only he could stay.

It wasn't long before he'd hurried back out, and up toward the mansion. There it was, at the top of the hill; its brick was cloaked now in the morning light, the kind of summer film that grabbed on early this time of year, and he could see his father approaching from the mist. Pa's stride was stiffer these days, though no less brisk, and he waved Ulysses over, cupping his hand to his lips. "Don't you dawdle!" he called out, clapping towards the waiting carriage. "What kept you?"

"I was minding the goats."

"Don't you lie now either."

Ulysses stepped among the dandelions and bowed his head as if he were still small. "Father – "

"No, Ulysses. Don't test me."

They were both on the carriage drive now, nearly eye to eye. For it wasn't just that Ulysses had grown, but that pa had begun to shrink: the legend that had once matched his proud silhouette already fading. Only his eyes truly retained their old vigor – fierce, certain, hinting at the fight still within. Ulysses held his tongue, lacking the courage to say what he felt, wobbling instead in the great man's shadow.

The trip into town was bumpy, and Ulysses spent it staring at his father's gray hair in front of him, full of stink from the powdered wig now dangling from the carriage lamp like a carcass. When they pulled in, he registered that the main square had grown: there was a milliner's, a granary, even a print shop. Dozens of families were lining the road – children waving pint-sized flags, parents singing *Yankee Doodle* behind them – and as he hopped from the folding step, he caught the eye of his friend Thaddeus, who gave a wave and a mock salute, though no one else seemed to notice, for already, folks had spotted pa.

Under their gaze, Franklin Brooke seemed to transform back to his old self, placing his wig back on, slapping their backs, commenting on the weather and the harvest and the latest travails in Richmond. It was as if the memory of war had awoken him, the pleasure of the past strong enough to call forth the value of the present. And when the parade began not long after, the buglers marching giddily by, drummer boys close behind, he quickly joined in with the other veterans, donning their old tricorns and frayed blue coats. Like aging gladiators they went – some on crutches, others with felt patches, most keeping their wounds hidden – while the lads leapt at their sides, the old-timers hooted, the women curtseyed whenever an old soldier glanced their way. Finally it was done, and Brooke and his men led the way to the tavern.

Even after all that, however, the day wasn't done.

For later, after they returned home, once the overseers were ordered to make themselves scarce, and the slaves directed to evening chores, it was time for Boxwood Grove's annual ball in the nation's honor. Ulysses was forced to greet guests with his family – all while seeking his chance at escape. Until at last, he spotted the Billings family coming up the main drive, and he offered to show Thaddeus through the side wing instead.

Tad took the hint. At once, they scurried away, leaving their families in their wake, racing down the hill behind the mansion, back to the tall grass of the quarters. They were different from one another, to be sure: while Ulysses brought a new flame to every brushfire, Tad was more like a hidden spark. But they both bristled beneath the weight of all that had been bequeathed to them. Ulysses knew that Tad's father was even more lost to the past than his own – never really returned from the war, folks said, his voice gone vacant, his words gone limp, looks that were dashing in the way of a marble bust rather than a living breathing person. It was this burden that had bridged the two boys, enough that they'd grown to confide in each other, and eventually joined in making ever more trouble: offering the slaves a helping hand in the fields, smuggling food to the cabins, even tutoring the young ones in letters. It was why Ulysses had found he'd been able to tell Tad of his friendship with Cato in the first place.

And there Cato was now, waiting amid the milkweed. He and Tad were the same height, and their eyes met in full as each extended a hand.

"Evenin'," Tad declared now with a grin. "What'll be your order tonight?"

"Soup of the day, if you please – and ham, good sir. Always ham!" Together, they doubled over in laughter, before Tad caught his breath and pledged to fetch whatever he could from the party.

Ulysses smiled as he watched. Not that he was surprised. Thaddeus admired authenticity wherever he could find it. In exchange, he offered something different:

a kind of ease, readily shared, knowing not only what to say, but just as much what would come in response. He'd long shown he was able to laugh with Cato in a way Ulysses never quite had, hooting at all the nonsense the slave often described: contests over counting maggots in the bread, witless slurs from the overseers, the way a visiting delegate from the Statehouse had shaken with fear when he'd been stranded alone too near the quarters. Ulysses had never seen a white man laugh over such things before – let alone a prince of the commonwealth.

In time, the sun dropped in full, and the two white lads knew it was time to go. With loping strides, they left their friend to re-join his people, as they went to re-join theirs. Although when the mansion came back into view, its windows like warm flames against a purple sky, Ulysses paused. He grimaced that while they could smell the roast fowl, golden butter drizzled across its crisped edges, Cato would have to wait – stuck behind them, with nothing but corn-meal and rotted beef.

***

The air was laden with scented water when they entered, as house-slaves fanned the guests with folded parchment and stood by the wall panels in liveries of red velvet. The ballroom piped with twaddle: lazy praise for Washington's inaugural, half-formed jokes about Federalists and their Jew-like appetite for money, while the two young heirs nodded hello as they walked through, registering the planters by their plump jowls, the legislators by their new-fangled tails, the merchants for their gratitude simply at being invited. It was as crowded as the tavern that afternoon, yet somehow even more hollow, as if every one of these ninnies was putting on a performance. Until at last, Thaddeus pierced it all with the precision of an archer.

"My lord," he whispered. "That brandy-faced lady just belched."

Ulysses spat out his punch. Sure enough, there was a woman near eighty, doused in rouge so thick she matched the drapes, and he laughed all the harder.

Peering past her, he saw something else too: a circle of belles gathered near, smiling and whispering and training their gazes straight upon him. Did they know why he was laughing? Had they seen him ruin his own cravat?

All three were in striped silk gowns, form-fitting unlike the older ladies' hoops, their skin powdered white, their eyes lightly shadowed with lampblack. They too were part of the artifice, he knew – the same as this whole affair – girls like that only eyeing him for his estate. Yet with the punch already plunging through his veins, he stepped forward. "May I introduce myself?" he inquired.

"You may," answered the one in the middle. "Though you needn't."

Ulysses smiled graciously. "It's a good thing, then, for absorbing such beauty threefold, I've already forgotten who I am!"

They laughed warmly at that, the middle one in particular. "Rebecca Vance," she offered, and he noticed her wide, interested eyes, the same shade as her dark hair, hanging loose over her gown. He found he was glad to have come inside, after all – learning they'd traveled from Richmond, that they planned on returning the following day: he was interested in that too, in city life, he told them, and whether it really was more ready for change. For a stretch, he stayed there, while Thaddeus was off fetching the punch, until the brawling chuckle of his father cut in, and Ulysses angled back to see.

It took a moment to spot him, turning down the second-story hall overhead, beyond the railing, without even the good grace to stick to the passageway's far side – a goblet of wine in one hand, a slave girl in the other. This one was young, no more than Ulysses' own age, dimpled cheeks and cocoa eyes, thick hair brushed down to her waist; father was guiding her just so from behind, his palm against the small of her back, his fingers curled beside the soft cotton of her maid's dress.

So that suddenly Ulysses wanted to fly straight up there, to scream, not just at his father, but at every last one of these deviled fools, loud enough, furious enough, that they all would hear. *Don't you see? Don't you understand? Don't any of you care?*

Alas.

He merely stood in place, empty glass against his lips, his voice gone mute.

Thaddeus returned now, and placed his hand on Ulysses' shoulder. Then the girl beside him – Rebecca, she'd called herself – stepped a touch closer too, almost as if she'd sensed that something within him had been stretched, nearer to snapping than ever before, and she lowered her voice to a whisper. "They say it's time for supper, did you hear?" She waited, and didn't look away.

He tried to acquiesce, knowing that his father had gone, that the banquet tables beckoned, that the only thing now was to join with the rest.

Rebecca tilted her head, as if to say more, to question what it was he was thinking. But when still he didn't respond, she just moved along with the rest. Finally, Thaddeus handed over the next drink. "Come along," he was saying, while Ulysses went back to eyeing the empty hall above. "Come," he said again – and when still Ulysses remained frozen, he nudged him from behind. "Let us nab what we can – we'll smuggle it down to Cato, and tell him of these fools."

CHAPTER 6

Scott's Landing (Scottsville), Virginia
July 1845

He blinked his tired eyes.

Was this old age merely playing a gag?

He peered up, past the judge's bench, and the mahogany columns that lined the wall flanking the chambers. The building's ribbon-cutting ceremony had been only a month before, and the courtroom still had the bite of barely dried paint. The floors scarcely creaked.

But Ulysses was focused on the faces. Their rumble grew as he turned – a buzz of anticipation, all for him – his countrymen, high and low, waiting for court to be called into session. But he didn't care about any of that, either. He looked only for what he thought he'd seen, amid all those bobbing heads, just there.

Finally, he froze.

Was it really possible? All these years on? Standing amid them like that, still lanky, still serene? Here was a figure in red waistcoat and knotted black tie, the same green eyes as ever, the same Adam's apple pressed out past his high collar, and wavy hair pulled off his brow, more gray now than brown. His face was creased by a life of good cheer; his posture gone hunched from all the worry that'd come later. "It can't be," Ulysses murmured.

And at that, the man seemed almost to hear him, nodding from across the way – just so, that no one else could see – and Ulysses could feel his own eyes watering, as his old friend nudged past the shoulders in his way, gripping a black walnut rail, no longer young and mischievous, but grown up and aged at last.

It was enough that Ulysses finally understood, as he couldn't have before, that he wasn't alone. That no matter what came next, no matter how often these brutes called themselves the law, they couldn't shake him. They couldn't make him forget what mattered – what his own boyhood had long ago pushed him to grasp. They couldn't erase what three young men had once devised: Thaddeus Billings, Cato Brooke, and him.

"*Hear ye, hear ye, hear ye!*" the bailiff called out, and slowly he turned back. "*All rise! Court now underway, this year of our Lord, eighteen hundred and forty-five! His Honor Thomas R. Breckinridge presiding! God Bless these United States!*"

The old magistrate's jaw was set, beneath craggy cheeks that hung like old sacks. Reaching the bench, he motioned that they all sit, and Ulysses frowned at their eagerness.

"I call order!" he proclaimed in a voice that stung, and a drawl he made bitter. "The case of Ulysses Brooke! Charged with larceny and trespassory against his fellow man. Suspected, though not alleged, over a period of decades." At last, the judge faced him directly, two gentlemen of the commonwealth, one puffed out atop his dais, the other reduced to cuffs. "How is it you plead, Mr. Brooke?"

Ulysses didn't flinch. He was caught, it was true. Yet his book of maps lived on, unharmed. "Guilty, sir," he responded, and his own voice surprised him with its force.

The judge wrinkled his forehead. "The discharge of your crime, Mr. Brooke, was of your own recognizance?" He was skimming now from a checklist. "You had no accomplices, not now, not ever? Is that correct, Mr. Brooke?"

Ulysses was sure he could still feel Tad's eyes behind him, and again he thought of Cato as well: never once hinting of running away himself, staying focused on their grander vision instead, always thinking of every slave there'd ever been, never just his own anguish.

"Well, Mr. Brooke?"

"That's correct, sir," he replied, letting loose a breath. "I was alone, your Honor. I was the one who saw what needs be done. And I was the one who did it."

CHAPTER 7

Richmond, Virginia
March 1802

It was near dawn, his city room cast in fine blue shadow, and Ulysses lifted a dried wax candle from his nightstand, shuffling to the embers still glowing in the fireplace, touching them to the wick. Slowly, the room came to life. The wood floor shifted loudly, frigid against his feet, as he fetched the day's clothes from his dresser, brushing the lint from his stockings, clasping the silver buckles on his shoes. Standing before the looking glass – flecked and narrow, nothing like the gilded ones back home – he tied his hair back, then peeked at the sundial on the sill. Grabbing his papers, he hurried to make the day's first meetings on time.

This was why he'd whisked straight from William & Mary to the capital, after all. And now he walked briskly, weaving among the carriages in every direction, skipping across more cobblestone than he'd ever seen. Jefferson liked to say Virginia was a land unfettered by cities, but that was ideology, not fact. Here were dark-suited men with purposeful walks, steamers curling in from the Atlantic, oyster sheds by the bay.

Ulysses stepped to the next corner, past red brick shining beneath new gambrel roofs – until his gaze froze upon a chained bundle of slaves. They were bound by iron, led by a tobacco-spitting yeoman in a feather-tipped cap, regular proof of the growing reports of runaways. One of them reminded him of Cato, back at Boxwood – the same steady, sure-footed gait that was a cloak for so much more – and he watched as the group trudged forward, toward the auction house, where they'd be registered with the overseas arrivals for sale. Ulysses followed, then listened to the sellers squawking, as they poured whale oil over the Negroes' arms to give them the proper sheen. One of the slave women shrieked as a girl in a shredded cloak was wrenched from her arms, and at last, he had to turn away.

These were souls he could help, he thought – if only he could sort out how. His official title was Counselor to the Governor, a position he'd managed quite easily through his name. Yet what did a title matter, if all he could do was write up empty tax proposals, and fashion tighter regulations for permits?

He didn't even notice, then, that someone had addressed him.

"Mr. Brooke?"

He blinked. It was a woman, her dark eyes shining as she spoke, her hair the color of burnt chestnut. When she grinned at his absentmindedness, it was a smile that seemed to bubble straight from her soul.

"But don't you know me, Ulysses? I daresay you look near the same!"

"'Mornin' to you, ma'am."

"We met some time back – at your family's property at Boxwood." She paused. "I'm Rebecca Vance," so that now, when she said her name, the memory flickered – and all at once, he realized he could recall her wide gaze indeed, the same amused smile then as now, the way she'd studied him as if there were actually something to glean, and not just power to be gained. "I don't mean to distract you from your concerns," but her short eyelashes fluttered, and her voice was tender, low but sweet.

He gathered himself. "It's my concerns that distract me from you, Miss Vance."

"Heavens!" She laughed outright. "Apology most certainly accepted. Come," she said. "Shall we walk?" Her dress was yellow, with a neckline of imported silk, and puffed sleeves that ended below her elbows in white cuffs. A bonnet dangled from her neck.

"There was a party, I recall."

"So there was, Mr. Brooke."

"Such was life at Boxwood."

"And now?" She looked interested. "Where is it you spend your time?"

"Here. With Governor Monroe." He saw her expression brighten, and surprised himself with his desire to impress her further. "I'm of counsel."

She eyed him closer.

"Mostly I fixate on things I can make right."

"Does that mean there's something wrong with me?"

"Merely your timing, Miss Vance," and he bowed, pleased by her wit. "For I must make haste."

"Won't you pledge to tell me more when next we speak?"

"A briefer interval than our last, I hope?"

"Why, that's up to you, Mr. Brooke." And with that, Rebecca Vance curtsied, and let him hurry on.

***

That night, he dreamt of her.

They were moving once more through the city, gliding side-by side across gleaming blocks, when they came upon a bank. It was impossibly tall, its walls freshly scrubbed, stone as bright as the sun. "It's the answer, you know," she whispered, and she pointed ahead.

He squinted back, unsure, not understanding.

"Target their banks," she seemed to be saying. "And you'll strike at their bondage."

He watched as her face blurred and blended into the city shadows. He wanted to stay there with her. To ask more about what she meant, how she was, whom she'd become. But Rebecca was spinning away, her voice becoming an echo. *"Go – it's time,"* she instructed. *"It's back there you're needed – it's there the fight's to be waged."*

Ulysses reached out his arm, but it felt jammed in place.

He sat up. Out of breath, baffled, he stared across his bedroom. Why had she been there, when he scarcely even knew her? What was it driving such dreams at all, making him this desperate, ever more inflamed? The cotton mattress shifted loosely beneath his weight – the city merchants had stopped offering hay, insisting this would get fewer mites – and he brushed the locks from his brow.

He blinked now, considering it, the meaning of this dream. It was true that ever since Hamilton had founded the National Bank, the legislature had been chartering new branches – dozens already, cropping up like weeds – enough that planters like his father were no longer forced to inventory their whole harvests on their own, selling them in parcel instead, with new cash coming in from the northern buyers, flowing out for deposit straight away. The banks, then, were as eager as any for the rank hypocrisy that welcomed them.

In the meanwhile, his own anti-slavery legislation had stalled yet again in the Assembly. He'd framed it for the delegates just the way the governor had requested – incremental, understated, compensatory – yet still they'd refused even a vote, accusing him of asking the tobacco plantations to let go their own lifeblood. Indeed, it had been at the close of the afternoon session just the day before, when he'd found the governor, with smarmy eyes and whiskers that had never fully grown in, awaiting him off the main parlor in the executive mansion. The man had always been overcautious, to be sure: it was why he would never gain the renown of his friends Jefferson and Blair. But that hadn't guaranteed a betrayal quite like this, gathered with the chief assemblymen, chuckling as they stood round the large chestnut table at the room's center – coming to a pause the instant Ulysses had strode in.

"Brooke, it's time you start up with a new fancy," he'd ordered. The mass of them had looked just like the oil paintings on the wall at their rear, wispy-haired, wrinkled old souls, oblivious to all, as they waited in their antiquated knee breeches. "Listen here. It's your burden to live in dull times, with no battlefield on which to prove yourself. It's that which makes you seethe – naturally it does," and Monroe had even looked sympathetic as he'd said so. "But you mustn't let it fire your passions."

"If I moderate any further, sir, I'll be moving backwards. They won't even hold a vote on my bills."

The governor had cut back in. "The commonwealth, young man, is not your plaything. Your father spoilt you, and that's fine – the price of his own success, and one I'm sure he's been happy to pay. But by heaven, we're not so easily smitten."

Thinking back on it, swinging his feet from the bed, Ulysses seethed indeed. They were old men like any other, clinging to their years as proof of their wiles, instead of testament to mere good luck. He'd hoped to fix the system alongside them, without driving them all away. Yet they wouldn't budge.

Was he delusional, then, to opt instead for advice from a dream?

CHAPTER 8

Richmond, Virginia
March 1805

Under a thin sun, the neighborhood outside was humming: locals chattering, markets crowded, boulevards jammed alongside the newest Corinthian columns and windows of octagonal panes. It was all part of the latest boom, from tobacco certainly, but now cotton too – that trespasser from down the coast, making known its might.

Ulysses closed the sash to shut out the noise. For months, he'd been putting in extra hours, and today had been no different, arriving at his desk barely past dawn, already scribbling away at the morning's drudgery: bulletins for the partisan rags, regulations for traffic at the port, banquet arrangements for visiting dignitaries.

Alas, it was all cover – a cloak for the vision that had been expanding in his mind, ever since that dream, the one he couldn't shed, the one that had come to refashion his very soul. His actual energies had been devoted to studying bank routes, taking stock of the drivers at the carriage houses where the wagons for the new cash shipments were stored, even joining along on some of their rides, on the pretense of cataloguing their speed for the governor. On such journeys, he'd sit quiet, attentive, passing by framed barns and brown hillsides, through air that was a mix of wood-smoke and hay. The grind of the axle was often the only sound for miles, the red squirrels the only living souls to be seen. After all, many of the grandest plantations, Boxwood among them, were isolated amid the foothills of the Blue Ridge, their only neighbors the endless pastures that served as their moats. It was why the planters all lived in such mortal terror of slave revolt in the first place.

Each time one of the wagons stopped, retrieving its cargoes of gold, feeding the horses, pulling aside for lavatory breaks, Ulysses would take note. He'd even begun to believe he could manage it: hiding the funds within arm's grasp of the slaves themselves, ready to be dug back up on his command – stealing, stashing, doing it again – creating a secret labyrinth of burials, treasures out of sight until the moment arrived. Indeed, it wasn't just the ambition that had been carrying him forward, but the clarity of purpose: a proper fund for a proper revolution. A measure to match the moment.

For he'd come to accept the truth. His country was a lie.

He supposed he'd sensed it, really, from the first moments he could remember: in preacher's sermons, schoolhouse lessons, lectures from his own father – all those high-flying words, and the blood of the whip always beneath them. At first, he'd nursed such thoughts on his own, afraid of them, ashamed even. But with each step he'd ventured toward sharing them – visiting with Cato, carping with Thaddeus – the more brazen his anger had become. As it'd turned out, he wasn't the only one who saw the truth.

In time then, the question had become not why he was the one itching to do something about it, but why all the rest remained silent. His spark had come from all he'd been forced to learn, nourished in the shadow of his father's self-satisfied ease, spurred by knowledge of his friend's fate, sentenced to a lifetime of anguish over nothing but the chance of birth – only what did it matter?

Until at last, Ulysses had resolved not to look backwards at all, to waste no more time wondering what it was had nudged open his sight, always questioning what was wrong with him, and not with them. Such piety was what the system required of its adherents, the bidding of the caste into which he'd been born. And so he'd made his move to Richmond instead, found his spot in the halls of power – it was to be a start, at least – fixating on what he viewed before him, pursuing finally what must be done. Their civilization itself was the crime, he saw, not any deed done in response. It was a realization that had led him toward molding the fire within him, tending it as fuel, rather than foe. It had turned some innate rage into action at last.

Abruptly, he looked up.

Two workmen had arrived at the door, thick-bearded, in homespun breeches, carrying a glistening portrait of Jefferson. He waved them in, and watched as they yanked down the old one opposite his desk. "What was wrong with it?"

One of them shrugged. "New term, new portrait."

He nodded and took in this latest version being unveiled. In place of the famous flame of hair, the president had apparently gone white – though still no wig, Ulysses noticed, as if his claim to be one of the people were alive and well. He pushed up from his chair. The nearest adjutant was just out in the hall, baby-faced in a black vest and no jacket at all – the performed informality of the new century on display. "Have a carriage brought round."

"Sir?"

"A livery. At once."

The boy did as he was told, and Ulysses turned back, dipping his quill, scrawling out instructions that the rest of his day's schedule be canceled. The governor was out of town anyhow. The meetings were all with men his junior. His absence wouldn't even be noted.

***

The ride ended up quicker than anticipated – mud season had been mild – and by afternoon's end, he was flanked by dogwoods, their budded branches boasting the first signs of spring. The mansion loomed like a throne, its upper chimneys silhouetted against a golden horizon, porches like a series of checkpoints. The stallions whinnied, and he jumped out, tipping the driver, directing him to an inn at the village for his night's stay.

Here was his mother now, already bounding out to greet him, her pleated gown swishing. "We've missed you," she declared as he got close, kissing both cheeks, leading him toward the house, where the front door swung open and revealed his father next: a wide newspaper dangling from one hand, brown-papered cigar glowing in the other. Ulysses noticed his hair had gone all the way white, same as Jefferson's. He was standing quite still, meeting his grown son's eye, until slowly, he folded the paper under his arm, and extended his hand.

An extra plate was brought out for supper – ham and sauced apple, squash and molasses – and they sat in the formal dining room, served by more slaves than ever, each one in velvet tails, as if Franklin Brooke had come to fancy himself some American royal. "How is it, then, working for that reformist boss of yours?" he asked midway through the meal. Governor Page had taken over for Monroe, and the old guard was displeased. "I must say, my boy – you've given the family name a bit of a spell."

"I'm sorry to hear that, father." Ulysses raised his glass. "It's the name, after all, that got me into my office in the first place."

The conversation ebbed from there, until the port had been served, and he decided he'd humored them long enough, declaring it time for a stroll.

"It's dark as Africa out there," his mother protested.

Ulysses shrugged. "Too many hours in the carriage."

His father, alas, was not so readily fooled – nursing his wine, squinting back. That's fine, Ulysses thought. Let them guess where he was headed. So long as they didn't know his reason. He let himself up.

Outside, there was a clatter of thunder, and the twilight had taken on a glow. The whole plantation seemed to seep with the smell of wet dirt. Still, with the overseers menacing, and harvesting season upon them, the slaves hadn't yet ceased their evening's work, and he nodded to some of the familiar faces as he passed them by. Eventually, he heard a chuckle. "What a disturbing sight!" And he turned to see Cato, wiping his brow between the lines of tobacco shrubs, strapping as ever. "Drowning in self-pity, whilst he wanders among his slaves."

Ulysses let slip a smile.

"The prodigal son returned."

"If only for an evening."

"Back to sneaking me scraps?"

Ulysses held out his empty hands.

"So then why've I deigned a hello?"

"Come, let's walk." Ulysses knew the overseers would be too cowed to question him. "Assure me the whippings grow less frequent at least. The tide turns against them in the cities."

"Someone ought to inform your men."

Ulysses sighed. All the world's progress: revolutions and parliaments, power looms and steamboats, and for what? Voltaire, Rousseau, Washington – all memories now. The new century was poised to be no more than a lackey of the old. "I'll speak with my father."

Cato snorted.

They traced the familiar paths of their youth, enjoying a moment of respite as friends – the way God must have intended, Ulysses thought, no matter what men had divined in His wake.

"It's not like you to collect your thoughts," Cato observed next.

"You'll say I'm mad."

"I've never been one to join the chorus."

Ulysses rolled his eyes and slowed. "The governor's office has taken on a new task. Overseeing cash shipments from the great plantations."

His friend looked back.

"The point is, Cato, I know where the shipments run."

"To what end?"

"They can be reached."

"You were right before. You do sound a loon."

"There's thousands in gold."

"You don't need the funds."

"All the more reason they wouldn't suspect me."

"No thief's ever started out aiming to be caught, Ulysses."

"Ah." He raised his finger. "But what sort of thief abandons his loot?"

"Beg pardon?"

"I wouldn't keep a penny for them to find. Even if they were to inquire."

"I don't know what you mean." Cato frowned. His oval eyes narrowed.

"Revolution."

"You're not serious." But now Cato had brought his voice to a hush.

"I'd draw up maps. I'd place the gold only where it could be retrieved by slaves – men whose cause is already my own. Not all would need to become soldiers. Most would simply flee, seed money in hand, for such flight would be rebellion unto itself. Those who stayed, those who desired, and were able – they'd take the next step." He caught his breath. "As I see it, revolutions require three fundamentals: men, motive, materiel. It's but the final piece that's lacking. This plan would provide it. Wagonfuls of cash, buried. Enough for muskets, food, whatever men would require – to remove the heel from your throats, and unshackle your wrists at last." Now, he turned back. "It's that which I came to share, Cato. That which shall shape the remainder of my years. That which to our own sons and grandsons will appear no more fanatical than the ravings of Patrick Henry do to our ears today."

Cato hadn't moved. "You mean all this."

"Most certainly."

"You aren't afraid?"

"What if I am?" Ulysses gripped his friend's shoulder. "Aren't you, Cato? Every day?"

"It's no choice for me."

"Nor for me any longer."

"Don't give me that guff."

"I thought you'd approve!"

"Naturally I do." Slowly, they resumed their walk. "But can I not also doubt?" The slave was shaking his head. "You were pampered inside that mansion, remember. Stuffed full with learning. Spoilt by satin and silk, university, the capital. You pretend we share a fate."

Ulysses absorbed his friend's words. "It's not bondage for me, I grant you." He exhaled. "But nor is it liberty. To be raised in a cathedral devoted to its own glory, knowing all the while it's but a den of thieves. That the Lord Himself must be sobbing."

"Spare me." Still, Cato appeared to be considering it. "It'd be blood money, you know. Stolen off the backs of the suffering."

"Our theft would be the thing to purify it."

"You're dreaming."

"Then dream with me." Ulysses realized he was clenching his fists. "There's a path that beckons. We must seize it."

They'd reached the slave cabins. In the silver light, the cramped buildings were smoothed by shadows, their anguish concealed by the pyrrhic peace of night.

"You say the shipments are frequent?"

Ulysses nodded. They were standing just shy of the porch now, where they used to meet as boys. "We'd mark down every treasure we'd got, and when all was said and done, we'd make known where we'd left them." He could imagine it already: posting the information in anonymous broadsides, tucking slips into the Bibles inside slaves' chapels, sewing them into their coats. "I swear to you, Cato. It's possible. They'll follow us when it's time."

"You speak of a lifetime's work."

"So long as I'm blessed with a lifetime for pursuing it, yes. And with some help along the way."

The grass, still dead from winter, crunched as they stepped to the cabin door. "Then you'll have it," Cato said finally. "Not because it'll succeed, mind you." He'd quieted. "Only because I know nothing else can."

CHAPTER 9

Site of Birmingham, Alabama – September

1885

The calendar said it was autumn. The black belt said otherwise.

Standing on the platform, staring out at an alien landscape, Sam gripped his book of maps, and stepped forward. He was soaked in sweat already, weary from the ride, yet he refused even another moment's delay. All those months since he'd first discovered the book, all those school terms spent scrounging wages for the journey, and now, here he was.

It was the South's latest hub, according to the papers, emerging like an oasis – from nothing, from nowhere – chattel and cotton no longer, said the boosters: now only smokestacks and ore. He'd decided he'd better get here before it was too late, before whatever treasure Ulysses Brooke had buried was swallowed up in the boom of cranes and steel.

Birmingham was where his dream would begin.

He'd packed a carpetbag of clothes, canteens, and hardtack, hired a buggy in Virginia, hitched a ferry down the Mississippi, then finally switched to rail in Selma. The women had been let on first, then the men, some in workmen's clothes like his, others in black coats and trousers, lastly the colored folks, directed to an unpainted carriage at the rear. Sam had never seen so many of them in one spot, a small boy among them, shoved down the aisle with the others, ears like saucers, a loose-limbed stride. The lad had tried for the open seat beside Sam, not yet knowing any better, only to be yanked by his smock collar when a conductor stepped in, as if everything the war had sought – all that Sam's father had died to enshrine – could be squelched in an instant.

After that, Sam had leaned against the window and stared. They'd passed through meadows of yellow, shredded cliffsides and mines, painted depots and whole swaths of despair – brick shops hawking pistols and cornmeal, boys in knickers patched with flannel, sprinting alongside the train – until he'd spotted the factories at last, pumping their steel for a salivating nation.

Now, hearing the locomotive's screech fade behind him, he glanced between the book in his hands and the vista that awaited. The world Ulysses Brooke had described was gone. There were no cotton patches like purple-streaked snow, no wooded valleys still bearing arrows from the days of the tribes. Instead, Sam saw only flat warehouses like giant crates, and smooth boulevards in between: grimy and gray, open to any soul who might be willing to join. And willing they were: dozens of men trudging from the station, hoisting mallets and augers, ready to barter their brawn. Tightening his own bag across his shoulder, following the map as best he could according to the slope of the hills, Sam joined them, ignoring their vulgar jokes and even more vulgar smells, spotting two locals offering directions. They wore heavy boots, and had beards thick as briar, and to Sam's surprise, when they spoke, it wasn't with the bark he'd expected, but in a pair of Irish brogues, the sort of melody he recognized from the immigrants back home. "How ya' fare, stranger? Speak the Lord's tongue?"

"I hope so, for my praying's sake," he answered, and they grinned. "Still hiring?"

"Wages by the hour."

"Can I start today?" Next to theirs, his own words sounded like a broken snare.

"A proper Yank!" came the reply – and they led him through, over to a bed of beams and a foreman yelping instructions, so that it wasn't long before he was blending in, keeping his head down until the supper bell clanged, and the others were hurrying off for bacon and beer.

He lingered after that, waiting as the voices faded, wishing the sun would follow their lead and drop. When finally it did, and the scaffoldings turned to shadow, he squinted at his book in the moonlight, matching the coordinates with his compass, counting his steps precisely, fitting the measurements to the page.

He paused at a trampled pasture, already staked for cement, a few loose lilies left over from summer. Then he slid his shovel from his bag, aiming for silence, grimacing every time he scraped a pebble. In time, he'd created a hole half the width of a train car, getting three feet down, until he was sure that he hit something.

He crouched close at once, like a dog after a bone, scooping the dark earth with his fingers now, feeling the cool of metal indeed. Iron, he thought – a rusted band across its lid – and he widened his stance, then heaved and stretched and plucked it straight from the ground, breaking the mud around its edges.

The moon rose higher, and the world grew bright once more.

The clasp was stuck, but he managed it with a pocket knife, and slowly, wishing it wouldn't groan so loud, Sam pried open the lid. The coins inside looked as though they'd only just been minted.

"My God," he managed to whisper. The Brooke treasure was real.

Still, he stared only a moment. Angling the chest against his knees, shuffling the coins into his bag with a clang, he straightened beneath their weight, resolving that in future escapades, he'd be better served with a wagon.

He heard a shout.

"Ahoy there brother!"

Sam turned. It was one of the workers: bowlegged in overalls, a thin wooden clipboard beneath his elbow. "You trailing me, friend?"

"Not to fret! No public privies in town: figured I'd do the lads a favor and get myself upwind!" The man glanced at Sam's shovel. "You in the same fix then?"

"Just finished up."

"A civilized Yank, I reckon!" The fellow laughed. "Burying your own dung!"

Sam shrugged, and let the man have his sport. Turning away, he gave a final wave – relieved the stranger stayed where he was – and picked up his pace back to the station, where the ticket window was still staffed. A young clerk was slumped behind the counter, mouth stretched wide in a yawn, taking no note of the dirt on Sam's clothes. "Next train's at daybreak," he all but murmured. "Where can I get you then?"

"Closest to Gotham that you're able."

"One way for a dollar. Return for a buck-and-four-bits."

"I'll take the one," Sam said, and reaching into his bag – tempted to use one of the antique coins, but staying careful – he paid his fare.

Ticket in hand then, he tipped his hat, and turned toward a bench down the way. His heart was pounding, he realized, and it would be some time before he could drift off. Pulling out a pencil instead, he turned to the page that had guided him through.

"*First success!*" he scratched across the margin, and leaning back, he waited for dawn.

1973

Amtrak's orange upholstery smelled of coffee and sweat. The air conditioning had given out somewhere back in the Carolinas. Wafts from the toilet came every time someone slid open the door. And as the train shifted on the tracks, a conductor strolled down the aisle, belly hanging over his belt, bright red bellbottoms that made him look like a clown.

Alvin turned away, staring off to abandoned hillsides and ramshackle barns, sloping porches and stacks of tires. In time, he was able to make out the contours of a river, and he squinted toward its muddy banks, framed by thin forests and rusted out bridges. So this was the deepest South, he thought.

It made him shiver.

The folder was on his lap, stuffed tight with photographs he'd clipped from the office. He'd used the bureau's lab to print Polaroids of the book of maps, then to get them matted and enlarged. Claire Calloway had raised her eyebrows when he'd submitted the budget – she'd scowled even worse when he'd applied for funding for the trip – but she'd had to agree. For how else to prove the maps were real? How else to show that Sam Billings had nourished his entire empire with spoils from a crime?

"*Success*," Billings had scribbled at some point, the pencil halfway faded. Below that, he'd doodled warehouse foundations and staked-out pastures – a construction site eager to become a city.

Alvin had already verified the information was real in broad terms from New York. But coming here, he hoped for something more – some layer of detail, however small – something to pave the trail for a jury.

The train slowed.

Pulling down his luggage, he found a canister of Brylcreem and crammed down the edges of his hair, aiming to look a touch more local. Then he joined the masses, amid a mix of sunshine and exhaust, entering into a panorama of office parks in heavy-baked air. Quickly now, he was moving through Birmingham's downtown, matching the hand-drawn etchings from Brooke and Billings with the modern road maps the bureau had provided. He soon found a neighborhood of front porches missing their rails, molasses-skinned locals in tank tops soaked through, guard dogs in steel-looped chains. It was enough to make East Brooklyn look like Fifth Avenue back home, and he quickened his pace.

The wool of his suit clung to him desperately, and at first he didn't notice the cops massing ahead, or the commotion beyond them: a young black fellow pinned against a Thunderbird at the curb, the officers snarling, spitting, keeping the peace. It was as if the old days were reaching out, eager to show they were still here, no matter the yellow cranes ringing the horizon like overgrown toys; these sheriffs might as well be carrying whips.

Alvin hesitated, but the noise began to calm, and he kept on, feeling a twinge of guilt at his own silence, before silencing that in turn, moving toward a stretch of faded brick and metal roofs, skipping over potholes-turned-pools after a recent storm, along a road angled just like the one Billings had sketched. He checked the coordinates from the photos' edge – numbers Ulysses Brooke had devised first, still clear, still precise – spotting the old factory straddling a whole block: dead ivy dangling like a forgotten scab, jagged holes in its window panes, the whole thing listing badly to the left, as if it had downright melted from too many years in the heat. He shook his head. It must have been a bare patch, slotted for construction, when Billings had arrived a century before.

No smoking gun, of course, but Alvin made a note.

1806

"When we were lads, down here was all still savages," Ulysses remarked.

"Thank God then for planters," Cato answered. And they both smirked, as their horses loped through endless waves of white on either side – Alabama cotton, lush and new – a replica of upcountry living. They'd reached the highway they wanted, and the air was like a hot wet cloth. It had been a long stint down, eating mostly squirrel and deer, steering east of Spaniards and natives – all after convincing Ulysses' father he required leasing Cato for the duration, flashing a copy of the governor's signature, acting as if it were an order from Richmond.

"You reckon they'll try and stop us?" Cato asked now. In fact, it had been his idea to grow the ambition of their scheme, venturing farther afield – to inject fear into the frontier itself, unsettling the whole of the South if they could, all while gaining more funds for its demise. Ulysses had agreed at once, deciding summer furlough was their chance, time enough for slipping away.

"They'd have to slay me first."

"It's me they'd slay, Ulysses."

They went quiet at that, then slowed as they entered a new patch of woods, hitching their horses by a brook, moving on foot towards the bank branch they were targeting. When they were close, they built a nest of tinder, laying twigs on top, and Cato notched the driest stick he could find, whisking it hard with his palms, while Ulysses blew in air from the side. As soon as it was ready, they sprinted back to the road just opposite. "There's only two men inside," Ulysses whispered, pointing to a breezeway down the building's middle. He'd learned of the place back in Richmond, sifting through the coastal cash routes listed in the governor's papers.

Already, the first curls of smoke were slithering toward the sky, and sure enough, there were nearby yelps of *fire!* soon to follow. To their relief, the bank's duo didn't hesitate, jogging right out, gripping their hats. Ulysses exhaled, Cato grinned outright, and together they pushed onward, Cato keeping two paces behind, committed now to the role of the obedient slave, as they stepped to the road and into view.

Entering inside, they confirmed the place was empty: a single counter to the rear, a pair of ladderback chairs, a painting of Jefferson just like the ones back home. Ulysses found a double set of keys hanging from twine, and a cupboard at his feet, and without a word, he unlatched it. Sure enough, the cashbox was within: squat iron walls, a brass padlock in front, and when the second key worked too, he gulped. For here was a true bundle of gold, newly minted dollar coins and more, Lady Liberty etched proudly across their fronts. The coins were local, it was true, but the metal would retain its value, and he wanted to shout in triumph and despair, that such riches were real, that they came on the backs of men just like Cato.

They hoisted the box up, keeping watch while a crowd of farmers pushed a cylinder pump right past them along the muddy road, heading over to douse the flames. Only then did they skirt safely back out, balancing the weight of the cash between them, swiveling their heads to be certain they remained alone.

They returned to the wagon in good time, keeping silent. And as they rode through a loose forest of pine, eager for nightfall to cover their tracks, they could make out plantations through the branches. "As good a spot as any," Ulysses whispered – there'd be thousands of slaves all around, plenty for when it came time for retrieving the box's treasure – and jumping down, distracting the horses with carrots, they slid it back out, into a grove of bluegrass between the trees. Working like oarsmen in shifts, shoveling hard in the dimming light, they heaved soil nonstop, until they had a hole half as deep as a man.

"Proper bank robbers then," Cato observed, hands on his hips, hemp shirt rising with each breath.

"Not robbers," Ulysses exhaled in turn. "Revolutionaries."

Filling the hole was quicker than digging it, and soon they'd re-joined the road. Ulysses lit the wagon's lantern, and grabbing a quill, the memory of the terrain still fresh, he opened up the diary he'd purchased with just this in mind. It had the tangy smell of new leather, and gold leaf that still gleamed, and with Cato soon snoring at his side, he traced a ruler, getting his map to scale, measuring the miles based on their horses' trot, checking his compass to make it precise. It didn't take long: a decent likeness of the topography, an arrow noting the plantations not far off, the burial spot itself marked with a cross at the center, and overlaying it all, the coordinates of his grid, marked out with graphs at the top of the page. It would be a fine guide, he thought with satisfaction, for all those poor souls, some already toiling, some not yet born, to follow in his path.

CHAPTER 10

Richmond, Virginia
October 1806

His first morning back from Alabama, Ulysses found himself confronted.

A breeze was blowing in from the water, chaises clattering down the cobblestone, and here they came, twirling out from right next door as he left his house not far past dawn, a man and a woman, about his own age. There was no avoiding them. They were directly in his path.

The husband was dressed impeccably – a bottle green waistcoat, white pantaloons, twin silk braces bearing roses and lilies. He lifted his walking stick as he waved, ivory-tipped, and offered a wide smile of greeting across his pale, pampered face.

His wife was a head shorter, curls above her ears, red ribbon around her bonnet, an ungodly long ostrich feather dangling from its rear. Her gown was muslin blue, she had boots the same shade, and her round little face was like a squat cup of fruit, painted and polished, a failing feint at beauty.

"Good day to you!" the young man shouted.

"To you in turn," Ulysses answered, lowering his hat in reply.

"Cyrus Thompson. And may I present my wife, Beth."

"A pleasure. New to Richmond, I gather?"

"Just Tuesday last. It's been a bedlam: carpet weavers, housemaids, carpenters too." This Cyrus Thompson leaned on his stick. "A funny thing, but I've not yet seen you passing by!"

"Been taken up with my work, I suppose."

"Oh? Where's that?"

"I serve at the governor's pleasure," and he extended his hand. "Ulysses Brooke."

Cyrus cleared his throat. There was a flicker of recognition in his eyes. "Not the son of Franklin? Heir to Boxwood Grove?" He laughed a bit too jovially. "I daresay I'd be grateful to make your father's introduction."

"You and the whole of the commonwealth, I'm sure."

"Indeed." Cyrus Thompson paused, as if he weren't sure whether he'd just been insulted, though his smile never left him. "If you don't mind the query, Mr. Brooke, how is it you've fallen toward city life?"

"Into the distemper of politics, you mean?" Ulysses returned his hat to his head. "As I often tell my father: our revolution's never really done. Someone's got to keep up its tending and care."

"You work closely with the governor then?" It was the wife speaking now, just as intrigued as her husband in forging a connection.

But Ulysses had had enough. He'd need to stay careful with these two, he was already certain: just the sort to remain keen on his comings-and-goings. "But forgive me," he parried. "What is it's brought you to our capital in turn?"

"Nothing near as glamorous as you," Cyrus explained. "Raised in Chester, made rich by cotton, like all the rest. I'm here to manage distribution."

"Ah. Godspeed to you then," and at last, Ulysses felt freed to go.

***

By the time he arrived at the governor's, he'd shed the irritation of their questioning – only to face one of the clerks on duty, pointing dramatically down the hall. "He requests all hands this morning," the lad declared breathlessly. "They're fixed to begin."

Ulysses frowned. This was unusual, and he stepped along the carpeting towards the parlor in back. Through heavy French doors, he encountered a crowd: every aide there was, gathered round the board table at the center. The executive chair – polished walnut, beneath a sloping red cushion – was empty for the moment; in the corner, double-hung windows were cracked to the courtyard. A sterling silver tray held tumblers of ale.

Governor Page strode in shortly then, citrus perfume wafting in with him; he scanned their faces with his tiny eyes, as if he were still surprised anyone might listen to what he had to say. He must know he's an unimpressive man, Ulysses thought – the type who maps his course only after he's certain others will follow. "Gentlemen," he began, sliding his spectacles down his nose. "A good morning to you."

"And to you, sir," they echoed back, no better than schoolboys afraid of the birch.

"Nothing too dire today, I'll warrant – yet neither a trifle." He stood beside his chair. "We've news from the commonwealth's northernmost bank, you see. Missing funds."

And suddenly, Ulysses' mouth went dry.

"Upriver," the governor was saying. "As of Christmas last. Across the county line."

Instantly, Ulysses knew it was his own doing. Ever since he and Cato had begun their work, he'd wondered when it would be noticed. The months had trickled by, and still it had been too easy – no postings, no capital chatter. The prideful piece of him had even grown impatient.

"I needn't explain to you that the banks must keep track of their gold," the governor went on. There were grunts of agreement, and fists knocking upon the table. "We can't have planters return to stowing cash in private lockboxes, hoarding wealth away from the greater good. As all of you know, absent a nourishing stream, no river can truly be sprung free. We'll have stifled our enterprise, whilst our northern neighbors are cultivating theirs."

"Hear! Hear!" they called out, and the governor looked buoyed.

"The bankers in question concealed this some months," he explained, "aiming to sort where the blunder occurred. They assure me such heedlessness won't occur again. I've assured them we must be made aware if it does."

Ulysses swallowed. *Scarcely a year of scheming,* he thought. *And nearly caught already.* Still, what else could he do? Playing by the rules had come to seem futile; only a fool would harbor faith in compromise and good cheer. And though the governor peered back at them all an extra moment, he eventually clicked his heels, and spun away, velvet tails fluttering.

***

The invitation arrived the next afternoon.

It came by post, a red wax seal across the outer edge, fine threaded paper within. The calligraphy was expert – shaded just so, loping across the page: *A Fall Luncheon*, it declared. And below that:

Mr. Ulysses Brooke is requested to attend,
At Capt. Vance's city home.
Saturday, 15th Oct. current, at 1 o'Clock, pm.

At first, Ulysses assumed it was something to do with the governor's office, another function, another request for a face to pad the crowd. It took a minute to recognize the truth. For this was the father of Rebecca Vance: the woman of whom he'd dreamt – who'd spurred him to his entire enterprise, then, without ever knowing it – who'd charmed him every time he'd come upon her. He recollected that he'd pledged to call, that before he'd distracted himself with Cato and their conspiring, he'd even meant to do it.

The rest of the week passed quickly after that. He came to recall her wit, her buoyancy when last they'd met on the roadside, even if he knew it meant she must harbor a kind of contentedness, a comfort with all that he saw as façade – enough that by week's end, he'd grown jitters. After all, it had been too long since their last encounter – it occurred to him she could even be betrothed by now – it was conceivable she wouldn't even remember him. Perhaps it hadn't been Rebecca at all who'd requested his presence, in fact, but likely her father, summoning him solely for his family name, one plantation scion to another, recognizing a man of influence when he saw one.

The luncheon was to be at the family's city home, a townhouse of burnt brick, bay windows, and a glass-enclosed observatory up top. And by the time the moment arrived, Ulysses was all but forcing his legs forward, finding himself bowing to the captain and his wife in the receiving line, questioning whether he ought to have come at all. They were a handsome couple: Rebecca's father shared her wide smile and searching brown eyes, her mother had her same fine hair, though rather than hanging ringleted, it was restrained in a bun. The captain wore his old military brass; his wife had on a high-waisted silk gown. They bowed and curtseyed in turn.

Behind them, the parlor room beckoned. There was a fireplace of white marble and walls of plantation art. Chrystal chandeliers lined the plaster ceiling; polished china bowls posed like trophies; and as he entered in, Ulysses registered familiar faces, staffers from the governor's office, a few fellows from school, his neighbors the Thompsons, their eyes flitting for a chance to chat with those of higher rank. The slaves, of course, swirled all around – silent, unseen, unavoidable – pouring carafes, mopping spills, while over in the dining room, the napkins had been folded into miniature manors, the vases were stuffed full with dried lavender and rose, and porcelain plates flanked silver cutlery. The air itself seemed soaked with pride, drowned with ladies' perfume, rosemary-and-brandy mostly, and the tang of the men's cologne.

And then – just as he was about to give up on the whole thing, to rush for the exit and a blast of icy air – Ulysses heard her voice. It was as bracing as the evening breeze that beckoned.

"You came."

She was smiling, her spirited eyes locked on his. She wore a pink sash, and a gown of cream; her shoulders sloped underneath.

He managed a smile of his own. "What sort of clod would forgo seeing you?"

"You tell me."

"Forgive me the past, Miss Vance." Ulysses felt his heart pound as she stepped closer, surprising him with its force. "I've found work all-consuming. To a fault, I'm sure."

"A man ought not apologize for his passions."

"Only for surrendering to them, then."

And when she grinned, he was delighted – filled with some kind of forgotten wonder. Was it her candor? Or the melody with which she cloaked it? "Shall I fetch us some punch?" she asked.

It was his turn to smile once more. "Do you oft recite a gentleman's lines in his stead?"

"Only when he can't summon them himself," and with that, she left him waiting, no longer fixating upon the party's indulgence, but swiftly recalling luncheons from when he'd been a boy. He thought now of how he and Cato would steal away for footraces, galloping down towards the quarters, never considering the trouble they might bring themselves.

Rebecca soon returned, delivering a flute, readying for a toast. They clinked their glasses. "I want to tell you something, Ulysses Brooke – though my father informs me I ought keep my notions to myself."

"Try me."

"I don't fancy I've met a Virginian of your stripe before."

He tried another grin. "So wealthy?"

"So wary." Her own smile had faded in response. "You're searching for something."

He looked back. "Maybe it's you."

"Mr. Brooke!"

He shrugged.

"You're very puzzling, you know," she said after another moment.

"What is it you'd like made clear?"

"Some glimpse of what vexes you. What you find so wanting in my family's home, enough that you were readying to leave before I halted you."

"You noticed?"

"Even a blind man wouldn't have suffered that grimace, Mr. Brooke." She tilted back her head, as if for another view. "And then – when I came back just now – a different look altogether. Sorrowful, even."

Ulysses realized he was staring at her lips. "I suppose when you put it like that, I sound a sad case."

She paused. "But you must be famished. Come with me. The cooks prepared stew and potato last evening – they've stored it the cellar – we've baskets of apples too."

"What of the luncheon?"

But she'd already started moving, and he stepped to follow. They navigated the crowds quickly, and over to a hidden flight of stairs below, empty but for a few of the housemaids, scattering upon seeing them. Soon, they reached a worn table by the home's basement hearth, and Rebecca ordered them a plate. Potatoes were resting in the middle, the apples in the corner. A pair of three-pronged forks balanced at the edge.

When Ulysses reached for one, their hands touched.

Instantly, they each pulled back, and looking up, he noticed her eyes appeared darker down here, cast in shadow by the table's candles.

The soup, meantime, was salty, the potato dry; but the apples were divine. "They're fresh plucked," Rebecca offered, reading his thoughts. "Those slaves are little durgens, but I'll be a devil if they haven't mastered orcharding."

"A pity we don't let them master something more."

"Beg pardon?"

"You must wonder at it yourself upon occasion, no?"

But though Rebecca frowned at that, she didn't protest; and together, they stayed there, eating, another while more.

CHAPTER 11

Scott's Landing (Scottsville), Virginia
February 1853

The cell at Albermarle County Jail had a cracked floor and a bloated ceiling, and Ulysses often imagined it might defy the laws of science at any moment, collapsing in on itself from both ends. It had to be a hundred years old, its front wall nothing more than rusted bars, its rear a concoction of sheared-off granite, with a tiny square window higher than his head. A dented piss pot sat in the corner. A bench of planks was also ready to crumble.

Still, he was accustomed to it by now: accustomed to the guards who'd gather in the hall, to the flicker from the single candle on the sill, and to the stench of sweat and stool, and the fading memories of company. It was morning, he thought – or perhaps afternoon. He'd been re-reading serials from *Frank Leslie's* – the guards left copies whenever they were done with them – dozing every now and again, dribbling urine down his thigh like an infant. His bowl was tilted by his feet, while a rat nibbled the mush at its edges. His joints were throbbing; his bones felt hollowed out.

When to his surprise, one of the men hollered in from the hall, a spindly fellow, with an officer's stripe. "You've a visitor, Brooke" he declared, and for a long moment, Ulysses simply stayed on the floor, making sure he'd heard right – until a new silhouette emerged from beyond the bars, and the guard's keys ground the latch, sliding open the door.

There, as fanciful as an apparition, was Rebecca.

Her hair was grayer, certainly, coiled into ringlets and a bun, tied in white linen. Her eyes, still smart, were dancing no more. But it was her. *It was her.* Even just standing there, it was clear she had the same mettle underneath, the same forward spirit as ever – staunch and determined, sharpening the whole space the instant she walked in. She wore a blue-quilted petticoat and a violet hoop dress, more color than this room had ever seen. Her cheeks were lined, the edges of her eyes gone red. Her hands were trembling, clasped at her waist as if that might keep them steady, and Ulysses tried to guess at what it was that shook them, or what he felt in turn: was this mutual rage, or pity?

After what that they'd each inflicted upon the other – look at her face! Aged now, and emptied – it was hard to admit this was the only woman he'd ever let himself consider, the one who might even have been his wife. And for just a second, he could see the years melt away: her hair grown lush, her visage the way he recalled it – lips not yet stern and stiff, but breaking into a knowing smile, that appraising gaze – and somewhere inside, he wanted to weep.

Instead, he stayed frozen in his spot, neither standing nor offering a bow – whether because of the pain in his legs or in his soul, he wasn't wholly sure. He merely cleared his throat, in the hope that his voice, once his best instrument, would overcome its rust; until at last he was speaking, uttering now, finally, what he'd always known he must. "*Why?*" he began – no matter that he registered the iciness of his own greeting, and how it startled him – "how could you have, Rebecca?"

When she reached him, he saw that there were indeed streaks of tears patted dry, like used up riverbeds. "Had you just lent me your ear, Ulysses," she answered, "just told me what it was you were doing – I'd have talked you straight out of it. I'd have saved you from this place."

"Instead of confining me to it."

"Don't be cruel."

"You deny it?"

"You were going to get yourself killed. For heaven's sake, you needed protecting, from your own folly, from assailing the very world that bore you!"

His old eyes shone anew. "I did what was right."

"Lying to all those you knew?"

"Enough then! Why come? Leave me to what's left of my life." And surprising himself once more, he clenched his fist as he spoke, and slapped his knuckles against the wall's stone.

Rebecca flinched and looked away. Her lips had begun to tremble, just like her hands.

And all at once, this was too much – the nakedness of everything they'd shared – to make any of his words match. He took a new, shaky breath, gathering himself, twisting back. "I was sorry to hear about your parents."

She kept her stance steady. "He warned me, you know. My father."

"I know."

"I was yours, Ulysses. We had an entire path unto ourselves. You knew it, yet you drifted off anyway – conflating me with all the rest." Her voice dropped. "Living as though you were Christ Himself." She could no longer conceal her crying. "You must have known such martyrdom would stain me too."

He watched her as she spoke, feeling himself wobble with every one of her sobs. "There's naught to be gained here," he only murmured this time. "You should've waited me out, 'til I was gone."

But she took another step closer. "All those years, fancying yourself a savior, yet what was it really, Ulysses? Only running from the world. From a career that might've done some good. Telling yourself you were the one with answers; that in time, we'd all see, that if you were just patient enough, you'd be proven good and true. And here you are, doing the same: imagining you made some mark, your character intact. That it was I who did wrong, naming what you really were."

"Do tell."

"A thief," she answered, and her voice was sharp once more. "A traitor. A common criminal."

"A man who broke your heart, you mean." He stared back, and felt his heart slam with its old strength. "You wished to live like all the rest, pretending at peace, denying our sin."

"Can nothing put a stop to your piety, Ulysses?" She pointed toward the wall. "Those rats scurrying – are they your only acolytes?" The veins in her brow had swelled. "You required only that slave friend of yours, I suppose. Now you lack even that."

So that finally, Ulysses had to brace himself, stooped, resting against the wall. "You came here to wound me."

"I came that you might listen."

"You mean that I might yet concede?" Suppressing a grunt, he yanked himself straight, like a reluctant piece of twine that had been bundled too long. "It was your own reputation that concerned you, Rebecca. That was all."

The guard's voice interrupted, the same fellow who'd let her in. "Time's up, ma'am" – and she turned, not even trying to keep from quivering. "Goodbye then," she said hoarsely. "You're right. I oughtn't have come." She gripped an iron bar of the cell. "Only just know that you were loved, Ulysses." She was stepping away. "Even after what you did." And as suddenly as she'd come, she was gone.

CHAPTER 12

Arlington County, Virginia
April 1807

The Vance property was at least as large as Boxwood, and even more valuable so near to the coast. The elm branches across its drive made for a tunnel into its other world, depositing Ulysses amidst a line of carriages just like his, their hoods stretched out like accordions, and he straightened his coat, hopping out, entering the glory of the home's foyer, where crystal-cased candles sparkled and the floor was freshly oiled. Fresh-picked bluebells dangled from porcelain, as sweet as if they were leaking sugar; an open-string staircase beckoned. Somewhere a pair of fiddlers had struck up a reel.

He had simply never met a woman like Rebecca, he'd decided, one who seemed to see through all the nonsense. It wasn't that she was angry about it, which he found baffling, but at least she was aware. That much was in her eyes – in their blaze, but also their restraint – in the way she nodded along when he critiqued their own people, or managed not to scoff at the way he spoke of the slaves. Other Virginia women fluttered through their lives, no more affectual than the breezes passing through their plantations. Not Rebecca. Her smile was beautiful, but real.

He hadn't seen her much since the luncheon at her townhouse. In the meantime, he'd filled his days putting together new schemes with Cato, consumed once more by their search for new opportunities – until he'd received the latest invitation, this time for an Easter ball, to be held at her family's plantation-seat, north of the city.

He found her now at her father's side, welcoming the arrivals, the height of fashion: a gown of gold lace, trimmed with pink pearls, her thick hair loosely knotted. When she saw him, her smile broadened. "Shall I show you in?" she asked as if he were the only guest there.

"What of all this?"

"Leave them to pa," and with a wink, she led the way across woven carpets, beneath endless portraits of New World nobles. Ulysses took in the frozen faces, perched like lords and ladies of old – as if America had never even happened.

"It's a wonder what the Revolution was even for," he noted.

"To free you up for making precisely those asides, Mr. Brooke."

"And them?" He pointed to the slaves by the wall.

"Ah – if not for our freedom, who should be left to ensure their bondage?"

He peered back, not sure whether she was joking.

"Do your politics never cease, Mr. Brooke?"

"Do anyone's?" They made their way in further, past waves of guests, and fetched goblets of rum, getting nearer the music, smiling at the awkwardness of being jostled together. Ulysses gulped down his glass and took another, as the shimmer from the chandeliers cast the whole scene in rivers of light. Why not oblige her at least a moment, he thought – if only for the duration? He sighed. "When I was a lad, you know, my mother would store lavender the whole season before Easter. She'd jar it in the cellar, then scatter it across the steps the evening prior. Come morning, we'd hang its leaves from the sills."

"That sounds lovely." The fiddlers had ratcheted up their pace, and couples were dancing, lifting their knees, hands at their sides, clopping forward and back. To Ulysses' surprise, Rebecca began stomping herself. "Happy Easter, Ulysses Brooke," she declared, grabbing his hand, taking a step forward.

"People will talk, Rebecca."

"I can't imagine what you mean."

"Your father." He spoke louder. "Your neighbors."

But she only smiled wider, and her brown eyes crinkled. "I seek merely to enjoy the ball."

So that finally, without quite meaning to, he slid across the floor right with her. In every direction, guests were clapping, expanding their circle, and it felt to Ulysses as if the music itself were becoming amplified, as he tilted back his glass once more. Gliding onward, he tried dodging thoughts of his next maneuverings with Cato, of the slaves on duty against the wall, of treasures yet to be purloined and buried. Somewhere along the line, someone delivered him another glass, and the fiddlers crescendoed. "Its melody lilts without warning," he remarked.

"Let me show you," she announced, reaching out her hand.

"We daren't."

"You wager anyone's paying us a bit of heed?"

"They'll all be too scandalized to protest!"

"You have to know, Ulysses, I've imagined a dance with you since the moment we met."

"That's the rum talking."

"It's not," and she brought her face to his. For a second then, it was as if the whole floor belonged only to them, as if some unknown force had swept down as a guide, with nary a thought for what was proper, or right. Rebecca's dark eyes were more alive than ever; there were soft dimples in her cheeks. She boasted her same smile as before. And succumbing further, he wrapped his fingers round her back.

CHAPTER 13

New York City
February 1886

Somehow, the wagon had made it intact all the way from Alabama. There'd been moments Sam hadn't been sure it would – when the axles had snapped during an ice storm in the Carolinas, and the spokes tore out on a stream bed in Maryland – but now, parking in a pile of black slush draped upon a New York curb, he'd managed it at last. He hitched his exhausted horse to a pole and hoisted down his carpetbag with the stolen treasure inside.

It was a constable, in a navy blue coat and matching stovepipe hat, who stole back his attention. The fellow was pointing right at him, barking through a bushy black beard. "What's in the parcel?" he demanded in an East Side staccato, fast-paced enough to come out as a single word.

"Shovel and spade," Sam improvised. "I'm with a gardening crew."

"In the dead of winter?"

He stiffened. He'd brawl if he had to. After all, it'd be easier to answer for a street fight with a nosy lawman than a sack full of antique gold. But facing front, he loosened the bag's rope, and pulled out the tip of his shovel – the one he'd used to dig up old Ulysses Brooke's iron chest of cash. The Alabama mud was still caked on its metal edge. "Wintertide bulbs," he declared with conviction. "Planted up through Madison Park. The mayor likes 'em ready by spring solstice."

The officer frowned. But he turned away.

Sam watched him go, and decided a stop at home wasn't worth any further risk. Gripping the bag tighter, he pushed past crowded stalls, and along the slick cobblestone, alert to thieving children darting through his legs.

When he arrived at the bank, it was grander than he expected. The wooden doors were framed with bronze-forged gargoyles. Inside, black-suited careerists were scribbling away, candles replaced by gas lamps, quills by gleaming fountain pens, each man glancing up when Sam entered, frowning at his threadbare clothes, as he scolded himself for not washing.

Still, he marched forward, scanning the faces, until at last he spotted the one he needed: cheeks gone rounder, chin turned to more of a crater. "Mr. Maynard!" Sam called out.

The banker turned back, and frowned. "But you are?"

"Don't you know me, sir?"

"Not without a letter of introduction, young man."

"It's me, sir. Sam Billings. Son of James." *Grandson of Thaddeus*, he thought to himself.

So that now, Mr. Maynard's eyes narrowed, as if he were trying to see through a patch of fog, and eventually his face relaxed into a pudgy smile. "Why, so it is, son! Why didn't you say so?"

"I thought I just did, sir."

Maynard laughed. "Please, Samuel. Come – come," and it was clear his suspicion was fading like the morning dew. Briskly, he led them through the polished stone and inky smell of newly pressed bills, asking after Sam's mother, recalling he'd been at William & Mary, welcoming him back to the city he dubbed the *"capital of capital!"* They moved up a tight stairwell, and past a tumble of black rubber cables – part of the new push for electrification, Maynard boasted – until they were in a private office, anchored by a rolltop desk and a set of mahogany chairs like thrones. The space had a strange glow, baffling Sam at first, until he realized it was coming from a filament lamp on the wall, the perk of an age he'd thus far read of only in the serials of science fiction. "Well go on!" Maynard declared as they sat. "What is it's brought you?"

Sam cleared his throat, focusing on the task before him, the necessity of getting it right. "I don't know if you recall, sir – how when I was a lad, you offered me counsel."

The banker raised his eyebrows.

"You told me of my father, sir. And the treasure he sought."

Maynard sighed. "A man should watch his tongue near youngsters."

"But that's just it, sir. What you told me – it was true."

"I don't follow."

He swallowed. The words were out now, there'd never be any taking them back, and in the instant that followed, Sam wondered if he'd been right to think he could trust this man, a fellow wielding just the sort of hefty handshake and threaded suits he hungered after for himself. "That treasure's why I'm here now, sir."

"Oh?"

Sam hesitated yet again, aware a man like Maynard was in no need of cash. He'd anticipated this, had pondered what it was he could deliver that others could not: an opportunity for cajolery, he'd decided, to nourish Maynard's very sense of self, a dash of well-placed flattery. "I can't pretend to sit here, sir, as anything other than a grateful guest."

"Do I detect some false humility?"

"No, sir. Mere honest brokering."

At that, Maynard's grin returned.

Sam sensed he needn't share everything – where the treasures actually lay, or how he'd discovered the book of maps that showed him their path – but rather, merely enough for Maynard to believe there was a plan. "There's near 1000 dollars in this bag," he announced suddenly. "I'll need your help, sir, if I'm ever to use it."

Maynard didn't bother to conceal his gaze shifting now towards the floor, and Sam unlaced the bag's top, revealing the coins piled inside.

"It's just the start, sir."

"Straight gold?"

"Plumb through." Finally Sam let slip a grin of his own. "Only it's antique, sir." He lowered his voice. "I don't consider what I'm doing theft, Mr. Maynard. I hope you see that."

"You're just not certain the courts will agree."

"I know how this would appear." He stifled a blush. "Coming in with coins like relics."

"Dug up no less."

"As my father designed."

"As he explained to me himself."

"Does that mean you'll help?"

"Ah." The banker sat back. "You're not the first to come in here with a secret needs protecting, Billings." He was squinting, pursing his lips. "You are, however, the first with a pa I considered a friend."

Sam felt the rush of connection. "I'd like to start an account," he pressed. "One I can draw upon at command."

"At regular interest, I presume."

"Indeed."

Maynard chewed the inside of his cheek. Then, without another word, he leaned round the desk, lifting some of the coins without permission, employing the kind of hushed reverence one would reserve for a newborn babe. After that, he retrieved an abacus, and a pad of paper, offering up an account number, a guarantee, terms of exchange – explaining that the coins' rarity more than made up for inflation, that Sam would even manage a profit from the conversion alone. Finally, Maynard pulled out a booklet of checks, and slid them across the desk, a soft whisper against the wood.

CHAPTER 14

New York City
January 1888

Outside, flakes drifted past the frosted panes. In the checkerboard of alleys and streets below, merchants pushed half-frozen barrels of still-jumping flounder amid their socialist rags. The steam from the new radiators snarled and snapped like gunshots, no match for the cold. And Sam rubbed his temples, trying to ignore it all: the wainscoting on the walls grown warped from frigid leaks, the noise from his men making a mockery of the flimsy horsehair insulation, the sign beyond the window clanging on its chain. *Billings Brokerage*, it read in stenciled black, threatening to crash with every gust from the river.

One day, he swore, they'd move uptown.

Straightening his collar, fluffing the patterned silk of his tie, he paused another moment. Then he rapped on the wood to signal the waiting crowd from the hall. As ever, they entered in on cue, gathering round like disciples – not a single oiled hair out of place, no pewter button dangling loose – and really, why should he be surprised? He'd lived up to his promise they'd each have a voice, critical cogs in what he assured them would soon be the city's standard shop in speculation. He'd plucked them from the finest firms across the city, tripling each of their salaries, and in return, they'd done as he'd ordered: taking risks their fathers never would, committing to everything and anything new – electric and gas, combustion and ballpoint, bicycles and phonographs – making their mark dollar by dollar, idea by idea, yanking profit from the old guard's sentries, those gray-haired fossils still sniffing the vapors of their youth, clinging to the twilight of this century they still called their own.

He only hoped their faith would hold.

The snow was shifting now to sleet, clattering against the glass like marbles on stone, and he began. "Gentlemen, I'll confess it. The lot of you counseled against today's meeting."

There was silence at first. None of them had yet mustered the nerve to protest to his face.

Then one of the youngest fidgeted in his chair. This was Archie Davis, cheeks still smooth, proud son of one of the nation's finest families – the Davises of Newport, engendering the brokerage citywide notice the instant he'd been hired – just the type to help Sam imbibe the glitter of the age. "It's the South, sir," young Davis declared now, with a voice like a trumpet.

Sam raised his eyebrows.

"The South, sir. You're asking us to invest in rebeldom."

"You must know it doesn't answer to that moniker any longer."

"Yes, but sir – "

Sam held up his finger. "Your nicknames slander nothing but ghosts." He leaned forward, meeting the boy's eye. "Would you refuse a slab of lumber, all on account of the faded blotch of a smoke stain? Would you worry over some wayward candle lit long before you were born?"

"If I may, sir, the war between the states was more than a spilt candle."

"Yet no less extinguished. I went to university with the men you call rebels. I assure you they're lads like yourselves, clamoring for the same grist that buoys us all."

It was Finn Hughes who spoke up next. He was the first one Sam had found, wearing pince-nez glasses at the end of a fragile nose, and a red necktie so crisply knotted it looked sewn to his lapels. He was too tall, Sam had thought, arms stretched like putty, elbows bent like a toy figurine's. But he'd always thought clearly. "We don't doubt the chance at profit, sir," he cautioned now. "Only whether it'll much matter, once it gets out what we're up to."

It was then, however, they heard the iron knocker downstairs. The men of American Tobacco had arrived, guided upstairs by the ladies tending to the front. They entered in, all grins and guffaws, banging snow from their rider boots, hoisting their canes behind them.

"Welcome!" Sam remarked at once, striding forward to greet them one-by-one. They were five in number, and he took each hand in turn. "My regrets for the frosty Yankee hello. You'll discover only good old American warmth in here," and the southerners chuckled agreeably at that, taking their seats as he led them in like ponies at the racetrack.

The fellow in charge had jowls encroaching upon a once-square jaw, and the surname *Lee* – a not-so-distant relation of the general's, he'd let them know – all rounded vowels and underperforming consonants, an unreconstructed accent to match the concerns that surrounded him. "We come here as friends," he started in, "partners-to-be. On account of our tobacco – an ornery pal of late, we know. Folks simply don't want it dribbling down their fine fitted threads any longer, staining their visage and vanity for their endless photo portraits." At this, he paused dramatically, drawing a thin reed of paper from his vest. "May I present you then, sirs, with the *cigarette*." He was holding it aloft, like a specimen of gold. "A modern mechanism, yet a tribute to tradition."

It was Finn who interrupted. "Let's cut through the evangelism, might we, Mr. Lee?"

The southerner laughed. "Why you're as eager as a March hare! But yes – yes! Your wishes are mine, my friend. And the fact is, our company's got licensing now." Suddenly, he sounded the part of the businessman indeed. "Our rolling machines have been patented. Where once we produced two hundred of these in an hour, now we do so in a minute –" there was a murmur of surprise at that – "leading us to our launch as a corporation. As such, we'll need stockholders in support. Forty-nine percent your way."

Sam had been waiting for his opening. He cleared his throat. "We'd be squatters on the ground floor." He meant every word. This was a chance to make a wave across the whole of New York – the whole of the nation if they were lucky.

Lee brushed back his gleaming hair. "We'll require a million in advertising as a start." The number sank in. "Double that upon our first quarter of sales."

Sam felt the others blanch.

Apparently, Lee felt it too. He shifted in his chair. "Which means it's your turn to talk brass tacks, Billings. Can you do it?"

Sam smiled. "It shan't be a problem."

The southerner's black eyes beamed. "It'll come back your way. I swear on my sons. It'll come back your way twentyfold."

"Sir, please-" It was Finn again. "We've already managed here quite well enough."

One of Lee's men snorted. "A few more pennies a year, you might even pony up for heat."

But Sam raised a hand. It was a risk, of course. That was why the rest of the city wasn't taking the bait. He glanced around at his underlings. "I'll tell you a tale, gentlemen, shall I? I spotted a fellow this morning trying to cross Broadway, looking both ways, two times each, before he managed even a step. In the time he waited, a caravan of wagons passed by, a mule got to kicking, he ended up splattered with dung, and all so he could be certain the path was clear." Sam met each of their eyes, landing upon Finn's last of all. "The only real gamble in life, boys, is not to gamble at all." He guessed he nearly had them. "The only men suited to that? Cowards and princes. And we, my friends, are neither."

Still – their eyes remained anxious. Something more was needed. Something specific.

He knew their devotion to him was up against something deeper: lessons from boyhood, worship of mortals mistaken for Gods, their own fathers, born but a generation sooner than they, transformed into heroes by a mere slip of timing. "By God, lads, my own pa fought for this Union, like yours. He was slain for it too." The men grew still. "Yet I ask you: what sort of Union shall it be if it stagnates? Sentenced to the same oblivion as those whose sacrifice it demanded?"

"And the Negroes, sir?" It was Archie, his brow furrowed. "Are we simply to ignore their return to slave days?"

Lee scowled.

Sam stood. "I don't see how they come into this one way or the other." Politics was the last thing he needed right now. It was the only force with the power to curdle money. He pointed out the window. "Look there," he directed, eyeing the newest immigrants below, not ten blocks off: a living quilt of patched heavy cloaks, and pushcarts crowding the muck. "Do you worry for them as well, Davis? Bartering after crumbs, whilst we're up here chasing millions? Do you fret beside your radiator at home, to think of them shivering by their wooden stoves?"

"Come off it, sir. They've got their opportunity, same as anyone here."

Sam nodded. "I see. We each of us harbor our moral compromises then, don't we boys? The anarchist still orders his children to their primers; the communist out there purchasing gems for his love; the suffragette who flutters her eyelashes." He snorted. "Too heavy a dose of scruples, and you lose your stomach for success. I assure you, gentlemen, this deal sees no blue, no gray – no, nor negro neither. It'll bathe only in green." He turned back to Lee and gestured toward the door. "Our attorneys shall prepare the papers."

CHAPTER 15

Scottsville, Virginia
September 1974

Alvin peered ahead, enjoying a memory of Faye in the kitchen, only vaguely aware of the soft hills that beckoned him now. He tapped his thumb against the steering wheel, keeping rhythm with the mindless rock and roll rattling the mesh speakers, appreciating the emptiness of the road – aside from one mucus green Buick, tracking along the same speed as him, a quarter-mile back.

He was glad to be here. He'd lost progress on the case amid the haze of Watergate and its endless ripples, dragged away from his work the same as every other agent, tracking down leads against the highest corruption there was. Now, with Nixon gone at last, he was freed to do his job.

He'd pledged to Faye it would be only one night away, and he was intent on making the most of his time. The rental was a white Rabbit, part of a run on hatchbacks after the oil crisis, with a sticky clutch and an engine that shook every time he clipped 50. Still, he'd been speeding, cracking the window, letting the southern wind tug at his hair.

Eventually, the roads turned single-lane. Forest encroached of ash and pine. *Welcome to Scottsville*, a sign declared in stock white letters, and Alvin turned off the music. Here were blocks of empty display cases, brick facades faded beneath a century of sun, and at the end of the street, an old city hall, small but stately, antique lanterns flanking the door, windows standing at attention. He parked right in front.

His hope was for a shot at this town's memories, some slice of lore from before Sam Billings was an American icon, and Ulysses Brooke a forgotten fanatic. Hell, it was Brooke's place of birth: a spot to find some truth behind the treasures.

Stepping out, he paused. He could swear he'd seen that same green Buick once more, coasting by on the main road. It was probably chance, of course. The targets of his investigation weren't exactly the types to follow him in turn – the nation's most esteemed philanthropists, and a pair of American ghosts. Still, he looked over one more time, before jamming a nickel in the rusty meter at the curb.

Inside, there was no lobby. Just a lone clerk and a thin counter. The man's sideburns were red, his polyester shirt royal blue; he was reading a copy of *Life*. The room smelled like a library mixed with a toolshed. "Apologies for the intrusion," Alvin began, deciding not to show his badge. "I'm working on a history of the region."

The clerk closed his magazine. "A professor in Scottsville!"

Alvin didn't correct him. "I'd love a look at some old warrants and arrests – whatever you've got."

The clerk, squinting back, pulled out a pad. "Name here," he directed, before leading the way to a room in back, with aisles barely wide enough for their shoulders, and books stacked to the ceiling. "No pictures," he recited, "no ballpoint, no carbon-copying, no removal of property."

But Alvin's eyes were already sliding along the maze that greeted them: marbled endpapers, folders clipped and clamped shut, dust that took over the air. "I'm after records on a former resident. Name of Ulysses Brooke."

The Virginian hooted.

"You have anything on him, or no?"

"'Course we do," and the clerk shuffled to the far wall, shoving aside a pile of plastic crates. Behind these, a card catalogue sat in hiding, as if its brass knobs had been deemed too showy for the surroundings, and the fellow jutted out his tongue, studying the drawers, yanking one out, retrieving a red tortoiseshell folder from inside. "Careful now, it's starting to rot."

Alvin thanked him, and opened the thing at once: yellowed sheets inside, scrawled with smudged script. Sure enough, these were the transcripts from Brooke's case – notes from a warden about his behavior (*"unobtrusive"*), his interrogations (*"unrevealing"*), his health (*"unreliable"*). Confirmation, at least, that he wasn't myth. The testimony from his sentencing called him every name there was, a fit of delusion, a traitor to his family, "an apostate," according to the judge, guilty of "terroristic and insurrectionary acts."

Then, at the close of the files, a visitors' log from Brooke's years behind bars: someone named Rebecca Vance, amid occasional mentions of the warden himself, but also, at the ledger's bottom, back from when the Civil War was nearly begun – when Ulysses himself was just days away from his death – somebody else. Alvin read it three times over.

James Billings, said the old script – and he turned to his briefcase.

The family tree confirmed it: that'd been Sam Billings' father.

Had that been the moment then? When Ulysses had transferred his book of maps? Was it proof Sam Billings would indeed one day enter the picture, and track down the stolen money, using those very maps?

Alvin looked back up. It was a link between Brooke and Billings at the very least; the plaintiffs Jack and Betty Downing had been right about that.

He returned the notebook and angled toward the exit.

"Follow the horseshoe of the river," the clerk directed him as he left. "There's some old-timers can fill you in proper: folks always happy to talk about Brooke. Hell, it's an article of faith 'round here that one of us might still get lucky and snag his gold."

Alvin nodded thanks, and feeling lucky, decided he might as well heed the advice. The day was heating up, and he slowed as he reached the houses up the way, squat and poor, with sagging porches like melted clay. He approached the first one that didn't look empty. Flowered curtains had been tied back in the windows up front; an aging Ford sat on its blacktop. He neared the door; and before he even knocked, he was greeted by a pair of large gray-haired ladies in matching blue sleeveless dresses. When they spoke, their garbled accents recalled those of the Downings. "We're innocent!" the one on the left exclaimed at once, and they both cackled.

"Read us our rights!" chimed the other.

Alvin smiled good-humoredly. "What was my tell?"

"Only feds wear ties in the heat, son."

He laughed in turn, and explained it was nothing urgent, that he was just hoping for a slice of the past – and true to the clerk's word, they were game. It turned out they were twins, Emma and Ruby Graham, spinsters by their own account, living right here ever since the last century.

Their kitchen had wood-veneer cabinets and green linoleum floors that'd buckled under the humidity. On the counter, a tiny TV with a fuzzy picture was airing baseball from somewhere distant. A stream of fly paper hung from an abandoned fixture, carcasses lining its plastic like raisins. The lone lamp stood under an opal glass shade.

"Sweet tea?" one of them asked. Alvin was grateful.

For several minutes, they chatted – about his drive down, about the humidity – and then he started in for real. "I'm trying to get to the story of Ulysses Brooke."

"Always keep your enemies close," Emma remarked at once.

"But your kin closer!" Ruby injected. It sounded like a well-worn localism.

"He was a thief," Ulysses went on.

"That he was."

"You happen to know if he worked alone?"

"Rumors say he had some partners. Never did hear it confirmed, though."

Alvin looked back, resting his chin atop a pencil. Out the window, he was suddenly sure he glanced the same green Buick he'd seen before – the stretched-out silhouette, the accents on the side! – he was certain of it now. And watching it go, he couldn't help but wonder: what sort of ghosts was he was up against?

"It's a wonder Ulysses didn't confide in a soul," Emma announced next. "Must've hated all his cousins. Hell, the Brooke clan owned half the commonwealth."

Ruby shook her head. "Some of 'em still got offshoots. Still sittin' on pots of gold, from what I gather."

"Which ones?" Alvin asked, re-focusing his attention. At that, Emma stood to clear the tea, creakily carrying the pitcher back to the sink. He followed with his gaze. "These questions are for my own background only," he added. "I won't share your names. I won't be using this as testimony. I just need information."

Neither one answered.

"Alright. Do either of you know a couple goes by Jack and Betty Downing?"

Emma snorted. "But they're not the ones you should be askin' about."

"Excuse me?"

"They grew up on the river – been too big for their britches all their lives. Descendants of the Brooke family, and won't let any soul forget it."

Now Ruby leaned forward. "Did they come your way, Mister?"

"And if they had?"

"They don't do nothing for their selves. Not without marching orders."

"From whom?"

"The other branch of their bloodline. Surname of Campbell. You heard of 'em?"

Alvin said that he hadn't.

"Only 'cause you ain't from here. Hell, everyone in this town knows the Campbells."

"Depends on them, more like," said her sister.

"You included?"

"Not us. Cleaned houses all our lives. Saved plenty." She shrugged "Those Campbells, they own half the franchises from here to Richmond – only as they see it, they've lost what mattered: they ain't got their old sway.

Whatever you're after, Mr. Starkman, I can tell you, they put the Downings up to it. It don't mean a whit to them that they still got it better than the rest of us, investing their trust funds as they did. The only folks they believe worth their time are the ones who came before."

CHAPTER 16

New York City
September 1974

While Alvin had been south, they'd changed the portrait on the wall. It was Ford's dazed letterman's grin looking back at him now, not Nixon's crooked cringe, and he turned away, impatient, listening for Jack and Betty Downing from the hall. Plastic bins were filled with gray magnetic tape against the wall, the bureau's latest bright idea for storing its data; quick-strip fluorescent bulbs intended a futuristic glow, though they offered nothing more than a steely, soul-deadening sheen.

The door finally swung open, and here they came. Jack had puffed out further since last they'd met: like a cake rising in an oven. His hair had been reduced to a jet-black comb-over; camel-colored stripes on his shirt stretched over the swell of his belly. His wife Betty was hunched at his side, with a neck like a chicken's wattle, and round eyes narrowed as if she sensed a trap. "A fine day, Agent Starkman," her husband announced before they were all the way in. "Here to show us our gold?"

Alvin shut the door, eager to catch them off-stride. "Who is it's backing you two?"

Jack Downing frowned. His wife stared.

"Should I ask again?" He took back his seat, unfurling his yellow pad, tapping the rear of his pencil.

"Somebody phoned you?" Jack was already starting to give.

"I'd prefer it if I do the questions today, Mr. Downing." Alvin leaned closer. "Who provided your train tickets from Virginia?"

Betty's scowl looked like she'd drunk from a lemon. "We shoulda known. Nice enough when we met you. Swindlin' us all the while."

Alvin ignored her. It was the husband who was going to break. "Who, Jack?"

For a moment, Downing remained stone-faced – until after a pause, his lips cracked, and he shrugged. "The Campbells," he sighed. "We're family, is all."

"I dislike being in the dark, Mr. Downing. I dislike all the more being asked to turn the lights on myself."

"Don't make it bigger than it is. They're heirs to Ulysses Brooke, same as us. Same blood pumpin' through their veins. Even if theirs is already laced with gold."

"They're using you, sir. To make themselves more sympathetic."

"We're kin."

"Great. Then why don't we have them over for a get-together?"

***

As it turned out, there were at least a dozen Campbells living in Scottsville, and loads more across the whole of the Tidewater. Alvin had learned they were bank managers mostly, a few doctors, even a judge. But the two that he needed claimed the label 'family trustees.' Any time one of their clan wrote a check for a local private school, broke bread with a mayor, or was listed in a program, it was they who were on hand. They were brothers – great-great-grandsons of some distant Brooke cousin – their own grandpop making a fortune in turn, down in Cuba on coffee. As far as Alvin could tell, they'd been living off the spoils all their lives, assembling the finest in degrees, vacation homes, political contacts too – known in Republican circles all the way back to Harding. Most recently, they'd funded the suit against Billings Trust, claiming the book of maps as an heirloom, pressing Jack and Betty Downing to become the face of their struggle, re-fashioning their efforts as a nice David-and-Goliath case, two poor souls up against a New York institution. Then they'd sicked their two patsies on the FBI.

The room felt full the instant they arrived. Alvin hadn't warned the Downings they were coming, and he enjoyed their collective flinch when the door opened up. Clay and Clem were the brothers' names, and here they were, both sporting linen white suits, one in a seersucker red bowtie, the other in blue, shoving in like aging cowboys through a set of saloon doors. Broad-shouldered, ruddy-cheeked, they offered handshakes all around, making remarks about the swampy air of Manhattan.

Betty and Jack Downing half-stood in greeting, then quickly returned to their seats, Jack tapping his thumbs, Betty crossing her arms. Entering in next was Alvin's boss, Claire Calloway. She was there only to listen, she'd assured him – though whenever any powerbrokers came by, she always seemed to wind near.

"How'd you poor saps get stationed up here anyhow?" the thinner one inquired now – this was Clay – all but lifting Alvin from the floor with his handshake. "Exiled from the capital?"

"New York's the largest field office in the nation, Mr. Campbell. I imagine that's why you sought after us."

"We came for your jurisdiction," and his words were languid and sure, southern syllables crafted exquisitely: not a one any less cared-for than any other. "At least you got the breeze on, anyhow. Tax dollars at work," and he took his chair, and smoothed his coat.

It was true. The room had a chill. Though to Alvin's mind, the new central system mostly just made the air stale, as if it had already been ingested.

Clay Campbell shifted. He had small eyes drilled into his face, skin drawn tight round his chin. It made him look like a ferret – overeager, sniffing – so that no amount of expensive suits could override the strain. "Why is it we're here, Agent Starkman?"

"You're the ones brought the case."

"Jack and Betty did that."

"You're the bankroll."

"Now don't you mean the brains?" This was Clem – quieter, handsomer – with a smile like a purr, and a drawl like a breeze. "Though you knew that, after your little fact-finding mission southland."

Alvin recalled the green Buick. "That was you then? Keeping tabs?"

Neither one answered, sipping instead from the water he'd provided.

"U.S. Code 18. Section 912. Look it up." Alvin glared at them both. "Tracking a federal agent is a crime." He noticed Claire glance up from her papers. "I'm not your puppet, gentlemen. The bureau took the case, and I've been assigned. But I don't enjoy being manipulated."

"Don't get cocky, Starkman. Remember, you weren't just assigned. You were requested – and the bureau told us yes." Clay placed down his glass.

"So you wanted to work with me?"

"Who said anything about wanted? Any notion of 'want' ends in boyhood. We just picked the best man for the job." Clay smiled slickly. "While we're reciting laws, by-the-by: the statute of limitations for theft doesn't go into effect until the crime is recognized by the state. Ulysses Brooke's treasures were taken unlawfully. We're his rightful heirs, and it's long past time they be returned. Open-and shut jurisprudence, Agent Starkman. No manipulation required."

"It wasn't Brooke's cash to begin with. He'd stolen it himself."

"Oftentimes from his own family – his own inheritance."

"Not all of it. Not nearly."

"That's conjecture."

"He was tried and convicted."

"By a planter class terrified of slave uprising, aiming to teach him a lesson."

"The conviction stands."

"Nonsense. It applied to only one of the treasures in the end. The courts never mentioned the rest." Clay cocked his head. "You our friend, Starkman, or ain't you?"

"I'm a friend to the law, sir."

"Why parse? The law's on our side."

"And to hell with Billings Trust?"

"Founded by a Gilded Age thief. Who covered up his sin with charity."

"They do good work. People are helped. That doesn't matter?"

Clem surprised Alvin now, speaking up from his brother's side. "Why should the law care a whit what Sam

Billings did with his cash once he stole it? So what if he chose to give it away on account of fearing his Maker? He was guilty all the while."

There might be a point there. Yet still, something ate at Alvin. He gazed back at the Campbells, sitting here in their 500 dollar suits, with gold-dialed Rolexes poking out from their sleeves. They didn't care an ounce about Ulysses Brooke, he concluded. They were just using his revolutionary lineage as cover for their own greed, the same way they were using Jack and Betty Downing. "Fellas," he concluded. "I'll do my job. But just so we're clear: it won't be because you tugged at my heartstrings with Jack and Betty here – or because I follow orders blindly. It's the law, binding us together, just as you say."

The brothers stood. Clem peered back with pale blue eyes. "You're not the first to get sore at my older brother, Starkman." And with that, as they turned to go, he started chuckling.

CHAPTER 17

New York City
October 1974

Billings Trust was still the most formidable charitable force in the city, and Charles Billings, Samuel's only son, was still the one in charge. The latest media accounts were as fawning as ever, hailing him for maintaining his father's legacy with aplomb, for preaching the gospel of improvement, for "graduating" the best of the best year after year: folks who went on to cite their funding as if it were an Ivy League diploma, then paid their investment back in full – first to the Trust, then to society. They were leaders in medicine, education, law. And every one of them prayed at the altar of Billings.

In the lobby, Alvin joined a fleet of America's nobles, all in black woolen coats and elegant maroon scarves. The air was an echo of sure-footed steps and stage-whispered conversation, and he moved briskly toward a granite counter where a pair of young women had frozen their smiles in greeting. "'Morning, sir," one of them offered – no more than thirty, Alvin guessed, with blonde hair converted from brown. "You have an appointment?"

"I believe Charles Billings is expecting me." The woman blinked, and her partner looked up too – same dye job, same satin red blazer. Alvin reached for his badge.

At that, the receptionist didn't argue. She went to a drawer, heaving out a hefty three-ring binder. As the pages flipped by, Alvin recognized dozens of names slotted for the day, precisely the types he'd expect: philanthropic reps, mayoral deputies, NAACP.

She was running her finger down a column. "Agent Starkman?"

"That's right."

"My husband's a cop too," she offered, and Alvin closed his wallet over his badge, as she led him to an elevator. They rode together in quiet, before stepping into a waiting room far above. Here were fabric chairs laid out in a grid, piles of *The Economist* stacked neatly on laminate tables, a burgundy carpet. The plaster walls were dotted with Murano glass sconces.

Into a wider hallway then, and finally, evidence of real work being done: gray cubicles like puzzle pieces, typewriters clattering, until the onion peeled even further. Alvin was deposited in a large corner room, its sofas stacked with red leather cushions, a desk evoking nothing if not the Oval Office. He stepped forward, and the panels creaked.

It was the turf of an older man, and he studied the plaques on the wall, bestowed by every university worth knowing, every government agency worth funding, every guild there ever was. Mixed in were ancient crew trophies from Harvard, a few photos of the Kennedy boys when they'd been young and alive, and there, shimmering above them all, an oil painting, in a puddle of light all its own. Looking down sternly from the portrait was Samuel Billings himself, founder of the whole place, with satisfied blue eyes, and a mane of gray hair tucked behind his Gilded Age collar.

It was then, as if in self-parody, that one last door made itself known, hidden in stacks of books to the side, and in walked Charles. Alvin could see there was another office behind him – an appendage to the appendage – boasting still more leather and wood, papers flung everywhere. But it was the man himself who drew the attention.

He was handsome, even after all his decades hording life. His cheekbones gave him structure, though not so much as to render him jagged; his eyes were the color of a summer sky; his face was the kind that looked better with age. His hair, white as snow, was combed straight back, and when he creakily lifted his arms, wearing a three-piece woolen suit, it was a practiced gesture of welcome. "So you're the young man with the bureau," he proclaimed, with a voice like distant thunder, in mid-Atlantic waves that sounded almost British.

Alvin cleared his throat. The old powerbroker had crafted a smile so friendly, it was hard not to feel like a plaything in his hands. "I know you're a busy man," he answered.

"Not too busy for a federal agent I should hope!"

"That's very kind."

"Now we're in danger of niceties." Another smile. They sat down opposite one another.

"I'll get to it then." Alvin exhaled. "I've been told your money is dirty." For a moment, the words lingered. "That it's stolen."

Charles Billings' thin lips parted. Then he began to laugh. His shoulders shook, and he clapped his hands in front of him. "By God," he eventually answered. "I told my people that's what this would be about! But you know lawyers: petrified as ever there'd been some tax oversight."

"I'm not sure I follow, sir."

"You're referring to the myth, of course." Billings winked. "My father's so-called discoveries."

"Scattered across the nation, yes."

"It was he who crafted such claims, of course." The philanthropist shook his head. "Alas, that only came at the end. And despite the facts. Poor soul spoke as if the whole world hadn't already been watching him work for decades." Billings chuckled once more. "We have records, of course – of his earliest meetings with banks, other brokerages, whoever would have him. Folks speak nowadays of credit scores; all that was asked of him was to march in there with a pitch, and talk the lenders into it. There was no trace of stolen treasure, I assure you! Back then, all he had was his word." He let his smile linger, and the lines in his cheeks were like crevices in stone. "I'd say he made good on their faith, wouldn't you?"

"And the book?"

"A historical trinket, naturally! My father got his hands on it and started doodling. Of no practical use whatsoever. There's not a court in the land that would deem it evidence of anything untoward. Certainly not on our part," and he pointed through the door, back towards the painting of the man himself. "He was the best of us, remember. Rather than keep his brokerage rich, he shifted every cent toward a brand new philanthropy. All of it."

Alvin didn't turn around. Instead, he glanced at the old man's glinting cuffs, and pinstriped sleeves. There was something calculated to this whole routine. "Can't help but notice, Mr. Billings, you've still made out just fine."

"Well why not?" Charles' gaze settled back down. "We've never claimed to be a non-profit here, my boy. Just the opposite. It was my father's revelation. Money drives the world – why not apply that to good deeds as well?"

Alvin nodded. He'd been reading up on the place: famous from the get-go, making its name in the lead-up to D-Day, prototyping the GI Bill before the government had even gotten the idea down on paper. Ever since, it'd been clinging to that same model, sending lucky recipients onto graduate programs, research tracts, study tours, all in the understanding that the investment would come back, plus interest. "There are those who say you've ridden the coattails of our country's finest."

"Hogwash. We're the ones who finance their journey."

"They couldn't have excelled without you?"

"Would you say the Bronx Bombers shouldn't scout the best talent?"

"These aren't ballplayers, sir. They're doctors, governors, soldiers."

"Ah. It's that last one, isn't it?" Charles folded his hands. "Your own father fought in the war, did he not? You must see that our ideals are the same for which he sacrificed. It's our alumni who are conquering disease, building interstates, working for those who've been left out. Women. Negroes. Jews of course." He stopped there, looking back pointedly.

Alvin straightened, taking in Charles Billings' vivid blue eyes in turn, a perfect match for the kerchief peeking out from his coat. "I've met with Jack and Betty Downing."

"I assumed."

"I met their backers as well."

"Oh?" Now the old philanthropist had arched an eyebrow.

"Clay and Clem Campbell. Brothers."

"Gilded side of the tracks, I presume?"

"Same as you, sir."

"Touché."

"I don't believe they like you much."

"No, I shouldn't expect so. They'd find it harder to demand my money if they did."

"They say it's theirs."

"And?"

"Why shouldn't I believe them?"

Billings smiled softly. "You're the investigator, Mr. Starkman."

"They answered my questions."

"You'd like me to do the same."

"Seems fair," Alvin shrugged.

"You really perceive the pursuit of justice in this saboteur's raid of theirs?"

"Mr. Billings – "

"Charles. Please."

Alvin nodded. "Hurting you – hurting this place – it's not my aim, sir." He paused, watching as old Charles Billings started tapping his fingers, wondering if this man had always been so impenetrable, imagining his younger version in his place – no less bathed in plenty, but with a whole future to play with, rather than a past to defend.

"You have a technique, Starkman."

"Just patience, sir."

Billings' laugh returned. And with a jagged wave, he beckoned Alvin closer. "Only – will you know what to do with the truth once you find it?"

Alvin stayed quiet. He was certain the old man was used to getting what he wanted.

"You fancy yourself a moral person, Starkman?"

"Is that at issue here?"

Billings shrugged, leaned back, crossed his legs. "I've often wondered whether a fellow like you might come knocking. Whether one day we might be called to answer for all this money." He crinkled his gaze. "Now here you are, sitting before me."

"And what do you see, Mr. Billings?"

"The right type of man, Starkman. The type who won't give up until he's got the whole story. Who'll go beyond his bosses even. Who won't just do the bidding of those Campbell boys."

"Hoping I'll do yours instead?"

"Not mine either, Starkman." Billings' voice grew more grave. "That of your own soul."

So that even as Alvin was aware he was being spun, he couldn't help but admire the instincts of power. Most men perched in an office like this one would long ago have lost their bearings. Yet here was Charles Billings, still crackling, as if driven by an ambition not yet proven, guessing correctly that Alvin had begun to bristle at the bureau's pressures, at Claire Calloway and political demand – that indeed, such things had made him consider that amid the statutes, there were real human lives. It was an itch that collided with his training, with the bureau's belief that the law was God – to be worshipped, never questioned. Still, he shook his head. "Moral progress doesn't turn a crime legal, Mr. Billings. If there's stolen money in possession of this Trust, it should be returned."

"And if it came first from slavers?"

Alvin frowned. Was Billings actually admitting it?

The old man cleared his throat, as if he too sensed he'd finally mis-stepped, going too far. "I mean it, Starkman. If you were to find our whole humble enterprise had been spawned by some treasure you'd been tasked with whisking away? What would you do?"

"That wouldn't be my call, sir." Alvin shifted. "Even if I wanted it. I don't have the right."

"Nonsense. Choice belongs to every one of us."

"To judge the law for ourselves?"

"To judge the past. And those who cling to it."

"Questions for poets, sir, not police." After all, who was Charles Billings to lecture him?

"Until next time then, Agent Starkman."

"Until then, sir," and buttoning his coat, he made his way to the door.

CHAPTER 18

Alexandria, Virginia – February

1975

The diners on Route 95 were always full, and this one was no exception, packed with truckers perusing menus as big as blotters, eyeing Puerto Rican waitresses in striped pink aprons and black heeled shoes. The twangs were nasal and loud and local, a reminder that for all of America's talk about being one-nation-under-God, it would take more than highways to flatten what had always been. Alvin had found a booth near the door, and he was letting the grease dribble down his chin, straight to the paper napkin crumpled in his lap.

He'd been driving south, scooting between browning farmland and the strip malls in between, new knots in the American tapestry, glowing neon, offering mostly gas and guns. Until at last, finally past Maryland and wishing he hadn't skipped breakfast, he'd pulled off for a burger. Now he was finishing up fast, busing his own plate, sidling past a teamster across the way, pot-bellied in a corduroy jacket, mullet as greasy as his meal, a crotch he couldn't stop scratching.

"Sir?" As usual, Alvin was trying not to sound like an FBI agent.

"You need directions."

"You bet. Which way to the richest part of town?"

The trucker chuckled, taking a slurp from a silver-cupped shake. He sketched a quick map onto his napkin, and passed it over, as Alvin thanked him.

Soon he was back on the road, the trucker's etchings in hand, rotating the dial between Christian preaching and high-pitched static – one and the same, as far as he was concerned. When he got off the interstate, holding the flimsy instructions against the wheel, checking their scrawl against the photocopied book of maps, he found quiet blocks of lantern-lined curbs, panes still twinkling with gas-powered flame, the kind of proud suburb with stenciled dates on its homes, like vintages atop fine bottles of wine.

He was certain Faye would sneer. "You can't get out of going?" she'd asked that morning, curled up next to him. "You can't just tell them no?"

He'd sighed, stealing a look at the blue slip sliding up her thighs, the brown cream of her skin. Truth was, he'd been the one who'd pushed for this trip. Claire Calloway had again been pressing him on budget, but he'd insisted on seeking out more burial spots nonetheless, proving to himself the maps truly were real, needing something that would convince a court of the same.

Faye had rested her cup of tea on the nightstand and turned, her dark eyes boring right into him, as if she could see straight to his fear and wanted to know why it was there: that Charles Billings had been right, that in the end, doing the bureau's business would crash into Alvin's own instincts. When he'd remained quiet, she'd straightened her slip and hidden her legs once more.

Alvin shoved the memory aside. He needed to get this done – the day's sun was already receding – and he parked the car. Stepping out, acting as if he were merely on a stroll, he quickly found the house in question. It was just across the street now, matching the address on his photocopied sheet. Its façade was faded, though not without charm: metal stars supporting gable-walls, an eagle-carved knocker, iron weather-vanes up top.

He took out his camera – every jury loved a good picture – and despite his ears ringing from the cold, and his nose starting to trickle, he stepped closer, past bare dogwoods lining the sidewalk. There was a driveway just ahead, a tan Mercedes at its center, and beyond that, a softly sloping lawn, rising to a small patio.

It was just as the book of maps described. "*Moss & brick*," noted the old caption, and sure enough, Alvin could see the red squares still intact: this, then, was the same stubborn place Brooke and Billings had come upon – civil war, civil rights, whole centuries plodding along in their wake – still offering that sure-footed peace that comes with money, a fortress preserved by gold.

He knelt down. They'd been in this very spot, he thought: Ulysses aiming to tear the splendor apart, Sam to make it every bit his own. Had they too watched their own breaths mist against the emerging stars? Crouched beneath these same street lamps as he? Had they paused by this very patio, taking in the casual boast of that slate roof, knowing then that whole destinies hinged on what they chose from here?

1888

The inn had come well-recommended: whitewashed brick and fashionable bow windows, black-skinned bellhops, a supper club off the vestibule – men munching on chops and caviar, voices like crackling flames. Sam stepped in to join them, ordering mushrooms and currant jelly, a cup of Bordeaux to help it all down.

"I say!" someone declared, as he rested a foot on the bar's brass rung. "Where from, old boy?"

He lowered his fork, taking in the fellow doing the shouting, wide-eyed and tipsy. "Started my day at a Manhattan rail counter – ending it on a Virginia bar stool." He offered a toast. "If that's not American progress, I don't know what is!"

The young man laughed and clinked his drink. "I'm Willie Koll."

"Nice to meet you, Willie. Sam Billings."

"Not of the brokerage?"

Sam grinned.

"By dickens – you're the spirit of the age!" Cheeks flushed, the fellow's smile broadened. "So you're the Yank managing what the whole war couldn't!"

"Not sure I follow."

"Riding Dixie tobacco to conquer Wall Street, from what they say. Forging a proper bridge between us. Born in blue, bedecked in gray!"

Another fellow caught Sam's eye too, leaning in like a lad seeking a better glimpse at a parade. "Name's Pollock," this one said. He had a thin face, and a thinner hairline. "Dispatcher for the *Examiner*, up from Richmond. Trouble you for a line, Mr. Billings?"

And though he was tempted – to think: they knew his name! – Sam flinched at the idea of being asked why he was here. "Your ink," he responded instead. "Your words." Finishing his meal, he left them where they sat.

Soon he was moving up the block. Here were leather-roofed carriages at the curbs, and privet hedges trimmed tight as whiskers. On every corner, new poles soared to the heavens, lead-sheathed cables curled overtop like snakes, electric light beaming from the houses, while the gas lamps on the sidewalks pushed back in vain – the flicker of the old century versus the coming might of the new. He spotted a figure: a lady – at this hour! – and her white-haired poodle at her feet like a prince. Deferring to an animal, for God's sake; the latest craze, this kennel-club obsession of the posh. Sam waited as she passed.

The air grew darker, and he moved on silently, eyes fixed on the home now coming into view, curtains drawn, a brass knocker out front. He pulled the book of maps from his shawl, confirming a sloping lawn ahead, the garden next to that, the terrace dividing the two, feeling as if Ulysses Brooke were right there, guiding him along. No doubt some local banker lived here, perhaps even one of the men back at the inn, and he held his breath, half-expecting someone to come out checking for intruders.

He reached the terrace, cloaked in moss that'd sprouted from its seams, and finding its edge, he started to dig. Scratching away, Sam scolded himself for not bringing his shovel – he'd worried it would draw attention – until eventually he was on his belly, arms buried to his elbows in soil. Then: the clang of metal! – the same as from the iron box he'd found in Birmingham – and though his fingers were growing raw, he pulled with everything he had.

If only the men at the office could see him now! He recalled how they'd gaped at his promise of two million, all for American Tobacco. And all at once, he felt a rush, even a kind of terror: not at the prospect of being caught, but at himself, an unexpected desire to draw these pieces of his soul together – as if he couldn't keep it all inside forever, couldn't keep from shouting it to the world. To let them know these torn hands were the very same that shook theirs!

He silenced the thought and stood.

Cash in hand, he shoved the pile of dirt back in with his boot, making it look as if nothing but a pair of foxes had rustled up the grass, knowing that newsboys and milkmen would be coming by soon enough. Then, with the metal box against his ribs, he started toward his buggy, reaching again for the book of maps, intent on making notes while they were fresh in his mind, a record of his work, a mantra to keep going – but also, he realized, his own way of giving thanks: to Ulysses Brooke, he thought, for making any of it possible.

1808

"You're trying our luck." Cato's eyes were intent, his heavy brow arched with incredulity.

Ulysses merely shrugged. Only yesterday he'd been back in Richmond, amid the sailors in their white trousers, and the gentlemen wedded to their fine silk hose: a life ever-beckoning, ever-distant, like some vista through a rain-soaked window. He'd fetched Cato at dawn – the overseers hadn't protested too loudly, not with growing season still weeks off – and they'd ridden without pause, trading naps, eventually reaching a wooden sign atop a sagging post. "*City of Alexandria,*" it'd said. A hub for flour and hemp. A prime spot for cash.

The traffic upon arrival had been heavy. There were colts guiding glass coaches, men in tailcoats, women in bodices. Every one of them had seemed to boast an overblown lilt, all bold vowels and up-tempo patter – "*oh dahlin'!"* – so that Cato had even managed a smirk, noting it was always the folks living nearest Yankeedom who compensated with the theater of Dixie. Alas, the roads had been just as jammed today, right up to the time of their theft, and in all the minutes since, and they were hurrying now to free themselves from the crowds.

When all at once, Ulysses pulled up the reins. "It can't be," he whispered.

He wanted to curse. For there, indeed, not half a link away, were the Thompsons. He was certain of it: his damned neighbors from Richmond, strolling right towards them. As ever, they looked dressed for royalty – the husband in a beaver hat, his wife in red muslin – here, no doubt, to make themselves more known among the city's merchants and mansions. "Brooke! Is it you?"

He forced a laugh. "And you in turn, Cyrus?"

"What brings you upland? With one of your hands, no less!" He gestured with his cane toward Cato.

"Here on occasion of the governor." Ulysses bowed as the wife curtsied. "Making a digest of the latest bank routes, ensuring they're secure."

"Ah, good for you then. You remember Beth?"

"Of course. It's my pleasure."

She nodded sympathetically. "More troubles, then?"

"Nothing too dire." And despite his nerves, Ulysses felt a small thrill to know the rumors of theft were spreading. It was gratifying to know folks such as these were proving unsettled. "Forgive me though. I'd best return this slave to Boxwood."

"You don't mean to ride through the night?"

"I've no choice," and leaving no room for doubt, Ulysses jiggled the reins, not willing to risk them spying the chest at his feet, pledging he'd see them back in Richmond. They moved on with a wave now, rounding the next corner, before there was any chance for further conversation.

As soon as they were out of sight, Cato grimaced. "That man'll raise queries."

But Ulysses scarcely heard him.

Up the block, he could see a freshly constructed house, its new brick walls all but shimmering, no grazing pasture out front yet, only packed dirt. It'd be perfect for what they needed, far enough on the outskirts of town, not yet occupied. They'd nabbed this round of cash from a bank just a half-mile back – the eastern ring of plantations all shipped their gold right here – locating a flat-bed wagon loaded to the brim, raiding it while the driver chatted inside. Now, they'd have a chance at completing the job before they'd even left the vicinity, before more attention could be called.

Cato nodded, clearly thinking the same, and they drew closer: confirming the property was empty, a half-finished terrace in the rear, the start of a raised garden. Eyeing the fresh bulbs of irises, like little blue marbles defying the frost, they rode right in.

CHAPTER 19

Richmond – Scottsville, Virginia
March 1808

Ulysses didn't often hesitate. But there was something in the power of Rebecca Vance's gaze – the way she lifted one eyebrow and not the other, the start of a squint to make her skepticism clear – that'd made him nearly spill every secret he had. "Go on then," she was saying, standing in his doorframe, the blue pleats of her dress brushing its edge. "What was it you were after?"

He'd already claimed he'd been in Alexandria on the governor's behalf, that he'd have returned sooner but for the late winter storms.

"Embellish the journey at least, Ulysses. Is that not what men do to impress?"

"But lady Vance, most men aren't impressive already."

She ceded him a laugh at that – brash, inviting at once – softening the questions that lay underneath. Still, no matter how drawn in he felt, Ulysses knew she was of the same world as he. It was the very world he ached to undo. "Where is it you're slated to next, at least?" she wanted to know. "Surely that's not cloaked in secrecy too?"

"Just home to Boxwood," he shrugged, and it was nearly the truth. In fact, he ought to have departed already; he would have done so if she hadn't stopped over – on the way to a dress fitting, she'd said. "I'll just fetch my waistcoat. I can walk you out."

She surprised him. "I can escort myself." She retrieved her gloves from her carryall. "You must know I'm not one to be trifled with, Ulysses," and she peered closer. "I don't mind saying, you've a fire in those eyes, Mr. Brooke. Always searching, simmering. I ask simply what embers lie below."

He watched as she turned. "Rebecca – " But it was no use. She was already stepping away. "Whatever I keep to myself," he called after her, "I pledge to you – I don't do it for lack of affection."

So that for just a moment, he was sure he saw a lapse in her stride.

***

By afternoon's ebb, he was again well out of town: brown hills ringing the horizon, green fields nearer in, slaves spreading wood ash and powdered manure across the seedbeds. There were hundreds of them, nearly a thousand: silhouettes hunched close to the ground, balancing their canvas sacks, nourishing their masters' profit – as formidable as any regiment in the land. Ulysses envisioned them dropping their tools, knowing it would take cash no less than courage: more than imaginings to topple this world, more than being right to convince people they were wrong.

The Billings estate was a staple of the boom times that'd come with Jefferson's sweep to power. Eager little guest houses had now sprouted round the mansion like miniatures, gardens mulched and seeded and lined with hedge, the whole place scented with citrus, leaked from lemon trees the family had planted after a grand tour of Naples – shipped across the sea and somehow still intact in their red clay jardinieres.

And Thaddeus. There – standing amid it all.

He didn't look so different from when they'd been boys, really – yellow hair clasped in a purple ribbon, boots of supple leather. He was taking in the day's warmth as only a young man of fortune could, languishing at the cusp of spring, lording over the manor that would someday be his. Ready for something new to fill his days, Ulysses hoped and prayed.

"Brooke the Believer!" Tad called over, his green eyes crinkling with pleasure, arms spread wide.

Ulysses hopped down from his horse. The pastures were overgrown, the soil set to renew. Over beyond the house, still leafless maples stretched like stalks to the sky. "You're every bit the same," he answered back.

Tad's smile widened, and he led them toward the hillsides – two lords of Virginia, surrounded by a harvest to come – and Ulysses felt the pry of his gaze. "It's true then? The capital's truly become your home?"

"More of a command post, I'd wager."

"The lord governor demanding that much of you?"

"It's not that."

"Then who?" Tad winked. "Might there be a blessed belle?"

"If only. I've been spending half my days with old Cato." After all, it was why he was here.

"You two prepared to be wed at last?" Tad howled at his own joke.

"Enough, Thaddeus. I've something to say."

"When have you not?"

So that now Ulysses lowered his voice. "I'm a thief."

Finally, Tad lost his grin.

"I mean what I say."

"You're a wealthy man, Ulysses."

"I'm not pilfering for my own sake."

His friend's smooth features stiffened further. "For Cato then?"

"In a manner of speaking, yes," and his voice slid into a whisper. "I aim to topple every bit of this."

Thaddeus stared.

"We ride off and nab what we can, you see. We bury it as near to slave quarters as possible – wherever we find them – mapping the way as we go."

"Cato has agreed to this?"

"With vigor."

"You coerced him."

"Not at all. He volunteered his labor."

"As he does for your father?"

"Come off it, Thaddeus. He deserves far more credit than that." Ulysses forced himself quiet once more. "Truth is, we've had some close rubs. We've come to agree we need some help."

For a moment, they stood silent. Tad exhaled. "And when you've finished your thieving?" He turned. "What then?"

"The gold's to be dug up. We'll spread the word." Ulysses recalled Cato's doubts too – his own friends, he thought, as warped by the mob's delirium as the rest, thinking it was he who'd gone mad, and not the world itself. "The slaves themselves shall recover it."

"To what end? Coloreds purchasing coloreds?"

He shook his head.

"What then, Ulysses? Revolt?"

Ulysses shrugged.

"You can't mean for them to start shooting?"

"If that's what's required."

Tad clasped his hands behind his back, tracing his boot in the grass. "It's treason."

"It's justice."

"Why not provide them guns directly then?"

"To allow them their choice. The gold is for whatever the slaves prefer: those who aim to run, yes, and those who prefer a fight on the way. It's choice that'll forge them the respect they've always been denied."

But Tad was bent over now, clutching the knees of his breeches, staring at the soil. A long minute passed, then another. Until at last, he seemed to locate his thoughts. He glanced up. "A Robin Hood in our midst, eh?"

"In search of his Little John," Ulysses answered, and he placed a hand on his friend's shoulder. "It's a chance at making good on what we've always known, Thaddeus. That the whole damned thing must come to its end – lest we spend our lives surrendering to hypocrisy, just as our fathers have done: honoring the Revolution, all whilst keeping men like Cato as trophies to prove it."

But Tad waved him off.

"You don't mean you're not interested?"

"In one of your lectures? Certainly not."

"In what then?"

They faced each other once more. "You mean all this, Ulysses?"

"Of course I do."

Tad nodded, gazing out across the meadows. "These fields have given me everything I've got," he offered next. "They're the only path that's ever borne me. Yet here you are, telling me I've another."

"Don't you believe it?"

Tad angled back. "You say you've already begun?"

"And then some." Ulysses didn't know whether to apologize for burdening his friend, or press him to be sure he'd heard.

"Surely you recognize the danger?"

"Why, Thaddeus, the danger is us!" And at that, Tad finally met his eye.

CHAPTER 20

Lexington, Virginia – September

1808

Cato's journeys from Boxwood hadn't gone unnoticed. The overseers were asking questions. The other hands had begun to whisper. Franklin Brooke had even urged Ulysses to purchase a city slave of his own in Richmond, that he might stop absconding with one of his father's and pretending the fellow was his. And so they'd decided: the next theft ought to be somewhere close, near enough that they could fetch Cato at Sabbath's start, and have him back before its end.

Ulysses had been tracking banking routes all through the commonwealth, until he'd come upon this one in Lexington: home to a small school for boys, tucked away but not too distant, with a credit union all its own. The kings of the low country even preferred this little hub's vaults to the national bank in Washington.

"Yonder," Thaddeus remarked now, as the three men pulled into town.

Tad hadn't agreed to join them right away: Ulysses had walked another mile with him on that day of his visit, telling him more of their schemes, eventually giving him time to sleep on it. But come dawn that next morning, Thaddeus had asked for another stroll, and standing opposite his friend once more, tall and steady in his fine fabrics, atop his family's fields, he'd declared himself willing, honored even to be asked. Ultimately, it was just as Ulysses had anticipated. Tad had always known what was in his own heart. He'd just had to hear it aloud.

Here he was then, along for the ride – Cato hadn't really believed it until he'd seen him that morning – pointing across the buggy's sidebars, past the local pupils hurrying along the quads: pony-tailed lads, pine pencil cases beneath their elbows, the blood of heroes in their veins – every one of them stiff-backed and smug. Cato steered clear of them, over to a stretch of storefronts, all creaky porches and fold-oak doors, brick cropping up in between.

It was here the local savings house resided, a converted old tool shed stocked with double-door safes – not much to look at, really, just another lean-to in need of a coat of paint, under siege from the rose bushes out front. A lone sentry slumped on a stool at the door, flintlock pistol looped in his trousers, one hand draped over its barrel while he snored.

The sun was low, glinting off a row of chestnut saplings that had been planted along the curb. The mud road was calm. It was the kind of place where every day matched the last. And together, they sat back and waited, keeping their eyes peeled for the week's shipment they knew would be coming.

It was nearly an hour, then, before a jet-black horse appeared, a full hand taller than their own, drawing a wagon sleek and low, the commonwealth's seal stamped along the wheel rims' edge. "Come then!" Tad urged, and Cato knotted the reins.

Yet Ulysses didn't move. They'd studied up before they'd arrived, it was true, knew the town's cutbacks, had made sure to use one of the slave buggies from back home – rotted, withered, in no danger of being recognized – had checked too there'd be no militia in a borough this scale: just the local sheriff, and a few evening watchmen over by the academy. Still, as he watched the money-wagon pull ever closer, he took in the slave at its helm, no doubt favored to be entrusted with such a task, his gray curls cropped short, a proper cloth overcoat, trimmed with lace. Except it was the color of the cuffs that had stolen Ulysses' attention: royal blue and gold – Boxwood's Grove's own coat of arms. "By God, Cato," he murmured. "We know that fellow."

Alas, before he'd even gotten out the words, Thaddeus was already off – angling suddenly up the road, circling to the wagon's side – pulling himself up by its rail board, cocking his fist, letting fly with everything he had: right into the temple of the old slave before him. So that even at a distance, there was a terrible crack.

Ulysses and Cato both gasped, watching as the poor fellow slumped, as Tad quickly took the reins, calming the horse before him. At that, he looked up sharply, gesturing that they come and help – and in an instant, knowing there was no going back, Ulysses sprinted over. By the time they were lifting out the gold, the injured slave was stirring – thank God Thaddeus hadn't hurt him worse! – and they skipped away just before he opened his eyes, treasure in tow.

The whole exchange had taken less than a minute, and the road remained empty. Heart pounding, throat gone dry, Ulysses met Tad's eye as they rode on, seeing him panting in turn, a river of sweat down his temple to the floor, splotching the dusty planks a soppy brown.

"His name was William," Cato suddenly announced. "Three score, if he's a day."

Ulysses squinted to recall it. "He's labored for my family all his life, no?"

"As he'll continue to," Thaddeus replied in turn. "I snuck the old boy but a single blow."

"A blow that was no part of our plan."

"You said you were thieves, Ulysses! Is this not what bandits do?"

The sun had sunk even lower, the scent of the season's last blossoms growing sweeter. Ulysses sat back, dabbing his brow with his sleeve. "You're certain he didn't spot your face before you struck?"

"Come now – the two of you fret like maidens! He'll be briefly questioned. They'll all presume it was local rogues."

"Still. We must take better care."

"To what end, Brooke? That we know precisely whose slave it is we're striking?" Tad snorted. "Whose gold it is we're heisting?"

Ulysses realized both of his friends were watching him now, two sets of eyes in the coming twilight, that Thaddeus was saying aloud what he himself had left unspoken: that he'd hesitated only because they'd stolen from his very own birthright. He pointed toward a hill, shifting the topic to where it ought to be. "The manors grow larger." On the bluff ahead, chimneys poked out from behind a lush grove of sycamore. And pulling out his book of maps, etching a portrait, he waited until they'd reached a flatter spot, and found a place to dig.

The world turned blue while they worked, that mystical bridge between dusk and dark, as a half-moon made itself known. So that by the time they were done – the cash buried, the soil tossed back on top – the air had filled with its nighttime chirps and croaks. Cato retrieved a five-stringer banjo from the carriage then, balancing its hollowed-out gourd against his shoulder, working to tune it. As a boy, he'd learned to play from the older men in the quarters, explaining that he liked to let his fingers do the thinking, even if they hadn't yet grown long enough to hit the chords. In those days, Ulysses would sneak down and listen, learning from Cato's haunted eyes, and human smile, that here was no base spirit in those who resided in the cabins, no separate species, no divine mistake – only a shared taste for freedom. And now as then, Cato started in, up against the red wolves' howls that echoed from the far side of the hills, with a voice both rumbling and smooth:

Tum, tum, tumbling down
Joshua fit the Battle of Jericho, Jericho, Jericho
Joshua fit the Battle of Jericho
And the walls come a-tumbling down.

1889

Even in this place, Sam realized with delight, the decaying book of maps was somehow working. Here, at the nexus between Old South and New, none of the roads were remotely as they'd been. Little Washington Academy had become Washington & Lee, a university in its own right, and the grounds had plainly swelled: prim brick paths, white pillars, playing fields in place of brush. But checking his coordinates against the grid, peering at the old sketches, Sam found his way, winding past plaques and statues, copper tributes to the glory of yore, and the bluster that had come along to join them: students in rimless spectacles and bright-checked trousers, traveling in packs like dogs.

"Lost your way, sir?"

He lowered his compass. Here was one of them now: razors for cheeks, flaxen hair like dried reeds. "Much obliged, son," but he gave a wave. "It's no matter, you can return to your books."

"Suit yourself, Yank – " though his tone had shifted at Sam's accent, as if to declare the stench of the war still resided here, had even turned sharper since Sam's own days on a Virginia campus, baking in the southern heat, bitterness reduced like cooked wine – Dixie's defeat merely a steppingstone on the way to Dixie's denial.

Sam spun off. A sweep of day-lilies beckoned, savoring their last minutes of light. Further up, a narrow chapel of brick stood at the ready, beneath a thin blanket of ivy. It was there, according to the rags, that Robert E. Lee himself was buried, namesake to this whole place, lifted directly from death into marble. What's more, if Sam's compass was correct, it was there that he needed to be, that very chapel erected just feet from where Ulysses had marked this latest batch of gold.

He fetched his shovel from the carriage and waited for the sun to set. His horse was snorting impatiently, trotting in place, while the lads nearby retreated to their halls. But in time, the grounds were cast in new stillness, and he started forward once more, parking beneath the small steeple in the milky quiet, ignoring the ghosts he imagined swirling in protest.

The soil was soft from the summer rains, and he dug quickly, one foot, then another, until he heard the telltale scratch – metal upon metal! – and switched to his hands. He caught himself grinning, another triumph at hand, hoisting the treasure out like a graverobber, the horse egging him on with a whinny, as he hid the chest beneath a heavy duck canvass.

When just as quick, he halted.

There, curling up the path, was a shadow not his own – thin and silent, and cloaked in gray. It might be a lone passerby, retrieving some item at the library, but Sam waited, until it had slowed in turn.

"Just as I wagered," a voice drawled now, shallow and eager, and Sam saw then it was the same yellow-haired lad from the afternoon: doing his level-best to sneer – laughable really – a self-styled heir to the cavalier class. "Typical Federal."

"Guilty as charged," Sam offered.

The lad smirked, a grin stretched weak, nothing resembling a genuine smile. "Why the shovel?"

Sam glanced over, silently cursing his carelessness. He'd meant to cloak it along with the treasure.

"Here to debase our heritage, then?" The words melted into each other, and the lad nodded back toward Lee's mausoleum. "I ought put you in the ground right there with him."

"Calm yourself, son. Don't you fight your father's war." Sam kept his gaze steady, using whatever years he had on this fellow to try and weigh him down, seeking something that might keep the poor boy sated. "I came here as a Union man," he sighed more steadily, ignoring the question about the shovel. "Union, not northern, mind you – as my pa was before me. To pay tribute to your side, just as I do his."

"By stealth of night?"

"By light of day – until you interrupted me earlier, as I'm sure you recall." Sam shrugged. "I waited a spell, that you might cool off, and now I'm returned. To finish my prayers." It was such a cheeky lie, he thought – profane in its sacrilege, cloying in its sentiment – that the lad had no choice but to believe it. And hopping up and snapping the reins, feeling not an ounce of guilt, Sam abandoned the fool beneath the stars.

1975

Raindrops hammered the car like broken little bullets, thunder rattling the roof, and Alvin waited out the storm with as much patience as he could muster. He'd been driving since dawn, stopping only once for gas, and now, in the campus' main lot, he was loath to linger any longer. Tapping the steering wheel, watching the windshield fog up, he took in the historic chapel ahead. Its flared steeple was shrouded in haze, and he sighed, tired of the humid little hatchback.

At last, the clouds eased, and he unbuckled his belt. The Virginia air was thick and golden, and by the time he'd made it across the asphalt, it was as if he'd entered the tropics, as he untucked his polyester shirt, and pulled the damp photocopied map from his jeans. Moving up a hillside, past a row of security phones glowing blue in the mist, he weaved among students emerging from their dorms, blonde boys in deck shoes and khakis, well-trimmed sideburns already on retreat, no matter the generation of longhairs who'd only just preceded them.

He arrived at the refurbished chapel, its red brick smoothed and stripped of age, a noisy air conditioner droning in the back. And for a moment, Alvin felt silly even coming, awed by how many college folks must have been through here since the treasures had vanished, how unlikely it was a single shred of evidence could have survived them. Still, he strolled forward, approaching the statue of Lee lying in repose, arms folded for eternity, stone bed underneath. There was a stack of fresh carrots on the ground a few feet away, Alvin saw with surprise: garnish, he realized, for a second tomb, marking the general's horse.

There were tourists surfacing now too, all around him, some bowing their heads in earnest, leaning on their umbrellas, paying tribute to all this nostalgia steeped in hate. They nursed a terrible longing, Alvin couldn't help but think – for a time none of them had ever seen, a time that never really was – mourners for a stillborn nation, making this their mecca.

Faye would spit on such hallowed ground. Of course she would. If he tried to point out the seductive power of an Eden already gone – the romance of it, even – she'd push back in a huff, he was sure, calling out this Confederate nonsense for what it was: a fable, a shadow-nation of slavers, overdue for extinction, indulged by posterity. It made its heirs just as delusional as their forebears, clinging to what might have been, telling themselves what might yet be – nasty, curdled dreams still begging to be let loose. Dreams that Ulysses Brooke had sought to topple for good.

Alvin looked up.

He blinked.

For how could it be?

Surely his mind was playing tricks in the heat. Yet as he peered past the chapel's edge, he confirmed it: a pair of men, skirting about as if they'd just graduated from an amateur course in sleuthing.

It was none other than Clay and Clem Campbell, the very brothers who were driving this investigation in the first place. Alvin stared now at their linen suits, the color of oatmeal – high beltless waists swelling against gargantuan red ties – each one strutting the same as when they'd come and brought the case to the bureau: Clay, the brasher of the two, and Clem, fleshier, quieter, both removing their sun hats in unison, holding them over their chests.

Alvin stepped forward, shouting out as soon as he was in earshot. "What in the hell are you two doing here?"

"Pleasure to run into you too, Starkman!" It was Clay who'd responded, chuckling, his fine accent tempering the blow of his narrow little eyes.

"You been tailing me all along?"

"Please, we're in town serving on a panel, you ole' cynic!"

"You take me for an ass?"

"Is everything a conspiracy to you types?"

Alvin wasn't sure if he meant G-men or Jews. "The bureau won't tolerate this kind of behavior."

But Clay just raised his eyebrows, and gestured past the chapel, where a gaggle of staffers were erecting a white tent. "I've already told you, Starkman. We're here on business. Our alma mater invited us for a word on investing, that's all. Gave us a title and everything – *The Cash Crop of Our Time.*"

Alvin didn't smile back. They probably saw in him everything the feds had ever pushed, everything standing in the way of all they held dear – busing and Birmingham, Bobby and LBJ – yet still they needed him to do his job, and they were clearly concerned enough to watch over him while he tried. "I mean it, gentlemen," he pressed. "We'll put this whole thing on ice if you keep it up." Though now he turned away. He didn't answer to them, after all. It was the bureau that'd sent him here, and the bureau to which he'd return.

CHAPTER 21

Richmond – Scotts Landing, Virginia
September 1810

It was unexpected, this swirl of nerves in Ulysses' belly, a thing he'd managed to leave behind during the robberies. Yet here he was, simply traversing his own city to meet Rebecca, and he could scarcely keep still.

He took in the capital's hum as he rode – merchants, assemblymen, carriage-drivers – and he rolled his eyes. He hadn't stopped trying to tell everyone, governor after governor, term after term, that it was puerile progress: that while the North raced on ahead, trampling its pastures with cement, unclasping its whips, their own idyll remained no more than a mirage, blinding them as they trudged on.

The mansion, at least, wasn't far: he could see the fine brick ahead, its fanlight door, the leisure garden at its side, and it was there he spotted Rebecca's mother, knelt among the green, humming in a corseted gray dress, gathering squash. "Mrs. Vance," he called from his carriage, stepping down to a lonely white gate.

She smiled, wiping the soil from her palms, offering a curtsy in return. "Ulysses! We've not seen you since spring!"

"Busy serving at the governor's pleasure."

It was then, however, Rebecca came bounding out herself, ringlets above her ears, a silk-satin bodice and rose sash at her waist, so that Ulysses had to blink to keep from staring; he couldn't help but wonder at the curves hiding just underneath. "Come, Ulysses," and her dark eyes flashed. "We're low on time if we're to beat nightfall." She'd clasped him by the arm, and now she waved to her mother.

"I'll see you later then," Mrs. Vance said. "Your father will be sorry to have missed the hello."

Ulysses bowed farewell in turn, and led the way back to the road, holding Rebecca's arm as she climbed into the carriage. A stagecoach buzzed from the other lane as he joined her, its irons splattering them with mud, and she started to laugh, wiping the mess. "I dare say, Ulysses – what muck!"

He was peering ahead, however, past crowds of women trimmed with pearls, pickpockets scurrying at their elbows, men pushing through with their canes. "Indeed," he murmured.

"Oh come now." Her smile receded. "You don't really mind it?"

"But of course, the muck runs far deeper than just a road," and he turned, meeting her eye. "Our Christian age, Rebecca – not nearly worthy of the name."

"What age ever was?"

"And thus we forfeit our claim?"

But she waved this off with a renewed chuckle and a sweep of her arm, her sleeve catching in the wind, as they rode the next blocks in quiet, exiting the city altogether, into the stillness beyond. The trip had been her idea, sent by post, urging that since her family had already hosted him, it was well past time his return the favor. Hesitantly, he'd agreed.

By the time Boxwood Grove came into view, she was slumped over, asleep, and the sun was barely clinging to the horizon. He nudged her gently, pointing toward the fenced-in fields as she woke, honeyberries glinting like sapphires, woodland crowned by fall's first hints of yellow. Rebecca stretched softly, taking in what the whole of the South would envy: curling steps of the veranda, pink azaleas still bright beneath the sills, crops and songbirds, blossoms and peace, the vast Virginia sky.

And every bit of it quicksand, Ulysses thought.

His parents soon spotted them, offering waves from the porch. They looked older than he recalled – his father's shoulders gone stooped beneath his cape, his mother's hair turned limp – though their expressions were eager.

Ulysses swallowed. Why had he assented and brought her? How long could he play at this game of pretend?

"So this is the famed Miss Vance!" his mother was calling out, as a gaggle of slaves approached to help.

"Welcome," his father announced. And with a bow, he took Rebecca's hand, leading her up the porch, and into the dining room at the rear.

Supper ended up filling half the night. There were porcelain tureens, and rows of fine silver cutlery, sauceboats as large as rabbits and centerpieces of bellflower, stews of yam, gumballs of sugar and seed, venison from the woods to the west. Though it wasn't until dessert – apples normally stored for winter, now stewed with molasses and cream – that it really became clear: everything had been ordered up on Rebecca's account. It was a shameless attempt to impress. And from her stifled smirk, Ulysses was sure she knew it too.

Finally, as the last plates were being cleared, his father came upon his favorite topic at last. "Is it true there's clamor for war?" he demanded, his voice sharp as ever. "Can our English foes be begging another comeuppance already?" Ulysses sighed, but to no avail. "What says your own father, Miss Vance?" Captain Vance had been chief of the capital militia, after all, nearly twenty years now, as famed a man as Franklin Brooke. Even without an official position in government, members of the Assembly, even the governor, constantly sought his approval.

"I'm but a lady of course," she answered adeptly. "He rarely confides."

Ulysses cut in. "War would be just another trap," and though he knew his words were fueled by drink, he was also sure what he felt. "To ensnare yet another round of men. That they can be told they're heroes, whilst offering up their lives for a broken land."

His mother's face tightened. "Really, Ulysses…" – though that was all.

His father was not so restrained. "Where possibly can such nonsense come from?" He pushed up from the table, scratching the floor with his chair. "You speak of a world that ought deliver you nothing but pride!"

Ulysses was ready to fire back in turn, to tell them it was they, not he, who refused to see. Yet as he opened his mouth to say so, his eyes brushed past Rebecca – shifting in her seat – and it was enough to give him pause. He caught his breath, letting them think they had won.

***

It wasn't until morning that he had his chance to explain.

He found her by the carriage at dawn, draped in a new shawl for autumn, a white gossamer fringe around her waist, idling below the day's first clouds. "No breakfast?" he asked quietly.

"There's still time to ruin another meal, you mean?"

"In a world already ruined?"

"Always so serious."

"Though never taken seriously."

She turned, and stepped nearer. So that all at once, despite his mood, he could feel something else: a sensation that seemed to sweep up over him, their cheeks near enough to touch, lips easy to imagine against his own, every pore of skin visible in the cool morning light. "What about now, Ulysses? Do all your troubles remain when it's just we two?"

"If only it really were," he answered. For indeed, here in the shadow of the manor, too early for the rest of the world to have stirred, it was almost possible to envision another life, one that could be all theirs. Was it really just the feel of her breath upon him that could have this effect? The thought of her touch? Could it be so simple, so base, as that?

She was smiling. "Shall we picnic?"

"What of my parents?"

"They dine unattended every day, Ulysses – I'm quite sure they'll manage."

And he laughed at that – eager indeed, he realized, to show he was more than his diatribes and fire. He clasped her arm in his, and led them to the rear of the property, past the kitchen yard and the current harvest, toward the unused pastures beyond.

"I can't know what to expect from you," she remarked, as they left the outbuildings behind. "The radical in gentlemen's garb? Or this, Ulysses: all sentiment and whim?"

"Are they not one and the same?" He paused at a patch of cardinal blossom, watching the hummingbirds atop the nectar, before motioning that they sit.

"My father claims you're distracted," Rebecca noted next, straightening her gown. "That you're taken over by your work."

"And what do you believe?"

"That he's wrong, Ulysses. That it's me who is the distraction, as you once told me – and your work that is your purpose."

He sat quite still a moment. "We never did fetch ourselves any breakfast."

"Is that all you can say?"

He squinted back. Somewhere, a pair of warblers had struck up a duet. "Why invite me out here, Rebecca?"

"The grass is dry. The sun not too warm."

"That can't be all."

"And because you're strange, Ulysses. Stranger than any planter's son I've ever met. Pondering all there is. Pressing me to ponder it in turn. Only what if I could offer you something else, by way of reply? A chance at savoring life itself?"

"I'd ask to what end."

"That you might allow yourself to admit the truth: a single sin needn't stain the whole of everything." She'd shifted nearer.

He was surprised. After all he'd done to shield his heart, she was peering straight into it. "I've been callous to you, Rebecca."

"No."

"You cast up nothing but warmth – yet still I flee."

She stayed in place, a large bee hopping between the blossoms nearby. The seconds turned to minutes. The breeze kept on.

"What is it?" he asked now, watching her hair glow copper in the sun.

"Whatever this is between us, Ulysses."

"And if one of the field hands were to pass by?"

"They'd have trouble finding us amid all these petals."

"They might be skilled – a tracker. An old scout." But he lowered his face to hers. Slowly. Carefully. Aware of every beat from his heart – in the sides of his neck, in his palms, on the bottoms of his feet. His breaths had grown shallow – his regular, racing mind seeming very far away indeed: thoughts of southern sin – of his parents and hers – buried deeper than ever before.

"Well?" she managed. "What say you, Ulysses?"

But though he opened his lips to explain, no other words came, and he made no effort to force them. Instead, he did only as she seemed to ask, allowing himself a lull, a hitch in his ire – enough that now, with each passing breath, all that came to exist was the sun overhead, the meadow underneath, and Rebecca just there.

He was tired, he knew – exhausted by his own ambition, by the secrecy woven into its every fiber, the danger he risked with Cato and Thaddeus at his side – muddling his mind, mining his thoughts, confusing his decisions no doubt. Yet was that reason enough to stop this? To deny a moment of content?

Until at long last, his throat gone parched, his stomach grown tight, he sensed he was ready. To stay, just here, the way they were.

"It's not that you feel obliged, Ulysses?"

He shook his head.

"That it's what expected of you?"

Again, he was silent. This wasn't the first time they'd sat together, or been so close. There'd been an evening once, when they'd been drunk. Other moments too, hovering near. But not like this, not holding one another's gaze. He watched her waiting. He saw her bite her lip.

And it was then that he kissed her.

One second, he'd been sitting, stationary. The next, he was grasping her chin in his hands, lips turned eager, pressed together.

Until, after a minute, she paused.

"We needn't go on, Rebecca."

"It's not that." She blushed, the first time he'd ever seen her do so. "Though – of course it's that too."

He nodded. "These lives of ours – intertwined as they are – " He took her hands.

"But are they, Ulysses?" She let him grip her fingers, but she slid no closer. "Tell me. You must. Is it me you're seeking, when you gaze out the window at your family's table? When you vanish on your journeys, returning with nary a word of where you've been? Is it my face ever swirling in your thoughts?"

He listened, waiting for more – then watching as she turned, and let slip her hands – as slowly she stood. "I want it to be," he answered. And that, at least, had the benefit of being true.

CHAPTER 22

New York City – October

1817

It had been the governor's decision to come here, and he'd invited Ulysses along.

James Preston was still new to the office – inaugurated just last winter – and had been leaning on his senior council for guidance, not least when it came to the notion of abolition. He'd gotten it in his head that gradualism might be the answer, had even proposed a study of its success in Manhattan: to see if Virginia might indeed follow the model and be slave-free by quarter-century's end. While Ulysses had come to see the notion as laughable – how could one speak of patience to a mother who'd just lost her babe at auction? – he'd agreed to the trip. After all, Gotham wasn't just a buyer of southern cotton, it was guardian to southern gold.

And what a city it was!

Every block made Richmond look like an abandoned stretch of Scotts Landing. "*Get it here!*" a newsboy was shouting, voice hoarse from repetition. "*Scandal! Infidelity!*

Under our noses! Read it, read it, read it!" Past him, endless corridors, each one dense enough to fill an entire village, and display windows as wide as crop lines. Horse traffic was everywhere: chimney sweeps on corners, ladies with parasols, merchants bundled up in wool, hauling crates of oysters and carriages of lumber, accents trailing all the while – West African, Dutch, Old English, French.

Ulysses had finally slipped out from the governor's latest round of meetings. It had been four days of sessions already, yet he'd delayed. After all, caution was paramount: word had continued spreading of all the missing funds, and without Cato and Thaddeus nearby, there was even less room for error. Still, the opportunity was why he was right here in the first place – why it had been worth coming alone. He'd gotten directions at the hotel – "*corner of Water and Wall Streets!*" the bellman had snapped – and now he studied the street signs with care.

Somehow, the crowds were growing thicker: workers rolling bales, bankers waving them aside like clutter, cobblestone smoothed near to nothing, and the horizon just the opposite: sails poking up from the wharves, brick chimneys from every rooftop, church steeples like flipped-over icicles. And there, at the center of it all, the counting house.

It throbbed at the city's heart, men in double-breasted coats racing back-and-forth across its steps, and Ulysses hurried in among them, past pink-cheeked portraits of Hamilton lining the walls, and fine, flickering chandeliers beneath pigeons in the rafters. Scanning the counter in back, he settled upon a nervous-looking fellow at its corner, not yet old enough to shave. The lad wore blue pantaloons bunched at the knees and had rusty brown hair parted against its will. His coat hung from his shoulders like a blanket. "Evenin', sir," he piped.

Ulysses smiled broadly and offered assurance. "'Evenin' to you, son. Call me Brooke – consort to the visiting delegation from Virginia." He let his own accent fly – all melody and ease – and to his delight, the young teller grinned. The newspapers had been covering the governor's visit with fanfare, and it was clear the boy was eager in any way to be wrapped up in its sphere.

"We're honored to be sure, sir."

Ulysses rested his hands between them. There was no time to waste. "I should be grateful for a tour." He let his smile go. "I'll be glad to regale the governor of your hospitality, of course. And the care being entrusted our funds."

For an instant the young man wavered.

Ulysses leaned closer. "Surname is Brooke," he repeated slowly. And from his breast pocket, he unfurled a standing letter of introduction from Preston himself.

So that now his victim buckled in full, lifting the counter's wooden flap by its hinges. "If you'll follow this way, sir."

Soon, the grand sweep of the lobby was gone, replaced by a jigsaw of narrow halls, each one winding its way toward the vaults. There were dozens of others lads too, fetching trays of coin, satchels of bills, cases of inkwells and quills. Ulysses distracted his guide with questions as they moved in among them – learning the boy had completed school that summer, that his pa had found him the job – confirming in turn his own identity: that yes, he was the son of *that* Franklin Brooke. Until, amid the chatter, he saw what he was after. There, stacked against the wall, a cabinet of letter files sat as tall as a man, each one dangling open and stuffed to the brim – bank notes piled high, not a one yet water-stained, each awaiting deposit.

He glanced at the teller, droning on about his hopes of visiting Dixie, then took note of a gaggle of others, bent in discussion. And seizing his chance, Ulysses grabbed a stack of the checks at waist level, a dozen at least, from drawers labeled Virginia, Georgia, the Carolinas too – tucking them into his vest in silence, striding on before anyone could notice. Finally he cleared his throat. "Beg pardon, young man – but the governor will be expecting me. Apologies indeed."

Without delay then, with his host stuttering in surprise – apologizing the whole way back for any offense he might have given – they were zipping along the same hall as before, Ulysses offering a hasty bow at the end, declining to sign a guest book, saying he really must hurry, knowing not all these lads would be such fools. He left the boy blinking, and retreated to the streets, praying nobody back in the bank would notice the missing checks for weeks, not until the planters down South sent inquiries regarding receipt. By then, with any luck, the coastal roads would be frozen, delaying the post, swallowing up more time. And stepping among the day's shadows, he looked down the block.

The next building seemed to reflect its patron's character: Aaron Burr had founded this competitor bank slyly, finding a clause in the national charter, a loophole for surplus capital, so long as it was mined from public interest. The Manhattan Company, he'd called it – a water-works, technically – offering plumbing to any who desired, all the while stowing profits and interest on the side. By all accounts, Hamilton had been furious. But no matter; Burr had finished the job. And here it was: a curb cloaked in mud, windows smudged, red brick turned black from soot.

Still, Ulysses had no choice. It was the only other bank in the city, and he wasn't about to snub it. He confirmed the checks in hand had been endorsed without specifics – southern lords treating New York as a single entity, just as he'd suspected – and he marched inside, gliding across a mosaic marking the floor. At his last stop, he'd sought youth. Now, he required desperation. He zeroed in on a fellow scribbling at a pine desk, wearing a velvet vest and shimmering buttons, a silk white kerchief, a red ribbon in his hair. He looked like a gift wrapped in too much tissue paper.

"You're a clerk?" Ulysses began.

The teller's gaze paused upon the checks in his grip. "And you, sir?"

"A traveler. An executor."

"On whose behalf?"

"The finest of Dixie," and he laid on the lilt even thicker than before. "Men desiring that I deposit their gold."

The teller wrinkled his forehead. "I must inform you, sir." His words were halting. "We require the signatories themselves."

"I have the checks. Even more pertinent than the people behind them, I should think?"

Another pause, and the fellow tapped his index. He was clearly absorbing Ulysses' manner, trying to get a look at the slips in his hand. Finally, he folded his arms, and pointed to one of the cushioned chairs before him.

"After deposit, I'd like to withdraw."

The teller shifted once more.

"With a cut for the bank, naturally. You name the rate, you can take it today." Ulysses steadied his gaze. "With the same amount for yourself."

The man swallowed, his eyes pressing. "Ten percent perchance? This would be acceptable?" His voice sounded shaky. "For bank expenses of course."

And though Ulysses winced at the corruption, he pushed the checks forward.

"This will be all?" The teller pulled out a feathered quill.

"Nearly. I require the cash before I depart."

Another hesitation.

"Forty-five hundred." Ulysses had calculated the sum on the way.

"Of course, sir, but again, without signatory..." The teller scratched his chin. "Perhaps – for an additional fee – we might yet manage."

"How additional?"

"Five percent for added labor, I should think."

"It's yours." Ulysses stood. "The rest, after interest, comes to me. No signatories then. No more questions. Specie only. You understand?"

This time, the teller didn't flinch. He was lifting another receipt, deducting the new figure. "If you'll excuse me," he declared, and Ulysses watched anxiously as the man pulled a key from his pocket, and made his way to a door in the wall behind him. Jiggling the lock, he disappeared behind the brick.

A moment later, his footsteps returned.

He was carrying a standard-issue iron chest now, grunting as he lowered it to the desk with a struggle. When he opened its latch, Ulysses worked not to gape. His hunch had been right: his exoticism – his performance of certainty – had done the trick. And without another word, before the teller could think better of it, Ulysses clasped the thing shut, and turned for the exit.

Gripping it tight, he moved from Wall Street's crowds, straight to the farmland uptown. There, gentler air and the maze of thickets stirred his memory of home, his conviction only growing as he discovered a patch of two-acre plots. They were filled mostly with cabbages and scraps, bought up by the speculators of the new century and marked by wooden fence posts, labeled with purchasers' names in sloppy white paint. The sun would soon be gone, and Ulysses, checking he was really alone, sought out one of the plots yet unclaimed. Then, bending to his knees, his trousers going cold against the hard northern soil, he started in.

He'd buried all the other treasures in the South of course, alongside the slaves he prayed would collect them. But here too, the lash wasn't gone entirely: chattel in woodshops and manufacturers were manning the port just a few miles down. And Ulysses dug vigorously, pausing only when a winter hawk floated past, circling, diving, plucking up a tiny mouse before it slid back to the sky – the lone witness to his crime.

1889

Stepping from his mother's door, Sam stashed the book of maps in his coat, and the shovel inside his carrier bag. He skipped over the scattered pigs grunting from the gutter, wary of clouds tumbling overhead. The rain had slowed, but the downtown blocks were still covered in mist, coaxing the stench of horse manure and rotted fish into a single stew, cloaking the new nearby Jewish stalls in wet.

He'd been a dutiful son, visiting for supper and then, when the storms had blown in, staying over. The nighttime hours had been spent alone by the light of a tallow candle, choking on its black smoke, hunched in his mother's kitchen, awaiting a drowsiness that never came. He'd been glad at least for the book of maps he hauled everywhere these days, growing absorbed as he'd flipped through it, settling on the page in question – its coordinates faded, its actual etchings grown irrelevant, reason enough why he'd never tried this spot before. For Ulysses Brooke had included no roads in this particular set of instructions, only a broad sketch of pasture and Dutch elms that couldn't possibly be there any longer.

Still, he'd thought, he had a free Sunday; he was no longer a churchgoer – too old for being preached at, he'd decided – nor could he ask the lads to come into headquarters on Sabbath. And so it was, he found himself weaving through the merchants stacking fish, wrapping their cigars, belting in languages he couldn't decipher a whit: not just the German and brogue from his youth, but barks and bursts he'd never heard in his life. It was the din of the expelled, he observed – fleeing pogroms and poverty, imagining there was some haven for them here – as if there weren't multitudes already in place, scrabbling for the same wisps of a dream.

He gripped the book of maps in his pocket – his own Bible, really, tending to his own faith – and traced its edge with his fingers, the worn leather, the gilded edge flaking away. Dodging the pushcarts, gramophones, potatoes and hanging meats, he ignored too the jumbled smells, the crackling smoke of sausages, sweet pies and puddings, a starched breeze advertising something called bagels. Proper brownstones beckoned a few blocks up, stained sheets hanging from windows, and boys on stoops – newer shops beyond that, all oversized registers and overeager clerks – until eventually, New York began to feel like New York again, not just some train depot jammed at the threshold of the world. It was then, as if obeying orders, the sun pushed aside the clouds, precisely as Sam crossed beneath the line of tracks, train wheels rasping against their casings, sparks like a show of fireworks: no more women in babushkas, or bearded men in lopsided vests, and he heard himself exhale.

The pushcarts were replaced by buses and trolleys now, and Sam even spotted a stalled steam carriage, a man scowling in Russian-accented English by its hood-stack, a colored fellow bent before him with a wrench. The bells of streetcars clanged amid the wrought-iron gates. There were men in heavy frocks, and women in heavier dresses, sidewalks wide and clean, trestles for the gardens, private roundabouts paved with stone. Even the fumes – the stench from the fat-renderers on the river, the fog of oil refineries next door – weren't a bother so far uptown. To him, they were the scent of progress and profit, proof that his own quest was worthwhile too.

He followed the map's grid like a captain at sea, navigating beyond Old New York's reach, and into this brand new horizon. Alas, as he slowed, the view ahead grew even less connected to Brooke's etchings than he'd imagined – offering a towering feat of sandstone, where there ought have been space, filling the whole block with gray. Here was somebody's house then, where once there must've been loose soil. The windows were all copper sills and flowing sashes, the rails sturdy and black. And as Sam peered through the fence, he found no opportunity at all, but rather a barrier, standing right where he still wished himself to be.

1975

Sitting opposite the color television he'd bought Faye for her birthday, resisting the urge to turn it on, Alvin gazed at the coffee table in front of him. It was ugly, all variety of oranges and yellows, a lucite carving of an African lion amidst an assortment of stars and sun. At least it hadn't cost them a dime, lying discarded on the sidewalk when they'd found it.

It was raining again, the patter on the windows muting the sirens from the street, and he stared at the photocopies stacked in front of him – the map on top from Ulysses Brooke's only trip northward, the product of a jaunt to this very city. Alvin had always presumed it the least useful of all the book's offerings: a century of skyrises and subways dueling for space ever since Billings had traced Brooke's steps. He'd even walked the block in question to confirm it, coming upon only a grimy, fluorescent-lit supermarket, no hope of finding the past at all.

Except that now, he read it yet again, feeling dumb.

Tucking his hair behind his ears, Alvin checked Brooke's description of unclaimed farmland against the note Billings had added: "*1200 4th.*" So that all at once Alvin clapped his hands and whistled. He'd long gathered it was an address downtown – 4th Street, of course – but now he wondered: what if Billings had meant Fourth Avenue instead? Wasn't that Park Avenue's original name?

Quickly, he grabbed his camera and sneakers – right as Faye stepped in from the bedroom, zipping a pair of knee-high boots, making her legs look finer than ever. "You leaving too?" he asked.

"C'mon, Alvie. You didn't even remember I was home."

He blinked, watching the way her Afro bobbed. "You want company?"

"I'm only getting milk. You'd have known that if you were listening."

"I know. I just thought maybe..." But she was already stepping out the door.

He returned to lacing his sneakers. Sometime soon, he'd need to make a better effort here at home, he thought – he'd at least need to pull back from working Sundays. In the meanwhile, he gave a stretch, and shook off his guilt. Deadbolting the door a moment later, registering that Faye was already out of sight, he stepped over a drunk on their stoop, and into the fallen paradise of the Upper West Side.

The rain had ebbed once more, leaving a pool of warm air in its wake, and Alvin rolled up his sleeves. He walked briskly, ignoring the vets in leather parkas huddled on corners, women in fishnets too, and the silent shops shuttered behind them – closed for the weekend or forever, it was never quite clear – steel shutters like death rattles every time the wind blew. These days, it was easier to tally last night's puddles of vomit than catch a clear square of sidewalk, and as Alvin hurried past the buses stained with smoke, and the rubbish bags colonizing the curbs, torn apart by rats or vagrants or probably both, it was hard to imagine that this was really the world Brooke or Billings had ever aimed to build.

He stepped into the park, scurrying past young men meeting for sex, more addicts lounging and dying, kids playing ball without nets. Cutting east, growing impatient, he eventually reached the block he wanted. It was filled by a single building, the front gates rusted out, sharp-tipped security fencing erected in their stead. Gargoyles on the roof had been blunted by acid rain, stone-framed windows had lost their stained glass. So that even here, where the wealthy still planted their flag, the city's aching bones were letting themselves be known.

At the same time, it wasn't the house from the map, Alvin thought now: for it was far larger than the one Sam Billings had drawn, and not quite as old. It couldn't serve as evidence, then, that the old scion ever been here – let alone that he'd nabbed any treasure from Brooke.

Alvin turned – and it was then he caught a plaque to his right: burnt bronze, faded script.

"*The Billings Mansion,*" it declared – and he read on: "*This limestone masterpiece, dating from the dawn of the American century, was a testament to the vision of its client, banker Samuel Billings, and his beloved wife Emily. Famed philanthropists. Vaunted New York patrons. Parents to Charles and Caroline. Among the notable features of the home, please note the recessed...*"

The letters wore away.

Alvin snapped a photo. Billings must ultimately have purchased the lot, he realized. Upon doing so, he must have set his sights on constructing something that would take the city by storm. No wonder he was famous.

By the time he got back home, then, Alvin's whole mood had turned, tantalized by another clue where he thought there'd been none, wondering just why Billings would have selected to build the home precisely on the site of one of the treasures. It was only when he saw Faye, cross-legged on the couch, that he recalled vaguely they were supposed to be doing something. She was in a red halter dress that let her skin shine, her hair pressed upon the cushions, dark eyes pressed upon him.

In a flash, she was standing. "That's what you're planning on wearing?"

He looked down at his torn jeans.

"We'll be late, Alvin"

"We'll be alright," but it was coming back to him. "Let's just hail a cab."

"You're paying?"

He re-opened the door. "What show are we seeing again?"

"*Chicago*," she sighed, and they stepped back out.

The ride was slow, and she spent it drumming her fingers against the vinyl, while the driver whined in a Queens twang about traffic and hobos and the steam from the sewers. Alvin tried to be polite, responding in grunts, alternately telling Faye how sorry he was for keeping her waiting, that he was excited for the matinee.

But she just kept her focus out the window. "Why not talk about your case, Alvin? That's where your mind is, anyhow."

He sighed in turn, and resigned himself to quiet, watching the city roll by, its crowded intersections jostling in rhythm with the cab's soft landings, the sharp lights of midtown, XXX marquees lining the way.

CHAPTER 23

New York City
November 1976

Scanning pessimistic headlines about the Knicks, picking at the last of a carton of sesame chicken, Alvin was near to dozing on the couch, when Faye closed her novel beside him. "Any progress on your case?"

He rested his fork. "If only."

She nodded in the lamplight, lifting her own carton from the coffee table, reaching to take his too. Standing, she tossed the rubbish down the chute, then faced him from the kitchen, fetching a half-filled bottle of wine. "You'll get there, Alvin – " she grabbed two glasses – "you're too smart not to figure it out." The wine was dark, and it purred as she poured; he watched then as she sauntered back, hips swinging seductively, effortlessly, beneath a pink cotton skirt.

"I'm sorry it's such a distraction, Faye."

"It's your job."

"Still." He took his glass. "You're patient."

"It's a part of you." She peered back at him. "I am too. I've got to make room for it. Or else where does this end up?"

He hesitated. "How do you mean?" Suddenly, he felt his heart beat like a snare.

She re-joined him on the cushions, putting down their glasses, taking his hands instead. "Tell me it's been on your mind at least."

"And if it was?" He absorbed her words. "That would make you happy?"

"Of course."

"The thing is, Faye – "

"I'm listening."

"It's not just my job that gets in the way."

"What then?"

"I just – " How to say it? He'd told her of his life, had even proposed having a Shabbat dinner with his mom and dad. But what about on her end? "I still don't know anything about your family."

She blinked.

"I'm sorry," he managed.

"Don't be."

"What then?"

She exhaled slowly. "My father – " she'd taken back her hands, and was smoothing down her skirt – "he doesn't have much of a life anymore."

"No?"

She shook her head. "He's in prison. Baltimore County, where I grew up. The same jail that's had him since I was six."

Alvin stared. "You never said a word."

"I was worried you'd think he's just another black man."

"C'mon."

"Your whole life is about putting people away."

"It's not. It's about justice – " But it wasn't time for a lecture, and he bit his tongue.

"I haven't even seen him myself. Not face-to-face. Not in ages. It's always just been the phone, for as long as I can remember. Even when I was a girl, he had to haul us to court just to show the judge he was some kind of family man." Her voice grew hushed, and she turned to her glass, rotating its stem between her fingers.

Alvin couldn't help but wonder what the man had done to draw in the law. "What about your mom?" he asked instead. "She was charged too?"

"She ran off." The sleet had picked up outside, driving Faye to speak louder. "She used to tell me she was ready for a man with a pension, not a parole. It wasn't too long before she found one – so long as it didn't mean taking me on in turn."

"Sounds like a real peach."

"I was sent to my grandparents – " and suddenly, there was a catch in her throat. "The visits dried up. Then they moved away altogether. To California. Eventually, it was just signed checks coming my way instead." She winced. "Straight through school, Alvin. Until word got to us that she'd passed: cancer in the lungs. Too many menthols, I guess. Meantime, Grams and Pops were getting old themselves."

"I'm so sorry."

"I shouldn't have kept it from you."

"I shouldn't have let you." He took back her hands. "You know I love you, Faye," he added quietly.

"You're a good man, Alvin – my father would see that." She wiped her cheek. "He'd see how much you care – about your work – about the truth." She took in a wobbly breath. "About me."

"Wouldn't he also see I'm white?" There was a hint of a smile through her tears. "I'd still like to meet him, though. Get his blessing. Maybe even figure a way to help get him a new start."

"I thought you don't bend the law."

"They give furloughs now." He shrugged. "For special occasions."

She raised her eyebrows. "Was that a proposal, Alvin?"

"More like an answer to yours."

So that this time, they both smiled, leaning their foreheads together, and she kissed him – a soft kiss that went on longer than he was expecting. The sleet crowded out the horns outside, and somebody dropped something heavy in the apartment above, but neither one of them glanced away. Instead, Alvin just kissed her back, with all that he felt – enough for marrying, he suddenly thought – enough for shunting out distractions and good sense and a nation taking way too long to catch up.

At some point then, they left the couch, and made their way to the bedroom, as he moved his hands down her back, along her sides, up her legs. He felt her body clench, her lips graze his, her hands lifting his shirt in turn, undoing his belt, reaching down and all over – until for just a moment, he stopped to look – to take in her lean face, gone golden in the streetlight leaking in from outside, until she brought him back in, kissing harder, faster, until many minutes had passed, and the sleet had softened at last.

So that when they were finished, they lay there in quiet, the city growing calm around them. At some point, he heard Faye talking to him. "You're really sure this is what you want, Alvin? I didn't push you towards it?"

He tilted back her way, resting his chin atop her hair. "I wouldn't trade it for the world," and he felt her nod, slowly, silently, her thoughts seeming to drift somewhere else, so that he knew he hadn't said enough. "Besides – " he moved his palms to her shoulder, rubbing her gently. "The country won't be like it is forever. That's why I'm at the bureau, Faye. I swear – it's why I took the job in the first place."

"To change the world?"

"And why not?"

"Oh, Alvie."

"Think what's already changed. Even since we were born."

"Think what hasn't. Beneath the headlines. Beneath the speeches."

"It's better than it was."

"For who?"

"For you. For me."

"We're not the country, Alvin."

He looked out the window beside her, to the city lights outside. "There's whole new generations coming up, Faye – folks who think it's normal to do what we do, to think like we do. It's the law that's on our side – the law that frees people up – lets them live how they want."

She gazed out the window too, up toward nighttime sky. "The papers say even NASA won't go to the moon anymore."

"So we're all supposed to stop trying?"

She nuzzled in closer. "Only I know you never will, Alvie," and her eyes were drifting shut toward sleep.

CHAPTER 24

Richmond, Virginia
October 1822

The robberies had grown, the attention too. There were reports plastered across the broadsides, and conversation transfixed in the capital: folks buzzing about cash shipments disappearing, planters so anxious they'd started hoarding gold, missives spinning out from the governor's office – some Ulysses had even written himself – pledging to apprehend the culprits.

He took in the view before him.

The new bridge over the James River was sparkling in the autumn sun, its logs coated with fresh splinters that waved like goose feathers in the breeze. Down below, fishermen lined the banks in knit caps and sloppily dyed wool, shad and sturgeon flopping, glinting, dying in wicker creels beneath their arms. Behind them, the city's brown rooftops sat like swaths of mud, his own home right among them.

For some time, he'd been keeping the book of maps constantly at his side, tucked tightly within his frock. Yet with the whole of Virginia talking, he was in need of a change. His new plan would bring new risk with it – the prospect of a fire, woodworms too – but at least if he were captured, the book would have hope of escape: to be re-printed and published, to spark the rebellion that still filled his dreams.

Ulysses found his tool chest in the parlor as soon as he arrived back at the house, then skipped to the second story and got to work. Leaning hard with a socket chisel, he pried loose the narrowest floorboard, ignoring the screech, yanking it free, and swiftly placed the book below, lodging it snug against the lime.

When all at once, he halted – certain he'd heard something.

He stood up and listened. There it was again: a rapping on the door, and he spun toward the stairs. He prayed it was no more than a peddler, come to hawk the latest trinkets from uptown – better-lasting horseshoes, tight-woven textiles ready to compete with northern looms – and tapping the heel of his boot upon the freshly restored boards, securing them in place, he brushed his trousers free of sawdust, and made his way down.

Damnation, he thought.

For here were the Thompsons, his neighbors, waiting on his stoop.

They were lifted straight from a fashion plate, as ever: Cyrus' overcoat so padded it turned him into an hourglass, Beth's silk printed with roses, her newly gray hair pinned back in a chignon. She was extending a tray of cold bread and chops. "We saw you blow in, Ulysses, thought you might require refreshments."

"The governor must work you like a field hand!" Cyrus added. "One journey after the next – and for what? That you might tally up another census? Mark a new road the rest of us shall never find?" He laughed.

Ulysses smiled stiffly, accepting the food to save himself something to say. The dough was heavy, the meat marbled and mellow, but it was at least an improvement from supper the night before: half-rotted squirrel, packed by Thaddeus amid their latest thieving.

Elizabeth curtsied. "You ought make time for more pleasures, Ulysses." She leaned closer. "For a family even."

"Fine counsel I'm sure," he answered, wiping his lips. "Though alas, I'd best return above stairs. I've a leak in my tiling, you see –" he was searching to explain whatever they'd heard – "rafters in need of a probe. Thank God they've withstood my pounding."

"Yes, we caught the din on our approach." Cyrus shrugged. "Pity you haven't a slave here to do it for you." His smile stayed frozen in place. "I mean nothing by it, of course, Brooke. Only that your support for emancipation is known to all. Surprising from the son of a planter, no?"

"One with an eye on progress, that's all." Ulysses clicked his heels. "I'll thank you for the treats, in any event. And I'll bid you farewell."

"Perchance I could aid with your leak."

"It's all but done."

"Have you always been so resistant to company, Mr. Brooke?"

"I've just never had such ample opportunity for resisting it –" though it was then that a new voice joined in their exchange.

"Ulysses!"

They all looked to see: and there she was, gliding over from the street in a fur-trimmed dress, violet waistband and white frills at the hem, aster blossoms tucked in her hair, the very picture of Richmond society. Her eyes sparkled as she skipped up the curb, and Ulysses, grateful for the reprieve, waved her near. "Cyrus, Beth – this is Rebecca Vance."

Rebecca shared a friendly scowl – "I dare say you've misplaced your calendar, Ulysses – you're terribly late! – " so that now he remembered: they'd scheduled tea with her family.

"It's we who should apologize, madam," and Cyrus bowed so dramatically, he nearly grazed the cobblestone. "For the intrusion."

"And to whom have I the pleasure?"

"Cyrus and Elizabeth Thompson. Proud neighbors to Mr. Brooke."

"Yet so humble in appearance," she replied in a flash, sharing a smirk that only Ulysses caught – waiting, patiently, as they said goodbye.

"I've kept your father waiting," he remarked, as soon as they were finally gone.

"Freshen up, though, won't you? Heaven above, Ulysses, I can smell you've been on the road."

He flushed, and skipped back in, splashing his face in the basin, stealing a peek at the giltwood mirror on the wall. The hair at his temples had gone gray, and his eyes were settling into new folds; in a bout of rushed vanity, he retrieved a pair of velvet breeches from the wardrobe.

Together then, they set out. All of Richmond seemed to have woken by the time they did: boys tossing hoops, milkmen shuttling buckets of bottles – though in time, the blocks calmed, as they reached the leafy mansions at the city's western edge. Here at least, life was quieter: polished stone lintels and iron fences, lilies and goldenrods still blossoming. And the Vance abode the grandest of them all.

A pair of red-coated slaves stood out front, to usher them past the columns and to the wood-trimmed dining room within. Here now was Captain Vance and his wife, waiting beneath crystal chandeliers and matching pendants on the walls, their plaster fresh, windows newly scrubbed. "We saw you ride in," the Captain announced, offering a terse bow. "I hadn't known a government hireling could afford such a chaise."

Ulysses doffed his silk hat. "Only those of us who don't depend on your tax dollars, sir."

The captain grinned, his wife curtsied and sat, and he snapped his fingers at the slaves. The food followed swiftly: creamed butter and fattened guinea fowl, parsnip and beets, grapes preserved from Spain. It was a stirring, salivating, sickening display, really – New World money in mimicry of Old World power, the revolution be damned, a feudalism born anew, Ulysses thought – all upon the bloodied backs of black-skinned serfs.

When it was finally done – small talk enough for a lifetime, chat of one-party rule, praise for the fall leaves outside – Rebecca escorted him out, only to surprise him by hoisting herself back into the chariot by his side. Ulysses started to laugh. "It's the gentleman commonly runs the lady home, you know, not the reverse. Surely you've read the rules of court?"

"I've just never pegged you as one of its adherents, Ulysses."

And he didn't argue that. The truth was, he'd be glad for the company, his hands beside hers on the reins, their legs nearly touching. It was enough that he never did ask where she'd like to be let off, nor protest when she remained with him all the way back to the stables, joining him next for the short stroll home. "I'll thank you," he finally offered, as he unlatched his own door.

"That's all then?" she wanted to know. "After all this time?"

And now, he simply stared.

For an instant he thought of the Thompsons – no doubt eyeing them at this very moment, through the windows across the way – growing tickled at the notion of scandalizing their very souls. Then, with a grin and a shrug, he opened the door, and led her inside – through the anteroom, into the kitchen, back through the hall – the soft clop of her heels behind his, breaths in between, such unfamiliar sounds against these old familiar walls. What was it they were doing?

They entered the parlor, and he paused. Her eyes were darker now away from the sun, her lips gone soft. Here, in this space where he'd only ever been alone, he realized, just below where he'd stowed the book of maps that very morning.

"Go on then, Ulysses – " and suddenly the room felt small. "I can't say I've ever seen you stumped." Her smile spread wide, and he could feel her breath on his chin, so that it made him shiver.

He shifted in place, the loose floorboards creaking, like ship masts at sea. "Only – " And it was then that he turned. "I can't," he heard himself say, half-buried.

"Tell me why not."

"If ever I could," he murmured – but still he hadn't faced back. "There's too much, Rebecca – too much you oughtn't be a part of. Too much you still don't truly know."

She lifted her arm then, surprising him, taking hold his chin, angling his face to hers once more – and he could see that her eyes were wet. "Must you reject all that comes near, Ulysses? First Boxwood, now me? Anything that might soften your anger, or offer pleasure in its stead?"

He opened his mouth to reply – even to explain: to trust that she of all people could understand, a mind keen enough to know what was right, affection as her guide. Yet the gamble of it! – the possibility it would undo the very future of which they dreamed, hollowing out his watchful eye, putting Cato and Tad straight into danger. And Rebecca right along with them. "My work," he managed. "My cause – "

Except she was shaking her head, backing away, as if trying to make sense of something. "All this time..." and she exhaled. "I don't know that I've ever misread a person so terribly."

"But you haven't, Rebecca." His response came swiftly, reflexively, sensing a hurt that had only just begun. "I admire all that we are – all that we've shared."

"And nothing more," she replied. "Don't you dispute it either, Ulysses Brooke. Don't you make me the fool any longer."

"No, Rebecca." But words escaped him. "No," he said again.

Yet her gaze, once eager, had gone to ice, and she bit her lip, and cast her face downward. "Like every other belle in this country of ours," she whispered, her voice descended into a quiver. "And me, too thick-skulled to see it. I only pray this other lady, whomever she might be, is worthy."

He gaped. "Please, Rebecca, you must believe what I say – it's not that – "

"Enough, Ulysses – enough now. I'm cleared of all pity, for want of all pride," and gripping a console table as she turned, she started off. "I expect I wished for something else – succumbing to fancy when I ought have heeded my father. When I ought have heeded myself."

Ulysses wished to scream. Could she really suppose his devotion lay with some mistress? Some light-footed soul, or worse, some concubine slave? And weighing his urgency against his fears, Ulysses stepped forward, then stopped once more, watching instead, extending his arm, somehow still managing nothing.

What had he done?

To have borne herself so fully, he realized, and now to have been rebuffed. Since the moment they'd met, he'd tried somehow to believe he might one day find a way – at the very least staving off the choice, until he need not make it at all. Now, he saw she had forced his hand. And watching her go, paralyzed between what he'd already wrought and what still could be recovered, he couldn't help but wonder: would she ever come back? Vanishing before his eyes, it seemed, the crest of a life he might yet have called his own.

CHAPTER 25

Scottsville, Virginia
March, July, 1826

How very like his father.

That had been Ulysses' first thought receiving the invitation, delivered on the finest white stock, with the finest penmanship in the district, bathed entirely in conceit:

> *Mr. and Mrs. Franklin Brooke*
> *request the pleasure of their son,*
> *Ulysses Brooke –*
> *Saturday evening next, at five o'clock –*
> *At their beloved home of Boxwood Grove –*
> *On the occasion of Franklin Brooke's eightieth year.*

While the rest of Virginia's citizens were preparing to honor the nation's birthday, here was one man eager to remind them of his own.

Of course, Ulysses knew his father would ride the coattails of youthful glory any chance that he got, that this moment was riper than most, with the semi-centennial mere months away. Back in the capital, patriotic bunting had already been draped from every balcony, wood-block laid down for the summer parades, new monuments birthed each time one of the Founding Fathers had died, and sometimes even before: Randolph and Rutledge, Livingston and Lafayette, Madison, Monroe, Jefferson most of all. Relics turned deities. And Ulysses' father, wanting all the more of it for himself.

On the way there, dusk was falling by the time Boxwood appeared, its willows waving languidly. From the main drive, Ulysses could hear the noise of the party cast upon the surrounding quiet, guests spilled out to the verandas – ladies' diamonds winking at the stars, men in tails – half the Assembly, probably half the cabinet too.

He hitched his buggy, and moved inside, spotting his father at once. No longer middle-aged, but fully stooped and withering, a half-deaf king upon his throne, leaning into the flattery, his old uniform far too large for his frame, a face like a discarded sail.

Ulysses was glad he was late.

Fetching a drink, he listened as the old-timers flogged the Stamp Act as if it were still new, and the buglers struck up melodies by the wall, until in time his father caught his eye. Raising his walking stick, he shuffled over, and gripped Ulysses' shoulder with a force of old. "You came."

"Of course."

"My son."

"Yes."

And now Franklin Brooke bent in closer, whisky and wine swirling on his breath, lips drawn tight, and though Ulysses had never seen the man ask for anything, it was obvious he required some aid easing down to the table. "This wretched state of affairs," he panted.

"I'd fancied you were having the night of your life."

"They honor me as they honor a statue." His cadence was antique – as staid as that of the Englishmen he'd once fought to expel – even if his bite was as sharp as ever.

Ulysses shrugged. "Father, please, enjoy it. It's what you wanted."

And for the briefest of moments, the old man's fogged eyes flickered, like crumpled-in storm clouds, lightning bolts deep within. "You know, I'd always hoped for a son who would have leapt to be my heir – " Yet his words trailed off there. At last he blinked, grunting as he pushed himself up instead of going on, offering a final clap upon Ulysses' shoulder, no longer the weight of a man seeking relief, but a gesture of duty, the sort of thing one does to fill the quiet, and carry on.

Ulysses watched him go then, knowing he wouldn't be coming back, knowing too it was time to stand in turn. Swiping scraps along the way – corn breads and calves' heads, custard and jellied pie – shifting them into his pockets like the thief he'd become, he aimed suddenly, desperately, to move away, free from this lowly theater of the highborn.

Quickly then, he passed from the main ballroom, and to the pastures beyond, the spring grass snapping beneath his boots, empty voices ceding to a sweet breeze upon his skin. Guided through the fresh-seeded tobacco by memory more than light from the moon, he soon reached the cabins below.

He rapped the corner-window in front, just the same as when he'd been a boy, the cup of his knuckle against the glass, and only a moment later, the hinges by the porch squeaked loudly, as Cato stepped out, scrap quilt around his enormous shoulders, a grin tucked in amid his yawn. "Are we off then?" he asked, rubbing his eyes. "Another campaign?"

Ulysses just smiled right back. "Not tonight, my friend. I've wine up to my chin. I came but to offer you this," and retrieving the food, he passed it over, as the sauces dribbled down his fingers.

***

The next gathering was even mightier. Another show of means. Another gathering of the proud, enough to make the other gods of Virginia envious. Only this time, Franklin Brooke couldn't pretend to resist it – couldn't even complain about the summer hail. It was coming in sideways, and Ulysses guessed his father might even have been pleased at these furious blades, pelting the gravestones like musket balls, colonizing the cemetery with puddles. He'd think it fitting, really. More dramatic even than rain.

He watched the pallbearers, retreating from the casket, laying wreaths at its side, their black crepe armbands sliding down from the wet. Behind them, the slaves were silent too, barefoot with permission, that they could balance in the mud as they dug; past that, what seemed the whole of the commonwealth had massed, spread out across the fields, sweaty and shivering at once, as if they'd been cast into some fevered state, penance for outliving the finest of them all. Only months since they'd last converged on his behalf, and here they were again. The tributes were endless, soaring, tear-drenched: words that said nothing for hours on end – "an American before there was an America!" – "a Virginian if ever there was one!" – right up to Governor Tyler himself, tipping his top-hat from the rostrum, nodding right toward Ulysses.

He soon brought the crowd to sobs, setting forth a picture of heaven, a homecoming for old Franklin Brooke, who'd preceded the hero Jefferson there by mere days. *"They endured, that they might mark the golden jubilee!"* he roared with all the drama he could muster – *"and with their creation secure, march toward paradise together: a Color Guard relieved from duty at last, granted furlough by the Highest Authority of all,"* his voice like fire, bleating out against the hail, capitalizing upon every hour of oratory he'd ever studied – making certain, Ulysses thought, that if there was a heaven indeed, his father would have no trouble at all cupping his ear to the celestial floor and listening in.

In time, the words seemed to meld together entirely, and Ulysses failed even to notice when the service had ended, or the condolences begun: old men delivering clasps on his arm, cousins whispering soft blessings, women swallowing thickly as they shared in his loss – and there, finally, his mother. Near a specter herself, sopping, shapeless, as she crumpled by the newest stone of them all, and wept with muted shaking for what seemed an eternity.

"Ulysses?"

He turned. For a moment, there was no face, just another veil. But he knew the voice, and soon indeed, Rebecca was lifting the thin black curtain from her hair, extending her fingers in greeting. "My deepest sorrow, of course."

He nodded.

"Though perhaps now, at last, you might shed the weight of his burden?"

The ice pelted down between them, and Ulysses squinted back. How to explain that the man had been less burden than spark? Reason enough for seeking the path he'd made his own?

He needn't have worried, he realized: Rebecca seemed to sense his response before he'd even found a way to utter it. "Freed at least from his shadow, Ulysses: from your need to placate, or rankle. From whatever it was you were after – to do now simply as you please."

He opened his mouth to thank her, though already the old veterans were approaching again, rustling his hair as if he were still a boy, leaving her to curtsy.

"I'll leave you to your mourning, Ulysses. And shall come upon you in the capital, I'm sure." Her tone was formal now, polite, and he wished they could just dispense with all this custom, running off together for a ride through the hills, as they might once have done.

Alas. Not when there were so many eyes eager for gossip. Not with her coming by as she had: thinking not of their past, nor of rewriting their future, but simply to show him some decency.

How could he expect anything more?

So he stayed put, as she trekked back toward her carriage, its rear wheels as tall as a man – surrounded by others just like it, lined up the road, all gilded doors and glass fronts, as if the funeral had been nothing more than a chance to prance and preen.

When something else flashed in his mind.

He studied again this line of carriages, their owners lingering, while the hail limped into mist, decorum preventing them from leaving just yet, lest they strand his mother with her despair: draped over the coffin now, no longer heaving, but quiet – even, perhaps, at peace – as if in her own mind, she were taking one last afternoon with her husband. The other ladies would eventually escort her home, of course – Ulysses would meet her there this evening – which meant he had a moment, that he wouldn't really be missed. Here then was an opportunity, he thought – to ignore it would be to ignore himself! – and sensing the familiar urge, pushing his worries, pushing Rebecca, aside once more, he took his first step forward: scouting the grounds, finding he was given his space. They were deferring as he'd anticipated, the son of the dead permitted to grieve on his own, and Ulysses quickened his stride. A minute passed, then another, and with that, he was away, cutting amid the poplar dotting the cemetery's edge, round the row of carriages to their far side, skipping up the folding steps that kept their hinges dry.

Muscles rigid, he sought what he could – a stray purse here, a stranded coat there – funeral goers having unhitched their wallets before stepping out, worried about the leather getting wet, leaving them on the carriage seats. There was no great treasure, it was true, nothing next to the shipments he'd been nabbing with Tad and Cato, but he felt in his soul this was right: with his father gone now, letting the Lord know that he, the son, was still very much alive.

Swiftly, he made his way, unlatching doors when he had to, moving from one to the next, claiming coin for his cause. Some of the carriages were occupied, slaves waiting in the drivers' seats, and he ducked hastily past, sorry it was they who'd be blamed, glad at least there'd be no evidence upon them.

By the time he came to his own buggy, his frock was bulging, and Ulysses dumped the loot to the floor. Then he pulled free, peeling off the main road first chance he got, onto the back paths he knew so well. The coins jingled, wallets sliding across the floor, enough to make him smile. Enough even to shake clear the thoughts of his father, and the age he was leaving behind.

Rich forests of cedar beckoned. Soon too, beams of golden light: like a missive from the heavens, eager to confirm they were watching, and that they approved. And Ulysses rode faster, no matter the bruising bumps, or the whinnies from his horse in protest.

There'd be no point in drawing up a route, he decided. Not this time. Not when a treasure so small would make nary a difference anyway. It was sufficient that Providence was already applauding – to know that in this case, the breach itself had been the deed. He'd seen burial enough for one day; why not, just this once, try for something else? And so it was he let go his thoughts of maps, and of his own grand aims, and lifted up the wallets instead, one, two, three at a time, with a mad dash of laughter, flinging them out the windows at his side, listening with relish as they landed in the wild grass, and skidded to a halt in the soaked ground below.

CHAPTER 26

New York City
June 1978

Here they were, the morning of the wedding, and Alvin was watching Faye on the edge of their bed, sunlight streaming in, turning her ivory satin to gold. She was like some avant-garde portrait, he thought: braided hair amid a tumble of pearls, laundry piled atop rumpled sheets behind her, a towel damp and forgotten on the bathroom door.

"Too tight?" He gave his bowtie a tug.

"Your nerves or the knot?" She grinned. "You didn't have to do all that legwork, you know."

"It was easy."

"Sure."

"I told you. Furloughs happen. Carter's made everyone soft."

"You a tough guy now, Alvie?"

"You practicing your vows?"

She laughed, and kissed him, and checked the train of her dress one last time. "Shall we?"

He noticed the new answering machine had a little red flash at its corner. Someone must've called while they'd been out for bagels, someone who wouldn't have known about today. "Work," he muttered.

But Faye was already through the doorway. "Don't you dare, Alvin. If it's urgent, Claire can tell you in person."

He hesitated. What if it was one of the banks, phoning to say they'd found a record of antique coins after all? Or some zealous young archivist at the bureau? Uncovering the latest oblique reference from the book of maps?

"Oh for God's sake, Alvin. It's our wedding!"

With a sigh, he let the door click shut.

It took only a minute to catch a cab, one of the new ones: mustard yellow, no checked pattern on the sides. The driver glanced back as they guided Faye's dress onto the seat; he had a mustache dyed black, a neck as creased as the permits on his smudged partition. "You in costume?" he asked, in a staccato that married Naples and Arthur Avenue.

Faye shook her head. "I'm the real thing."

"Then this one's on me," and he switched off the fare box with a grin.

Alvin thanked him and gave the address of the synagogue. It'd been important to his parents that they marry there, and like a saint, Faye had agreed. As it turned out, the rabbi was a liberal, quelling their nerves the instant they'd met with him, offering a word about his work with Dr. King a decade before – pedantic, Faye said afterward, but welcome – sporting a white beard and a voice tinged with Yiddish, as he'd toured them through the Hebrew etchings in the lobby, and boasted about the cast-stone façade as if he'd built it himself.

Now, when they arrived and entered the sanctuary – chuckling as the cabbie honked a congratulatory farewell from the street – they quieted. The air had a soft, warmed-over smell, and they moved down the aisle, past plain brass chandeliers and heavy wooden pews, admiring plaques listing members on the wall: surnames from the Old World, fads of the New – *Kowalcyzk, Ken; Rosenblatt, Jeff* – and there, two-thirds down, Alvin's own parents, *Starkman, Emil & Miriam*, members since 1916, the year they'd both been born. The rabbi was rehearsing with the cantor in the corner, and reaching the chuppah, Alvin and Faye waited, watching the guests come trickling in.

Toward the front were veteran-pals of Alvin's father; past that, the younger set – friends from school days, mostly – and bureau colleagues buttoning and re-buttoning their blazers, WASPs no doubt visiting schul for the first time. Among this last lot, Claire Calloway seemed the only one unfazed, clasping her hands, taking in the scene with interest, and Alvin supposed encountering Jews was nothing really, not compared to being a woman in charge at the cocksure bureau.

His side of the crowd, alas, was thin.

Too many guests had mailed in apologies – making excuses about surprise medical appointments, even sudden funerals – the instant they'd learned the bride was black. All his life, Alvin had worked at dodging his own status as an oppressed: no yarmulke, no beard, no honest-to-God threats to be dealt with. Even when folks knew he was Jewish, they could nearly always think their way past it. With Faye, however, things had turned different. And while she'd told him this was to be expected, that the wedding would bother far more people than he guessed, it was only now, taking in the whispers, that he saw how right she'd truly been.

Alvin squinted hard now for an older black face among the rest. He hadn't gone into the details of the furlough with her, the sheer logistics of getting a man freed: a warden delivering plane tickets, prison nurses drawing up a schedule, color-coding pills, checking blood pressure, even a set of beat cops serving as chauffeurs from the airport. "*Name of Dexter Williams,*" he'd kept reminding Claire Calloway. "*Yes – you already asked me,*" she'd remind him in turn, "*your fiancé's father*" – as if pulling strings was a frowned-upon part of their business, and he ought to be grateful. But now, facing this crowd, Alvin wondered if he'd been dumb to trust the system.

The only photo Faye had shared was from the '30s, ribbed and faded and black-and-white. Her dad had been a young man then, in a wide-collared shirt and flat cap cocked to the side, his face half-visible behind the dust: the same narrow chin as his daughter, the same smarting eyes. Alvin tried imagining him as he must be now.

"Maybe he's just slow-moving," he observed aloud.

But the rabbi cut in from their side. "Whenever you're ready, folks."

Faye turned to Alvin. "So long as he gets here in time for a toast – that's what he'll care about." She paused. "This part would be strange for him anyway."

"You're really sure?"

She was nodding.

Alvin nodded to the rabbi in turn.

The ceremony was brief, at their request. There was a blessing upon a goblet, and a sip of terrible wine, followed by a stint in Hebrew. After that, the kiss – the crowd perked up at that – and then the cantor woke everyone for real, stomping until they joined in and clapped, his *tallit* fringes fluttering, black beard to his belly, a baritone fit for Broadway.

When it came time to break the glass, the rabbi knelt as if he were on the gridiron, holding the flute in a heavy white napkin. Alvin lowered his heel with vigor – he'd practiced with a set of light bulbs the night before – and earned a raucous round of *Mazel Tovs*, after which his father waved everyone toward the exit. "Let my people go!" he pronounced to crests of laughter, and the exodus to the street began.

The reception was at an old neighborhood standby, soaked in the smell of brisket and beer, square tables laid out in groups of four. In one corner, the buffet. In another, the klezmer band, men who looked plucked straight from the century prior, all wire-rim spectacles and long black coats, though their tunes were infectious. Waiters whipped past with hummus and cucumber, cantaloupe and lox, kosher pigs-in-a-blanket. Checks were handed off. Children squealed. Someone even started blowing a *shofar*.

Between congratulations, Faye pointed past Alvin's shoulder. "Look how happy they are," and it was true. His parents were twirling each other by the elbow.

"And you?"

She smiled gamely and gestured toward the band. "I think I'll put in a request for *Love Train.*"

Still, even as she joked, Alvin knew she was distracted. Dutifully, she was accepting the hugs and handshakes, listening graciously through the condescension – "*how lucky we are to live in a better world,*" one white-haired woman whispered in her ear; "*I never knew how it was for you people,*" another exclaimed through chomps on a cough drop, "*not 'til those Freedom Riders went down to help, nice boys, like your Alvin here*" – yet all the while, her eyes hadn't much left the door.

Alas, it was his father, not hers, who eventually shuffled over. He nodded toward the empty seats – more last-minute RSVPs, joining the coward's train of protest – and he peered at Faye. "I come to offer apologies."

She took his hands and leaned in. "Maybe we should tell them I'm Jewish after all?"

So that now, Emil Starkman guffawed despite himself, eyes twinkling. "Would you mind if I stole that line?"

"I'd be flattered."

The older man lifted his glass then, clanging it with his fork, silencing the room. "Poor Miriam," he began, getting their attention. "I never did tell my wife that Faye here was a *goy*," – and sure enough, it worked. A new bubble of laughter took over, as the guests rocked in their seats, the oldest among them repeating the line for one another, in phlegmy waves of Yiddish.

From there, Emil grew heartfelt. His eyes went moist as he looked to his son, speaking of *beschert* – beloved destiny, he explained – and of Faye's grace and crackle. Finally, he paused again, coming upon the cousins in front, their shirt sleeves riding up their wrists, faded blue numbers tattooed inside their arms, and he thanked them especially, lowering his head, leading all in prayer. In the end, he raised his glass once more. "Some might call this marriage a step toward progress, or maybe even a challenge. Friends, you call it anything you like. I just know what it'll be for me: a blessed addition to our family."

The applause emerged, and Faye came up to greet him, reaching for a hug, toasting to the night, and to the rest of their lives. It went on like that for some time then – drinks, catching-up, cavorting – until at some point, Alvin caught up with Claire Calloway. She was with the other agents he'd invited, wide ties loosened, coats on the back of their chairs, and he wandered over with a beer. "I appreciate you coming," he said, raising his bottle high.

"C'mon, Starkman. Not just here to kiss up, I hope?"

He smiled. "No, ma'am."

"So?"

"Any word on Faye's pop? He still hasn't shown."

Claire looked surprised, her pale eyes gone narrow. "Want me to make a call? I can check on that plane."

"That's alright. You've done plenty." He hoped she'd follow through on it anyway, but knew he shouldn't press. "Enjoy the rest of the night, ma'am."

"You too, Starkman." She offered up her glass in turn. "You're a lucky one."

"Appreciate that, ma'am." He nodded thanks, and glided back to his table.

"What was that about?" Faye wanted to know.

"Just saying hi."

"Tell me it wasn't about the case."

"Which one?"

"Don't play the fool, Alvin."

"Come on. Let's dance."

It was the right thing to say, and soon they were in the center of the floor, swaying to the melodies and the moment. He could smell the citrus of her shampoo, and feel the curve of her hips, and he wrapped her closer, slowing his step. "I'm sorry he's not here, Faye," he offered quietly, and she nodded into his shoulder.

Later, when the party was finally winding down, and in time there was no one left, he called another cab, and they stepped out together, winding home through the amber streetlight, exhausted and enriched, past the scurrying rats and shadows of graffiti, back to their apartment for sleep. Except that when they got there, and Alvin had moved to the bathroom, he heard Faye tap the answering machine button he'd noticed all those hours before. He shut off the faucet.

"This is for Miss Faye Williams," the voice began. It was a gravel-voiced man, coming in fuzzy from the speaker, introducing himself as an officer from the Department of Corrections, and Alvin halted in place, staring absently into the mirror. "We're awful sorry to tell you, Miss," the message went on. "Your father has passed away. It was in his sleep. This morning, at the hospital. He never did make it to his furlough." At some point then, the fellow asked for a call back, and started going on about arrangements, but Alvin didn't really hear the rest.

Instead, he spun slowly back, swinging open the bathroom door, finding Faye standing right there. Her skin had drained to gray. Her bottom lip was shaking. "I wanted you to like him," she said, in no more than a whisper. But Alvin simply heaved in a breath, and welcomed her back in his arms, holding her tight, his new wife sobbing against him.

CHAPTER 27

Alvin missed the keys of a proper typewriter.

At Faye's encouragement, he'd surrendered and bought one of the electronic ones, all soft whirs, no real air of permanence. Still, as she rested on the couch, working her way into a Saturday nap, he could at least appreciate the neutered quiet of the thing, and he trudged on through his latest report for Claire.

He'd been at it some time, the pages growing bleary before him – dates, dollar figures from travel, details of interviews – when he noticed Faye was napping no longer, but rather standing in front of him, foxy as ever in her navy blue pajamas. Alvin blinked. "Sorry," he murmured, recognizing it was getting dark outside, that the long winter night had begun.

"Is this our marriage, Alvin?"

"With a husband who adores everything about you?"

"With a husband who can't let up on a case that won't break."

He pushed back his chair. "It's a tough one, Faye, that's all." Someone had started shouting outside, cursing about a stolen parking spot. Alvin tapped his thumbs together, glancing out again, noting that flurries were starting to swirl. It was supposed to turn heavy at some point, the radio had said. "It's not just a matter of cracking it," he added now. "It's what to do once I figure it out."

She folded her arms, sitting on the desk's edge. "Tell me."

"These trips I take." He leaned his head against the cracked plaster behind him. "They've been a kind of hunt."

"For what?"

"For treasure." He watched as she began to smirk. "I'm serious, Faye. Honest to God."

"Whose treasure?"

"Well that's the question." He considered the bureau's obsession with confidentiality. Hadn't he been stifled long enough? Why shouldn't he tell her why he kept speeding off? "Samuel Billings claimed the gold was his."

"Sam Billings the founder of Billings Trust?"

"You got it. Only he wasn't telling the truth, you see. Not to start with, anyway. It'd been hidden a whole lot earlier, by a fellow named Ulysses Brooke – "

"The abolitionist?"

"You've heard of him?"

"You hadn't?"

Alvin shrugged self-consciously. "I recognized the name."

She was standing once more. "You're saying Ulysses Brooke's treasures were found?"

"Maybe."

"After he was convicted?"

"Long after. If the story's true, he'd already been dead for ages."

"And Sam Billings was the one who did the finding?"

"That's what I need to figure out."

She looked at him.

"Because if he stole that money out of the ground –" Alvin took a breath – "then it never belonged to his philanthropy in the first place."

"And so everything they give away..."

"Exactly."

"Who would the cash go to instead?"

He cleared his throat. "Descendants of Brooke."

"Ah." It was her turn to pause now, peering ever closer. "And are these descendants proud of their abolitionist ancestor?"

He hesitated a moment too long.

"Alvin."

"I know."

"Ulysses Brooke stole that money for a reason!"

"Money's always stolen for a reason."

"It was supposed to be for a better world, Alvin." Her eyes had grown piercing. "The kind of world the Trust is fighting for."

"That doesn't change the law."

She crossed her arms. "And if the bureau succeeds?"

"These folks will get their money."

"Slave owners."

"Descendants of slave owners." Now he stood too. "Look, Faye, I'm not a lawyer. I don't pick my clients. I can't just switch sides, and declare I'm suddenly for the Trust."

She was scanning his desk. Alongside the typewriter, stacks of photocopies awaited him, images of the antique maps themselves. "You're leaving for another trip then?"

"Richmond."

"I've never been."

"Me neither."

"You want company?"

"You mean it?"

"Why not?"

"It's the South, Faye."

"You think I don't know where Virginia is?"

"You know what I mean. It's just – things haven't changed as much as advertised."

She met his eye. "You really shouldn't have waited to tell me all this."

"It's an investigation. I shouldn't be telling you now either."

"Have some faith, Alvin!" Her voice tightened. "Or do you think I need you curating the whole world for me? Making certain my delicate Negro eyes can handle it?"

"Please, Faye. I'm learning. I'm trying." He took in her silhouette against the window.

"You want to know why my father spent all those years in jail?"

"I'm sure he didn't get a fair shake, if that's what you mean."

But her pupils had grown wet.

"Faye." He stepped forward. "We don't have to talk about this."

"But we do." And wiping her eyes, she pushed on. "They said he raped a white lady."

Alvin nodded. It had been Jim Crow's favorite line. They used to fling it around like shoplifting.

"It wasn't true," she continued. "He was with me and my mother the day they said it happened, visiting cousins.

We weren't even in the state." Her voice was bubbling forth now, like a kettle of water, ready to boil. "That was life as it was. You so much as peered at someone cross-eyed, and they had you. Ma said he was lucky they didn't kill him in his holding cell, that the jury was a sham too: eight Klan, four of them sheriffs, all white." She shrugged heavily. "Most folks, when they think Maryland, they think Baltimore. They don't know about the rest. But it's the South, Alvin. The same South you wanted to tell me about. The same South you tell me is rough."

He felt his cheeks going red.

"Our road was paved with dirt," she explained. "Every time it poured, the whole thing washed away. And nobody gave even half a damn. We'd go into town, the heart of Calvert County, and mom would keep her head down, pa would step off the curb if a white man even walked anywhere near: tipping his cap, knowing it couldn't ever be enough." She swallowed. "At my school, some had grandparents who'd been there since slave times. Broken fans in front, broken heaters in back. Three Valley Schoolhouse they called it, as if that made it sound pretty. A single room for all of us, asbestos siding, cracked roof, termites in the corner. In the end, the only way I got out was grandma made sure of my grades. She drove me into the city center for interviews when it was time; stole me a nice pink dress from the family whose house she cleaned – they had a daughter my size, she said – said I could wear it that one time, and if I got so much as a single speck on the fabric, I'd get a *switchin' like I wouldn't believe*." She almost smiled. "I was so nervous, Alvin, and when I was done, she made me change right there on the sidewalk, so I wouldn't brush up against the rust on her car."

"I didn't know all that." He bit his lip. "I didn't know all that, Faye."

"I never told you." She extended her hands, lowering her voice to quiet. "She never did get to see the world change, Alvin. But I have. And it wasn't because I was protected. I know what it is I'm getting into. I know what it is you're up against. I'm just asking that you let me be there for you, while you're at it."

CHAPTER 28

Richmond, Virginia – September

1979

Fall retreated into summer as they drove. It was like watching the world on rewind, rusted foliage melting green, apple blossoms giving way to myrtle, so that by the time they reached Virginia, Alvin had flipped on the air conditioning, and was checking the engine gauge to be sure it hadn't overheated.

The city arrived, and it looked scarred. A few high-rises were clumped at the horizon, as if they'd been quarantined; the patches nearer in were lost to time – projects, squatters' digs, drug dens – men draped atop benches and wheelchairs, flasks in paper bags, pins from Vietnam dangling from their denim jackets. Others were too lost even to beg, buried in sleeping bags on the curb, clustered on the median, ranting beneath marble statues that towered like cruel gods.

Then, emerging from the poverty: a boulevard, wide and tree-lined, *"Monument Ave,"* Faye read aloud – an Appian Way for a republic that never was. There were more statues now, with names that sent a shiver – Davis and Lee, Stuart and Jackson – and on either side, as the slums receded, rows of fine mansions, the city's wealth at last: humiliation turned to denial.

Finally, Alvin found what he was looking for. *Patterson* and *Ridge*, the next corner's street signs declared. These were the names he recognized from the book of maps. He parked, as Faye squinted ahead. "What is it you think you'll see?"

He only shrugged. "Some trace of Billings and Brooke, if I'm lucky. Who they were. What they were after."

Instead, two blonde teenagers loped by, each in a sagging tracksuit, awkward as they passed, taking note of the white man and the black woman stepping from their car. Alvin ignored them. The folds of the past were everywhere, and it was in their crevices he hoped for a clue. He picked up a stray pebble from the sidewalk, skipping it aimlessly down the concrete.

"Alvin," Fay said now, in a voice as quiet as the wind. "We're getting noticed."

But he held up his hand, and crouched.

"We should get to the motel," she added, a touch louder, and finally he glanced back. A new pair of men was watching from a driveway across the road, leaning against the side of their pickup, a brown Ford idling steadily, belching black exhaust. One had a smashed nose, the other an ill-cut red beard; they were both beefy, in overall jeans and no shirts underneath.

Alvin cursed silently. This was just the type of nonsense he'd tried warning Faye about. Still, he aimed at ignoring them. Up ahead, shy of a stretch of developments, a rectangular stone slab seemed to beckon, half-buried in the grass.

"It's getting dark," Faye cautioned.

"I'll be quick." And he scurried over to see. The rock's edges had grown smooth, but as he brushed them off with his palm, there was something more: stenciled into its side – slim, slender typeface – the year *1826*. At once then, he began rifling through the photocopies he'd been carrying in his pocket.

"Alvie. Enough."

"I'm getting close to something, Faye. I can feel it."

"I'm glad," she replied. "Meantime, we need to be getting farther away," and she gestured up the block, at the pickup, still growling in place.

Again, he waved her off. For hadn't Ulysses visited this spot that very same year as the cornerstone was marked? What would count as proof? How would he know? Finally, hearing Faye close the passenger door behind him, he reluctantly turned back, joining her again at the car, sidling in.

"Drive," she suddenly urged. "Drive!"

He checked his mirror. He saw the pickup coming their way – and peeling away in turn, he gained more speed. Soon he was ignoring a stop sign at the corner, as the truck came along with them, staying in his rear view: the two clowns had their heads out the windows now, hooting and hollering and cackling as they followed.

This was no time to wonder if they meant real business, or if it was just a lark. And spotting a sign for the interstate, forgetting the motel they'd reserved, Alvin gunned it as best he could. He could hear their whoops even more clearly now, like some horrible scale shredding the hot autumn night, when, at last, there was Route 95. Faye was pointing frantically. "I see," Alvin said. "I see," and he angled right, pressing his foot down as if he were trying to take off – until, thank God, they reached the entrance ramp, and the pickup turned away.

Alvin felt himself exhale, and he looked at Faye, muscles clenched, sweat on her temples, while headlights zoomed past in the other direction. "I'm so sorry," he managed.

"So am I," she echoed back.

They raced along, making their way north, stopping only for gas and crackers, then keeping at it, driving as if to eternity.

When to his surprise, she spoke again. "It's my fault, Alvin."

"What're you talking about?"

"I forced you to take me along."

"It's their fault, Faye. Not yours. Them, and everyone who came before them."

Only she'd begun to cry. "I knew better," she managed, wiping her eyes. "It was me, Alvin – I was stubborn – "

"It's this whole damn country," he cut in. This country that was his employer, he thought – that'd been his own family's salvation! – and yet still: the blasphemy he uttered was truth. He knew it in his soul, did he not? That the America his father had served in war, that he'd exalted in peace, was a notion, not a nation. Alvin gripped the wheel, and wondered if it was that which Ulysses Brooke had known all along, that which Sam Billings had come to learn. He reached over for Faye's hand, as she leaned against the window, and shared a shaky sigh.

1826

Ulysses had arranged the rendezvous with care, distant enough from the coast that yeoman cottages still dotted the valley: dual chimneys casting gentle shadows, quiet meadows split by old rail fences, no passersby to speak of.

Except now, he cursed aloud. For the bank's wagon was pulling in early.

There were cash routes springing up aplenty these days, and this one angled down from the next bluff. He spun his pocket watch with his fingers, fidgeting in the shadow of a wide red cedar. Thaddeus was to have fetched Cato at dawn, leasing him from Boxwood for errands, with ample time for beating the evening's shipment. Yet there the cash was already, unmistakable, snaking in from the horizon, turning up a cloud of dust, and the two of them nowhere to be seen.

Ulysses stayed put, still tucked from view. He could feel the years in his gout – in how he squinted when he read – and had noticed them too in Cato's glide slowing to a gait, and the strands of white turning up in Tad's blonde mane. But his fire had only grown. After the endless summer bashes, the toasts to the Declaration's fiftieth and the tolls of liberty bells, it was harder than ever to accept the fraud all around him. Money was still needed. The revolution was not yet realized. And chances like this couldn't be permitted to slip.

The bank looked to have hired a freight wagon, the same type the settlers were using on the frontier. Its floor would be sloped to keep the gold from shifting, its top secured by rope and wooden hoops. As usual, two drivers were visible at the front. In a moment, they'd pass through the next bend, and the horses would pick up their pace. Taking a breath, Ulysses knew he couldn't wait. Silently, he slipped from the tree, and skipped to the wagon's rear as it went by him, working hard at keeping his footing, reaching swiftly for the nearest bowline knot – the wheels were bouncing louder, the pebbles flying faster – then yanked hard while he still could, aiming to grab a clump of money bags from beneath, pulling out the first ones he saw.

When to his horror, the tarp flapped up loudly.

Its rope was unbound in an instant, like cotton unspooling from a reel, and the drivers both turned round – beards the color of coffee, startled grunts like those from a pair of frogs – and Ulysses ducked, cloaking his face with the purse now in his grip, listening to the men elbowing past one another. On instinct, he sprinted to the side, right back to the trees where he'd been. Ignoring his swollen joints, pretending he was as young as when all this had started, he spotted a ditch amid the brush, and darted towards it, sliding to a stop.

At first, there was nothing.

Then: a sharp pop from behind the slope. A fallen branch? A swallow mending its nest?

Or had the drivers jumped down in pursuit?

Something flashed through the leaves – a pistol, he realized – and jumping back up, Ulysses was pushing again through the thicket, skipping over fallen limbs, dodging branches and stumps, trying for quiet. Heaving for breath, he dragged himself forward, knowing this stretch of forest had to end soon, that he was nearing the main city, where he could work to blend in.

Then, sure enough – poking out from the woodland: the peaked steeples of the capital. So that carefully, he wound through the undergrowth and onto a sprawling dirt boulevard, praying not to be noticed, scanning the locals, tradesmen carrying baskets of goods, women chatting by hitching posts, a muddy intersection a few yards down.

Just past it, a row of half-finished foundations stood as part of the city's latest boom. Brick columns circled patches of dirt, lonely rafters hung overhead, men in workmen's vests straddled their edges and checked on their levels. The closest plot looked to be the start of some proud commercial property, maybe even another town bank, its laborers staring skyward, bickering over the best way to hoist the next beam. It wasn't ideal, Ulysses thought: too far from a plantation, hard to approach without garnering attention. But with holes already dug at the edge, it offered a chance.

He advanced toward a cornerstone only just laid, dropping his money bag in the groove that surrounded it. It took but half a minute to scoop a mound of dirt over top, and when he was done, burying it in full, he saw with relief the workers hadn't turned back. His mouth was parched, his nerves wrung raw, but he'd done it, and he stepped away.

Only he'd scarcely moved a yard, when there was a hand on his shoulder.

Ulysses' heart clanged against his ribs, and he spun back.

Here was a sheriff indeed, a silver-star badge on his collar, skin bronzed and pox-marked, gray eyes fierce. He'd stepped right out from the scaffolding.

"Might I help?" Ulysses offered. He knew the type: bastards who needed the whole world to know they were there.

"I'm sentry on this site." The words spilled out in a twang. "And you're trespassin'."

"With no ill will." Ulysses offered a hand. "Name's Brooke."

"Why you covered in dirt, Brooke?"

"Just muck of the road, I imagine."

The sheriff was quiet a moment. The workers behind him had paused too. Then one of them spoke up, young by the look of his meager shoulders, though with a beard to his chest. "I saw him whiskin' about, deputy – rushin' off as though he was a'feard."

Another worker inched forward too, an older fellow. "I spotted him also, sir – fixed with a bag, I could swear it."

Ulysses frowned. "Beg pardon, sheriff. But this fellow must be mistaken."

"I ain't one for mistakes."

Now, needing a new tactic, Ulysses bowed, and let his frock come open. He saw the sheriff hesitate, eyes settling upon the silken vest peeking out. "If you gentlemen are done, I'd best repair back to the governor's mansion. Perchance we can walk together, whilst I explain?"

The man paused. "No need for that," he said at last.

And keeping his voice from wavering, Ulysses thanked him, and turned to go.

1890

Even now, the city seemed stuck in the war's shadow.

That's how it appeared to Samuel anyway, as he slowed the horses to avoid the potholes at Richmond's edge. Sipping from a tin drum canteen, he stared at the old charred bricks, and the line of empty plots still waiting for permits and construction crews. It was only as he entered the city center that there was any hint of renewal, and even this seemed blistered by the past. For here were statues, flanked by workmen on stepladders, being sculpted before his very eyes: rebels frozen in time, shredded bodies made whole again by granite and bronze. '*Monument Avenue*,' they were calling it – a revelry of shame, really, yet a new creed at that: if truly we must be chained, they seemed to be saying, let us at least gild the links.

He rode on, past a few pillared porches and fountains bubbling – proof there would always be kings, even in a desert – and lifted the book of maps. He'd been studying it straight through summer, ever eager for more backing, propping up the investment in tobacco.

And then, the intersection he was seeking: a deserted corner lot, a blackened wall, a meadow of fine rye grass. *Paddington* and *Ridge*, the signs said, and he yanked at the horses, and hopped down with his shovel. Some vagrants began to swarm as soon as he arrived, holding out tin cups for coin. It seemed unlikely the map's treasure could really still be here, Sam thought, amid such rabble as this. But he caught sight of a rectangular stone by the curb, past a pile of fallen roof slates, and a heap of manure with fat flies buzzing – the remains of some proud structure, brought to ruin by the war between Brooke's visit and his own. *1826*, read the old cornerstone – just as the map directed! – and ignoring the gazes nearby, he bent into the dirt, and started to dig.

The crowd was growing, and he worked quickly – discovering no iron chest this time, just a badly rotted leather bag – and using the shovel, he pried it loose. Removing his coat, he slipped it round like a blanket, shredding the leather the second he grazed it, then, squatting like a strongman at Barnum & Bailey's, swung its towards the carriage, delighted by the heft, shooing away the scrum.

Still, even as he left them behind, exiting the city, coming upon a sloping hill and a clump of round-topped trees, something in the quiet gave him new pause.

What possibly could be calling to him now? Sending a sudden chill across his skin?

Until gradually it became clear: a story from boyhood, he thought vaguely, a snippet of memory from school, from supper table conversations with his mother, from boisterous toasts at the veterans' hall back home. He hadn't recalled it on the way down, he concluded – hadn't let it distract him anyway – too focused on the task at hand, too wrapped up in the book of maps. It was only now, taking in the unused road up ahead, the winding fieldstone walls at its sides, that he found his mind had room to breathe.

These were the very fields, he realized, that had taken his father.

They were the same valleys and brooks where men had been gunned down by the thousands, no better than fowl, hunted and felled, to be buried where they lay. And his own pop among them – who'd found the book of maps in the first place, only to come here and die.

Sam leaned against the wall of his carriage. And though he was not a praying man, he found himself speaking aloud. He felt a loon at first, but the sentiment came naturally, as if it were Providence that had nudged him, and Providence that now demanded some tidings of acknowledgement in return. "Pa," he heard himself saying. "I only hope you can hear me," and he grew louder. "That you might take some solace in a life cut short. That you might have knowledge of a son at least, treading the path you ought have called your own."

He took a breath.

The sky grew darker, and the breeze picked up, and the moment seemed to pass.

Sam wondered what the lads back at the brokerage would make of him now. Or worse – what the veterans themselves would say, haunting these fields still, cursing for eternity the war that had flung them aside. Until lifting the reins once more, he carried on past clusters of dandelions growing naked in the wind, and listened to the gold clanging at his side, as if spurring him onward, reminding him that this was what his father would have wanted. Not for his son to dwell upon some empty Virginia field, receding into the past, but to charge ahead into nightfall.

CHAPTER 29

New York City
September 1899

Twirling his fountain pen, watching its shadows dance across the leather blotter, Sam wondered how long he'd been at it. He glanced at the gingerbread clock on the mantle, and reminded himself to have it mended: a gift from the mayor, a fine floral headpiece, only it didn't tell time. On just its second day, both hands had frozen at midnight.

The receptionist's bell clanged. "Let them in!" Sam shouted, and the door handle turned.

The furniture had arrived: an oak sideboard for drinks, a matching rolltop desk, a set of whitewashed bookshelves, for a dash of the modern. The moving men were a mix of coloreds and Italians, in peaked caps and stained bracers, drenched and barking at one another in their dialects, so that Sam could scarcely believe he'd once lived amid such types, watching as they removed the newspapers they'd used to wrap the shelves.

He stood and peered out the window while they worked. These new offices stood on Madison Avenue, above sprawling sidewalks scrubbed clean, and chocolatiers lining the block. No longer just carriages either: horseless motor-wagons too, combustible engines sputtering as they thumped over the manure, growls and hisses echoing off the cream-colored limestone.

Farther off, there were purple smokestacks past the Hudson, Jersey's flatlands gouged out by warehouses storing tea for export – a picture of the future itself. Profit from profit, he liked to tell the clients: the panic of the last decade receded, the investments pouring in, closing out this wondrous century with such triumph, it was hard to imagine there was room for another.

Meanwhile, summer was at an end. Social season was marching in to take its place. The parties had come to seem more normal to him, it was true: a part of keeping up, no less than neckties or promptly posted tax forms. But this, the first of the fall, was to be hosted by the Townsends over on Fifth, and he'd rather not be tardy.

They were the sort of family he'd once only read about in the society pages: descended from both lines of New York royalty – Hamilton on one side, John Jay on the other – and though their earliest fortunes had come from coffee plantations in the Indies, more recently they'd set up shop on Wall Street, like all the rest of the stars in Manhattan's galaxy. One cousin had been mayor, another was vying to be Senator. But it was Robert III who remained their patriarch, reigning alongside his wife, a blueblood coincidentally named Roberta, famous for donating to the suffragettes and proclaiming to the papers: "just *take the 'a' off my name, and I'd have the vote.*" To which her husband had famously quipped, "*she only wants it dropped, that she can sign my checks!*"

The *Herald*, the *Sun*, even the *Times* – they'd all led with the gala's announcement.

So that by the time he was tipping the workmen on the way out, Sam found he was eager. He reached the sidewalk and entered his own horseless carriage, leaning against the upholstery, gazing through the smoky light of the oil lamp fixed to its door. The ride was short. Upon arrival, there were men in white ties surrounding the townhouse, women in sleeves as swollen as pillows, terrifically low necklines to boot, and he stepped out among them, ascending the carpeted stairs toward patchwork tile beyond, trading his invitation for a dance card, passing his gold-topped cane to an usher. Chandeliers, wired for electricity, provided the light. Black-skinned waiters offered flutes in the vestibule. Someone grazed his arm.

He turned, as a pair of rouge-cheeked women curtsied. "So it's you!" one of them exclaimed. "We recognized your face from *Harper's!*"

"Samuel Billings," he bowed. "The pleasure is mine."

With a parade of others then, they were ushered into a mahogany elevator, before they could flatter him further, and on up to the upper ballroom, where mirrors lined the way as if it were Versailles. It was all like some fantastical scene from Jules Verne: emeralds like extensions of the women's flesh, men's hair so greased it looked as if they'd been for a dip. The air was a symphony of self-satisfied laughs, and as Sam entered, one of the waitstaff handed over a sterling silver spade, and directed him to a trough of white sand at the wall. "Party favor," the fellow explained, pointing to where the other guests were already digging like children at Brighton Beach, giggling as they unearthed their prizes – gold-ringed watches, ruby rings, diamonds encased in woven gems.

Soon his name was declared, and there was a genuine hush – not just the distracted intrigue he might've attracted a few years before, but real stares, and bounteous handshakes – and he dove into the sort of small talk with which he was now well versed: tips on the market, platitudes about besting Spain in Cuba, appreciation for the shift in weather.

Until there was a clinking of silver spoons, and the Townsends themselves were announced, emerging at the top of the marble stairwell in the ballroom's corner. Robert and Roberta were stately in their matching silk – he in a winged collar, she in a train that scraped the ground. A smile parted his beard as they descended; her little eyes were like crystal themselves, sharp as butchers' knives.

Yet Sam wasn't looking at either of them.

For here came their daughter too, gliding down at their rear, her shoulders peeking out from beneath cream yellow lace, her gaze both deep-set and guarded. She'd let her hair all but fall free in loose black waves, scarcely held back by pearl-lined pins, and it softened her frame. And as she lifted her gloved hand, guiding the crowd back to conversation, she paused, if only for an instant – and her dark eyes seemed to settle directly on his.

Sam supposed he'd grown accustomed to ladies taking notice of him, and not just on account of his cash. Since university, he'd taken on weight without looking fat, and now with a touch of gray, he was sure he'd grown downright handsome. Still, this was somehow different – she was different! – and he swallowed, stepping forward, startled by his focus.

"Mr. Billings, I gather?" This near, her olive skin seemed to shimmer beneath the electric light, her eyes amused before he'd even shared a joke. "Not to worry, sir – I'm no mind reader. I was merely taking in introductions from above," and she held out her hand. "Emily Townsend. I'm surprised we've not yet met."

"Until today, I'd not yet been invited."

"Ah." She lowered to a whisper. "By night's end, you'll come to wish you never were."

"I doubt that very much, my lady."

"Emily, please. And I swear it's true – " she flung a wrist across the room – "each one of these get-togethers more vulgar than the last!"

He could tell she didn't quite mean it: such disregard was just another set-piece, no less than the banana mousse soon to be passed about, or the peacock-feathered rugs. It was the luxury, he thought, of forgetting one's luxury. "After all, Miss Townsend," he responded, "what is America, but the liberty to be vulgar?"

She laughed at that, and it left him elated. "How rare to meet a stranger to all of this, Sam Billings."

"I don't aspire to stay one for long."

"No, I don't imagine so. This way, then. For between my old money and your new, every soul here shall want something from each of us." She led them to a set of stained glass overlooking the park, its brackets still open from summer, the panes framed in silver, boasting a portrait of oversized lilies. "Terribly ugly, no?"

"My lady?"

"Surely you aren't too timid to agree? They say you're a fellow unchecked by bashfulness."

"Who says so? The newsmen? Your parents?"

"All New York, Mr. Billings. As well you know. That you built your firm from naught. '*An alchemist for our age!*' The man who discovered the secret to conjuring gold."

"And all the while, they await my fall."

"You know your city well."

It was his turn to grin now. For here was a woman as interested in forward motion as he.

"I do hope we'll meet again, Mr. Billings."

"And I hope you mean it."

CHAPTER 30

New York City
October 1899

In the span of a single month, Sam observed, young Archibald Davis had proven more use than in all his previous years at the firm put together. It was true his surname had always fetched them clients and credibility. But now, he'd also provided counsel.

For as it turned out, in the maze of high-born courtship, Sam's book of maps could offer no aid. Thus it was he'd knocked on Archie's door late one afternoon, explaining, all but stammering, to this fellow who usually sprinted to do his bidding, that he wasn't sure how to go about contacting Miss Townsend.

To his relief, Davis hadn't even smirked, but had simply beckoned him in, and the two of them had drawn up a calendar. In the days that followed, they'd purchased theater tickets for the latest Weber & Fields on Broadway, rung up Archie's cousin to serve as chaperone, even penned a formal letter of introduction to Emily's father. From there, and just before each rendezvous, Archie had reminded Sam the rules: that he might offer his arm but never his hand, that he mustn't linger saying good evening, that he could never, ever be seen taking note of another gal on the street.

Sam had absorbed every word, fixed as he was on Emily Townsend, and the tenacity he was sure he'd seen in her: a kind of fortitude, really, no doubt borne of thinking herself superior, and being resolved to stay that way. Finally, with autumn breaking, he'd been invited to her family's home once more – this time without all society there to join him. Guided in by a butler, he'd entered the private dining nook for Saturday lunch, taking a seat at the far end for grace. It was an exquisite room, naturally: ringed by rose-printed wallpaper and a crowded circle of footmen, linens so fine it was impossible to see their threads, polished porcelain carrying stuffed duckling and beef, carrots and gravy, even bowls of imported cherries.

Outside, the horses' trots were interrupted by the whine of engines – a strange new rhythm to the city's old racket, and apparently enough to make Mr. Townsend perspire. When one of the gasoline carriages stalled right beside the window, grinding its gears and screeching, he even slammed the table with his fist. "Imagine if such buffoons had been tasked with saving the Union! We'd all be warbling Dixie!"

Sam focused in on his plate. If Robert Townsend had been anyone else, he might have pushed back: *is there nothing beyond the Blue and the Gray?* he'd demand – *can you not admire any bit of the new?* But he was quite sure there was nothing to be gained from arguing.

"What say you then, Mr. Billings?" Townsend had jabbed his finger forward. "How to guard against this sinking ship of state?"

"By waiting for it to capsize, I suppose. And making sure my clients are still afloat when it does."

The older fellow paused, then grinned. "Good man," he concluded. "Good man." He turned to Emily. "A survivor."

"More than that, father," she responded. "A pioneer."

Sam pushed back his chair, sensing his moment. "Might I divert your daughter then, sir?"

"A pioneer indeed!"

"Oh let them go, Robert." It was his wife now, sipping her wine. "As if he were anything less than the goliath of Gotham!"

"Don't go reciting the rags at me." But lifting his glass, Emily's father waved them off. "Returned by sunset of course," he called – though they were already on their way.

They stepped from the mansion to Central Park across the street, and wound amid the herds of sheep grazing upon its southern meadow, moving uptown from there, until they'd reached the Museum of Art. It looked as if it'd been plopped down from one of the glittering capitals of Europe, straight into the sod of the New World, taunting the wooden homes still scattered opposite. The entrance had the air of a carnival: women in high shoulders, men in knotted ties – children bounding along in pleated skirts and sailor blouses – and Sam and Emily made their way in with the rest, tickets soon in hand. "It'll vaunt us upon the world stage," she mused, tilting back to view the soaring ceilings.

"And why not? Are we Americans to be weary of our own ambition?"

She paused in her stride, as they quickly came upon a wall of impressionists, and faced him instead. "You must know I'm aware you were born to nothing, Samuel."

He hesitated.

"All creation knows, Sam. Your story's no secret."

"I suppose not."

"Yet nobody minds, you see," and she stepped closer. "Me least of all."

He started to look away, but she held his gaze.

It didn't mean he could let her in entirely of course. But it seemed an invitation on her end, nonetheless, and he swallowed as she stepped in closer – close enough that anyone passing by would assume they were married. He could feel the warmth of her breath, and see the small patchwork of lines beside her lips, and suddenly he wanted nothing more than to wrap her in his arms, custom be damned. Stepping back instead, he steadied his heart, and cued by better sense, they turned away together, toward the shimmering brushstrokes and bustling hallways that greeted them now.

***

It wasn't just courting where Archie Davis had provided aid.

For in the quiet of his office, Sam had been chewing through the season's latest biographies: tributes to the heroes of the age – Carnegie, Rockefeller, Pullman – romantic tales of greasy-haired boys drowning in pluck, grown into silk-threaded men drowning in gold. By virtue of their cash, certainly. But also, he'd learned, by way of their clubs.

And so he'd consulted Archie once more, only to be startled when the young man had looked back from his desk with nothing but a shrug. "Look here, Sam," he'd offered, like a bored schoolmaster explaining spelling, "you donate the right amount, and by Christ, they'll come knocking so quick, you'll think you're the one taking queries."

In the end, the Union Club was the one he'd picked: birthed during the war and famous ever since, favored watering hole to the city's least thirsty. It boasted every name worth knowing, took dues so inflated the numbers sounded like a mistake, had grown so entrenched it might as well have dated to antiquity – just like the swaggering nation itself, Sam had thought, harvesting a claim to tradition, before its seeds of memory had even been planted.

The new headquarters was overdone, more navel-gazing palazzo than a staple of privilege's restraint, endless cornices and arcades, rows and rows of glass and pillars. Not that Sam minded, taking in the sweet smoke of cigars, admiring the balusters on the stairwell, coves lining the woodwork, grilles and rosettes etched into the wall, new members' names burnished in bronze already: his own at the very top – *Billings, Samuel, 1899* – whether for its spot near the start of the alphabet, or the extra deposit he'd delivered, who could really say.

The tour began almost as soon as he'd stepped in. They moved first to the card room, then right into the library – old-timers sipping brandy, some dozing over treatises taller than bricks – the billiards corner next, the drawing rooms, finally the dining. It was here the newbies were brought to mingle among titans of the century nearly past: former mayors harrumphing in the far corner, aging generals in their old Union blue, even the current governor.

Supper was oysters and pheasant casserole, and Sam chatted with his tablemates, sons of founding members mostly, plus a lone physician famed for his vaccines, before finishing up in the smoking den, where the voices echoed even louder, and the air was gray and tumbling like a storm in miniature. Men's heads bobbed on the leather sofas, and jokes turned ribald at mistresses' expense, as Sam wound in among them, taking in handshakes and claps on the back, a room full of mustaches of the old style. "Our latest J.P. Morgan!" one of them bellowed when he got near, cheeks so ruddy they glowed like embers. "Where you from, Billings?" He was prying, Sam was sure.

"Manhattan, by Jove!" he clamored back. "Born and bred."

"Can't say I know your father."

"Felled at Petersburg."

"Ah. Good man." The old fellow sipped from his flute, bags like silver dollars beneath his eyes. "And your schooling?"

"William and Mary."

"Surely your pa was no rebel?"

"No, sir. Union through and through."

"Yet Virginia sirened away your youth?"

Not Virginia, Sam wanted to say – *a book of maps.* "I answered its call that I might view defeat firsthand," he explained. "Making certain I'd never trip near it again." And as they chuckled, he handed out calling cards for appointments. Until there, right before him, was Robert Townsend.

The old man raised his considerable eyebrows, and stared through a monocle.

"Evening, sir," Sam offered, stuffing the cards back in his vest, aware of the others leaning in.

Townsend let loose his tobacco smoke between them, picking at the flakes on his tongue. "You've no real family, then?"

"Here on my own merits, if that's what you mean."

"On your gold, more like." There were some grunts nearby, and Townsend lifted his cigar once more, its tip glowing red. "Our new age indeed."

"Is it really so different, sir?"

"I never journeyed South like you do, son, I'll say that. Not 'til they made me, anyway."

And now Sam understood. He was being chastised yet again for investing in Dixie, Townsend's own love for tobacco aside. "Of course the war's over, sir."

"I was one who helped make it so."

"That we might one day know our enemies, if I might say so, sir: citizens of the very Union you and my father both fought to save."

Finally, Robert Townsend released a long, raspy breath. "I go too far," he sighed, and gradually, the other men shuffled back to their own circles, as if a matador and his bull had retreated beneath the seats. "You're here, Billings. I'm here. I shan't pretend otherwise."

"Nor should you want to, sir. If you'll just give me my chance."

***

It was only later, however, after Sam had emptied several rounds of glasses – after Townsend had moved fully off – that the night truly left its imprint. For it was then, past the ornate bar, back down the stairs, among the butlers and doormen in front, that he spotted Emily.

She was standing as near as women were permitted to enter, just inside the revolving doors, her slender face still flushed from the wind, reading the latest edition of the *Ladies Home Journal*, checking a silver clock pendant hanging from the clasp of her coat. Probably impatient for her father, Sam thought.

He didn't realize he was gaping until an usher glanced his way. "Might I help sir?"

He blanched, but it was too late. Emily had started grinning. "Look at you then! All cockeyed on whiskey!"

"I wager I'd be staring cockeyed or no."

"Now I *know* that you are, Samuel."

He felt himself blush. "Just surprised to see you here," he said dumbly, descending the last of the steps. "Your father didn't mention it."

"No doubt he was caught up interrogating you." Still, she was smiling. "Shall he be exiting too?"

"Not just yet, I'd imagine. He had designs on another tumbler as I left."

"Ah." Her voice echoed, unsurprised. "Perhaps you'll keep me company then, Mr. Billings."

He blinked.

"Whilst I wait, I mean."

"I'd be delighted," and she stuffed her magazine in her handbag, beckoning that they step outside, away from the ears of the staff.

On the sidewalk, she paused. "You know – we haven't always had money," and it was clear she saw the surprise in his eyes. "We act as though we have, it's true. For we had it once before. I'm sure it's that which gives my father his gall."

"He has every right," Sam managed, his curiosity sparked, the scope of his imagination challenged. He worked at picturing the Townsends empty of their fortune.

"I've told this to no one, Sam."

"Yet now you've started."

She offered a nod. "My father had an old spinster cousin, is all," and she tilted her head as she spoke. "As anguished as could be, they say – cousin Rebecca they called her – all but left at the altar. She eventually married some old-timer instead of her true love, 'til he up and died, and left her on her own once more. We were trained not to speak on the subject, you see, for the shame of the story behind it, for the stain it could bring upon our name, especially after the effort my father put in at the bank, building back our fortune. Poor woman, really. Cursed to have fallen for a crook – a planter's heir, no less! Well-known for his time, I gather, a real Virginia legend."

Suddenly, Sam's heart picked up its pace.

Emily shrugged. "Too distracted by his own schemes, apparently, to make good on a betrothal."

"What schemes?" Sam cut in, before clearing his throat. "It's just – I'm not certain what you mean – "

"In his own mind, he was a luminary," she sighed. "To the rest of Dixie, a fanatic and a danger. 'The Devil's Spy,' their papers called him! – thieving from their own kind – and our cousin too heartsick to move past it all, so the story goes. She'd be seen visiting her would-be bridegroom in his cell, anguished, never checking her accounts as she aged – all whilst the estate managers were inserting their talons, and siphoning away her gold."

"Surely she noticed?"

"Far too late, I gather. By then, her parents had passed on: she was forced to hire solicitors all on her own, discounted in court even still – the ravings of a lonely, fallen woman, one with no man to back her, no husband, nor brothers neither." Emily lowered her voice. "Father says she went down by her own hook: lost her temper, cursed the bench before the whole of everyone, that the judge had her committed to asylum. Heaven knows if it's true. The records are gone, the war was already begun. It wasn't 'til Appomattox she was shipped back home, only to come upon her manor's charred remains, all the pride of money, yet none of its comfort."

"Poor woman."

"Only don't let father hear us saying so! He was the closest thing to male heir when she died – second cousin, once removed – just finished burying his own ma. He found every one of the properties ruined: a house in Richmond burnt to a crisp by Grant's men, the plantation nearly as bad. He sold them for pennies on the dollar, then used what little he had to start anew."

Sam blinked, piecing it together. "So then your pa's got southern kin himself."

"It's why he acts so righteous over being a Yank. He's afraid folks will doubt him if they learn the truth."

But Sam was too stuck on the story to dwell on any of her father's hypocrisy. "Where in Virginia was the crook from? Do you know?"

"Does it matter?"

He shrugged. "Only on account that I studied there."

Emily rubbed her brow, as if to coax out a memory. "As I recall, some backwater called Scotts' Landing."

Sam faced her. Was it really possible? The hometown of Ulysses Brooke himself? That Brooke could have been the very man Emily's old cousin was to have wed?

"What is it?" she asked. "Do you recognize it?"

"I've heard of it, I suppose." He was tempted to share everything: to confide in her as she had in him. Yet what would she say, knowing he'd benefitted from the very crimes that had left her ancestor forlorn? Might she view it as too much coincidence to be ignored? Some kind of warning from fate, rather than an endorsement from the heavens themselves? "Do tell, Emily. What more of that southern coot your cousin loved?"

"Oh Sam – it's nothing but family lore!"

"All the more reason to explain what makes you doubt!"

"If you must know, it carries with it a whiff of sentiment and fancy. An abolitionist, they claim! – and the rarest breed at that: borne in Dixie's darkness, come to God's light nonetheless. Burying his loot that he might one day re-purpose it, for charity, or an uprising, or both." She smiled, and shook her head, as if she couldn't believe her own words. "Not that we can ever know, Samuel. He was jailed before he ever got the chance."

"And his name?" Sam was trying to stay patient. He thought he could hear the men from the club now, traipsing nearer with their cigars, voices tumbling, far drunker than at evening's start. "I could swear we learnt of just such a culprit in our primers, as lads, back at school."

"Did you then? My father's told me as much, though I suspected him guilty of grandeur, propping up our own family's weight." She rolled her eyes. "Brooke was his surname, in any event."

"Given name Ulysses?"

And she laughed. "You must have been quite the pupil, Mr. Billings."

"Emily – wait." She glanced back, her black hair shimmering in the flicker of the streetlight. "What if the tales were true?"

"Come off it."

"To have lasted this long? Perhaps they've some merit."

"And perhaps not. Perhaps my cousin was merely forsaken by some mud-drenched, backwoods robber, someone my family couldn't stomach, so they made him lofty in the telling."

"Be that as it may – " he took a breath – "is it not a cautionary tale?"

"Not to lose track of one's money?"

"Not to lose track of one's love."

She smiled once more.

He stepped close; he could see his reflection in her dark eyes, everything she'd told him, everything there was left still to do, suddenly vanishing in this space where they stood.

"Go on," she said then, her gaze intent, as if she knew his aims, and was awaiting them.

And it was in that instant, before the men had come upon them, before he could think better of it, or she could either, that Sam leaned down and kissed her indeed.

CHAPTER 31

New York City
May 1900

Another year, another Memorial Day. And the nation trotted out its veterans for another parade. Passing the colored dockworkers on his way from the brokerage, Sam watched them stacking milk bottles from the upstate farms. "Off to honor the devils that set us free, Mr. Billings?" one of them shouted over, and the others sputtered.

"Here I was thinking you'd be invited yourselves!" he called back. And because he said it with a wink, or because they knew he was a man with power, they laughed all the harder.

Emily had saved him a seat on the bleacher boards, and by the time he found her, north of Columbus Circle with the other bigwigs of the day, the veterans were already marching past, standing straight as they could muster, while the cheers cascaded down upon them, so that for an instant at least, they could become themselves once more.

To entertain himself, Sam focused on all that the music and marching were designed to disguise: flecks of manure on the curbs, rats hissing in the rubbish, the ghosts of those who weren't even here – those like his father, long since shat out by the maggots who'd taken them in.

Emily nudged him to return his watch to his vest and offered a touch of snuff to calm his fidgeting. Yet even as the crowds stood in approval, stomping their feet, peering over one another's shoulders, he kept his seat – the same practice he'd been following for years, one small protest against the stranglehold of a generation.

"What is it, Sam?"

She was standing with the rest, a bit ridiculous beneath the stuffed hummingbirds atop the brim of her hat.

"Old habit," he shrugged, and for the moment, she nodded, letting him be.

Only later, as they were making their way below the park, after the marching was done, did she bring it back up. "People know you, Sam. You ought remember that. They see you."

He glanced over. "The parades, Emily. They're nonsense. I trust you can see that."

"More than the dinners and soirees?" Her eyes glimmered in the sunset. "The homes vast enough to house whole villages? Your own club, for heaven's sake?"

He managed a smile. "You know I adore all that." But he pressed on. "It's the war, that's all. My pa, running off to get himself killed, even after his own father had left the anger of Dixie behind – same as yours, Emily – pushing free of the plantation rot and aristocracy of old."

"It was a call to arms, Samuel." A gust of wind blasted down the avenue, and she gripped her hat to keep it from blowing off. "Surely you don't wish slavery were back upon us?"

"I only know its vanquish stole my father away from me." He took in a breath. "I won't succumb to all this. I can't. For I don't owe them, you see. I won't straighten up for them either."

For a moment, she stayed quiet. "Alright, Samuel," she said at last.

"Alright?"

She sighed. "Just don't tell my pa."

He agreed to that, and offered his arm. The evening stayed warm. The air, laced with the perfume of petroleum, sat heavy on the avenues. Irish doormen tossed out Memorial Day greetings as they passed, soot-stained beggars held out their hands, officers in stiff blue blazers made way.

Sam waited until they were in the quiet of uptown. And there he unclasped their arms, digging into his pocket. For the truth was, he'd been carrying a ring some weeks now, never knowing when the moment would present itself; it was a Kimberley diamond, offset by blue sapphires, fastened in a platinum band, tiny seashells etched on the sides. He'd spent a quarter's earnings at Tiffany. "Speaking of your father," he began. "I've met with him."

Emily's dark eyes welled. "You asked him for my hand?"

"He said yes." In fact, Robert Townsend had hesitated far less than Sam had expected. It turned out that even new money carried sway, when there was enough of it. Townsend had offered his blessing over drinks at the club, as soon as Sam had asked – by then having read up on the firm.

"Then I'll say the same," Emily answered now, though her normally sturdy voice wobbled – and slowly, she took hold of the back of his neck and kissed him. Here, away from the arteries of midtown, the city felt still, the moonlight scarcely visible amid the corridors. And they stayed glued there some time, until it was Sam who backed away, only an inch, and placed the ring round her finger.

"Come," he offered. "I'm keen to show you something more."

Normally she'd have asked where, but now she only smiled.

He knew the way well, a few blocks right, then north, and there it was: the manor he'd found with his book of maps – the only one of its pages that didn't point to Dixie. The gray stone had turned black since his first encounter with the place, its old majesty laid waste by the very epoch it'd helped usher in, clouded by grime, subsumed now by neighbors on all sides. He slowed by its gate. "What do you think?"

"I think you've gone mad, Sam Billings."

"It's a fine lot."

"It's not half as big as my father's. The porch is rotted straight through!"

She was right of course. Sam could remember well how it had appeared when first he'd come here, not so long after university, still nurturing his plan anew – seeing even then that he'd need to dig this lot up, if he were ever to pursue Brooke's etchings and uncover what lay below. Now the place seemed merely a fading sentry from the past, prey to this city's boundless appetite: chipped pillars, green copper gutters, a lonely rear chimney missing some stones. Its gardens were a patch of yellow grass. There'd be no grand flushing toilets inside, no electric bulbs or phonographs playing marches. Just drafty halls, and stained fireplaces scattered straight through.

Still.

He looked back at Emily. "It's begging to be developed. Think what could be built in its stead."

"Fit for the new century, you mean?"

"Why not? There's acreage aplenty." He was hiding his real motive from the woman he was to marry, it was true. "You deserve the finest home in the city, Emily."

"So you're a realtor now too, Sam Billings?"

He laughed. The fact was, he was thrilled it was finally on the market; he wouldn't even mind if the asking price ended up larger than the treasure below. For he'd come to see that he couldn't just sit by. Not when he knew of a trove of unclaimed cash somewhere right there; not when there was a possibility someone else might encounter it if he did not. He couldn't stomach the thought of another soul coming upon this glimpse of Ulysses Brooke's gold – comprehending it was real – growing to wonder at what had become of the rest. He turned, and saw Emily still gazing back his way.

"Always with an eye to the future," she remarked quietly.

"The only way to value the present," he shrugged right back, and she laughed right along with him.

CHAPTER 32

Southern Piedmont, North Carolina
December 1836

Thaddeus was whistling as they rode, his languid green eyes taking in the landscape, still treating every bit as an adventure. Cato was in the middle, hunched, silent, staring at his boots. Ulysses was all but alone beside them, nerves frayed after another heist, and from the argument they'd had in its wake.

Alas, even after all their success, it'd been time again for travel, away from the prying eyes of Virginia, where panic over Nat Turner had never receded, and prickly paranoia had become the new normal. This time, they'd taken on an oversized coach, cutting it off with their own carriage, while Ulysses had ducked to its rear – a practiced sleight of hand by now – unfastening the knot, lifting the canopy, lugging out the nearest chest just as the driver and horses had started back up. At that, Thaddeus had jumped down too, and holding the chest by either end, they'd hurried silently off the road, into a bed of blue orchids for Cato to meet them. He'd done a lap, before arriving but a minute later – the bank's wagon already out of sight – and working as one, they'd managed a hole in no time, placing the box inside.

Only then had Ulysses realized his heart was racing, as he'd followed the others back to the road. "Be quick about it then! Get these mounts moving."

Cato hadn't budged. "There's more gold to be had on that wagon, Ulysses. We'd catch it if we hurried."

"Have you gone mad? We'd be pressing our luck." He'd looked at Tad. "Help me here, friend."

But Cato had responded for himself. "Don't ignore me, now." His words had rippled in the quiet. "Don't go acting the master, Ulysses."

Ulysses had caught an edge in his eyes indeed – an impatience he was sure he didn't recognize. Surely, it hadn't been simmering all this while. "Now look here," he'd said next. "We mustn't court danger, Cato. You know it as well as I. For the cause, remember."

"Your cause."

"Our cause, Cato. Yours more than mine, I dare say."

"What's that to mean?"

"Only that you're the slave amongst us, naturally."

For a moment, his old friend had been silent. "Are you so unwilling to see what comes next, Ulysses? That I'll never be free? And that you'll be caught?" He'd stepped nearer. "Or is it that you've grown addicted to these journeys of ours?"

"It's absurd to even suggest."

Finally Thaddeus had moved between them. "Whenever you two hens are done clucking," and he'd stretched out his arms, pushing them apart, before tying his hair back with one of his ribbons. "We launch northward either way. If we catch another sight of that wagon, let us try again. If not, let's onto Richmond."

Cato had grunted, and lifted the reins at last. Ulysses had joined him. Thaddeus had hopped up next. They'd been riding an hour in silence ever since. The road had turned to pasture and sod, and with no trace of the bank's men, they'd eventually slowed.

Now, however, Ulysses stiffened once more. And amid his concern, he angled back his head and tried to listen. For hadn't he just heard something? At first, it sounded a mere scattering of stone – just a prowling bobcat perhaps, or some unseen stream – but then, a carriage's squeal. He squinted harder to see, Thaddeus doing the same, hunching down in the darkness, in case a shot rang out.

Then, despite the clatter of their own wheels, they caught the yelps of men – no more than a quarter-mile back, snarling instructions, shouting something sharp – and Ulysses clutched Cato's arm, pointing at the steeds. "Whip them if you must!" he urged.

Cato obliged, retrieving the switch from below, risking being heard. "A slave with a lash," he murmured, and he struck the horses yet again.

To the left, they all spotted a cutaway at once: just off the main road, scarcely visible, crowded in by pine. The wagon tilted sideways. Ulysses feared they'd go toppling as the axles groaned, the soil giving way, but they jostled back down. Here it was even darker, the forest reduced to shadow. But the air, thank God, had gone still – only a chorus of tree frogs, and the occasional hoot of an owl. They rode further, until at last, Cato guided the horses to a trot.

"You wager it was the bank's watchmen?" Tad whispered.

"Just young locals," Ulysses answered. "Coursing about for a night's fun."

"Slave-catchers," Cato cut in. "After a local runaway."

"It was the bank," Tad concluded, answering his own query. And this time, neither one of them argued back.

The moon never brightened after that; the horses grew weary. But they kept at it, in time reaching a small hut. Faint light leaked from its windows, and Ulysses studied the weeds in front, battling for space among beds of spinach, a line of sleeping chickens wheezing in a coop, a slanted porch under a lantern at the rear.

They parked, right as the front door flopped open, a lone woman standing in its frame.

She wore a one-piece dress, fastened with hooks, long sleeves rolled up, linen apron folded down. Her hair was hanging loose; she was gripping a musket in her fists – cocked, Ulysses saw now, and angled right at them.

"Hold your fire," Thaddeus announced, stepping from the wagon, arms raised, even a mischievous smile – could it really be? – the same one he still used for flirting back home.

Ulysses looked again toward the woman. Younger than them, he thought – thick hair, no streaks of gray – eyes of midnight blue, swimming like an ocean in the dark. He sighed. Really it ought to be no shock Tad was flirting. Even here. Even after all these years. And if it helped them get shelter, why not?

"Who's the darkie?" the woman barked.

"Our hand," Tad answered calmly, moving toward the porch, removing his cap, showing off the red ribbon in his hair. "Might you fancy an introduction?"

"I might," and though the musket was still up, the woman's voice had grown easier.

The leather reins dropped. "Call me Cato," came the answer from the wagon. "Cato Brooke. Property of Ulysses here." And together, they waved.

"Alright," she replied to them both. "I'm Abigail Hughes. My sister's above stairs, fixing her own rifle on you all as we speak, studyin' on whether to believe a damn thing you say."

It was hard to catch every word. They were fired in staccato, crackling and untoward: that special yeomen breed of talking Ulysses had encountered all his life, and that might as well still have been foreign. He glanced upwards, searching out the second musket, finding only potted periwinkle outside the sills, a chimney stained at the edges, hillsides to the back, no doubt rows of corn already plucked and sold off.

"We'd be grateful if we could stash our wagon," Thaddeus was saying.

"At this hour?"

"You'd have us wait 'til morn'?"

"You don't fancy I'm worth it?"

Ulysses blinked, shifting his gaze back down. *My God,* he thought. *She's actually flirting back.*

"There's a stable out front. Have your slave steer the wagon acrost. He can give your mount some of our feed. Meantime, the two of you – slowly now," and she gestured them inside.

They moved as she said, into the yellow glow, the porch creaking below their boots, then toward a small table in the kitchen. In the light, the woman looked older, Ulysses observed, lines at her lips etched deep, eyes less blue than he'd realized.

He spun round at a scratch from the hall.

"That there's Elizabeth," Abigail remarked, and a woman with the same face, and a second musket indeed, came to join them.

Ulysses stayed standing. "You should know I'm in employ of the governor in Virginia." He kept his voice steady. "Anything we might do for your betterment, you need only give word."

But the sisters Hughes were smirking – and Thaddeus right along with them. "You're awfully brazen then," said the one named Elizabeth, her accent like a brushfire, even stronger than her sister's.

Thaddeus chuckled outright. "You don't know the half of it." And at last, the guns were lowered.

Ulysses took in a smell of old wood and mashed apples, and eyed the countertop cluttered with thick-handled can-openers, spice grinder, peelers too, absorbing the sheer know-how of the place.

Abigail chortled, as if reading his mind. "It's you who need help, boys – not us. What is it you're after?"

"Proper shelter, is all." Ulysses cleared his throat. "And our slave shall require it too." There was a silence. "If that's a refusal, then we'll thank you much – but take our risks on the road." Ulysses still hadn't shaken Cato's anger from before, he realized: he felt an urge to do right by him.

"Odd request for a planter," came Abigail's reply.

"I'm merely a planter's son."

And at that, they smiled once more. Elizabeth even laughed. "Come in then, planter's son. Just don't ask your man to mealtime. He can 'sup in the stables, and slumber on the floor."

CHAPTER 33

Southern Piedmont, North Carolina
December 1836

The whole of the county, it seemed, had come looking for the latest stolen funds.

Not that it should have been a surprise. Thanks to the growing spate of thefts, planters were more alert than ever for losses, and word spread quickly of gold gone missing. Apparently, the wagon driver had heard the canvas flapping soon after Ulysses had unhitched it: sauntering back to re-string the rope, noticing the absent chest, he'd ridden straight to the local sheriff.

Constables had appeared at the door the very next morning. Thank God then for Abigail, by then fully smitten with Thaddeus and pleading innocence, never mentioning the men hiding upstairs, already knowing what they'd done. To Cato and Ulysses' horror, Tad had made their crime plain to her, but neither she nor her sister had seemed to mind. Abolitionism meant nothing to them, it was true, but the notion of stealing from the aristocracy: now that had given them a thrill, and from then on, they'd treated their guests with a new dash of respect, serving fresh warm milk at dawn, even laundering their linens on Saturdays.

In the weeks since, they'd been scanning the broadsides together – reports of man-hunts, suspects, dead-ends – until at last the search had seemed to ebb. In the meantime, they'd settled into something of a routine, storing carrots and potatoes in the cellar for winter, tending to the hogs up the hill, sharing cups of ale by the evening fire. The cottage had grown familiar, bedchambers above, kitchen below, the hiss of the charcoal stove making it all the way to the narrow porch out back.

It was there the men found themselves now, while the sisters readied supper, three fugitives wrapped in woolen blankets, looking out upon soft brown hillsides and winding stone walls. The air hinted of old nectar and ash, and Ulysses, breathing deep, rested his hands on his lap, resisting the notion that maybe here was the answer after all. For could it really be? That after years preparing for revolution, real solace could lie in just shutting out the world, living as well as possible, for as long as possible, away from all that boiled beyond those bluffs?

"It's been some weeks," he noted, letting the words seep in.

Tad nodded. "I can keep a calendar same as you."

"Our trail has cooled."

"You mean then to return home?"

He blinked. "Don't you mean to say 'we'?"

But this time, Tad didn't answer.

The sounds of the world seemed suddenly to cede to the moment, the chatter of sparrows fading, the breeze itself ducking notice. Ulysses almost laughed. "Tad, you'd grow restless by first frost."

At that, his friend faced him, his green eyes stopping their usual dance. "Abigail's kin would never favor the match. Nor mine, naturally." He smirked. "We've made plans to move north instead. To New York," and he patted Ulysses' knee, as if the latter were an old pup, to be consoled before being put down.

A long moment passed. Ulysses had certainly seen how intoxicated Tad had become by Abigail, as fiery a spirit as she'd first appeared, holding him to account with ease. They'd vanish together for hours at a time, loping off to the woods, sitting in pastures and beneath the pine. But this? It was madness. "Come now, Thaddeus, she has youth enough to beget a child! A whole destiny yet undefined."

"She's merely a score younger than I."

"I stand corrected then. Near an elder herself!"

"Now you're being cruel."

"And you're neglecting who you are. Set to be a bachelor for life, I'd thought."

"No, old friend." Tad sat back. "That was always you."

The door squeaked open, and they turned to see Abigail, looking down upon them, hesitating. "Ah," she offered. "So he told you then."

Ulysses was quiet.

"Blessings are in order," Cato managed.

She nodded. "When you're ready, gents, steamed grits are waitin'." And she turned without giving them a chance to stand, letting the door bang loudly shut.

"Well that might've gone better," Thaddeus announced. No one laughed.

It was Cato who sighed in the quiet. "This whole enterprise was always a romp to you, there's no use denying."

Tad looked gently back. "And you? Will you be glad only after we've all been sentenced? Sacrificed like Christ Himself?"

"Better Christ than a coward."

"Oh for heaven's sake! It's enough, from both of you. Cato, I could have you free'd straight away. I'd offer payment to Mrs. Brooke – as I ought have done the instant Colonel Brooke passed." His gaze hardened, as he faced Ulysses instead. "As you should have done yourself."

"Come off it. My mother knows I oppose the whole institution. She'd keep him in stockades simply from spite."

"Not if you overruled."

"Even then any sale would be blocked by the estate, and held as bond. My father left too much debt as it was."

"Tell yourself what you must."

"As you do, Thaddeus." So that all at once, Ulysses felt an anger like a sudden storm, twisting itself from the sea, words coming now like the driven rain. "Sitting there smug, abandoning your friends atop your cause! Fancying this as anything more than it is – flirtation, seduction – bedding your yeoman minx, and calling it love."

Tad stared. "'Master Brooke,' is it? By God, I'd forgotten I was to live by your command."

"Stop it there, Thaddeus. Don't dare compare your plight to theirs. It's beneath you."

"Then perhaps so are they," Tad muttered – only to turn away at once, flushed, swallowing, straightening his vest, shifting his chair loudly against the porch. "I didn't mean that," he offered next, glancing toward Cato. "Only that we've done what we can, that we've time enough left in our lives for living." His words picked back up, and he looked between the two of them. "Cato can be free. You can distribute the funds, Ulysses – slowly, clandestinely." He waited. "In the meanwhile, I'd best inquire if they need help serving," and he stood with a clipped bow. "I'll see you in there."

Ulysses crossed his arms as Tad went inside, then stretched and crossed them again – regretting already his quick-tempered barbs. "And you?" he finally asked, spinning towards Cato, while voices grew hushed from within the house. "Will you really stay on? With me?"

"Is it not what you want?"

He rubbed his brow. The question laid out the truth, even more starkly than Tad's anger and arrows had done. "I can't ask you to turn from freedom, Cato. Not even for the sake of others."

"No?"

"No." He peered back up. "Nor can I ask it on my own account."

"As friend, you mean, Ulysses? Or as owner?"

"Would either one change your reply?"

"I suppose not." Cato's next words came slowly. "For real freedom isn't granted by one man to another, is it? It's a thing I've already got within." He reached out his hand. "I stay now, because I choose to. Because I know my life's purpose, just as you know yours, Ulysses, each one of us the same."

Ulysses felt a wetness in his eyes at that. His chest surged, filled with a grace and gratitude more sweeping than any he'd thought possible, and for some time then, they sat there together, as the evening birdsong faded and the nighttime chirps began, as the last light went for good. Until eventually, they stood, and moved along, to eat with the others.

CHAPTER 34

Richmond, Virginia
December 1836

Another journey complete. Another page logged in his book of maps.

Only this time, a homecoming without their friend: after farewell to Thaddeus, they'd ridden in quiet, hitting a hail storm in the mountains, eventually dropping Cato back at Boxwood, explaining the slave's absence with talk of burdens in the capital. Until finally, Ulysses had pulled in here.

Cyrus Thompson was looking immaculate as ever, as though sufficient layers of velvet could fool the world into thinking he was still a young man. "Out on the road a whole month this time, Brooke!" he chortled, bowing at the door uninvited, a new set of jowls crumpling upon his collar, while his wife Beth looked on, a fine-woven sash no match for her growing heft.

"Not to fret, Mr. Brooke," she wheezed in turn. "We tended to your shrubs."

"I was gone on account of my mother." How many lies had he told to these neighbors over the years? "Her eyes have dimmed. I was there at Boxwood aiding with the dockets." And though he tried to shrug, he couldn't shake his unease. Their meddling seeming to grow with every burst in their stature – new slaves, new carriages, even new accents, more trills than ever. "If you'll excuse me now, I'd better rest. All that journeying." Managing a nod then, he moved back inside swiftly, and poured a tall whiskey. It was merely the regular Thompson prattle, he told himself, and he sank into the nearest chair, shutting his eyes to the questions, the gossip, the coming adventures with Cato, the memories of Thaddeus abandoning them both.

In time, his head slouched, his tumbler resting on his thigh, and he let his dreams usher in new company. In place of the indoor air, there was now wind like fire; in place of the lantern, heavy bouts of smoke, and artillery shells screaming across an orange sky. His thoughts turned cloudy at the strangeness of it all. For this wasn't just the old Revolution, he decided: there were no Continentals' vests here, but rather blue uniforms of felt – new soldiers, suffering some new war – until he looked up towards a bang. Then another. Even more after that. Ulysses opened his eyes, realizing there was someone knocking on the door yet again. He nearly tipped his drink as he went over to see.

There, before him now, was Rebecca: hands on her hips, hair tinged gray as if by clouds. She sighed. "It's true then, Ulysses. You've returned."

"Only just."

"Some hours past, I should think."

"Is the whole of Richmond so keen to know?"

"I made a query of your neighbors."

He took a sip from his glass. Was this why Cyrus and Beth had come round that morning? Were they simply doing Rebecca's bidding? "I'd have written, but I was weary from my travels."

"Travels to where, Ulysses?"

For a moment, still shedding his dream, he felt cornered for the second time that day. "Come in, Rebecca. I'll fetch another drink – " and he spoke as they walked. "Merely pursuing my work for the governor's council. Nothing more intriguing than that."

"The Thompsons say the rest of the council stays put, that you're the only one who journeys."

"They're gossips is all. Always have been."

She raised an eyebrow. "Will you never tell me of your work, Ulysses? Truly? Shall we make it to the grave in silence?"

He took in another sip and turned back her way. Since last she'd come, Rebecca had been married at last – briefly it was true – to an old widower, who'd made her a widow in turn: a lonely, onetime cavalier, from what Ulysses had been told, losing his family to fever decades before, making Rebecca all the richer in exchange for a kind smile to see him off to heaven. Only what of her? Had it merely been a way to fill her days, in place of the marriage she'd truly wanted? Or was it worse: a way of pleasing her father at long last – doing what she was supposed to do, just like all the rest – just as he supposed she'd always done? Could he have stopped her? "There are other men, you know," he remarked now. "Others who would yet find you considerable dashing."

She smiled softly, letting him change the subject. "At my age, Ulysses?"

"Your beauty hasn't left you."

"Is that all you see?"

"It's what they would see. I know it."

She exhaled, rubbing the back of her shoulder, as though there were some pain there that she couldn't quite reach. "My father's not long for this earth, you know. He asks after you, advises he'd like to keep up ties." The floorboards shifted beneath her. "Even if your affairs of the capital must still prove as secret as you say."

Placing his glass atop a sideboard, Ulysses paused. Was that really the reason she'd come? Had it not also been for her own sake? For both of theirs? "I include you in every thought I ever have, Rebecca." He imagined what it would be to reach out and touch her. "You must see that. Every deed I've ever done."

"I think you even believe it, when you say so." She was stepping nearer. "Be that as it may, Ulysses. My father mentioned supper this evening."

So that now Ulysses met her eye, and softly shook his head. "Perhaps another time." He took in her familiar gaze in the dim light, across the empty patch of room between them, and the flickering oil lamps he'd lit before sunset.

"Are you really so different from other men?" she asked him.

"Surely I'm not the only one to claim so."

But she afforded him no smile. "Well you're as blind as any of them. Never once taking the time to see that I might admire your despair, Ulysses, that I grasp the rancor in your eyes at your fellow slaveholders – the pain when you pass upon a slave."

"And yet you do nothing in turn?" He found himself itching more than ever to explain. For how many women could look at him as she did now? As she always had: actually listening – even wanting to hear! She'd have been a distraction, it was true, putting herself in danger to boot, just as he'd long ago concluded. Yet he'd never given her a chance to say no.

Alas. The secrets all piled atop one another, a whole life in hiding. It was far too late now, was it not? How possibly could she forgive him the years? The life they might have had?

She'd started twisting back. "Oh, Ulysses," – and his name, uttered a thousand times, seemed suddenly to catch in her throat, her voice muffled against the walls. "What is it's happened to make you this way?"

He opened his lips.

"What then?" she pressed – though when she looked this time, it was as if a shadow had passed between their gazes, no matter the dark. "Please, Ulysses. You must answer." Her mouth was drawn tight, her eyes gone moist, no effort to try and shutter them any longer.

"The life of my father..." he murmured at last. "I never wanted it."

There was a pause. She nodded slowly. "All Virginia adored him, you know. Folks used to say he'd have been a fine as president as Jefferson."

Ulysses hesitated, scuffing his boots upon the wood of the floor. "I'd wager perhaps they were right," and he glanced back up. "He was brave, and intelligent, I'm sure. Everyone always said so."

"Yes."

"He always wished I'd stay. It was my duty, he told me. And I refused him. We mustn't always do what our fathers demand, I wanted to tell him – but rather what we think is right. Even at the expense of Boxwood Grove. Even at the expense of a family of my own."

"And that was all, Ulysses?" She swallowed. "That's all there was to it?"

"That was all."

CHAPTER 35

Charleston, South Carolina – September

1981

Already Alvin's dress shirt was sticking to his chest, and the sun was barely even up. There were ramshackle shotgun homes as far as he could see – the bureau far too cheap to have gotten him a room by the bay – walls battered, locals shouting at him across dirt-strewn lawns: black men in white tank tops, some readying for work, others with transistor radios buzzing R & B by their ears. *'Howdy honkey!'* – *'Loosen that tie, fella!'* – *'You lost, Yank?'* – nothing too vicious, but more than enough for confirming the city was split in two, that whatever visions of justice had brought Alvin to the bureau hadn't accounted for history's ever-sprawling rot.

Then, only a few blocks more, and the rough edges were receding, the rot abruptly papered over with bloom. The cracked curbs became sidewalks. Pit bulls on chains ceded to golden retrievers beneath hammocks. In place of foreclosure notices, here were customized postboxes. Until not long after, the mansions themselves started their reign: Palladian piazzas and Corinthian columns, gardens with views of the sea. Three – four – five stories high, ivy stretching up the walls, slate roofs sporting copper weather vanes like crowns, clay-potted chimneys dancing in pairs.

Out on the water, the ferries were docking, ready to usher the day's visitors toward Fort Sumter: a safari of graves, another affront to the ghosts still haunting them. Alvin smirked to think of Faye scoffing when he'd invited her along. "To go and visit a movie set?" she'd fired back. Now, looking upon the place, he understood what she'd meant. It was all just a cloying, candied diorama – and probably always had been, put in place to muffle an entire people's cries.

He walked along the shoreline, and came upon the largest estates of all, porticoes round their midsections like fat men's cummerbunds, playsets and climbing gyms on the lawns, treadmills in open carriage houses at their sides – southern ease made fashionable once more. It was easy to imagine that soon this whole place would be like one of those medieval mountain towns of Europe, villages sustained by voyeurism, pickled and set aside solely for their visitors' sake – no more than postcards in motion, all special fares and old-timey balls, as if to animate a still-life, when what they were really doing was propping up a corpse.

Alvin took the photocopied book of maps from his briefcase. The fact was, he'd been putting this city off for ages, along with anywhere else like it, doubtful there'd be anything left to find. It was too much of a hub, every stone long since unturned, sailors and senators and storms all making this port their own in the years after Brooke and Billings had been through themselves. Yet here he was, with these maps still commanding his faith, never offering salvation in return – and him, doubling down like Job in response.

He found the address he was seeking: faded sketches transformed into three dimensions right before his eyes – a stenciled iron door, limewashed ochre walls, prodigious live oaks in front, and there, a sloping lawn, just like the drawings said. It was exactly the sort of spot Ulysses Brooke had aimed to overthrow.

A collection of midwestern tourists was riding by at the moment, oohing-and-aahing aboard a mule-drawn carriage, flat vowels like chalk on a blackboard. Their guide was a local high schooler, gesticulating as though he'd built the city himself, all but doing an impression of Scarlett O'Hara for their benefit.

Alvin turned.

Here now was a man about his own age, wearing a pink-striped polo, khaki shorts, penny loafers sans socks. He was striding over from the very driveway Alvin had come to see. The fellow had a swoop of brown hair, and a chin sawed from stone – a Brooks Brothers catalogue come to life.

"I saw you gapin'!" the local announced, in a tenor high and smooth.

"Apologies," Alvin answered, deciding not to mention the bureau. The guy seemed at ease, no need to make him jumpy.

"Not to worry – you're far from our first gawker," and the fellow grinned, extending his hand. "Name's Bradford. First name Jamie."

"Alvin Starkman. Pleasure's mine."

"Welcome to Charleston, Starkman." Swaddled in the local cadence, each vowel took up twice its regular time. "Care for a tour?"

"You mean it?"

"Why not?"

"I'd be grateful."

"Whereabouts you from, Starkman?" They'd started down the gravel driveway, cutting in across the lawn, towards the porch.

"New York. Brooklyn-born. Manhattan-corrupted."

Bradford smiled wider, showing off a gleaming set of teeth. "A Yankee in our midst," he sang. "I've wanted to get up there – just too caught up in this old pile of lumber, helping my grandma fix up whichever piece just broke." They reached the porch. "Mind the third step there, Starkman – it buckles to the left," and he laughed. "Case in point."

They did a lap along the rail before entering, taking in a picture-perfect guest cottage to the side, just refurbished, painted sky blue, a river rock fireplace at the rear. Its white shutters clapped softly in the breeze; lilacs scented the whole place with heaven. "Old slave quarters," Bradford announced cavalierly, and the words hung in the air.

The mansion, meanwhile, turned out to be more rickety indoors than out. The smell was of antique leather and mold, the light uneven, thanks to a line of smudged sash windows up top. Somewhere behind the rafters, rodents were scurrying. Past the vestibule, missing panes of stained glass had been replaced with thin cuts of plywood. "Lost 'em way back," Bradford explained. "Apparently we were in the business of hiding officers, and the boys in blue came firing."

They started toward the library and came upon shelves listing beneath endless gilded bindings; then it was to the kitchen, where a mop and a yellow bucket sat atop a mosaic of blue tiling. From there, the central parlor awaited, anchored by dueling soot-stained mantles –

portraits over each showing the original owner in a proud white wig and satin breeches. Alvin studied the chipped frames, and held back a sneeze, taking note that whatever money the Bradford clan retained had been reserved for the views from the street. Even in the dining room, the floral wall fabric had faded from purple to gray, the crown molding cracked straight down the fore.

The second story was the same: four-post beds and long-abandoned wood stoves, rusted chimney pipes dangling off the ceiling. Bradford focused on the architecture rather than the decline – a double stairwell like a two-trunked tree, pediment and pilaster at every entryway – offering only a few throwaways about the place's history: the cotton fortune and its crash, a gaggle of cousins gone off to Colorado, his grandmother's recent move to a nursing home. Finally, when they'd circled back down, Alvin nudged for more: "I was actually studying up before my trip," he began. "Learning about these houses – the stories they have to tell." He held off another moment, but his host said nothing. "Any small chance you ever heard rumors of treasure?" There, he thought: he was out with it, even if as soon as the words were uttered, Alvin knew they sounded kooky. He shrugged sheepishly. "Reports of theft, I mean – near the war?"

Now Bradford surprised him once more. "How in hell's bells did a Yank like you ever hear about that?" He shook his head. "It can't have made the guidebooks?" He led them toward a pair of slat-backed rocking chairs on the porch. "Come – sit."

The sidewalks were picking up ahead, men with polo shirts and paunches, their wives in high-rise jeans, a few go-getters on morning jogs in the salty air, portable cassette players at their waists. Farther off, the sun was revealing ever more of the water, crumpled waves against a winding coast of crags and cliffs, its mild temper hinting of something more.

"You ask about rumors." Bradford leaned back in his chair, the very picture of a man with a fading trust fund, head tilted, eyes cast toward the splintered beadboard ceiling. "I always assumed it was just grandma and her pals runnin' their mouths. There was a Virginian thief, they used to say. Still a bit famous – name of Ulysses Brooke."

"I've heard of him," Alvin replied. *If only you knew*, he thought.

"Robin Hood without the following. Stealing from rich folks whenever he could."

"Including this house?"

"Well – that's where the history shifts to legend. Schoolbooks never mentioned his coming down here exactly. But old-timers always insisted he did. Most said to this very spot."

"How'd they know?"

"Somebody, sometime, swore they'd seen a fellow at the bank matching Brooke's description – dartin' eyes, quick steps, like he was up to no good." Bradford snorted. "Not that anyone thought it worth sharing 'til the guy was already on trial: no doubt just gabbin' for the attention. It made for a good yarn, at least, and folks kept re-telling it, some even claiming an old Bradford up the line had seen Brooke himself, duckin' about right here, ridin' off with his slave."

Alvin raised his eyebrows. "They were sure it was a slave helping him?" For that was a surprise.

"Don't take it as gospel, my friend. It's just one family's little notion: that Brooke was a hypocrite, ordering one of his own to do his bidding – name of Cicero, or Cato, or somethin' like it. That wasn't all, of course! Folks were always adding new pieces: tales of trespassers coming through, hungry for treasure, as if Brooke really had stashed some here – phantom figures, always spotted in the night with shovels and spades – like ghost stories growing over the years. My grandpap even told me of trying to dig some cash up himself when he was a kid, wrecking his mama's flower beds, getting the switch, never finding a thing."

Alvin was eyeing the bay again now, eager not to betray all that he knew, to unravel this man's trust in him.

But Bradford sat up in his chair, eyeing him in turn. "Only here I am rattlin' on. Tell me, Starkman – where was it you said you picked this all up anyhow?"

"Just some teens going off at my motel." Alvin scratched the back of his head. "Local guides I think. Offering tourist-catnip, for when we passed by your house."

"Ah." Bradford sounded disappointed.

"But I've taken too much of your time."

"I enjoyed it." They stood together, and walked down the steps. "That's the place there," he added, pointing to a dip in the lawn, just shy of the cottage. "Where the trespassers were supposed to have gotten spotted. Between you and me, I'd bet it was just a traveling greenskeeper or two. These gardens used to be something, you know. They've got photos at the Historical Society, though black-and-white can't do it justice. People used to come miles just to see."

Alvin looked where he was gesturing: merely a clump of orange day lilies now, and some overgrown rye grass, and in the rear, a wall of rhododendron thicker than any he'd ever seen. Still, he zeroed in. For wasn't this section marked in the book of maps? And for a moment at least, he could almost feel them, Brooke and Billings both, urging that he was one step nearer to proof – still coming up short nonetheless.

1837

Ulysses awoke from a doze, and it took a moment remembering where he was. A dusty road stretched on ahead, and dawn was approaching – the horses trotting past meadows and huts, cattle barns of unchinked timber, hogs slurping at troughs – and he supposed they were getting close.

Peering past Cato, he saw more of the dimly lit fields, speckled white as if by frost: cotton bolls cracked for harvest, and halfway-plucked. Hillcrests loomed behind them too, mansions larger than any he'd ever seen – grander even than the ones west of Richmond – silver stone walls and iron verandas, pineapples and palms etched over the doors, porticoes like outdoor ballrooms, and slaves, of course, waking for work by the thousands.

Ulysses met the gazes of those nearest, massing now amid the white tufts, and he was embarrassed for his own liberty, wishing he could tell them, somehow, who he was, why he'd come: that the overseers didn't even blink when he picked up Cato these days. That this was the crown jewel of the southern crown, and it was past time he strike it.

The city arrived upon them like a summer storm, sudden and swift, the fields seeming to vanish at once, yeoman cabins cropping up in their stead, stables to follow, cramped gardens of cabbage and carrots, the smell of seaweed caressing the air. Black-eyed Susans were soon snaking their way through picket fences, potted white roses in between, the soft clatter of carriages too – and a few blocks past that, the city's wharf: blue flags rippling above the docks, oak-hulled ships gliding in from calm seas, steam and sail together, as if testifying to the port's strength, proclaiming so it had always been, so it would always be. Ulysses could hear the shouts of sailors, already loading their pressed bales of cotton, trading jokes about the ladies they'd met, and the ones who hadn't yet had the pleasure.

Richmond's competitor indeed. There were gentlemen with their house slaves and women at their sides, in ruffled sleeves as large as their heads, feudal lords for the modern age, trading morning pleasantries in a language all their own – "Aren't you lookin' the viscount this mornin'!" – "and you, I must declare!" – empty words that swooshed the same as their silk: lavish and languid, a cloak for their savagery.

Cato was shaking his head – only just so – but Ulysses was certain of the horror that drove it: the same horror that seeped through every crack of this place, there between the gleaming churches and open-air creameries hawking the day's eggs, printed for all to see on the broadsides tacked to the posts and promising rewards for the runaways, etched in the corner signs advertising the auction houses. It was there, most of all, beneath the shingle roofs, in the merchandise itself, mothers wailing, voices shredded hoarse for good, children panting from scurvy, men staring out from their rags, chests dark as ink, eyes rigid and wincing at once, faces more like wounds, straight to their ruptured souls. All of them standing in their rusting chains – refusing to sit, or forbidden to sit, or both – despite their knees buckling, and their muscles that heaved, drenched in their urine and sweat and stool. Right here in the city's heart, not even tucked apart, the way they did it in Richmond, cruelty so entrenched it didn't even qualify as embarrassment. The buyers were pulling up now too, planters in rows of flat-bed carriages, with large spoked wheels – money, more money – greedy grunts as white men slapped the black men's backsides like meat, and eyed the chained girls beside them, not seeming to notice them shaking in return, lowering their cash into the palms of the eager yeomen, while Ulysses and Cato moved past, finally reaching the purpose of their ride.

Charleston's central bank awaited.

Past the auction houses, and the next line of market stalls selling beefsteaks and beans, it stood on its block like a temple. Unlike the backwoods outposts, this was a proper affair, gray stucco front, molded cornice at either end, a golden leaf eagle pointing toward the sky. Yet wasn't it also just the same? No more than a holding cell for the sinners' money. And waiting with Cato at the corner, Ulysses scouted out the lonely guard – doughy, yellow-bearded, taking a lap every half-hour to ease his legs – and then waited some more.

It was quarter past three when their moment arrived: a wagon coming from the west, tar-caulked walls, a draft horse that looked bored. Its driver was in no hurry either, tugging his sacks of cash over the curb, through the doors and toward the vault inside. The guard was off on one of his strolls. Ulysses leapt down without a word, eyes fixed, while Cato trailed from behind.

He got there in seconds, sliding one of the sacks from the wagon for himself, angling back across the empty road, passing Cato as he went, holding his breath – almost arrived – almost done – when:

"You there!" came the shout. The voice was clear. "Halt, boy!"

Ulysses swallowed. The word "boy" couldn't possibly be meant for him, and he didn't dare turn, not with the evidence still in his arms, continuing on as steadily as he could, mouth gone dry, blood racing, the short walk suddenly an ocean's crossing.

Sure enough, he could hear Cato stammering behind him – "I'm but passin', sir – I swear it –" and hoping his poor friend could forestall another moment, reaching the curb in the meantime, he heaved the coins now into their own carriage's rear.

Finally, he faced front.

There was Cato indeed, just feet from the bank's steps, and the guard himself, returned quicker than anticipated, arm raised, finger jabbing straight into Cato's chest, free hand reaching for a pistol beneath his buckskin coat.

"What in blazes?!" Ulysses shouted at once – and they each looked over, as he strode back, scowling furiously, as though he were disappointed in them both. "The boy's with me."

The guard spat. "The boy's got no pass."

"I'll vouch for him direct," and Ulysses reached inside his vest. "I ought have placed it on his body." It was a thin certificate, crumpled from the journey, and he handed it over.

Being accounted for, this Negro slave, named Cato Brooke of Boxwood Grove, is hereby granted right and title for travel –
Signed <u>Ulysses Brooke</u>, <u>Master</u>

"I ain't recognize it," the guard muttered, and Ulysses guessed he couldn't read.

"It's Virginia-granted."

"A Virginia buck, scoutin' a Carolina bank?"

"Surely you don't aim to interrogate me?"

"I'm interrogatin' your boy."

And Ulysses sighed, completing the performance. "Now look here: I've given you my word as a gentleman. That's more than plenty." He took Cato by the collar. "He's a faithful boy, prone to getting lost, is all."

"He's uppity. You ought teach him not to look a white man in the eye."

Ulysses peered back. *How about striking a white man in the eye instead!* But he merely nodded, already moving down the block, reaching the carriage, lifting the reins and passing them over.

"They'll count the cash," Cato whispered, as they started off.

Ulysses knew he was right. "Toward the bay," was all he said, aware of the guard's gaze still upon them. If they were quick enough in getting to next steps, they'd at least be empty of the money before any pursuit. It was still bright outside, but they had no choice, and on the very next block, moving out of sight, they started hunting for a spot.

Here yellow ivy wrapped around stone walls by the roadside; potted ferns and formal rows of myrtle lined the streets like royal corridors. In most of the gardens, there were ladies taking tea, hoop-skirts twice as wide as the benches beneath them. But then: a house on the right, one of the largest of all, a fine double door, lime-washed walls the color of dirty clay, lean live oaks out front. It wasn't the home's size, though, that grabbed their attention, but the endless windows – every one of them closed, still shuttered from summer, owners apparently away, no doubt tending to a plantation nearby.

They pulled into the driveway and hurried down the carriage steps, fetching their shovels, giving the horses blinders to keep them put. From there they entered a garden that smelled of heaven: pink camellias, magnolias, wooden trestles crisscrossing in between. Ignoring the beauty, they walked toward a low-down clearing at its edge, half-expecting the owners to show up after all, screaming, firing even, the bank's guard racing over in turn. When the silence continued its reign, they began digging their hole, soon shoving the treasure inside with practiced efficiency, smoothing the topsoil, returning the shovels to the carriage the instant they were done.

"No soul will ever check here," Ulysses remarked as they returned to the road, sketching out the scene before he forgot it. "It's too far up their own 'arse," and they both chuckled. The sun was lowering at last as they made their way north, snacking on cinnamon bark and cured pork, splashing their heads with water from their canteens, turning onto forest paths, as soon as they found some.

"You were convincing," Cato remarked, once they'd made some distance and were sure they were away, dabbing his forehead, breaking the lull. "Claiming back your 'boy.'"

Ulysses nodded. "I had to be."

But at that, Cato only looked away. And they kept on in quiet.

1902

Sam had been pleased when his advisor Finn Hughes had booked this trip. "That was American Tobacco on the line," Hughes had announced. "Still hankering to have you down, sir."

He'd grinned outright. He could have said no, certainly, but the fact was Charleston was in the book of maps, and he'd long meant to reach it. He no longer required buried treasure, of course – greasing the markets had long proven easier than darting through steamy southern fields – yet why turn a blind eye, when opportunity fell straight into his lap?

That very evening he'd told Emily he'd be departing, and she'd approved. With the wedding approaching, extra time with her mother would be welcome, after all; there were invitations to be designed, a gown to be sewed, attendants to be selected. Sam knew it went beyond that too. For she adored money as much as he did: her brown eyes had lit up when he'd assured her this would only mean more.

He sighed.

It was all a welcome recollection – a reminder of the life that awaited him upon his return from these twilit, reconstructed streets greeting him now, desperate in their plea to be taken seriously, hollow nonetheless. This city's wealth remained, to be sure. It was in the sheen of the sidewalks and coral stone, the eternal spring of the gardens' lilies. The problem lay in the aims that simmered underneath. Trying to halt time, he'd decided, and even worse: to turn it back.

For indeed, the cramped blocks had been overtaken by Confederate battle flags, bullet-ridden and long since faded, not to mention the buglers lining the curbs, trumpeting *Dixie*, all part of a reunion parade only now reaching its ebb. He'd learned of its scheduling only that afternoon, when he'd come upon the rows of veterans, boys of yesteryear garbed in gray. They'd looked as rusted as their weapons – crinkled faces, uniforms drawn tight – bowing and waving the same as the geezers back in New York. So that in their pining, if nothing else, America's old men had at last found common cause.

At least the tobacco men were willing to break free, Sam thought, hosting him with aplomb, touring him that morning through a stretch of warehouses on the city's western edge – modern, utilitarian, a welcome escape from the nonsense. There'd been rolling machines lining the aisles, electric bulbs overhead, mechanized knives, copper tubes stuffing the cigarettes to the brim, paper conveyer belts gluing, slicing, packaging in perfect synchronization. As he'd bid them farewell, offering his congratulations, accepting theirs in turn, he'd been baffled why the rest of these people wouldn't simply move on too.

He stepped more quickly now, farther from the parade, and nearly collided with an ancient dark-skinned fellow, trying to sell him a mug of tea. "Help an old slave out," the figure slurred, with a smell that seared Sam's nostrils, and a voice like torn up leather.

"Only I'm not thirsty," Sam shrugged back, racing on before the man could pester him further, down a short slope that shielded him from the last of the parade's noise, toward blocks of smaller houses painted pastel. Above, the dimming sky idled, coating the plum slate roofs in blue, shadowing the walls crumbling at their sides – too many of them not yet repaired from the war, marble bird basins at their corners cracked and filled with mud – ruins, really, here in the cross streets, proof that the city's boosters were no more than snake-oil quacks, not just bathing in lost glory, but letting the dirty water run down its back.

By the time Sam had come out the other side, the sounds had grown quieter still, and darkness had arrived, so that he pulled the book of maps from his vest, and squinted to check the next road. In the moonlight, it looked haunted. He listened to the echo of his own boots against the cobblestone, and the lap of the ocean farther off, and he winced again at the stench, manure this time, as he took care stepping past the hogshead barrels jamming the merchants' doorways. Finally, he exited the maze of alleys, and saw at last the mansions overlooking the bay.

They were as big as those back home, though here they seemed oversized, losing all trace of purpose, as if nursing the same longing as the parade. Sam wandered over to the address he was seeking, wisps of moonlight cascading across its yellow walls like loose twine, an iron door towering in blackness. Sure enough, there was a garden at the side with a dip at its edge, precisely as the drawings had pledged, a crumbling fence past that, pockmarked by holes that shimmered with termites. One of the chimneys was surrounded by plywood-scaffolding; the old slave quarters in back had fallen into disrepair – window panes shattered, poison sumac manning the base – the oaks in front far thicker than what Brooke had drawn. It was all just another relic, Sam concluded, like a blind, proud old mare, with ribs protruding from its mane.

Stuffing the reliable old maps back in his pocket, he pulled out a spade from his waistcoat. Tiptoeing now, wary of overeager servants, he knelt in the garden's dell, exactly at the spot Ulysses had underlined, and pushed the blade straight down. The ground gave way at once, and he kept at it, deeper than he'd anticipated, eventually growing concerned that perhaps the book of maps wasn't quite as perfect as he'd wanted to believe – until at last, something clanged, bright and high-pitched. It felt different than the iron chests to which he'd grown accustomed, sinking further when he made contact, and he reached down with his hand.

The coins were loose, he realized – old half-eagles, he saw now – minted at five dollars, worth far more at this point for their gold. He leaned in farther, scraping the earth with his fingers. Now there were more – whole piles of them, in fact. There must never have been a chest at all, he decided, just a carrying-sack of some sort, its canvass long since rotted away – and digging through, he confirmed it, fragments soft and thin, threads spun delicately through the earth. In a hurry, Sam scraped the coins up, jamming them into his trousers and his coat, near to overflowing. Wishing he'd brought the carriage, no matter the dark narrow alleys from the hotel, he shuffled back to the road.

When out of nowhere, he realized he wasn't alone.

The outline of a man had appeared on the property behind him, an unkempt beard at his jaw, cotton overalls smudged with dirt, a wooden rake in one hand and a set of dibbers for bulbs in the other: a gardener, it seemed, eager to outsmart the heat by working into the night. He was eyeing Sam in turn, his gaze fixed on Sam's spade and the coins bulging in his clothes.

So that all at once, Sam presented himself as he knew that he must. No more than another gardener under the moon, with the same bright idea for getting through his tasks. It was too dark for his silk tails to be revealed, or to rely upon the class deference that he'd come to expect. Instead, he simply gave a small wave, and to his relief, received a hesitant one in return. Who would possibly guess there'd been a pile of loot here, anyway? So what if there was suddenly a new hole in the ground?

The fellow was a mere laborer anyway, Sam thought, as he walked off.

Leave it to him to fill the damned thing in.

CHAPTER 36

New York City
May, June 1903

The clatter at the tables was as raucous as on the streets outside. Here were young clerks on their lunch breaks, waiters crashing, electric bulbs buzzing like locusts. Sam was rolling his eyes. "I'm not so old as all that, mother," he declared, and he poured himself another glass of iced tea. He'd never even heard of the drink before today. But the bow-tied fellow who'd poured it had insisted it was the latest craze, and who was he to argue? Why should syrup and lemon be any more a shock than the rest of the old neighborhood?

He'd come down just before lunch, taking the El, hands clamped tight upon his money-purse to keep from being pickpocketed. From the station then, he'd made his way through the hue-and-cry of this newest New World: newsboys, candle hawkers, butchers, blocks of his youth changed more than he'd even imagined, even denser now than a mere decade past. So that for every boarding house that'd once loomed, there were three new ones smashed together; for every lost soul, at least a dozen more; for every old dialect, a new language entirely – Italian, Chinese, everything in between – Yiddish most of all. Yellow brick synagogues sat on double-wide lots, klezmer ditties bubbled from gramophones, a mad rush of new smells invaded, meat-fats fried and roasted, sweat and piss and sweat some more. There were laundry lines draped like cobwebs, children like squirrels, razor-edged shouts pinging like sleet – churning, toiling, jostling, elbowing – enough that somehow, Sam thought, they were even something like Americans.

His mother had been waiting at her door, hair coiled in a bun, cheeks sagging like wilted petals. Though when she spoke, her voice had been sturdy, a chirping mid-century accent as insistent as ever. "If I'd known we were dining high-falutin," she'd cracked, eyeing his dotted tie, "I swear I'd have worn a gown."

Back through the masses they'd gone, amid gurgling sewers and come-ons from the vendors, forced into single-file at the first corner, and he'd taken note how she still fit in: a two-toned gray skirt hanging loose over her ankle boots, an edge to her aging strut. No matter his standing offer of a home uptown, she'd never find the will to accept it.

In time, the crowds had thinned, the racket returning to English. Coffeehouses had sprung up like dandelions. And Sam had given his name at the first presentable one he saw – *Rufus Spice & Teas*, said the sign – quite sure his mother was smiling as they'd been led to the finest table at the rear.

Finally, he'd explained why he was there. For a moment, he wasn't even sure she'd heard. Just opposite them, a crowd of Germans were loudly discussing their Kaiser; a game of dominoes had erupted beyond that; somewhere, a bulb's filament had given out with a pop.

"Did you catch that, ma?" He leaned forward now. "I'm betrothed."

And this time, she nodded. "I should say it's past time, Samuel."

"For God's sake, I'm not yet forty." She was the last one in the world dared still speak to him this way. "You'd have me remember Washington himself!"

"It's you this young lady desires, Sam? Or your gold?"

They're one and the same, he wanted to say. "Her name's Emily Townsend."

She lowered her cup.

"That's right, ma." The room seemed to swell from the tobacco smoke and steam of Turkish coffee, and he waited as the waiter delivered a platter of liver and cheese. "I've made you an appointment, at Altman's for tomorrow afternoon."

"Uptown?"

"On the Ladies' Mile."

"Because you're ashamed?"

"Because I mean to show off."

"Those are their scruples, not yours."

"To the contrary." Sam tore off a slice of the liver, salty and wet and brown. "It's the age in which we live, mother. We're all playing our part."

"It was this for which your father was felled?"

"That I might have a proper life, you mean? When he and his fellows could not?" Sam pointed to her plate. "I beg of you, ma – finish your lunch. Enjoy it. And whilst you're at it, enjoy your dress-shopping tomorrow. Enjoy the wedding too, if you can."

***

When the day arrived, he found her fidgeting in front of St. James as his carriage pulled up, catching his eye from beneath a cast-iron lamp. Her gown was violet and slim at the elbows, with white trim at the seams and a lace shawl wrapped round tight; her hair was tied in a braided chignon – and for a moment, skipping down to greet her, Sam wondered at the turns his mother's life might have taken, had there ever been a man tending to her properly. "The seamstresses knew their work," she acknowledged.

"They had a worthy client," he smiled back. The guests were inside already. Emily was on her way. "You're fixed to go?" So that she nodded gently – no more argument, it appeared – and he guided them into the church. She even gave his elbow a squeeze at the crowd: clients, colleagues, jammed across the whole brownstone nave.

The music emerged right on cue – the swell of the organ, the choir spreading out on top – and they moved up the aisle together, beneath the slender columns grasping skyward, while the guests grew hushed, and a black-cloaked rector stepped to the front. He was a doughy, dimple-faced man, with a kind smile and the hint of a stammer, and after Sam had deposited his mother in the pews, the fellow lifted his hands, and the bridesmaids glided in next, in gowns of gold, followed by the crochet-capped flower girls, and finally a smattering of withered Townsend relatives too: old enough to recall when weddings like this had been the province of royal European courts alone.

Finally, in came Emily herself.

Draped in orange blossoms, escorted by her father, she wore a veil thinner than seemed possible, and when she saw him looking, Sam was certain that she blushed. In later years, he would scarcely remember the exchange of the vows. He wouldn't remember the sound of the priest's voice, or how his mother dabbed at her eyes despite herself, or the way the steaming temperatures rose. He would recall only that this was the moment he felt truly complete, the moment when what was happening on the outside seemed to match what was within: his whole soul shaking with the approval of the city he called his own.

***

It was many hours later, then, after the guests had headed home – blue uniforms and black tailcoats tumbling into the dark, hoop skirts on the older wives, gowns on the younger – with no one able to remember a more glamorous or better-attended occasion, that the newlyweds at last found themselves alone. They shuffled upstairs to the top of the Union Club together, not far from the Church, along Persian-carpeted steps and toward the bridal suite above. Sam closed the oak door and turned. Emily wore a new bow necklace of diamonds, bestowed by one of her aunts downstairs – and he exhaled.

"I take that to mean you're contented?" she asked quietly.

He slid his arms around her sides, cool silk against his palms, kissing her gently on the cheek, and on the lips. "I've waited as long as I could," he whispered.

"I as well, Samuel."

And feeling her smile against him, he stepped to the four-post bed at their side, kissing her neck and shoulders and back as well, leading her to the quilt, sliding it away. Carefully then, he undid the bows that kept her dress together, and when his fingers fumbled, she slid from it herself, letting his eyes trail down from her face – until a moment later, she'd taken his shirt in turn, holding him tight, kissing his forehead and chest, and soon every other place.

In time, they lost all notion of being quiet, laughing when Sam's shoes fell to the floor, as he was able, for once, to focus on the here, the now – no thoughts at all of what was to come – perhaps because she was both. He kept her wrapped in his arms then, delighting in her soft hips as he'd always imagined he would, breathing in her scent, wanting never to leave, as she pulled him ever closer, and guided him inside.

CHAPTER 37

New York City
September, November 1903

Sam tapped his foot at the threshold of the apartment, looking between the lift and the entrance hall. He'd purchased the place the week of the wedding, one of the new Park Avenue standards, telephone booth by the door, electric lamps in every room, a grill house for whenever they called. It would be enough to hold them over, he'd thought, until the new home was ready, smoothing their first days together, offering whatever comforts they desired.

Alas. If only that'd been all they required!

He needed to go in there, he knew – to see her. But he took another breath first, eyeing the crown molding, steeling himself for what was to come. Only a week since the return from their bridal tour – traveling the Great White North, from Niagara to Montreal – and now, here he was. That morning, he'd been in the study, perusing the latest files from Hughes, not wanting to rush off while Emily was in the washroom, not without a proper goodbye.

Eventually, he'd stood, fastening his vest, gathering his bowler and cane, pacing by the door.

He'd given her another five minutes, then another ten – finally, a full half-hour.

Until the door had opened at last, and she'd appeared like a ghost. Her hair had hung limp, her face had seemed empty: cheeks sallow and sunken, eyes like smashed coals, lips weighed down from the aftershocks of sobs.

But the blood.

That had been most dire of all.

In an instant, it had turned to rust: like a dying fire, still dangerous, still crackling – still spreading across her silk gown, like muddy water in unsuspecting snow.

He hadn't even known she'd been pregnant.

"Emily," he'd managed, softly – firmly – fixed in near this same position at the door, still holding his cane, still wearing his hat. "I'm so terribly sorry."

She'd begun to weep in full, unable to bring herself closer, cut down to nothing.

So that he'd swallowed, placed down the cane at last – had moved straight towards her, had held her by the shoulders. "We'll be alright," he'd whispered then. "You'll be more than fine."

"But the baby," she'd mouthed. "There won't be any baby – "

"There shall," he'd assured her. "Of course there shall," he'd said. "Not now, not yet, but in time. Yet come, please – Emily –" And he'd taken her around the arm, and led her to the chaise lounge nearest the corner, at the edge of the living room, opposite the door, while he'd stepped back to the study, and phoned at once for a lady's doctor and nurses. They'd arrived in minutes, straight from the new offices at Mt. Sinai, satchel and instruments in hand, and Sam had breathed in relief as the team of women had turned to propping Emily up, getting her clean, while the physician had pledged she was in the most professional of hands.

He'd waited for the examination, had gotten it confirmed that the best thing now would be for her to rest and recover. It'd been then he'd stepped back towards the bedroom where she lay, lifting up her hand while the nurses had given him a moment, leaning over, kissing her cheek.

"You're not leaving?" she'd asked at that, her voice turned into barely more than a squeak, sounding like a poorly played flute.

"We'd better allow the ladies their work. They'll tend to you far better than I."

"Only that's not true, Samuel."

"But of course it is – you're in some delirium, Emily, naturally – but they'll help you eat, and drink, and I'll be with you soon my darling. I swear it," at which she'd nodded slowly, for of course he'd been right, and even in her state, she'd appeared clear-eyed enough to see it.

Somewhere in his mind, he'd wondered if perhaps somehow he was wrong instead – if what she needed most of all was simply to know he was there. But he'd thought better of that, brushing aside any hesitancy as mere sentiment, and had soon eased off, one last kiss atop her brow, rustling the edge of her dark hair with his breath.

After all, his aim in departing in fact lay far beyond her care. He'd stridden from the room then, and into the steamy late summer of the city, arriving at the office, nodding greetings to Finn, and Archie, and all the others, making all the calls he'd originally planned.

For after weeks of pressure, and years of waiting, he'd confirmed it: the property he'd sought, the one with the old house upon it, the one where Ulysses Brooke had buried his treasure, was finally his. By afternoon's end, he'd left his aides to conduct the day's shorts and sells without him, and had taken the walk straight up there, shaking hands with the laborers, checking on their schedule, until finally, when he was sure their work was under way, he'd allowed his mind to return where it ought always to have been.

Here.

His hand was already on the knob, and at last he pushed it open.

She looked up slowly from the bed, blinking through sopping eyes. Her hair at least had been combed – her nightgown from the morning gone, replaced by a clean silken one without creases – and when she saw him, she tried to swallow back her cries, wiping her face with the back of her wrist.

"It's alright," he offered, unable to find new words from the morning. "It's alright," he said yet again, pushing off the urge to walk back to the life outside, amid folks off to supper, and theater, and vaudeville, and pubs. "You needn't pretend, Emily."

She nodded against his chest, gripping the tweed of his suit, hair loosened once more upon his shoulder, and he leaned his chin atop her head, closing his eyes, waiting a long minute, then another – breathing deeply, slowly – wondering if he ought just keep quiet, before finally tilting back, and meeting her eye.

"I have another bit of news."

She blinked. "Not another journey?"

"Not that, no." He paused. "Something good. Something grand. A new chance, Emily, I swear it. A new life." He lifted her hands to his, and held them close. "I've started on the property at last." And though she still didn't react, didn't give him near the smile he'd hoped for, Sam was certain it would do her good – do them both good – and he brought her in close once more, and held her there, to stay until night had fallen, and sleep had come, and this terribly laden day had released them at last.

***

The icy breeze seemed appropriate, as the last of the old house came tumbling down, copper sills crashing like dried up twigs, splintered porch planks warped like blown glass, all of it turned into a bundle something like barbed wire. Men were hauling bits off in their steam-powered carriages, leaving only tufts of soil, brown and splotchy and wet, like crop mounds missing their harvest. There were cracked stones too, from the ruined foundation, dug up and spit out, all part of Sam's heaving, desperate, exorbitant fixation.

And now, he knew, every last bit of it for naught.

Emily was at his side, narrow chin tucked behind her cashmere scarf. It was a new ritual of theirs, really, wandering up like this on weekends, standing here amid the damp New York air, eyeing the mass of machines and men – black and white together, sweat-drenched despite the chill – bespectacled architects too, scurrying over with their blueprints, each trying to out-impress the others, showing where this or that portico might go, how a tower could stand, whether there ought be a chimney here or there.

At first, Sam had tried it the old way, just in case: following the book of maps, scraping the dirt himself, on the chance there might actually be a buried box of iron or a pile of antique coins. Eventually, he'd resorted to what he'd gathered from the etchings all along, that Brooke's treasure had never been beside the old house here at all, but directly beneath it, that the only thing left was to tear the whole thing down, no matter that winter was near, or that plans were still incomplete for replacing it. Ever since, he'd been passing extra cash to the contractors every chance he could, asking them to keep an eye out for anything odd – a chest, a sack, even century-old tools – urging them not to discard any scraps, explaining he was simply interested in the history of the place, knowledge of the grounds, he said, to share with future guests.

Now, he frowned at the emptiness, an oasis at the heart of the city's wonder. And not a hint of treasure.

"I still can't fathom it, Samuel."

But he waved that aside. "You deserve a finer home than any that exists, my darling. As I've told you." He could hear the tightness of his own voice, the dishonesty woven in. "We'll wire the entire thing. We'll install elevators on either side."

"For heaven's sake, what more is left that you must show off to the world?"

"There's always more."

Yet Emily's eyes had flitted away. "What about those, then?" She was pointing to the hydraulic excavators, bordering the old foundation. "Are they too part of some contest? To see which of you bankers and brokers can plant your footprint the deepest?"

He shrugged, and tried a smile. The truth was, he'd ordered the whole property re-graded, bribing the city regulators to look the other way, while he lowered his entire block. He'd justified it to the contractors saying he aimed for a wine cellar – had ordered the most powerful diggers yet invented, steam cylinders only, no cables or chains to hold them back – all in the name of making sure for himself that the treasure really had been lost to time. It was becoming his own private Moby Dick, he'd thought.

Perhaps he ought to be relieved then. To see the truth at last: that he needn't ever have concerned himself with this plot at all. That whatever had been here no longer was – probably dug up ages ago – some fellow no doubt finding himself rich many years before, a builder perhaps, who'd helped construct the original home, taking his secret all the way to Heaven. No chance left, then, for someone to discover evidence of what Sam was actually up to.

Or maybe, he'd started to wonder, here was a deeper signal altogether. A terrible hint that he was losing control, a warning at least, that soon enough he would be, unless he escaped his own obsession. He didn't yet know how he could, but there it lay before him: some new kind of purpose, he thought, percolating at the edges of his mind. Some new, better way for moving forward.

"I promise you," he offered now. "We shan't regret this." He winked. "You believe me, darling?"

"I love you," she responded. "And I suppose that's enough."

Sam nodded. And though he knew the workers would see, he gave her a fine kiss at that.

"Just tell me we'll move in by Christmas, Sam."

He grinned. "If it's next Christmas you mean, then you have my word," and chuckling for the first time in a long while, he led her back to the street.

CHAPTER 38

New York City
November 1904

He'd surprised himself with the urge to cry.

He couldn't even remember the last time he had. Perhaps not since the war, not since being a lad himself, missing his own father, maybe even when he'd learned the old man was gone.

Now, though, Sam found himself shaking: hiding like a skittish mouse, in the dumbwaiter corridor of the new central hall, one hand on the rope pulley, the other cupping his forehead, blinking back tears all the while, catching his breath as best he could. He'd kept himself in order all evening, sipping from a wide tumbler of whiskey outside the bedroom, keeping it slow so he wouldn't be drunk, nodding at updates from the nursemaids, clenching his fists with each new sound. Even when news had finally arrived of baby Charles' arrival, well past midnight, he'd stayed composed, offering cigars to the butlers, clapping the doctor on the back, bounding in to go meet his son.

It was then, though, something had changed – from somewhere deep in his chest, surprising him, gripping his throat – so that he'd had to clutch the wooden base of the bed, and Emily had even asked if he was alright. He'd mumbled something about not having eaten, his eyes fixed all the while on the scrunched little face, burrowed in her arms, the crocheted blue quilt beneath that tiny pointed chin – a touch like hers, he'd managed to think – and for a single, overwhelming instant, the whole of the night, and all the nights before that, had come rushing down upon him.

How different life had become! – since his own first moments, since he'd been an infant himself: when there had been war in the air, and doctors with no idea at all how to help. His own mother had spoken of how the church bells had clanged that day, the lines stretching out from the Western Union offices as news trickled in from Washington. The winds of war had been blowing for weeks of course, but on the very day of his birth, all had finally been lost: Virginia had joined its Dixie brethren. The news had traveled up from the streets, boys hawking headlines the instant they were written, voices shriller than ever, crowds denser than on the busiest market days. None of the usual haggling over fruits and rents, or arguments between the Germans and the Irish, no sailors telling tales of ports, or schoolchildren squealing over jacks and hoops: every conversation instead funneled into one, rumors of a draft, announcements about where to enlist.

Sam, then, had entered life straight into chaos: a nation that no longer knew its own soul, news so big that the only two people in the world who'd cared about his arrival were the ones who'd been right there with him. His mother, panting with joy; his father at the door.

There'd been a very tall bed apparently, oil lamps on the mantle, bright violet wall paper, still some money coming in from the furniture shop back then. The smell of blood, metallic and heavy, must've been relieved when a nighttime breeze finally came blowing in, snuffing out the candles – while pa, accepting congratulations from the hall, must just as certainly have grown distracted himself, wanting to know what Lincoln had to say, how many troops would be called up, when they'd be reporting, enough so that he'd had to have been called in twice, then three times, just to bring in the matches. At last, mother had always recalled, he'd paused at the bed: waves of dark hair falling across his face as he'd leaned in, gently cupping the face of his new infant son, softening the little lad's sobs, as the boy had looked up in reply. "I'm glad I made it back in time," he was said to have whispered. "To have gotten to meet you, little Samuel. For whilst I was off making plans, you were the object of them, you see."

And now, Sam thought in turn, here, his own son: staffed and served already, scarcely another babe in the world born into circumstances as luxuriant as this – after the miscarriage, and more waiting, the fears that time had passed them by – and he suddenly wanted to punch through the space before him, to scream in triumph and exhaustion and terror and grace that his was the one, the boy who'd have it all. The sobs convulsed him louder, wilder, the more he tried to keep them quiet, until at last he brought a rolled-up sleeve to his eyes, and took in a long, wobbling breath. No longer just Sam Billings, he realized, the man he'd worked so hard to become, but rather the father of Charles, as he stepped back into the hall.

The passageway gleamed. There was gray quarried stone from France, and Indiana lime for the floor;

chandeliers from crystal ropes, and ribbons made of glass. The radiators were clanging, maids' quarters situated straight through, and Sam imagined how it all would look to his young son: endless secret pathways, spinning off like a labyrinth, to be discovered with wonder.

As the next run of days and nights passed by, he spent them in a similar state, making arrangements for Charlie's future – new trusts, wills, testaments – overseeing the last of the house's touch-ups too: paint in the nursery, more nannies, cooks, gardeners. He marveled at Emily all the while, as she stuffed the crib with 'Teddy Bears,' the newest fad ushered in by the president himself, worked to face the baby north, his nervous system to be aligned with electrical currents, made sure to buy the finest of soothing syrups at the pharmacy. Sam could feel the tug of the brokerage, to be sure, the questions from his advisors pinging away, a hankering, now that the house was done, to find something else to build, and expand his fortune ever further. Yet even so, when they were all three together, gathered in the soft light, or watching Charles sleep, it was as if he could almost understand, finally at least, what it was he'd actually been striving for.

It was nearly Thanksgiving then, when his mother came unannounced. She'd met baby Charles already, but Sam had been off at the firm, and now, on a Saturday afternoon, the butler rang that he should come on down. He readied himself for asides about all the extravagance, and whether it was too much, reminding himself she had a right to visit, forcing a smile, opening his arms to greet her.

She appeared even frailer than usual. Her shawl was matted to her shoulders, the same gray as the clouds. Her white hair had been loosed by the wind, cheeks chapped from the chill. "'Morning, Samuel," she said, and he could see her struggling not to gaze past right past him, toward the spiral staircase and its ten-foot railings, the painted ceiling, and the muffled patter of servants.

"Charlie's sleeping," he explained. "Second story, then to the right, you remember."

She offered a clipped nod, and stepped in. "I'll sit with him 'til he wakes. For time is fleeting, Samuel – you musn't forget. No matter how vast a man's fortune." And she removed her shawl, ignoring the footmen who'd emerged to help.

"That'll be fine, mother. No lecture required."

"It's not that I don't honor your success, Samuel. To the contrary. I still can't fathom how you did it – " and for a moment, she was looking at him harder than before, so that he wondered: was she asking? "Only are you happy, Sam?" she wanted to know. "For any of it?"

This time, he scoffed, aware of the staff, ears ever attuned. "You just said it yourself, ma: I'm the face of the age."

"And that's happiness?"

"It's what's possible." Though it was then the baby let out a wail, lungs crackling, voice piping and shrill, and they both angled their heads. "Go," he said next, more softly.

And with a new warmth in her eyes – as though she'd recollected something lovely, and distant – his mother turned now indeed, and went up to see.

CHAPTER 39

New York City
March 1905

He hadn't been here since the wedding.

That had been Sam's first thought upon entering: that he ought to at least have attended services for Christmas and Easter. And now, looking up at St. James' dome, he couldn't help but think the gray stone was blander than he recalled.

He blinked, and faced his shoes once more, running through the last time he'd seen his mother, unable to parse if she'd known then that she was dying – or whether she'd been planning on telling him. Probably not, he thought. She wouldn't have deemed it worthy of the trouble.

The news had arrived over the wire, soulless, and to the point. He recalled the ink smeared on his desk, jammed up against the other letters delivered by the clerk. The poor woman had died alone. With all his damned resources – the telephone code of every doctor's office in the city, funds to buy her a whole hospital wing of her own – she'd died in her tenement, stubborn to the last. The coroner's slip had cited lung fever, and sepsis. But to Sam, it had been simpler. The cause had been neglect.

He didn't suppose a grand funeral could make up for that. But he'd set out to try. All along, she'd resisted his life uptown. Now he could say he'd gotten her here in the end. Half the city seemed to have shown, festooned in mourning dresses and tails, faces solemn, and Sam was satisfied. That he could beckon them, and they would come.

He turned and faced Emily, rocking a sleeping Charles in her arms, patting his round little shoulders, and the pink of his neck, and he imagined his mother had once done the same for him.

Then, when it was time for the burial itself, he marched in procession with the rest, eastward to the cemetery. Plots in Manhattan had become endangered, but he'd written a pair of four-figure checks, and had managed a family vault: a mausoleum at the far edge of the yard, its marble as wide as a cottage, the finest of pilasters, cherry blossoms engraved in high relief. "BILLINGS," the center slab declared, for upon purchase, he'd decided to honor them both.

This wasn't what they'd have imagined, of course: his father, bleeding out on some forlorn Virginian field, no doubt begging the heavens for mercy; his mother, scoffing at any such pageantry at all. But was it not what they'd earned? "*In dedication to an American soldier,*" the inscription read. "*Who laid down his life, that others might flourish in theirs.*" Sam had written it himself, steering clear of any flag-waving – enough of all that, he'd thought, all the rivers of blood, and libations poured to the idol of war – saying what he meant instead. "*And his devoted wife, Eliza. As fine a lady of New York as could be, bearing its struggle, and its strength."*

And he watched now as the workers hauled in the gleaming iron casket, using thick bights of rope, lifting the new stones like precious blocks of ice.

CHAPTER 40

New York City
September 1913

Word came by messenger that Sam was wanted at the bank. Its headquarters had transferred uptown, and the cab ride would be brief. What's more, this was an invitation from the man who'd first helped him; he owed his whole life to this bank and the fellow Bart Maynard behind it – keeper of secrets even now, depositing every cent of his antique cash. Still, Sam had never actually been called in unprompted before, and as he entered the gleaming lobby, a towering behemoth more like antiquity's temples than any American countinghouse, he steeled himself for bad news, even confronting the notion that a piece of his funds had somehow been misplaced in the bank's move.

"Mr. Billings!" Here was a young, anxious chap, in a red bowtie and sparkling spats. "This way, sir."

"Do tell, young man – you were awaiting me?"

At which the fellow looked back with surprise, blue eyes darting, as if seeking out exactly what it was Sam wanted to hear. "We're receiving all of Mr. Maynard's clients this week, sir. You were fixed right at the top of the list, if you don't mind my saying."

They moved swiftly then, down a maze of mahogany halls, stopping at an office in the rear. A fine walnut desk was at its center, glass-shaded lamps crowding the corners; on the mantle, a radium clock, dispensing an unnatural green glow.

Then, coming in from the far side, a figure Sam didn't recognize. He had a cleft that made his chin look split in two, and a nose near as big as a fist. His gray hair was thick, his winking gaze bright, and he sported a bold-striped shirt as he extended his hand. "Sam," he began, in a voice that snapped like twine. "You don't remember me."

"Where's my usual man?"

But the fellow exhaled. "My father's passed on."

So that now Sam stared, and found he had to lean against the back of a chair – suddenly confronted by a vague memory, images of a bounding boy from his school days, young and sharp-tongued, nothing like this beefier picture standing before him now. It was enough that for a short, impossible instant, every moment since then seemed to flicker, and fade, and vanish away, as if not one had been more than a mirage.

"It's me," the banker nodded. "Bart Jr.," and he gestured that they sit.

"My condolences," Sam managed, even as he cursed himself inwardly. He'd always assumed Maynard Sr. would've retired, that there'd be some warning at least, were he ever to fall ill. Some time for getting affairs in order. Nothing like this. Nothing without any warning at all.

"Not to worry, Sam," Bart said then, as both of them lowered down. "I'm a faithful son."

"You've been toiling at the bank all this time?" Sam couldn't remember seeing him – couldn't recall Maynard ever once mentioning it.

"I was in our Newark branches, over in Jersey; my father felt I oughtn't advance solely on account of my connection." He shrugged. "Yet here I am."

"Here you are."

"I expect we'll see you at the funeral?"

"Most certainly. With a heavy heart."

Bart nodded once more, hands folded atop the smooth desk, face in shadow. "Well, Samuel. You should know in turn: I'm content with the arrangement you already had with pa."

"Which was what?"

"Come now. I've said you needn't worry."

"Words that usually portend the opposite."

Maynard chuckled softly. "Your 'treasures,' my father called them."

And crossing his legs, Sam took a breath. He knew when he had no leverage. After all, it was a rare enough sensation.

"Spinning your antique loot into proper gold, Billings, dispersing it through the bank's coffers without a trace. All whilst your reputation bloomed. He adored your American tale, Sam, 'a gentleman of his own making,' he liked to say – had faith I'd keep it quiet too, once he'd roped me in. Even thanked me for introducing you two in the first place. Or don't you recall that either?"

Sam wasn't sure that he did. Either way, he thought, he'd been betrayed.

Bart was scratching his chin. "I'll ask no extra odds, then." His eyes hadn't budged. "That is, aside from the allowance pa already made his own."

But at that, Sam swallowed stiffly. There'd never been any allowance for Maynard Sr. – not as far as he knew anyway. He'd monitored the interest all along, had confirmed the conversion rates aloud, had even looked past the occasional discrepancy since the coin values weren't precise. No library or ledger was capable of agreeing upon inflation figures from generations before, after all. And so he'd never raised it.

Besides, hadn't it been the old man who'd made everything possible? Taking Sam under his wing – fondly recalling Sam's own father – even planting the very notion of the treasures in the first place? Sam could picture the firm clasp of his hand, a free offer of counsel, pledges of discretion: all those years ago, inquiring after his studies, checking in on the brokerage. Could it all have been for the chance at a little extra gold on the side? A mere deal between associates? Grooming Sam as his mark?

And all at once, he began to feel the fool.

As if frozen in youth's credulity, he thought. Already, the wound was beginning to fester, his instincts moving into gear to contain it. He felt himself nodding – his decision winnowing into place, rationalized, ready to be executed – with the same purr and efficiency of the city around them. For he was nursing a new anger now: not at these Maynards, he realized, but rather, towards himself, as he smoothed the top of his trousers, cooling his thoughts, facing his own mind.

For what if it had indeed been a transaction all that time? An illusion of goodwill?

Then so be it. Transactions were where he thrived.

"Very well," he exhaled. "The existing rate. But from here on out – " and he sat forward, and met his new banker's eye – "I desire it in writing."

Bart Jr. merely shrugged and opened a drawer, pulling out a wooden dip pen with a golden nib. Swirling the ink, he simply wrote out the number "*4*" on a small square of paper. A record of their deed, too vague ever to bother either one of them in court, yet clear enough that neither one could ever forget it. "Four percent," he said aloud, scribbling his name. "My services for converting old money to new. Counted against the sum you receive in turn."

"It's high."

"It's matched to treasury."

"General rates were closer to three when I started with your pa."

But Bart ignored him, and passed over the pen.

CHAPTER 41

New York City
November 1982

There were days when New York got in the way. Days when the wind was bracing, yanking at Alvin's hair, revealing his receding temples for the whole world to see, while the stench of rotted fish butted in from every corner. Days when he'd been spat upon by the smack-addled vets at the subway, and forced to flash his badge before it got rough; when what folks called a melting pot, just seemed like noise.

Not that any of it would have bothered him, if he weren't still smarting from the latest meeting at the bureau. "It's time," Claire Calloway had snapped – as if he were a child, and she were performing the role of grizzled old cop. "It's been time for far too long, Starkman. You need to be fighting honest-to-God crime."

"There's still a path toward justice," he'd countered.

"By going after men long gone? By hounding Charles Billings? And wrecking his philanthropy?"

Now, re-playing it in his mind, registering that Calloway had clearly tired of funding his pursuits, Alvin barely noticed when he'd reached home. Not until he looked up, and saw Faye sitting on their stoop. She wore a paisley scarf atop her sweater, and her hair was crowded in by earmuffs.

He smiled, despite his mood. "It's still just fall, you know."

"Fall always ends badly."

"How 'bout some hot chocolate then?"

"Is that what you're calling me now?"

He laughed. "So what is it? Why you out here shivering?"

"I didn't want to say something 'til I was sure." Her face was vivid in the gray. "It's been three months now, Alvin."

He stepped closer, studying her expression. "You're not serious."

But slowly, she was taking his hands, placing them gently above her waist. "I see the doctor next week. I've already taken one of those new tests."

And it was then the world seemed to swoon. He swallowed, searching for new words. "Aren't you happy?"

"I want to be."

"But?"

"What if we can't do this?"

He gestured down the block. "Look at all the idiots. Raised by idiots. Raising idiots."

Her smile, however, was gone. "You still don't see, Alvin. Not really."

"See what?"

"What it's like to be me. In this city, Alvin. In this country – " he'd opened his mouth to respond – "Don't." And she let go his hands. "Don't try and explain. I already know what you'll say."

"Well you'd better tell me then, Faye, so I can know too."

"You still believe in people. In this world of ours." She looked back. "In America."

"And you don't?"

"How can I?"

"After Richmond, you mean?" He thought back to those men in the pickup.

"After anywhere. Haven't you noticed I've never gotten promoted to a better desk at the museum? That your salary's been lapping mine?"

"So we do what we can to fix it. You, me. It's why I work at the bureau in the first place."

"So you always say."

"To make it better for that baby."

She snorted.

"To make it better for everyone. We've seen it happen already! In our own lives. Real strides – " He saw her turn away, but tried to press on. "Because we know how things used to be, Faye – how we can't ever let them be again." There was a tear in her eye, he realized, and he paused.

"Why not start by being here with us, Alvin? By being with your family?"

Again, he hesitated, knowing she was on Claire Calloway's side when it came to letting go of the case.

"I take that as a no, Alvin?"

"I can't."

"You won't give up the traveling?"

He took back her hand. "No," he answered. "I won't give up on believing."

***

Her water broke in the restroom of a restaurant.

They'd gone to "Curry Hill" for lunch, a line-up of Indian canteens west of the Flatiron. The doctor had said there'd be another week to wait, but a girlfriend at the museum had given Faye an article about the power of spicy food, and she'd decided why not give it a try?

The meal had been a revelation: lentils rich as chocolate, sauces bright as Christmas, and at some point, Faye had ordered them extra peppers, so that Alvin had requested a whole new pitcher of water. She'd burst out laughing and excused herself to the toilet.

He'd gulped from his glass while he'd waited, losing himself in the view out the window. A city in search of its old whimsy, he'd thought: bars on the doors, graffiti on the walls. Hippies grown up and erased, hatchbacks on the curbs stripped of any fun. Until he'd turned around and seen Faye shuffling back. She was standing in front of him, one hand on her hip, the other holding her purse atop her belly.

"You alright?"

"We'd better go." She'd yanked a twenty-dollar bill from the purse, plopping it down without waiting for change.

The cab ride to the hospital had been quick. From there, the first hours had gone slow, Faye sipping from an enormous plastic mug, even reading a magazine, while Alvin had paced. It hadn't been until the city was quieting outside that her labor had begun in earnest: an escalation he'd later recall in snippets – a doctor, gray at the temples, a tie caught in his lab coat, a nurse with a cough, urging Faye to breathe – the moment when the room had suddenly grown full.

The doctor had tapped a small button on the bedside, and Alvin had watched the door open from the hall: new figures swarming in, some with clipboards, others wearing white gloves. "What's all this, doc?" he'd pressed. "What are they all doing here?"

Until finally, from beside Faye's bed, someone had muttered the answer in his ear, "please, sir, let us just do our jobs," while someone else – med student? another nurse? – had leaned over and announced, "you're in good hands." All the while, more folks were coming in, and Alvin stretched past their shoulders as if he were a boy again, straining for a glimpse at a parade.

Faye was panting – cursing – and he tried to catch her eye, to offer a clumsy wink, and stupidly, a wave. His own stomach was churning, his heart thumping back at him. When suddenly, the doctor in charge was lifting a pair of forceps, tugging and twisting as though he were yanking out a mere stone and not the most precious thing in the entire world – until then – as if by magic –

Wet hazel hair, chestnut skin. And silence.

Alvin stared, lost at sea: the world split in half – every moment up to this one falling away – the doctors gone quiet now too, even the beeps from the machines seeming to have stopped. And like soldiers lifting a limp flag, they hoisted the little body onto an aluminum tray all its own, placing the brand new boy down like a rag doll. His thin little lips were blue, and Alvin, laid bare by the whisper of hope, blinked back.

He hadn't even seen the tray enter – had someone wheeled it in? had it been there all along? – and gradually, it dawned on him that the whole team had shifted places: only one person standing alongside Faye now, smoothing back her hair, monitoring her numbers on a black screen, while the rest were moving as one, like birds across the sky, wedged so tight round the baby, that Alvin couldn't join in.

Faye was opening her mouth, wanting to ask something, he realized, eyes soaked, sweat caked against her cheeks, and he knew he'd remember this instant forever – the pale gray of the walls, the blaring light – as he murmured something about it turning out alright, as he glimpsed one of the men sliding – jamming – a tube into the infant's tiny throat.

When as if from nowhere, he heard it.

A yelp.

A perfect little yelp.

It was from the baby, he was sure. And he felt his whole body stiffen, Faye's hand gripping his own from the bed, tighter and tighter, so tight his fingers turned numb, and then the baby was being wheeled out, off to another floor, and someone was calling back, "he's going to be okay," so that Alvin wanted to shout after them with gratitude, managing only a quick nod instead, looking back at Faye, and repeating it – "he'll be okay" again and again – not sure if she'd caught it too, needing anyway to hear it himself – "the nurse said, he'll be okay."

He watched her eyes close then, one final doctor behind them, lingering, filling out a form, making sure the numbers were right. For several long minutes, Alvin just stayed hunched, not sure when to move, or even if he should, when at last, that doctor was gone too, wishing them a good night.

He found a restroom then, making his way in, closing the door slowly to the stall. Ignoring the industrial toilet, he leaned against a green-tile wall at its side, surprising himself as he felt a sob come down upon him, engulfing him, echoing off the corners – wracking his body: the relief of what had happened, the terror over what nearly had not – and deciding to let it be, he buried his face in his sleeve, muffling the sounds as he leaned against his own knees, and waited until he was done.

***

They met their son for real that afternoon.

Faye was rested, propped up on a pair of starchy pillows, assigned to the hospital's tenth floor, above the white-cresting East River. The windows faced the twin towers further down, ugly imposters on the old skyline, Alvin observed, striving arrogantly toward the sun.

The room's door squeaked open, and he turned back.

It was the gray-haired doctor from before – the same man who'd done the delivery, who'd later come back in, after the birth, and explained that the baby's shoulder had gotten caught, that he'd be healed in no time – only this time his tie was newly loosened, his white coat unbuttoned. And with a flick of his hand, he motioned Alvin to come to the hall.

Dr. Beck was his name, and he nodded as they stepped out together. He was taller than Alvin had realized – vain too, his skin bronzed from a tanning bed, pale, ugly half-moons beneath his eyes. "The baby's just fine," he said now, with the command of a network newscaster. "Breathing, crying, taking formula all on his own. They'll be wheeling him over any time." Only then did he pause. "I did, however, want to be sure someone told you – sooner rather than later," and his voice dropped lower – sterner, colder – into that same tone lawyers and cops and judges all shared too, usually for when they were about to bring down the hammer.

Alvin folded his arms.

Dr. Beck cleared his throat quietly, and peered down his long nose. "Your wife won't be having any more children," he said at last, holding his words steady, as if he were intent on keeping this just a business chat between men. "The delivery was complicated, as you know."

"Why?" Alvin answered at once – not quite meaning to raise his volume.

"Her canal's a touch narrow," the doctor went on, with a hint of a sigh, as if it were almost something to be expected.

"You're not blaming her?"

"Certainly not," Dr. Beck replied. "Some things, sir – they just aren't meant to be."

Alvin squinted back.

"If you'll excuse me – I'll leave you to consider it."

"Just a minute, doc." Alvin blinked, as a new thought bubbled to the fore. He was aware of Faye waiting behind them, back in the room, and all at once, it was as if he could recall all she'd ever shared with him, all she'd ever told him about white folks the way that she'd seen them. She'd warned him about this, after all – warned him it would affect their new son – and here it was, on the boy's very first day of life, the rest of Alvin's life too, he realized, and he stepped forward. "What about Faye, then – my wife? Won't you be telling her the news as well?"

"We do have nurses, sir: ones we assign, those best able to speak with her, you understand."

Alvin understood indeed.

He took a breath to stay calm, tasting bile in his mouth, not sure what more to say, knowing a flash of his badge would do nothing but make an enemy he didn't need.

Except then – had he been too quick to judge? – something seemed to shift in Dr. Beck: he was watching Alvin in turn, meeting his eye. He waited – and instead of continuing on his way, he rubbed his chin, and exhaled. "Look, Mr. Starkman – "

"Agent Starkman."

"NYPD?"

"FBI."

Dr. Beck nodded once more. "I hope you know – whatever my own views – I would never let them affect the care I provide."

Alvin listened, gaping back, wanting to punch the fellow square in the jaw. The guy spoke as if he deserved a damned medal for doing his job, praise for not penalizing a patient for marrying across the color line, for God's sake. It was as though he were the victim of circumstance, and not the perpetrator himself.

What would Faye say to any of this, he wondered? But he only bit his tongue further, and extended his hand. Not because he didn't believe in the fight, he realized. But because he wanted the best for his wife, and his new baby. "I appreciate it, Doctor. I'll thank you for taking care of us."

Beck delayed an extra moment, as if he couldn't quite detect whether that was sarcasm.

"My wife will be alright otherwise?"

"She will."

Watching him go, Alvin finally turned back, and peeked again into Faye's room. Sure enough, a nurse was now seated at her side, just as advertised – a black one, to be sure – chatting softly, holding hands. He stood in the door a long moment, watching this conversation just out of reach, Faye's eyes growing moist once more, as it became clear she understood: that this baby, the one she hadn't even yet held, would be her last.

The nurse stood back up – a short woman in blue scrubs, possessing more years than the two of them put together – before offering Alvin a brief nod as she passed, her chunky white sneakers squeaking against the linoleum.

He walked over next, taking her place, and saw the swirl of tears darkening Faye's pupils.

"They told you too?" she asked.

"I'm so sorry, Faye," and he lowered himself down, and kissed her softly on the forehead.

She bit her lip, and looked away, and they stayed there like that in quiet, listening to their own breaths – until once again, the door swung open behind them, and the baby was carted in.

He was wrapped tight, sleeping, breathing just fine now, a hint of pink behind the soft brown of his cheeks. And as the nurse passed him over, Faye began instantly to weep. "You're beautiful," she whispered, right as the baby opened his eyes to see, then arched his back as if trying to look all around, making a sound somewhere between a fart and a gurgle.

Despite themselves, they both laughed.

"He's ours," Alvin murmured.

"He is. A little boy."

Alvin petted the baby's brow, smoothing back the dark waves of his hair, so thin he could scarcely feel them. "What'll we call him?"

Faye didn't look up this time. She nuzzled her nose down instead, rubbing it against their son's little temple. "I did have a thought."

"After your father?" Alvin had sensed it, he realized, before she'd even said something. Her pop's name had been Dexter – a sturdy name, a strong name – and gazing upon the fragile, scrunched face before them, he was certain: the right name too.

Faye was nodding quietly. "Welcome to the world, little Dex," she said. "It's not such a bad place, all this," and she glanced over. "Your daddy even likes to say it's sure to get better from here."

CHAPTER 42

Gloucester, Virginia – September

1983

Alvin had resented the bureau's new sessions on counterfeiting, part of the endless training they were all being shoved into these days, no matter their expertise: reviewing ink color and check size, paper strength and sturdiness. It had been a full week long, every minute of it in a seminar room without windows, with a sleepy-eyed lecturer who'd spat when he'd talked.

Little had Alvin known: it was also about to change everything.

For after it was finished, and another week begun, he'd confronted something new, a notion that he'd missed something – something he couldn't quite place – something he hadn't even known to look for. The original book of maps had been sitting in the Evidence Room all these years, decaying ever further in the bowels of the bureau building. But with the seminar fresh in his mind, and sensing he'd learned something despite himself, Alvin decided to go and see the thing once more.

He signed it out and brought it to his desk. And it was there indeed – reaching the back of the book, when he was almost done flipping through – that he found just what he was after: a double-width sheet. One he'd simply never noticed before.

He gripped it tight between his thumb and his forefinger, using the training he'd only just completed, and carefully, delicately, he dabbed with his nail, prying loose the brittle material without making it crumble. It was like petrified wood – browned, melded together – but after some time, he managed, getting his nail underneath a drooping corner, then its entire edge, peeling it back, eventually undoing the whole length of the binding.

He stared.

On the back, he could see a whole other map, apparently torn away, then glued back in, so that it hadn't looked separate at all. *Gloucester, Virginia*, the caption declared, its etchings long since faded, too faint for shining through to the other side. It'd been drawn entirely in Ulysses Brooke's hand, Alvin realized. Nothing in Samuel's. And he wondered: could it really be?

He raced to the photocopier, then phoned Faye, pledging he'd be back in time for Dexter's feeding at midnight. And so it was: he was soon cramming his foot against the gas, shooting down Route 95, until Virginia's loping green hills were sprinting by. By then, he'd been pulled over twice – using his badge to escape the tickets – each time quickly rattling the engine once more. Past ramshackle gun shops, and half-hidden signs for corn, overgrown sunflowers and hedges of briar and berry, the colonial roads were all long gone, grown over with fields and sliced through by shops. But the coordinates were alive and well. And trusting his compass, Alvin arrived upon a gravel lot at last, less than a mile from the spot where he needed to be.

Gloucester Pie, a homemade sign declared, hanging over a glorified shack, with a shingled roof and a pair of screen doors. The air was softened by late summer. Distant lawns were speckled with brown silos and crumbling barns; dented cars had been left to sunbathe on un-mowed lawns. Young folks were wandering in, with flared jeans and heavy-metal t-shirts, ordering at a pizza counter amid wood-paneled walls; inside, the air was soaked with salt and burnt yeast and the simmer of tomatoes; college kids were doing the serving. They all looked like hippies, beamed in from Haight Ashbury a dozen years before: long hair and bandanas, tie-dyed aprons, earrings on some of the fellows as well as the ladies.

Alvin ordered a slice for himself. Then, fetching his shovel, he stepped from the lot, over a two-tiered fence at its border, and into a sloping meadow of wild grass and purple blossoms. Brooke had marked a line somewhere near, a nexus of forest and field, sketching in a woodland of elms, amid rolling bare farmland. Now, Alvin felt a shiver amid the warmth, almost as if his body knew he were gaining on the steps of a ghost – for the first time without another ghost in between to block them.

He found a stretch of barbed-wire, twisted, low to the ground, wholly untended, and realized he was holding his breath. Somewhere, a wren was bellowing, rasping and endless, undoing the peace, and he looked all around. No longer any forest to be seen, it was true – but what if these wire remnants tracked some old wooden predecessor? He checked the grade of the land, counted his paces, re-checked his coordinates too, did everything possible to follow Ulysses Brooke's instructions.

Then he started to dig.

It was easy going at first – caked top-soil, tufts of grass flying back – though when the ground firmed up, he had to jam his sneaker upon the shovel's edge, pushing with his chest, until eventually he was down on his knees, using his hands, careful of the wire at his side. His fingers cramped, and he spat to moisten the red earth. His breaths grew labored. Out came pebbles and worms. Finally, he grazed something smooth.

Sliding his fingers along its edge, Alvin shifted his strategy once more. He raised the shovel back up, working to get under it, to wrest the whole thing loose, leaning on the stem, ignoring the sting from his sweat – when at last, just as he was worrying he'd never manage, there was a small pop, and the earth let go.

Alvin let the shovel drop. This was some kind of metal, he thought, cloaked in rust and soil, and he wrapped his arms around it like a graverobber lifting his loot. He stumbled then, nearly fell, and started brushing it off. The walls had gone brown; there were streaks of black at the corners. Latched belts gripped the top, a kind of hammered iron. He undid the fasteners one at a time, tapping their tiny hitches to knock loose the dust, shimmying the top, and slowly, the lid creaked open.

He peered closer.

There were stacked coins inside – so tidy they looked to have been laid down that very morning – wrapped in thin sacks of brown cloth, nearly rotted through. Each one was the size of a quarter, some of them oxidized at the edges and turned to smoky gray, others with muted green splotches like pellets of rain, every one fully intact.

He reached in, and one of the drawstrings came undone at his touch, the old twine crumbling to nothing. He raised the first coin up, letting it see the sky. *Five dollars*, the lettering said – block capitals, slightly off-center – with stars round the rim. The word *Liberty* was stenciled in as well, and when he turned it over, he found the outline of an eagle, spread wide, ushering in the nation's name itself – *United States of America* – right across the top.

He looked back down and did the math. There was a fortune here, even by modern standards, enough that Ulysses Brooke really could have managed a revolution with it, and plenty for Sam Billings in turn – had he ever made it down here – all in this box alone, in the one spot Billings had never found.

It was all a jury would ever need.

The book of maps was real. It was more than mere pages, scribbles and rumors, empty journeys or wishful thinking. It was a blueprint. Drawn by a radical. Used to fuel a brokerage, and finally, a Trust.

Alvin sat there some time after that, letting the sun burn him, blinking in a daze: at the work, the leads, all the years – wanting to feel like an inmate finally freed, wondering why instead he felt like a man exiled.

For what was he to do now?

After all that, if this was what was true – then how, now, to get toward what was right?

1842

It was on account of Cato's knees, Ulysses thought, that he'd had to leave his friend behind. Ulysses was old himself too, of course – tired – though until his own knees gave out in turn, he knew he'd never quit. So it was, he thought: he was alone. For the first time in ages.

His mother – ever more infirm, all but bound to her bed and cared for by the house slaves – had been reliant upon him for years, managing Boxwood's ledgers in full. Now it was finally time for making good, seeing through on this next step, the latest, truest step in his scheme.

Ever since he'd been granted executor power, he'd withdrawn the family's funds gradually, steadily, in small sums so as not to call attention – pulling them from scattered counting houses along the Piedmont, storing the arriving cash in a compact iron chest, at the corner of his father's old study. Until finally, when its inner compartment was filled entirely, the coins secured in tasseled canvas haversacks to keep from jostling, he'd known he was ready.

That morning, he'd ridden out at dawn, lugging the treasure from the study, towards the carriage in front. Some of the slaves had watched him, but no matter – what could they possibly suspect? That he was stealing straight from his own home? Hell, as he ought to have done all along? His mother had remained oblivious. He'd bade Cato farewell next, delivering him a sack of calves' heads from the butcher in Richmond, plus herbs for planting. Then he'd headed west.

Watching the sun turn orange, he recalled now how anxious he'd once been, riding on his own like this, back before he'd shared his vision with Cato, or with Thaddeus, back when he'd had only his nerves for company. Now, he felt peace: knowing the book of maps was full, that it would make sense even without him, guiding his revolutionaries to all he'd left behind.

The air was steady, the clouds non-existent. Sloping hills flanked the road, clumps of flat-topped trees at their edge, leaves still lush and happy, fat off a summer of rain. Pink aster blossoms beckoned in every direction; knee-high grasses waved; hawks as wide as wagons soared. He passed a few villages, just circles of wooden shops really, a few white churches lording over them, then nothing after that.

In time, the lane grew all but hidden amid the field, and Ulysses knew he couldn't ride much longer, not without getting lost, or risking his horse. With the plantation centers far enough behind that he needn't worry about being spotted – still near enough that their slaves could make it to this cash – he sought out a spot.

Slicing from the road, he sent a flock of wrens away in a panic, bumping through the meadow and toward the forested edge. This was public land, he saw, marked off for shared grazing. It was littered with clumps of manure, winding paths where cattle had trampled, a fresh timber fence to keep them free of the trees.

Still, there was no one about. And removing the book of maps, he sketched onto one of the blank pages in back, copying the scene all down, overlaying it with his regular Cartesian grid, so that even if the place were torn up and built over, his map would work, its guidance and hope still intact.

Buoyed by all the years of know-how behind him, he pulled out his shovel. The digging took the better part of an hour, dusk falling by the time he was struggling with the chest itself, sliding it out of the wagon, balancing it so the metal latches in front wouldn't slip apart. The temperature was dropping, the gnats already swarming, and he slid the dirt in on top, next marking his paces in the book, stomping upon this new grave until it was secure.

He turned back around.

And it was then that he cursed.

For there, twenty yards up, where the hill flattened out, a wagon had paused.

He could spot three figures inside – parents, and a wisp of a child – saluting him as he walked closer. "Howdy old-timer!" the father called out, with eyes that were narrow, and a beard a dull brown. He was wearing yeoman's garb, front trousers of hemp, boots to his knees, though he wasn't armed, and his voice was cheery enough. "This is my land, don't you know, public no longer! I was riding in, aiming to trace it through with my boy."

Ulysses tipped his cap, as though he'd already gathered as much.

"Bill of sale went through Thursday last," the fellow continued. "You're the surveyor?"

"Beg pardon?"

The man pointed toward the book of maps, still in Ulysses' grip, the compass pressed against it. "I saw you sketching, marking down your figures. You drawing up boundaries?"

Ulysses cleared his throat. "Just ensuring that your fence is rightly located."

"Well is it?" The man had shifted forward in his seat.

"I'd wager so, friend." Ulysses was readying to go, to lure them away from the burial spot.

"May I see what you wrote?"

"Just grids," he shrugged. "Mapping the terrain."

"You'll be sharing it with the county?"

"Naturally. And with the commonwealth."

The man dropped his reins. "No offense intended, stranger. I'd just be sated to know you didn't shrink my borders."

Ulysses nodded. He daren't hand over the whole book, he thought; he resolved in an instant that next time, he'd better leave it safe, back where it belonged, back beneath the floorboard at home.

The local's wife was fidgeting now. His small son looked bored.

Sensing a chance, Ulysses opened to the page in question, bending back the binding, tearing it straight out. Let the fellow have a quick glance, he decided. So long as he didn't peruse it too closely, the images would look harmless enough – a map, coordinates – just what he was expecting. At the very least, even if he suspected something, even if he made the page his own, aiming to check it with others, he'd possess only the one loose sheet.

Handing it over, Ulysses jammed the rest of the book back in his coat, waiting. To his horror, it took longer than he'd anticipated, and he held his breath as the man began nodding, squinting down sternly – even theatrically – until Ulysses realized: the poor fellow couldn't read. He was making a show of it, sure, matching the sketches to the landscape, but thank Heavens, never deciphering a word about the burial. At last, he handed back the page. "You've made a fine likeness, sir."

"My thanks, to be sure," and Ulysses started again toward the wagon.

"But won't you be returning it to your ledger?" The fellow was pointing, and Ulysses saw that in his nerves, he'd begun crumpling the sheet between his palm and his waist. "I only mean, sir, if those records are for the village seat, I'd hate to see my own claim left behind."

"By all means," Ulysses answered then, and looping to his wagon's rear, aware of the family's eyes upon him, he lifted out a cannister of fish-glue he'd stashed for stamps, and smeared it now in haste, straight across the page he'd ripped. Too late, he realized he'd applied it to the paper's front instead of its back – right across the map he'd just drawn.

Damn, he thought.

The etchings might yet be visible, at least – faint but decipherable, he decided – if held up to proper light; and with his thumbs, loath to draw any more attention, he simply pressed the page into place, albeit backwards and facing in, while the group watched from afar. Then, with a small shrug, he held the book aloft, and extended a wave.

The farmer waved back. "I'll thank you for your service."

Night was drifting in from the east, and Ulysses hoisted himself up, spurring his horse without looking back again. The treasure was safe.

CHAPTER 43

New York City
November 1919
May 1924

Bart Jr.'s office sparkled brighter each time Sam visited. While the rest of the city dug out from the ravages of flu and the aftershocks of war, Maynard's bank only flourished, its stately stone like a fortress, clerks like members of its own royal court. At the center of Bart's desk these days, a silver stenotype machine stood planted like a flag. He never seemed to use the thing, shoving it aside whenever he actually scribbled a note, but he referred to it as though it were his own invention: "just like our bank, Billings!" he'd declare – "visionary, vital, full of vim!" Electricity, meantime, shimmered from every angle, a yellow porcelain lamp at the stenograph's side, brass chain fixtures dangling overhead. There was even a push-button lock for the wall-safe, wired to the lamps, so that for no reason at all, Maynard could switch the whole room to life at once.

He looked more like his father by the year, Sam had decided, only clean-shaven: broad and proud beneath his wide lapels, blood vessels popping from too much drink, gray hair tumbling forward in waves. Gleaming. Prosperous. Just like his surroundings.

The problem was, he was intent on prospering even more.

"You already bumped me to six percent," Sam began, forgoing any salutation, ready to get this over with. "During the damned war, no less."

"You slander me a profiteer?"

"If it walks like a duck..."

"Mind yourself, Billings. I knew you when you were no more than a mash of soot."

Sam rolled his eyes. He wasn't even in the business of hunting treasure any longer. He'd cleared the whole book of maps through. Yet still he remained beholden to this fool. For as long as there was a Billings fortune, there would always be a Billings secret. And already, Bart Jr. had upped his cut, demanding a monthly fee, raising his rates further from there, all on the grounds – never spoken, perfectly understood – that such was his charge for keeping silent.

"It's extortion."

"It is, yes."

"For God's sake, Maynard. We grew up together."

"Yet you aimed to leave me behind."

"You and everyone else."

"All the more reason you can afford this. Seven percent, then. It's what I want."

Sam blinked.

"Well?" Bart's expression stiffened. "I risk my career, you know."

"As did your father."

"He was compensated. Even if you never knew it."

"With the decency at least to avoid my humiliation." Sam lowered his voice. "You have the upper hand, I'll grant you. But I'm not without recourse. If ever you dared try and ruin me, you'd lose your golden egg in turn. I'm more than acquainted with every newsman in the city, as you know. Every politician too. Hell, with every fellow who has account here. I could set their ire alight, even on my way down." Though even as he sputtered, Sam was retrieving his wallet, laying out the bills like a pile of cards. "Seven percent. No higher." He pushed himself up from the hand-carved chair. "In future, just extract the sum from my reserves. No more of this unpleasantness, then."

***

Alas, it was that very evening when the terrible dreams began. Sam had the first one, in fact, not long after returning from the bank; and from there, they only increased. Before long, it was getting so that he felt more surprised if he woke up in peace than when he was disturbed in the night.

Such was the case now, certainly, as he sat up stiffly, rubbing his temples, breathing fast, jerking his head, as his eyes darted across the dark room. Jagged honks rattled the air. The rumble of the underground trains shook the walls. Nearer in, a radio blared static out a window. It was enough to make him long for a time when nightfall had actually meant quiet, and he sat up straighter, realizing he was panting.

Swallowing back his heartburn, he tried to recall what the dream had entailed this time round. A copper had been trailing him, he thought, racing across the avenues – no, not an officer, he decided, but a man he knew. For hadn't it been Maynard Jr. himself, from the bank? The figure's wide shoulders had been heaving, arms pumping, ready to strangle Sam by the neck. *"Thief!"* he'd been calling – *"thief!"* he'd said again – nearly catching up, all but on top of him.

Until Sam had opened his eyes, and found himself here.

He stretched now, and swung his weary legs from the bed, seeing he wasn't alone. Emily was in the door, in a cotton lace nightdress, like a ghost. "I heard you call out."

He tried to chuckle. "Look at me – padding about in the night, darling, when I ought to be sleeping. I grunted as I sat up is all – no intention of waking a soul."

She ignored that, and stepped nearer. "Are you unwell, Samuel?"

He scoffed.

"For God's sake, Sam, you're perspiring – you're soaked straight through."

"Not yet accustomed to spring, I warrant."

"It's too much. You've not come down with fever?"

"Enough." He lay back. "Back to bed with you. With both of us."

And though she hesitated, she eventually retreated with a sigh.

He lay still another minute – another hour – piecing together his nerves. Finally, as the sun made its approach, he slid out of bed for good, dressed, and moved downstairs. He thanked the cooks for the boiled eggs and bacon, and loitered through the early edition of the *Times*, looking up only when the chimes rang, and one of the new butlers shuffled in, favoring one good leg, the other gone limp in the latest war.

"I'll receive him in my study," Sam remarked without waiting word, checking his watch, standing to go.

It was Charlie who was scheduled to come: just finished Harvard, with a baby boy of his own now, asking for a meeting, just the two of them. That was why Sam hadn't yet gone into the office, baffled as to what it could be, wishing he knew Charles better. It'd been the governesses who'd done the raising, of course – boarding school, off to Harvard after that – Sam always assuming there'd be time, that the brokerage would eventually settle into taking care of itself. Somehow that moment had never arrived.

Charlie entered in a tweed suit, white kerchief beside a red silk tie, yellow hair and blue eyes, a graceful stride the perfect echo of his mother's, and that gaze that still danced, as if he could anticipate a joke before it was even told. He stepped smoothly through the door.

"Leave it open, son."

"Yes, sir."

Sam pointed at the marble clock. "You're on time."

"Are you surprised?"

"Though not disappointed."

Charlie grinned, and made his way over, while Sam waited behind his desk. Slicing the tip of a cigar, he offered up a second, and for a moment, they sat there and smoked, each eyeing the other, the air growing cloudy between them.

"I'd better just say it," Charlie announced at last.

Sam raised his eyebrows, folding his legs, leaning back. "Out with it then, boy-o."

"I'm done living in your shadow, you see." He shrugged. "Done living as you might expect."

"I wasn't aware you'd yet lived at all."

"It's no slight, father. You've been a fine example – as fine a father as I could hope for."

"You flatter."

"I lie."

"Good then. We're being honest." Sam saw the lad wasn't entirely Emily after all: that there was some of himself in there as well, in that swagger of a voice, the bluster turned to banter, nerves transformed to wit. He took another puff. "If you don't fancy the brokerage, Charles, that's more than fine. I'll fix you up anywhere you like. You needn't be shy." Except now the lad was shaking his head, his blonde locks coming unglued, and Sam frowned. "You ought comb in more brilliantine, son. You look like a flapper, letting it shimmy so loose."

"Don't be antique." Charlie's smile had faded, and he balanced his own cigar between forefinger and thumb, so that Sam grew quite sure the lad must've practiced the pose at school. "I fear I haven't expressed myself ably, father. The fact is, I'd rather follow your model than wallow in your charity." His blue eyes shone.

"Nonsense. Take what I can give – what my own pa never could."

"I'm here for counsel, not for cash."

"Oh for Christ's sake, Charles, don't sound so pompous."

"Precisely my problem, father! You've spoiled me. Yet it's not the spoilt scions whom this nation honors."

"No – just the men in the trenches instead. Would you rather be lying legless and bloodied?" Though as soon as he'd said it, Sam wished he hadn't. Was a father to serve as the millstone upon a son's neck no matter what? After all, Charles had been too young for service – but it'd been Sam who'd forbidden him lying about his age. And whatever this was between them had widened ever since. "Every successful man you've ever met has been aided by giveaway and gift, Charles. One way or another."

"That's not what you say to the papers."

"It's what I say to you."

But Charles stood now, dashing as ever in his brown suit. "I'm moving west, pop," and his voice was firm. "That's the long and short of it. I'll be starting on an enterprise in California, running taxis from the rail stations."

"Do tell."

"There's already transport out there, but it's ramshackle. More men reach the Pacific every day – they're modern frontiersmen, father – they deserve better. Why not take some of our New York know-how and apply it for their sake? Standardized rates, trained drivers."

Sam found he was listening.

"In time, we'd get in on the vehicles themselves, paving the roads too, funding the lights. The market's never roared like this – you've said so yourself." He paused, taking a breath. The smile had returned. "You approve, father – I can see that you do."

Sam glanced out the window. It was true, the taxis here in New York were taking on profits. GM and Ford were making a play, Checker Cab company too, operating new fleets, arming themselves for a war over turf. He could see them this very moment: knobby headlamps out front, medallions on their hoods, all those lanes that had once roamed free. Why shouldn't it work just as smoothly out west? "It shan't be easy, though, Charles." He turned back. "You'd have to find permits, sit down with union men, carve out appointments with the commissioners." He could feel his own muscles working into gear now. "Even if it works, son, you'll encounter challenges anew. The rail companies will want a piece – there'll be bandits – protection required for your drivers. Accountants to file taxes on their wages. Petrol stations on your routes – "

Charlie was holding up his hand. "I've thought of it all, father."

"And you really won't let me deliver you a boost?"

"I'm already sound."

"Regard it as a loan."

"I can visit a bank."

"An investment then, from the brokerage. I'd task Finn Hughes with the plan."

"I'd rather curry favor from men not in employ of my own family."

"Everyone knows you're my son anyhow, Charlie. You can't make anyone forget that."

"No. Nor should I want to."

So that finally, Sam paused. It was clear – this wasn't to let up. And instead of arguing further, he leaned back at last, and lit them another pair of cigars.

CHAPTER 44

Richmond, Virginia
June 1845

It had been the capital's finest crowd, he supposed, crunched into every pew in St. John's, tumbling from the nave, right onto the muddy grounds. And Ulysses had been there with the rest of them, ducking the temptation to up and leave town, glad at least when it was done. He'd sat with his mother, frailer than ever, while Cato had waited in the carriage.

He suspected she'd brought Cato as some kind of gesture: a recognition really – without ever saying so aloud, of course – of the affection Ulysses had for his lifelong friend. And he was grateful for it, even if he resented that she still jointly owned Cato's deed all the while, even if it had taken her all this time to acknowledge, however implicitly, that Cato was more than chattel.

Now they were returned to his house in Richmond – mother was staying the night, before the ride back to Boxwood – he and Cato on the porch, while she was already indoors, when a noise from the road made him turn. A black-draped carriage had arrived across the way, and Ulysses sighed. For that would be Cyrus himself, coming home a widower for the very first time.

They'd grown to ignore each other in recent years, thank God. Having bested society – owning the very best of the merchant houses on the port – his neighbors the Thompsons seemed to have decided they didn't require Ulysses' connection after all. Whatever suspicions they'd harbored over his comings-and-goings had faded in time amid the fruits of their ambition; for why stir trouble, when the city was already theirs to boast of? He'd embraced their blind eye in turn. When Beth had taken ill, he'd sent a card certainly – had even stopped in, though she'd been in delirium – had, in due course, made arrangements to host his mother for the funeral. But in the end, Ulysses realized, his and their time together had been one of life's passing currents, more like a drizzle barely recorded in *Richard's Almanac*, than the tempests to be recalled by the bards.

Gamely, he shuffled out to the curb. He saw Cyrus' gout had given him a limp, his handsome face finally grown puffy. But he was still a man of manners, even in his grieving. "Ulysses. I'll thank you for attending."

"My condolences, of course. I only take solace the city came to savor Beth as you did."

"You're kind in saying so." Thompson peered over his shoulder at Cato. "I know that one."

"Indeed. An old family slave. He's been with us from the start."

"The best sort." Cyrus sighed, and though his gaze lingered an extra moment, he offered a bow. "Well."

"If there's anything I can offer, you send word."

"I shall, Ulysses." He twisted away.

Ulysses spun back in turn. "What now?" he asked as he returned to the porch, and saw his friend's glare. "Oh what was I to say, Cato? That this here is my dearest associate, my accomplice, my aide-de-camp in our unrealized revolution?"

Cato didn't smile; his brow simply creased. "I gather not, Ulysses. Even now."

"Time is no cure for this world. You know that."

And together, they let the night come.

***

For his next trip out of town, Ulysses knew he'd need to take care, of course – to make certain he didn't venture far, that he didn't push his knees. He'd settled upon a return to his old stomping grounds, just east of Boxwood, tracking the routes he knew best. When the day had arrived, he'd made sure to place the book of maps beneath the floorboard at home, and packed only a single night's supplies: water, cured bacon, a can of beans. The air had been light – spring still staving off the anger of summer – letting him make good time, humming old tavern tunes in the absence of company, even enjoying the sun.

At some point, he'd yanked the reins and slowed: thinking he'd heard a branch rustle somewhere off the road, a small stone tumbling from the grass. But searching for tracks, he'd come upon only empty dirt and mounds of uncut pasture. And he'd kept on.

After that, the theft itself had gone smoothly, even easier than anticipated, years of experience making themselves known. He'd waited at a bend in the highway, eyeing the newest coach stop from Richmond. It was a mere cottage really, a single clerk hawking dried fruit to travelers, and Ulysses had hurried over at just the moment a fine carriage had parked, making his move while the driver was inside, stealing a sack of coin, returning to his own ride in a matter of seconds.

A minor heist. An uneventful one. Yet enough for a thrill, he'd concluded, to re-spring the coil in his soul. Whistling quietly then, he'd headed straight towards Boxwood, with a mind toward showing Cato his haul, to accept his congratulations, even to bury the loot right there, on his own family's property, for when the time came.

It'd been only another few minutes, before he'd noticed the traffic.

It was nothing too striking at first: a line of well-appointed carriages, coming from the opposite lane. Guests for some evening ball, Ulysses presumed, even as he marked that the men were wearing plain blue vests, and checkered coats, none of the usual bright velvet he'd expect from Virginia's most proud. He should have taken into account how this stretch had grown so busy of late, it was true: the way the stones of the road were mashed down, the grooves from wagon wheels deep as crop divots, brick homes scattered along the way. He considered that perhaps his senses had been more dulled by age than he'd wanted to admit. Still, at least the hard part was already done.

And yet – this growing commotion on the road gave him pause. In time, it even seemed enough to change his mind: Ulysses figured he'd better not press his luck by pushing all the way to Boxwood after all, and he lifted the reins instead, angling into the next patch of meadow. He knew this terrain well enough; he'd be able recall it just fine for jotting down in his book of maps, and he lowered himself carefully so as not to turn an ankle, lifting the sack of coins along with him.

When all at once, a scurry of shouts filled the air.

Ulysses looked up, and saw the carriages converging suddenly – leaving the road by the same path he had, scaling towards him with great speed. He saw too that the men were pulling badges from their frocks – that several of them had pistols hoisted to their belts – and he cursed his faded eyesight that he hadn't made those out before.

Then he nearly stumbled in place.

For there, in the very first carriage – sitting at the rear – pointing his way and glaring, was none other than Cyrus Thompson: wrapped in a woven woolen shawl despite the day's warmth, white hair grown stringy, once fine features sagging like melting ice in the sun. He was shaking his finger, his mouth tilted awkwardly, no longer the refined gentleman who cared most for elegance, but a snarling, angry creature, as debased as any of the rest.

The wagons slowed, and Ulysses felt his tired heart picking up its pace, his nerves insisting he race away, his mind counseling that he was far too old. At least the book of maps was safe, he thought – his whole plan, his whole life! – and it was that, he realized, which gave him a new calm.

One of the men leapt down. Then another. Finally, from a carriage at the center, with a loping swagger and tobacco rolling from his lips, a burly fellow strolled forward, badge affixed to his chest, mustache the color of ripe tomatoes. "You're under arrest, Brooke," he thundered, as though he were the Lord Himself. "By the authority vested in me under the commonwealth, and at the behest of Governor Gregory."

Ulysses knew the procedure. He'd helped craft it. And dropping the treasure where he stood – knowing now he'd never bury another – he raised his hands, then gazed up at Cyrus Thompson, still sitting in place. "Why?" he asked simply, aware this had to be farewell.

Cyrus was watching as the sheriff latched his wrists. "Because I have pride of place, Mr. Brooke. And because you never did." Some of the other men had grown quiet, almost sheepish, as though it were occurring to them that they hadn't, in fact, been needed in pursuit of a stooped, gray-haired thief. "Because a lot of folks have been itching mad for a lot of years. And because it was my own wife, may God rest her soul, who took note that you were gone every time a new incident was reported."

"Yet you delayed?"

"To the contrary. We went to the sheriff some long time since – even straight to your parade of governors, Brooke. They'd scowl, tell us to be gone, that there was nothing even to be discussed, so long as our only proof was suspicion. Some had a thought to arrest *us*, mind you, for daring to besmirch your name." Cyrus snorted, and had to wipe a string of drool from his chin.

So that now, Ulysses swallowed, and looked away.

Not at what he was hearing, really, but at what he was not.

For if it had been such a challenge to find proof, then how had they done it at last?

In a flash, he recalled now that he'd recently written Rebecca Vance – a note telling her he was off to Boxwood for a spell, that he'd like to see her again when he returned if possible. He'd mentioned it had been far too long, and that he missed her. Writing hadn't been necessary, of course. It was merely an excuse for contact – a way to let her know he was still considering her after all this time.

Yet she hadn't written back.

Ulysses glanced back up, keeping his gaze steady, swallowing a sudden shudder. She couldn't have, he thought. She wouldn't have.

Not Rebecca. Never.

There was a shove against his back then – a grunt – the shackles now locked in place, and he realized he was being moved toward a waiting wagon, with bars round its sides. "Was it just you, Thompson?" he managed, even as he was being twisted away. "Not a soul else?"

But Cyrus merely pursed his aged lips, and spat straight where Ulysses walked.

"Answer me," Ulysses barked, suddenly needing to know, no longer masking the unbearable. "Go on then, you old fool! You'll be dead and gone before I can ask again."

But it was the sheriff who smacked him to be quiet – once – twice – twice again – so that Ulysses all but fell as he neared the step to the carriage. "There's no need," he muttered, even as another smack descended. "No need for that," he tried again, wincing at another blow.

He could feel the world going blurry, the blood rushing straight from his head, and he watched as the faces above him began to spin. He worked to block the next strike with his arms, but the shackles held him back, and down it came, enough that soon everything was fading, and he was swiping his bound wrists only at the air, trying merely to keep steady.

It was no use, he suddenly knew. The world was coming at him in waves, topsy-turvy, the sky underfoot, the grass somehow floating above. There was a terrible onslaught of nausea – a sharp slice through his mind – his arms going limp –

And at that, the world went black.

***

On the morning he'd entered the world, too many years ago now, it had been snowing.

Every bit of the landscape camouflaged: carriage lanes undetectable; the slave quarters virtually buried. In the distance, forests to the horizon, blanketed, softened. And everywhere, just quiet: that special quiet that comes with fresh snowfall, so that to anyone passing by, it would have felt more like a painting than the very center of a brand new nation's trade.

Until he'd let out his first infant's cry.

The soldier at the door could hear the yelps even before the midwife had stepped out with the news. Buttoning up a battered blue coat, he'd folded the slip into his pocket, ready to brave the storm toward the boy's father, encamped with Washington, pursuing the independence that Jefferson had declared for all of them that summer. And so it was: that before the lad was even dried, news of his arrival had been off at a gallop, past the oaks lining his birthright and straight to the coast, where passage northward would be easier that time of year.

In the meantime, he'd been wrapped in light wool, bound with ribbon, tucked into the arms of his ma. One of the nursemaids had ordered a slave to feed the hearth, as the flames crackled and red coals throbbed, while clumps of men had entered with stacks of chopped maple, and piled them high by the wall. At some point, she'd stirred, and gestured to be cooled, and the slave woman had shuffled from the corner to the window and lifted it so that it squeaked and shook, the carcasses of last summer's horseflies tumbling down from the frame, a draft of icy air swirling in, guiding mother and son back to sleep.

They'd rested then, with dark beams overhead, and an oil portrait of Ulysses' father gleaming atop the mantle, his celebrated face frozen in oil, his torso stained by smoke. The mattress had been of straw, the lush carpet boasting an image of a vase and vines; on every wall, yellow candles had burrowed deep into their cast iron holders.

Or at least –

That was the tale Ulysses had always been told.

He blinked now, and the years fell away.

He couldn't recall a lick of it, of course – relying instead upon inherited images, seeking respite, as he did now from the back of this jailer's wagon, when it was needed.

He looked about, as they jostled along the road. The sky was heavy, the horses ragged, brown and hunched and dragging their hooves. A junior constable held the reins, his collar stained brown with sweat, rolls on his neck the color of plum juice, wide-brimmed hat fighting the sun.

The wagon itself was rotted, its flatbed empty. At Ulysses' feet, a feeble gray mouse nibbled at his boots, and he kicked it over the plywood wall. They were on their way to the stockade, past cottages and privies in disrepair, through the stench of excrement and the perfume of blossoms, each fighting for the upper hand.

The constable was shaking his head. "I just can't figure it." His words came out splintered, his voice an ugly rumble. "A fella like you, cast so favorably...."

Ulysses looked up.

"The whole of the world in his grasp – turned against the very folks that gave it to him."

Now Ulysses merely grunted.

"I'm sorry for you sir. Truly I am. Encounterin' Judas in your own lair."

But Ulysses turned away. Until in time, the holding cell came upon them: a red brick citadel, half a day's walk from the prison-house up the road, and he was escorted from the wagon by a crowd of new deputies, and shunted into a cramped stone hall, weeds curling up from its corners, rusted bars marking the rooms lining its sides. He shuffled along at the men's command, legs shackled by iron as if he were a slave himself, when eventually they stopped at one of the doors, and someone pushed him through. The air smelled something rank, the hinges swung shut, and he took in the view: a lone window up top, damp stone all around, the squeak of rats hard to ignore. And he let himself crumple, resting his head on his knees, working to make sense of it all.

CHAPTER 45

New York City
December 1983

Alvin was up early, finishing the brief. He'd been putting it off all week, knowing he needed to loop in Claire Calloway, that he couldn't keep this antique box here forever, with all its gold coins still inside. He'd cleaned the thing since digging it up in Virginia, its iron belts no longer caked in mud, but it sure looked odd in the apartment, next to the plastic rollers on the window, like some looted museum artifact on layaway, ready for the black market to come calling.

He didn't notice Faye watching him from the door. Not until she stretched, sporting one of his button-downs and a pair of flannel pants for sleeping, bags beneath her eyes, curls jutting in nine different directions.

"Did I wake Dex?"

She brought her finger to her lips. "Not yet," she whispered.

He nodded. "You're beautiful," he mouthed, though she rolled her eyes, stepping toward the desk, looking over his shoulder.

"You're really going to tell them?" she said after a moment.

"I have to."

She was leaning over now, lifting the chest's lid before Alvin could stop her. Reaching inside, she retrieved one of the old coins, rotating it, squinting in thought.

"You want me to break the law?"

"I want you to listen to your own heart, Alvin."

"Not so simple. I have a case. I have plaintiffs."

"And now you have their evidence."

"Yes." He sighed, as she lowered the coin back and sat on the desk's edge, ankles crossed, arms folded. "Evidence I can't conceal, for Christ's sake." He paused then, letting that sink in, but she didn't move. "Oh hell, Faye – you can't mean it! I'd be party to the original crimes. No different than Brooke and Billings, taking what wasn't theirs."

"And if the courts say this is proof the whole Trust came from stolen goods?"

"Then so be it."

"Alvin!"

He took a breath. They'd been fighting about this since he'd returned: over whether he really should turn the thing in and risk dismantling the whole Billings operation – unleashing the press against the city's largest philanthropy, assailing its reputation, even grabbing its cash for the Campbells and Downings who'd brought the case in the first place. Could he really justify all that with the technicality of the law, Faye wanted to know? Would Ulysses Brooke himself have accepted it, she'd asked – would a judge even go along? "You know I answer to the bureau, Faye."

"You're answering to the southern bastards who put you up to all this."

"You don't know them." He could hear the strain in his own voice. "You don't."

She peered back.

He faced down, examining the treasure once more. "My father used to tell me this country was perfect."

"He wanted it to be, Alvin, same as you do. It's what he fought for." Little Dexter suddenly gave out a yelp. "Those men of yours – Brooke and Billings, chasing each other, chasing this nation; and now you, chasing them all in turn. It's time you make this story your own, like they did."

The baby unleashed an outright cry.

"You hear what I'm saying, Alvin?"

"Sure," he answered. There was yet another wail from Dex's room, and Alvin shared a smile. "Though now I'm mostly hearing him."

She turned. "Let's go in together, then."

So they did.

***

Aside from a portrait of Reagan, his hair just as coiffed as when he'd still been in Hollywood, a grin etched as if already frozen in marble, the bureau's board room was mostly unchanged. A round-faced clock was on the wall, like the ones from school when Alvin had been a boy, its second-hand shivering with every twitch, moving right past 9 o'clock. He waited, gazing through smudged windows into the sleet outside. Crowds passed along the sidewalks below, a mash of black umbrellas and matching trench coats; red traffic lights and yellow Chevy taxis battled in between; puddles sloshed curbs the color of coffee and smoke.

At last, the door swung open.

The years had not been kind. The Campbell brothers strode in arrogant as ever, but their thick shoulders had gone soft, their reddish hue turned fleshy and blotched, their paunches swelled. They were both wearing boxy double-breasted suits, gray pinstripes, the same fat red ties as always, and Alvin stood, aware they were studying him in turn.

Clay was in the lead, his face still a touch narrower than his brother's, and he jutted out his hand like an over-eager bird. "You're no kid anymore," he barked through a phlegmy chuckle.

"You neither."

"It's an odd thing, ain't it: a fellow still feels like himself."

Alvin nodded, as they joined him at the table. A moment later, the door opened again, and in came Jack and Betty Downing.

He was glad. He'd invited them as the original plaintiffs in the case – no matter that the wealthier Campbell cousins had put them up to it – and had been hoping Clay and Clem wouldn't somehow block them from coming. Jack Downing was wearing a checkered blue button-down, half tucked in, crusty jeans and black sneakers well past worn out. His wife Betty was in a Christmas sweater two sizes too small, and ten shades too bright. Her hair had thinned, while his had magically grown thicker, betrayed by dots like ink blotches lining his scalp, some hideous combination of plugs and brown dye.

"Good to see you, Mr. Starkman." Jack smiled anxiously, while Betty's blue eyes were opaque, cloudy from cataracts perhaps, or maybe just shielded all on their own. The capillaries in both of their cheeks were like city maps penciled with blood, their skin deflated, like old balloons. It occurred to Alvin that while money might not buy them happiness, it could at least be a down payment toward health.

Not that the Campbells could be trusted to share a dime.

Alvin flattened his tie and steeled himself for what was next. Faye had been right – he wasn't their pawn. But he wasn't to be their enemy either. Not if he still believed in the law the way he was supposed to. She was furious with him, of course. Hell, he was furious with himself. "I'm glad you're all here," he started in. "Better for everyone to hear this."

They waited – Clay like a tightly coiled cat, his brother Clem leaning back, silent – the Downings unnaturally straight, as if trying to impress.

Alvin folded his hands. "What if I told you we'd finally hit some proof of what you folks allege?"

There was silence at first. Just the horns outside. The ticking of the clock. The muffled voices from the hall. He could hear Clay Campbell's breathing, like the hiss of air escaping from a tire, his brother tapping his fingers on his chair.

Then Betty stood up, moving toward a counter where a day-old pitcher of water was waiting, pouring it into a plastic cup. The men in the room all watched. "Proof would be good news," she said.

The room relaxed. Clay opened his briefcase.

There were stacks of sheets inside. Affidavits. Alvin could see his own name printed at the bottoms, next to a signature line. "You anticipated this?" he asked.

"Why else would you call us in?" Clay was lifting out the pages. "We're requestin' you sign these straightaway, Starkman, confirming what you just said: that the money is to be ours, and ours exclusively. Not Billings Trust's. Not anyone else's either."

"Well now hold on, Mr. Campbell. The next step for us is to go to court, and see this through."

"That wasn't our agreement."

"That's the legal process."

But Clay was already sliding one of the sheets forward.

Alvin scanned it quickly, skipping down the jumble of paragraphs to the bottom: *I do swear, as acting investigator, that all the above is true, that this money was stolen and has been recovered, returned to its rightful owners, that no more need be done.* He looked back up. "This is absurd. It's way beyond my parameters."

"You're the man who knows this case best, Starkman."

"And I'll testify to what I found."

Clay extended a ballpoint pen, clicking its tip. "We want it in writing. We've been very patient, Agent Starkman. Just help us feel a touch more secure, won't you?"

"Mr. Campbell – " he wasn't even sure yet what this was, but something in their sudden restlessness, the edge and hunger behind it, made him reflexively want to pause – "all these years, watching me hit dead end after dead end, you never once asked for a transfer to some other agent. Now here you are, still doubling down like I'm special, insisting on a personal vouching. Tell me why. Why stick with me?"

"Don't let it get to your head." It was Clem this time, sighing, growling really. "Your ego's already big enough. Bred into you, no doubt."

Alvin squinted back, working not to get distracted by what sounded like Jew-baiting, to try and see instead what was really happening here. "What's that got to do with anything?"

"What good is smarts, when you can't trust 'em, Starkman? It's simple: if you don't sign, who's to say you won't go back on your word? The way you types do?"

Alvin nodded, recalling now those whoops he and Faye had encountered down in Richmond, spooling out from that pickup truck, and it occurred to him these men would have delighted in all of that. Still, it somehow went deeper too, didn't it? For these weren't just regular mud-dwellers coming to the law for a hand. They were after its perversion instead, trying to strip it down to an earlier, uglier version of itself. They'd been trailing him, manipulating him all along. And he sensed they were still doing so now, their bile seeping from their smiles. "You're not really calling me the one with ego now, are you?" He'd met Clem's eye. "When it's you trying to take money away from doing any actual good?"

It was Clay who cut in. "That's enough of that, now. Both of you. Clement here's just eager. We've spent years on this, Mr. Starkman, same as you. It's time to put an end to it. Just sign, and we'll shake hands as gentlemen."

Alas, it turned out his quieter brother, once rolling, wasn't so easily stopped. He'd jammed his finger to the table. "Just because it's our people built a whole nation, Starkman, doesn't mean you get to be ashamed of it."

"A nation that took my own family in, you ignorant ass. Who said anything about shame?"

Clem's lips grew rigid. "We slingin' names now?" His voice, newly tightened, sounded ever more ready to erupt. "You think we don't know who you are? You think we don't know your lifestyle back home?"

Alvin took in a sharp breath.

There was a phone in the corner for security, and he wondered if he'd need to use it.

He didn't want to.

Instead, he gazed back, knowing he'd helped escalate things, no longer caring, as if for the first time, he was seeing them in full. "My lord," he muttered all at once. "That's it then, isn't it?" His own voice had turned to stone.

"Come again, boy?" Clem glared. The Downings glanced between them.

"That's it," Alvin repeated, and he was shaking his head. "That's why it's got to be me. That's why you stuck with me all along...."

Clay was clearing his throat. "Starkman, my brother is out of line. I grant you that."

"No," and Alvin leaned forward. "He was telling the truth. You're right: you do know who I am. You always have. You knew when she and I met, didn't you? You were watching, right there at the start."

"Met who?" Jack Downing suddenly asked.

"My wife," Alvin answered, letting the words linger. "I'll be damned," and he glanced Jack's way. "You see – your ancestor, Ulysses Brooke, he didn't work alone. He had help taking all that cash, didn't he?" And he paused, slowly facing back toward the Campbells. They were each frowning now, more than before. "You came to the bureau for justice, didn't you, fellas? Well, taste it. Smell it. Go back home – and tell your people what it looks like."

***

They left a few minutes after that, Jack and Betty near ready to weep, Clay and Clem newly silent and boiling. Alvin stayed in his chair, knowing it wasn't really over. Not while the evidence still existed. Not when he'd switched his position on a dime, and had allowed such men to humiliate themselves: tempting their souls right out of them, watching as they came crashing, splintering down. He had no doubt they'd return, in fact – sooner rather than later – demanding fuller answers about the proof he'd mentioned at the start, and what exactly he'd uncovered.

When he exited in turn, Alvin had a frown on his own face too, a swirl of nausea underneath at what he'd heard, a spike of relief at what it had done for his resolve. He hurried then: past young agents in the hall – hunched over fuzzy gray footage, scanning overstuffed shelves, stretching phone cords as far as they would go, pacing and pleading and prodding lawyers for leeway, judges for warrants, witnesses for information – all that effort, he thought, just for buying a small-time bust here, a delay over there, occasionally even a headline. It was a picture of forward motion, with good guys in badges, and bad guys in cuffs, no matter that the real criminals were still out there: the world no better, no purer, no safer, the nation no sounder for its children, for his family, for his own son.

Yet he knew too it was what he needed to see: confirmation indeed of what he felt now, what he was choosing to do, abandoning all this precisely for what it was, voices buzzing with their own inertia, a collective – a battalion – unthinking, unmoving, stationed amid gray cubicles like jigsaws, window shades drawn tight against the world they were supposed to be helping. It was no more than mere theater then, a show for justice and for America, progress so slow, so bumpy, so handicapped by compromise and technicalities, there was never any knowing if it was actually on anyone's side at all. They weren't just ineffectual, then; they were complicit. This plodding rhythm, this echoing into nothing; and Alvin knew now, the same way he'd once known this was where he'd wanted to be, that to do what was right, he couldn't stick with them. It was just as Faye had urged: he'd need to face this place down, no different than he'd just faced down the Campbells.

His heart sped up at the thought. It would violate his oath, and the law itself. He could even end up on the wrong side of the ledger, in the interrogation room himself, answering for what he'd done. And he tried to grow calm, angling back to his own desk, keeping Faye's counsel in mind as he mapped out his next steps, suddenly finding himself imagining the faces of Ulysses Brooke and Sam Billings. It was as if he could hear their ghostly voices, as if he could finally listen in, while they reached out across time, and asked him for his help.

CHAPTER 46

New York City
January 1984

Alvin tapped a pen against his steel anchor desk and watched through the interior glass. Claire Calloway was snaking closer through the cubicles. She hadn't scheduled them a meeting, yet here she came, and he stood up as she got close.

She wore the same padded blue blazer that she put on every Tuesday and Thursday – red for Mondays and Wednesdays, black for Fridays – a checkered turtleneck beneath, trousers too baggy at the ankle. She'd never been one to depend on clothes for her command.

When she entered the room, Alvin steadied his pen. Even after all these years, she put him on edge. It wasn't just that she was his boss. It was because she was smarter than him too – smarter than anyone, he'd come to see – and that she'd never bothered to hide it. It was how she'd become a deputy in the first place, really, why she'd soon be the point-person for the whole tri-state area, if the rumors were to be believed. Never a friend, yet never petty either, like a bureau handbook come to life. And while

Alvin still didn't know a thing about her personal goings-on – still wasn't even sure where her apartment was – he knew enough about her mind: her insistence on no wasted time, that the pragmatic was as worthy as any ideal, that he better wait now in quiet, to hear what she'd come to say.

"How's the baby?" she all but barked.

"Sleeping much better." He knew she'd asked only because it was expected. "Faye's been a saint."

"Good for her." Claire took a seat, and ended the pleasantries with a sigh. "You met with the Campbells before Christmas."

"And Jack and Betty Downing. Yes."

She nodded stiffly. "They've been calling. Threatening to go up the chain."

"They got pretty angry."

"They hate you, Starkman."

"I know."

She slid her hands apart, setting them on the desk, flat, steady. She'd finally reached the age she always should have been, Alvin decided: hair gone gray, voice solid and sure when she spoke, her display of strength reinforced by the years now behind it. "What do they know that I don't, Starkman? What happened in there?"

"I told them the case is closed."

"Excuse me?"

"The Billings case. It's done. I figured you'd be pleased."

"I was praying it'd go quietly. Not that they'd be asking for your head."

"They didn't want to hear that there's no evidence, that's all. And if I'm honest, ma'am, I made the mistake of leading them on at first. I was aiming to show I'd really tried, that I thought I'd come close. I overpromised." He worked to look sheepish.

Her gaze narrowed. "You're leaving something out."

For a moment, Alvin's heart panged. He was leaving everything out. The treasure he'd found. The fact that the Campbells had been right all along: that there was a case to be brought indeed, a chance for them to get their money from Billings in court. That they still wouldn't be able to do it, however – not unless his very own family renounced any claim to the money themselves.

For indeed, after the meeting, after he'd gone off to fetch Dex from daycare, had put him down for a nap, had paced the apartment and waited for Faye – ready to burst by the time she'd come through the door, flinging down her bags, unbundling her scarf, warming her hands by the radiator – they'd begun putting it all together. "It's frigid out there," she'd exclaimed.

Alvin had nodded slowly. Waiting as long as he could, joining her on the couch. Taking her in. "Your father, Faye," he'd finally said.

"What about him?"

"He grew up in Baltimore."

"You know that he did."

"And his family was always there?"

"I think so. They were city slaves back in the day."

Alvin had paused at that, wondering if he was nuts after all. "What about your mom's side?"

She'd shrugged. "They came up from Virginia – after the first world war. Had enough of sharecropping, apparently." She'd looked back at him. "Why you asking?"

"Where'd they call home, Faye? Tell me you know the name of the town."

And though she'd squinted a moment, she'd come up with something eventually. "It had a first name in it, I think. Stephen, Simon – something like that."

"Scott's Landing?"

"How'd you know?" She'd started smiling. "You been checking up on me?"

Except Alvin had gone quiet.

My God, he'd thought.

There really had been a slave then. Thieving alongside Brooke, just as he'd suspected. And the Campbell boys had known all along.

More than that: they must've traced that very slave's lineage all the way down to Faye. It was the reason they'd acted as they had, growing so interested in Alvin in the first place.

There, on the couch, he'd searched for words to explain it, filling her in slowly but surely. When he'd finished, she'd been near to tears.

That very night, they'd reserved a spot at a motel in Virginia, then had spent the weekend traveling. Back to Ulysses Brooke's hometown – to the town hall Alvin had visited a decade before – this time researching not Brooke's own narrow path, but the ledgers listing his slaves.

Then – sure enough – they'd found a name: recorded again and again in the logs, year after year, a man entered in as 'Cato.' He'd first appeared the same year as Ulysses' own birth announcement, as a new property of the Brooke family plantation – Boxwood Grove, a hell of a euphemism for that sin of a place – then, too, in slave rolls right up to the Civil War, his death notice coming three years before the peace, no offspring listed.

It was a sister of his who'd had kids of her own. According to the census, she'd stayed in town after emancipation, dropping the surname 'Brooke' on a maternal line, sharecropping for decades to come, free in law but never in practice. The family had stayed local to the end of the century, until eventually, the only surviving member had married Faye's grandfather. The two of them had migrated to Baltimore.

Alvin had stared at the microfilm of the census that proved it, cracked beneath the lens, while Faye had sat at his side, the whole story deepening out before him, this tale of Ulysses Brooke that he'd thought he'd known so well. And he'd come to understand, how upon learning of this themselves, Clay and Clem Campbell must have worried Faye would discover it in turn and would one day realize that if they could claim to be heirs to a stolen fortune, then she could too. Indeed, as soon as the brothers had sorted out Alvin's connection to her, had seen the relationship grow, they must've thanked the heavens and re-doubled their approach: for who better to drive home their case, than a man with such a rock-solid interest in getting in its way?

In a daze, Alvin had returned home, no longer seeing that case as his job, nor even his cause, but as his family. Striding back into the bureau, he'd flipped through pages he'd thought he'd never peruse again. This time, he'd understood the recurring references to the slave Cato Brooke, the importance of scribbled margin notes across the whole book of maps: *"CB picked up at noon"* – *"Cato fed horses prior to discovery"* – notes he'd always moved past before, far too interested in geography, and the coins themselves.

Together then, he and Faye had sewn together the truth: that Ulysses had entrusted a man whom he'd also owned. That this man had been Faye's own ancestor. That this was why Alvin had been pegged by the Campbells, wanting him not just because he'd find their proof, but because once he had, they could fool him into helping them claim the gold all for themselves: disowning Faye's status as an heir to the cash, simply by signing their lousy affidavit. It was to be a piece of paper designating all money to them, affirmed by the white-skinned husband of its only other potential claimant. Even if he were to renounce it later, that would mean going back on a sworn statement; they'd have claimed he was motivated by personal riches alone.

It was enough to make him boil all over again.

Not that Claire Calloway had sorted any of that out. Not yet. Looking back at her, unflinching, he knew he'd have to tread carefully. "At least the bureau won't be seizing philanthropic cash, ma'am."

"We'll get bad press anyway. The Campbells can't be quieted. They'll say we didn't work hard enough, that there's still proof to find."

"Better to take incoming fire from them than Charles Billings."

The desktop phone rang loudly. But Claire reached over, tapping one of its endless buttons, silencing its rattle. "I'll have you file a report of course."

"Of course."

"Shouldn't take more than another day. Then we can get you back to work on other matters."

Except at that, Alvin shook his head.

"What's the problem?"

"No problem, really."

"But no case work either?"

"That's just it, ma'am." The words felt crisp, heavy. "I'm retiring."

"Stop it."

"I am. From the bureau at least."

"You're barely 40 – you're a decade from pension at least."

"I can't stay."

Claire frowned. "You're serious."

Alvin reached in his drawer for the resignation letter he'd prepared. It was staid, and formal, and had been sitting there all week – though until this moment, he hadn't been fully certain he'd actually be taking it out.

Now he knew that he had to, sitting here, looking back at Claire, blocked from admitting aloud what was actually burning through his mind: that he could never trust himself again – could never go on with his job and pretend he'd never strayed from the law. Not after what he'd already set in motion.

"Now look here, Alvin." She watched as he slid the letter across the desk. "You can't let one failed case push you away."

"No, ma'am. It's all of them."

"But they don't all end this way. You know that. Most are clear-cut – they've got answers."

"Only that's just it, ma'am. I came to work here for an ideal, not answers alone. This case – it's just helped me remember that."

***

It was a week later – the following Monday, first thing – that Alvin found himself in an elevator he vaguely remembered: freshly scrubbed, with new security mirrors installed in the corners. Charles Billings had been away, fundraising as ever, according to the papers, but he'd returned on a red-eye, and his secretary had arranged this slot for as soon as he was back.

They'd arrived here in a cab – Faye accepting Alvin's invitation to come along – avoiding the subway, thanks to their cargo. Nearly late amid rush hour, they jogged the last block with traffic at a standstill. It was a relief to be inside then, ears popping from the ascent, tinny saxophone music pumped in, as the buttons lit up the wall. Alvin undid his coat and folded up the black garbage bag he'd stretched over the luggage case. Faye let out her breath with a whistle.

"What?"

"You still think I should be here?"

He took her hand. "You've got a truer connection with him than I do."

"He might not see it that way."

"Let's find out."

"His ancestors owned people like me, Alvin."

But the doors opened before he had time to reply.

Here now was the waiting room, lavish as always, clay-potted plants as tall as children, ceramic lamps lining the sideboards, more crowded than Alvin recalled: stuffed full with visitors, young men mostly, in wide-shouldered suits and overblown suspenders, tapping leather shoes against the carpeted floor. It must be a presentation day, he thought, folks applying for the Trust's sacred funds; the nerves were contagious.

Up ahead, the floor's receptionist was waiting. She wore her white hair in a bun and sat behind a chic waterfall desk of rosewood, in a violet blazer to match. A smile washed away her years. "Agent Starkman?"

"Former Agent."

"Mr. Billings will be with you straightaway." So that in an instant, the whole room seemed to hush.

Alvin wheeled the luggage case around, and tapped his fingers against its handle. Faye folded her coat several times over, smoothing it down, eventually draping it over her arm, just in time for another receptionist, appearing from nowhere, to gesture them toward the inner sanctum. This woman was younger than the first, with glossed lips and a beige blouse, and she led them past rows of assistants, then alongside all the shelves lined by books and awards and black-and-white photographs, straight into the heart of the Trust itself, where Charles Billings was waiting.

The old man had reached that phase of life when the body begins aging in dog years. His dazzling white hair was thinning at last; there were new creases too, turning his long brow into something like grooved cement. His smile was warm but weary, as if it had taken him some effort to put on, borne not of reluctance, but of rust.

He was anchored behind his oak desk when they entered; his ocean blue eyes were as rich as his suit. And despite the lines in his face, and the tremor as he extended a hand, he still gave off a kind of sure-footedness, as if pain were no more than a foreign-tongued stranger, and age was to be savored just the same as youth.

Panel shutters had been drawn down over the windows. A brass desk lamp offered a narrow puddle of light. "My apologies. It's these eye drops they give me – too much glare, and I see triple." The accent remained an artifact, his vowels boasting of the money that had raised him. "Welcome."

Alvin nodded. "Before we begin, sir – I'd like you to meet my wife."

Charles Billings stood. It was an effort, to be sure – one he tried his damndest to conceal: gripping his armrests, moving in a quick, fitful burst, still bent even once he was upright. But he made it, and he took her hand. "The pleasure is mine, madam."

"Mr. Billings." Faye smiled. "I feel as though we've met before."

He raised his eyebrows. "The perils of fame..." But he bowed his head appreciatively, sitting back down. "I hope you don't find my lair too horribly archaic."

"I happen to think it's cozy," Faye responded, glancing toward books enough to feed a lifetime. "Feels like a home."

"More like a cave."

"You must be a pretty comfortable bear."

Charles' smile turned to a laugh. "Well, Mrs. Starkman. I beg you to sit. You too, Agent Starkman."

"Actually, sir, I've left the bureau."

"Oh?" He angled his head, and peered back as if from a great distance, trying to get a better view. "Can I presume you're not here to arrest me then?"

"I expect you already knew that, sir."

"Tell me anyway."

And Alvin, in the chair now, sat forward. "I met with the Campbell boys last week, to let them know I finally had proof of their case."

"I beg your pardon?"

"When they heard, they wanted me to sign a document. To pledge they were the exclusive heirs to all that buried money."

"Well?"

"No doubt you'd fight it in court if I had."

The old man's smile had faded. "We'd hope to settle with them. I'd wager they'd be afraid of our legal arsenal – happy in the end if we offered a mere cut."

"That, or they could end up erasing this entire place."

Billings cleared his throat.

"Not to worry, sir. I didn't sign." Alvin reached over. Slowly, he unzipped the luggage case still at his side, pulling out the antique box that had been waiting. Using both hands, he lifted it, and lay it gently on the desk. The rusted iron glinted red beneath the lamp. "A donation for the Trust," he said simply.

Billings reached forward, knuckles more like blades, and with a jagged grip opened the clasps. The old coins were arranged the same as when Alvin had uncovered them in Virginia – though now they stood only in stacks of half-height, piled like miniature silos. In place of the rotted canvass, he'd stuffed the day's newspaper, to keep them from shifting.

"I don't understand."

"I think you do, sir."

Billings' blue eyes moved slowly back up. "The book of maps?"

"A lost page in back. It took me to Gloucester, Virginia."

"Proof after all," he murmured.

"One more thing, sir. This box was full when I found it."

Now Billings blinked. "Won't you tell me of the other half?"

It was Faye who answered this time. "With its rightful owner, sir."

She sat back. For she and Alvin had arrived at this conclusion together, in their apartment late Sunday afternoon, admiring the coins as they shimmered in the winter sun through the blinds. The fact was, Alvin had spent most of the week trying to convince her to take on the whole sum, reminding her it had originally belonged to long-dead planters they couldn't ever know – that the best thing was to recognize herself as one of its proper beneficiaries – impressing upon her how much she could make off the profit. In the end, she'd settled on half: acknowledging she warranted it, insisting that the wider world – that for which the thieves had intended it – did as well. They'd scooped out her share then, while Dex had played with blocks on the floor, occasionally reaching over to grab one of the coins for himself.

"You see, Mr. Billings?" Alvin was explaining now. "The Campbells liked having me on the case because of who I married. By getting me to sign off, they aimed to block any claim by Faye. They knew she was descendant to a founding conspirator."

"By God." Billings hadn't moved. "And here I thought that was my own trump card."

"Excuse me?"

The old man's smile tilted just so. "My own great-grandfather." He shared a shrug. "Or didn't you realize?"

Alvin swallowed.

"Name of Thaddeus Billings. Friends with Ulysses Brooke, you know."

"I didn't." How had he missed it? Hadn't the family had long been in New York? "You're kidding," he managed. "Sam Billings had his own claim to the funds?"

Charles chuckled lightly, even as his words still hung in the air. "Why else would Brooke have given my family the maps for safekeeping in the first place?" He looked again over at Faye, whose own smile was once more at the corner of her lips. "Tell me though – what have I done to deserve your fine treatment?"

"It's what you've done your whole life, sir," she replied. "Working toward the kind of nation that my ancestor, Cato Brooke, would have wanted to build."

Finally, the old man's façade began to crack. "I fear you think too highly of me." His gaze wavered. He shook his head. "I was always too busy fixating on the role my own great-grandfather played in all this, ever to consider the notion of another. All these years, young lady – your own family as deserving of wealth as my own."

Faye's smile hadn't left. "Both of us descendants of thieves then."

Billings paused. "I'd always preferred 'vigilantes.'" Now he pushed up from his chair one more time, and stepped carefully across the carpet, towards one of the bookshelves on the wall. There, high above the endless tomes, sat a series of silver frames – more black-and-white images like those lining the hall – and reaching up, his suit jacket riding up to expose a withered, blue-veined wrist, he reached for one in the corner, lowering it down so they could see.

Here was a portrait in soft glow, a young man in soldier's uniform, pins decorating his khaki lapels, tie tucked smartly into his shirt, clear intelligent eyes beneath fine slicked hair, and cheekbones like stilts. He was greeting them with a guarded expression, a smile just as restrained as Charles' grin was now, and looking between the two – the antique photograph and the living breathing legend before him – Alvin wondered when exactly that cutting, young figure had grown old. "I wasn't aware you'd served, sir."

"But I didn't," came the quiet reply. "It was my boy who went off to fight, not me." Charles lingered on the frame another moment. "I lived like my father, not my son. No war of my own. Forced instead to craft my own purpose, to leave others to do the fighting for me." He eased the photo back up, methodically, intentionally – like a sacred Torah at the altar, Alvin thought – not that Charles Billings would know a thing about that. Its spot on the shelf was smooth, he noticed, with none of the dust mites that surrounded the other frames, from all the times Billings must've reached to grab it. From all the times he'd reached to mourn.

When the old man turned back, his blue eyes were welling, and he cleared his throat. He gripped Alvin's shoulder, speaking more hoarsely than before, his shield of a smile returned. "You're like me, then, are you? Spared from our great American project of war?"

"That's right, sir. They missed my number when it came round."

"Though your father was called up."

"He was."

"Parades and attention and all that." He angled back toward the desk, using his hand for support, sidling to the chair. "That was the philanthropy for me, you see. I'd once assumed I would hand it off. Alas, my sister Caroline has passed. Her children I scarcely know. My daughter's got a life of her own out West – a producer for the pictures, if you can believe it. And my son..." He offered a slight shrug. "He was my father's favorite, of course, the eldest grandchild. Thank God the old man was already gone by the time the war had its way." His words slowed, as he seemed to recall some distant scene, as if he were conjuring it back. "Had I listened to what my father counseled, the lad would've been saved. Instead, I helped my boy enlist, thinking it the very chance I'd never been granted myself." Billings clasped his hands once more on the desk. "With this Trust I've tried to make up for it ever since."

CHAPTER 47

New York City
November 1932

Against his better judgment, Sam had allowed for a Board of Directors.

He'd resisted for years, of course. It was only once he'd begun drifting off during afternoon sessions at the office, his own forgetfulness about appointments undeniable, that his hand had been forced. At least Charlie was one of the members, he often thought. At least the meetings afforded a chance to spend time with his son.

Still, today had been his idea: kowtowing to the fad of moral capitalism, no longer just through donations, but with some action of their own. They were to dedicate a new monument to New York's old Union heroes, now that the last of them would soon be all gone. Despite the board's protest, he'd insisted on the firm donating the funds in full, using his share of the vote to steamroll their dithering. He didn't yet tell them he had a far bigger plan than this – one with more of a splash than they could imagine. Better first to get this little endeavor out of the way.

Frankly, what could they say? That he'd spent a lifetime fleeing the memory of his own father? That he was aiming to make up for it now? They wouldn't dare. In the end, they'd ceded voicing their concerns to Charles, who'd merely patted his shoulder, nodding earnestly with those shimmering blue eyes, as if Sam need only see reason – before surrendering easily.

So it was he sat now in the back of the Model J – its plush red leather customized to his specification, a colored chauffeur up front – gazing out its rain-soaked windows. He'd spent the whole ride listening to old Finn Hughes whine. "If you could only explain to me, sir, how a war memorial might possibly increase profits."

"It's do-gooder stuff, old boy. Lands the sculptor a commission. Scrounges up some good press right when they all despise us." He leaned his head against the fogged-up pane, and spotted the statue coming into view. "Ah. You see? All this time, and it lives on."

"What's that, sir?"

"The damned war."

"It's only a decade past."

"Not that one," Sam muttered.

Emily at least had agreed it was a good idea. "The firm's fragile in the public eye," she'd concluded. "After the run on the banks – the bread lines – the latest numbers."

"Yes. You understand."

She'd nodded. "Give them a new image. Remind them of who you are. They've invited you on the pretense of honoring others: they'll end up honoring you instead."

They were arriving at the park now, and he peered out at the cutaway off Third Avenue, where rows of wicker chairs had been assembled and heads turned to see him step out. The car slowed; the rain, thankfully, had stopped. One of the aides opened his door, and he obliged the crowd. It was audacious certainly. Dedicating a war memorial when he hadn't even served.

Emily was already there, in a wrap of finest monkey fur trim, extending her arm, escorting him up the dais to the statue of the hour: an American soldier, in a uniform vague and timeless. Behind her were the children, Charlie and Caroline, each with sons and daughters of their own now, too small to be paying attention – except for Charlie Jr., blonde and clear-eyed, knees locked in the front row, knickers freshly creased, so that Sam couldn't help but smile. He took his place before the crowd, men in dark suits, women in furs like Emily's, new titans for the new century, ready to prostrate themselves upon the altar of the old.

***

It was later that afternoon, resting in his study back home, when the double doors rattled, and Sam looked up. The afternoon light remained strong as his son came treading in, shutting the door tentatively – the same as when he'd been a boy, as if he were afraid of disturbing important work – making his way past the shelves, across the padded Afghan rug toward Sam's desk. He looked rather different from when he'd left for California, and Sam shifted a container of crystal pens aside to get a better look. The boy's brow had been creased by the western sun, his fine yellow hair turned a touch gray. In truth though, it was something deeper – something humbled, something chastened – that was all too evident in his fine blue eyes. They still danced as he nodded hello, but there was an edge to them now, as if he saw more than what was in front of him: not just opportunities, but the sucker punches that lay in wait around every corner.

"You picked up the style out there," Sam observed, as Charles crossed his legs, revealing a pair of white leather saddle shoes, a perfect match for his linen suit.

"I've disappointed you, father."

"Not in the way you suppose, dear boy."

"I don't follow."

"Only in that you turned your back on what was yours." Sam placed his pipe down in its brass stand, molded to look like a galloping mare. "It's hard enough to make it in this life. It's nigh impossible if you don't squeeze out every bit that's offered."

His son sat forward. "The taxi business was a fine model. It should've worked."

"A useless sentiment in the world of dollars and cents."

"It was the engines. They weren't suited to the dry air."

"You needn't explain it."

"We were in need of a bigger fleet – and spares of everything: tires, casting parts. Only by the time I realized it, the investors wouldn't bite, not even with my name." His voice grew hollow. "Not with all that's occurred."

"You could've come to me."

"After you'd warned me off?"

"Ah. But it's past now, Charlie." Slowly, Sam pushed up from the desk. He met his son's eye. "I asked you here for a reason."

"Yes?"

"You've mentioned the country's troubles. They're on my mind as well."

Charles was nodding. "People are starving, father. I saw it on the transcontinental. Children waving, holding out their palms for crumbs. It's why they look to Roosevelt for help."

But Sam brushed that off with a wave. "The Progressives have been touting their wares since Theodore was the only Roosevelt there was."

"You've something better?"

"We establish a philanthropic wing of our own – here – now." Sam let the words sit a moment. Folks would assume it was his old age, he suspected. The New Dealers would brag it had been the strength of their arguments on behalf of collective action. But he knew the truth: that he'd never truly accepted how he'd gotten here. That in the end, a part of him still wanted to try and get somewhere else. "Recipients for aid would apply, of course – men we'd recruit to compete. Those selected for a grant would be supported, educated, placed in apprenticeships. Not granted mere jobs, mind you, but proper vocations. The other charities – Red Cross, Henry Street – they're operated by reformers. They offer only handouts – no prospects, no pathways to status and station. We'd meet people where they are, at the East docks, in back of their delivery trucks, outside their Yiddish theaters, treating them not as lost souls, but as our bottom line."

"You sound cold as ice."

Sam laughed. "Not at all. It's the same profit motive as ever. That's what'll set us apart. For it's profit that's purposeful, and do-gooding that leads to bug-eyed children by the rail tracks. We'll tell them outright they're an investment."

"And if they don't earn enough to pay back their debt?"

"We'll have them sign contracts. Enforceable by law. We'll use higher standards than any bank: requiring letters of introduction from their schoolhouses, foremen on their sites, chiefs of their union squads. We'll administer tests to boot – I've already hired Columbia's men to help us write them – interviews too. We'll be offering partnership, not aid." Sam grinned. "And you, Charles. You're the man I need."

His son's jaw tightened.

"This isn't what you wanted, I know, accepting my help." Sam stepped round the desk. "But come," he announced. "You'll even have your own headquarters." And he beckoned that they go, before Charlie could question further.

They passed down the hall then, and into one of the new automated elevators to the street. A signal system had been erected on the corner, an ugly little lighthouse, square and bulbous, but Sam ignored it, no matter the cars blasting their horns. "Let them grumble," he proclaimed. Together, they clutched their fedoras, braced against the dropping temperatures, past an army of beggars that lined the way: curled up on church steps, bindle sticks as pillows, the stench of human rot soaking the breeze. Until the air opened up, and the light diminished. Their striving city was growing up, Sam thought. Some complained about the claustrophobia – how once proud boulevards had become cramped back alleys – but to him, that was nonsense. Man's ability to block out the heavens was a testament to his prowess, not an indictment of his vanity, and he craned his neck, careful not to lose his balance, taking in the jagged horizon like a dreamscape: water towers like basilicas, radio antenna like new stems of spring, windows melding with the sky.

The building looked like a palace already, nearly complete: dwarfing the flats winding off at its edge, stained brick tenements waiting to be bought out, more like antique toys than neighbors. His own walls were all spotless splendor, smooth limestone he'd shipped from the backwoods of Indiana. The facade gleamed, the bronze doors too. "'Billings Trust,'" he explained. "Old Finn Hughes took care of its naming this morning: as of opening bell, validated by the Revenue Act, sanctioned by the New York Council."

Charlie raised his eyebrows. "What'd you knock down to make way?"

"No big loss, my boy. Just a set of old stables – losing money by the minute."

"Someone's livelihood."

"A collateral of capitalism."

"In these times no less?"

"Especially in these times, Charles." He pointed upwards. "At the start of the fiscal year, you'll control fifty percent of all our funds. When I meet my end, that figure doubles."

"I thought this was merely to be a wing of the brokerage."

Sam lowered his voice. "When the time comes, this 'wing' will subsume the whole enterprise. I've already had my barristers draw up the papers."

And now Charles turned. His lips were tight. "I won't disappoint you, father."

"It doesn't bear saying, son. You never once have."

CHAPTER 48

New York City
December 1941

Sam resented Christmas. He always had.

He resented the whole season really, enduring it like one enormous Sabbath that simply wouldn't end, and he leaned against the lace curtains of the parlor room, tapping his fingers on the sill, reminding himself that his family was gathered, that his days at the firm were behind him, that even the philanthropy's coffers weren't his for fretting over anymore. A new couple had just rounded onto the block below, he in cheap single-crease pants, she in rabbit fur dyed to look like mink. Their arms were linked, and inevitably, they slowed in front of Sam's gate, salivating over the stonework. So many of his peers' homes had been swallowed up: easy conquests for museum boards, schools, foreclosures too – fortunes no more than sandcastles in the end.

"Father?"

He blinked.

"Father – please. You oughtn't stand there – the draft is too strong."

He turned. It was Charles, grown fashionable in middle age, fine hair slicked back, pocket square folded just right, brown border over its white silk. Even his handsome face was no longer a distraction, taking on an earnestness at last.

If only Charlie Jr. would hurry up along the same path. Here came his grandson now, joining from the next room, a force of striving energy that reminded Sam of his own. His blonde hair was a touch too long; his blue eyes seemed constantly to be smiling – just like his pop, really – looks that made it all too easy.

Sam reached for his tumbler and eased down to read. Alas, even that was no solace. For of late, even the *Journal* was alternating between obeisance to Churchill and Roosevelt. "They always forget," he murmured. "Every war – every single one – all just the same."

Charles smiled softly, condescendingly.

"Boys of every century..."

Now his grandson wandered over. "Well why not?" he grinned. "Who else to defend the world from itself?"

Sam stared back up. "You don't mean it."

"I do." Another pause. "I've enlisted, grandfather. It's time you know."

"Come now."

"Don't be angry."

"What of Harvard?" He straightened up from the chair with a grunt.

But it was Charles who cut back in. "I'm on board with the boy. I didn't stay at Harvard myself."

"You left for business, not war!"

"At your insistence."

"Limbs intact, silk threads glistening. Yet still you complain!" Except it was then that Sam stumbled. It lasted only a second – his hand found the armrest – but there was no covering what had occurred.

"Father." Charles' voice changed in an instant. "Shall I take your drink?"

He waved them both away. These two men before him – his replacements, he suddenly thought. "Certainly not," and he turned toward the next room and the stairs, already sifting through names in his mind: luminaries he would call come morning, men who'd long ago tripled their investments thanks to his firm. Men who'd make certain young Charlie Jr. stayed at a desk for the duration.

For now, he simply needed rest. His chest was throbbing, and as he gripped the balustrade at the stairwell's base, his head grew light, and his mind wandered, grappling with what his grandson must think, working to recall what it had been to be his age. There were flashes of his own boyhood then – flashes from before the days of the firm, before the book of maps, before even his own father had been killed. Until at last, Sam reached the next story, and moved toward the bedroom – to catch his breath, to still his heart – to close the door, and muffle the chit-chat from below.

He lay back, feeling the leathery folds of his chin, listening to his wheeze come out in stitches, studying his wingtip shoes, his arthritic fingers atop his waist, his knuckles like paper clips half-straightened. He'd long since known the humiliations of his years, yet somehow still they shocked him, and he closed his eyes.

The ache in his chest traveled to his head. Was it guilt over Charles Jr.? Or did it go all the way to fear – that after all he'd built, all he'd accomplished, he'd somehow ended up an old man like any other: his charm come to nothing but a shadow of times gone past, his own grandson ignoring his every word?

He could make out Emily's voice now, floating in amid the others. She was showing off the latest curtains, pointing out the maids' clothes dryer, skimming the surface of life as surely as ever, never bothering to inquire what held it up. And yet – hadn't that always been her strength? Every napkin folded, every spoon gleaming, every silver strand on her head intact.

He ought to have told her more, he thought. He ought to have delivered the truth about what he'd done, sat her down and shared it directly. He'd always assumed he would one day, yet always too there'd been reason to wait, the sense she wouldn't believe it any more than anyone else; worse, that if she did, she'd turn away.

He opened his eyes once more, and took in the bedroom. Here, in this city as grand as any since Rome, diamonds and sapphires sat atop the dresser, gilded mirrors on the wall. For a moment, he wondered vaguely, distantly, if he should try and sit back up, keep his eyes open a few minutes longer. To see even if he could.

But no. He was tired, and so he curled up like a boy once more – a boy that was still somewhere inside, he thought vaguely, beneath the liver spots and varicose veins, beneath the sags and crags and pathetic wisps of hair.

Escape was at last upon him. And he let himself be.

CHAPTER 49

New York City
Present Day

Faye walked in from the kitchen, more agile than she'd been in years, thanks to the new hip. Her white hair was pulled back and wrapped in a band of turquoise beads. She wore a purple, wide-knit woolen sweater down to her thighs, using it to dry wine glasses from the night before. "There's someone at the door."

"Probably the press," Alvin sighed. "The last one asked me to let him stop by."

"You said yes?"

"I didn't think he'd follow through." He stood. "I could still get in trouble you know. There's no statute of limitations on concealing evidence."

"What about taking evidence for yourself, and living off the interest? You think the press would like writing about that?"

"Don't even joke."

"Oh, Alvin – they want a puff piece, not a hit job! Think of the headlines – '*Former agent protected Billings Trust! Stood up to bigots!*'" She was laughing. "You'd be hip."

"Not to the bureau."

At least the requests were calming down. When the Campbell brothers had first gone to the papers, he'd gotten nearly a hundred calls a day, always answering "no comment," refusing even to admit the legend of Ulysses Brooke was true. Clay and Clem had started slinging their accusations on cable news – asserting he was on the take, bribed by the Trust to keep quiet – that he had secret proof that would get them their money.

Thank God no one had believed a word.

In time, their story had grown tired. Eventually, they'd both died, and the press had drifted on. Now, with Charles Billings gone too, Alvin had assumed the attention would fade for good. Mostly it had.

He went to the door. There was a young man out on the stoop – barely ready to shave, a tweed blazer too light for the chill. Alvin frowned. "May I help?"

"Mr. Alvin Starkman?"

"Go on."

"I'm Bill Basley – we spoke on the phone." The fellow pulled out a card, solid, engraved, stenciled with a hotshot masthead from the *New York Times*.

"A big fish!" Alvin chuckled.

"You mind if I record us, sir?" Young Basley held up a fancy little machine.

"All you like," Alvin answered. "Though I've still got nothing to say." At that, something buzzed in the journalist's pocket. "You know, young man, back at the bureau, I'd never have let myself get distracted from a witness standing right in front of me."

"So you're a witness, Mr. Starkman?" He'd looked back up. "Does that mean there was a crime?"

"Nice try."

"And what do you say to those who allege your own wife's family took part in the original heists?"

Alvin laughed. He nodded goodbye, and closed the door.

Back inside, he saw Faye had returned to the kitchen, and he paused, looking toward the built-ins closer in. There, in the upper corner, nestled between frames of Dexter growing up, was a biography of Charles Billings. Alvin had bought it on a whim. The cover showed the man as he'd been right around the time they'd met, stately, already snow-haired, in a blue blazer and a scarlet tie. "When's the last time we mailed off a donation?" he called out.

"To Billings Trust?" Faye answered back. "Couple of weeks."

Alvin nodded. "Let's send another." And though he wasn't sure if she'd heard, he moved toward his desk, took out his checkbook, and found a pen.

***

It was the following winter that found Alvin watching through the window as Dexter stepped from his car, a sporty little sedan, and made his way from the sidewalk. He was elegant these days – taller than Alvin had ever been – with coffee skin, close-cropped hair, eyes that were never fooled. Just like Faye's.

The bell rang, and he answered it at once. "How was Birmingham?" he asked with a hug.

"These conferences are all the same, pop."

But Alvin merely shrugged, and took his coat from the hook. "Tell me about it anyway."

"I had *tapas*."

"Spanish food?"

"Took a tour of the synagogue."

"We still talking about Birmingham? I've been there, you know."

Dexter chuckled. "Kids were marching for gun control while I was in town."

"No tiki torches?"

"Stop it."

"The cops left you alone?"

"C'mon pops – that's mom talking, not you."

"Proud to deliver her lines, then," – and despite himself, Alvin grew misty.

They'd reached the car.

"You alright, dad?"

"It's three months next week."

Dexter nodded. "I know."

It had been sold as routine valve surgery – though of course there was nothing routine about pushing 80. Alvin recalled how she'd been on that last day, holding his hand tight even then, from the hospital bed, asking if he might find a way to visit the Met without her. "Remember?" she'd mouthed. "Remember it all?" She'd gestured for water – wanted to know if he could re-fill the bottle.

When he'd come back, her eyes had been still, her hand drooped down at the mattress' side. The machines had started beeping.

"Dad?"

"I'm ready now," and he opened the passenger door, sliding in. The radio sprang to life; he hit the knob to silence it.

The drive was just a few blocks, past parents and strollers, hipsters nursing coffees near the shops, and Alvin recalled how much it had all changed. When he'd been Noah's age, every one of these corners had echoed with pink Spaldings – stoopball, stickball; he'd race home from the other boys only when his father made him.

Of course, that had only happened for special visitors: strolling over from the IRT, a few with their Studebakers parked a foot off the curb, hoods red and sleek in the fall afternoons. The only other folks who'd ever come by were Jews of course, fast-paced and familiar, and always from Brooklyn. Not those special fellas: they spoke like newsmen – consonants like waves, voices like their engines' purrs – some even traveling down from Westchester in their loose-fitting slacks. They were what his mother had called real Americans; "Atta boy, Emil!" they would call out, patting his father's bushy-haired pate, making fun of how malaria had taken half his locks back on the front, sporting proud paunches and tortoise-rim spectacles, even juggling an unloaded Luger that one of them had brought back from the Rhine.

One morning, Alvin's father had found him in his room, and had clapped his hands to his knees. "We're off to our luncheon, Alvie," he'd said with a grin. "Anniversary of our homecoming, son," and he'd paused. "How'd you like to tag along?"

He'd raced out the door.

The legion hall back then had been located in the very same school they were visiting today, Alvin was sure – P.S. 266, home to his own sixth grade, and to his father's job at the high school. The gym had been draped with flags, its whole floor hidden by tables. Alvin remembered how when they'd entered, the vets had been singing the anthem, and how he'd piped loudly along, hearing his own voice amidst theirs, knowing they were in this together, just the way his grandmother had always told him: recounting how she'd landed at Ellis Island on the last day of the last century – "all so you could grow up free, *bubbala* – " her eyes crinkling so tight they were almost invisible.

Only when he'd rejoined the men for the ride home that afternoon, had the spell been broken – and only then because a nearby engine had backfired, nasty as a firecracker, and he'd felt them all suddenly flinch. The knuckles on the large fellow next to him had even gone white, as the other vets patted his shoulder. "What's buzzin' there, Jack?" one of them had asked. "You okay?"

"Thought I spotted Gestapo, is all," he'd cracked, and after a moment, the others had roared.

It would always continue like that when they returned to the house – more jokes, more back clapping – right into their farewells, when Alvin's father would thank them for coming, and they'd hug their goodbyes. "It was a dandy of a visit," his dad would remark, his glasses fogging up. "I hope you saw so, Alvie. I hope you saw that."

He blinked.

The car had stopped. The years vanished. Dexter was looking back at him. "We're here," he said – and Alvin nodded, glad they were still in the neighborhood, he realized, grateful to his son for moving the family so close.

"I just hope I don't bore these little ones to death," he answered now, shaking free his thoughts, urging his mind back to the moment.

"Just tell them about what you've seen – about the twentieth century, what it was all about."

"You make it sound like ancient Rome."

"It might as well be."

"Noah knows I'm coming?"

"He's thrilled most of all." Dexter turned off the ignition, undoing Alvin's seatbelt for him – leading them in, signing in with a receptionist, moving toward the classroom.

It was the same as it had always been really, mid-century cinderblock, watercolors lining the halls. Not so different from his own time, Alvin thought: maps on easels, one-piece wooden desks, a teacher asking the students to gather round, offering a round of applause for their guest.

He spotted Noah among them then, beaming proudly, and noticed they were all holding tablets. "Today's a day for listening, kids. Let's put those down." It was his classroom for the morning, after all, and he'd teach them as he chose. "Easier to pay attention this way, is all," he explained, next asking for a show of hands. "Who knows what country this is?"

"America!" they clamored. "The United States!"

He laughed. "That's right. And I'm here to tell you about how it's changed. To let you know it's not done – that it never will be. And to show you that's what makes it special."

CHAPTER 50

New York City
March, June 1864

Sam's pudgy legs couldn't quite make it over the chaise, little knees like indented cushions themselves. Yet young as he was, he already knew the truth of his father and the men like him. That it was up to them to save the nation. To forge a land of liberty, absent venom and mutiny. To stand for patriots everywhere.

Until now, he'd known pa only through the studio portrait on the mantle, its wooden frame worn dull by how tightly his mother clutched its sides. But here was the picture come to life, brass buttons in full color, brown locks too, mouth unfolding into a smile. On furlough before the spring campaign, father had raced home on the very first wagon convoy he could find.

He spun back now, and little Sam squealed – enough to make his pa chuckle in turn, bending down, nuzzling his knuckle between Sam's cheek and his shoulder. He lifted the boy up, and together they sang the latest sensation: *Battle Cry of Freedom*, just the same as the soldiers marching toward the 'rebs.

It was the happiest moment of young Sam's short life, and he could barely keep up the tune, laughing too hard instead, gasping for air amid his delight. His father's hands, impossibly large, curled round his belly, his voice seeming to make the whole room vibrate. Sam was too young, of course, to know any better, and he grinned with the ease only a child can summon, free from any sense of an end.

Except that end it did, and all too soon. For it was only two months later, when spring resembled summer, and Sam's fourth birthday had passed, that he was back on that same chaise, watching the older lads through the window. It was the fifth inning of their game, and he'd relished every pitch: boys gangly and jagged and barely older than he. The roadsides were jammed with pushcarts, but to him, it might as well have been the Colosseum, and he gaped as they threw the baseball the whole length of the block – until his mother hurried in for their regular trek to the telegraph office. He followed at her knee then, palm smooshed against hers, dodging trouser cuffs and hems, eyes stinging from manure flung up by the men's boots.

The building impressed: trim cornice, wick lanterns, ladies within. Its air was singed with burnt copper from the wires, tickling Sam's nostrils until he giggled, and his mother had to smack his brow to keep him still. The sounds were everywhere: clicking, clacking, like a million little echoes, connecting this one corner by magic to every other one in the world – and there, at the center of it all, the man in the straw-ribboned hat, bellowing atop his raised platform, holding the square of paper that had only just been inked.

His voice was staccato, cold, and Sam had trouble paying heed, distracted by the tiled ceiling, the hooks for lamps, the smudges of bird waste on the rafters. So that when it arrived, he missed the tally from a place called Petersburg – then the name *James Billings* called out with the others – and the curdling sob that escaped his mother's lips.

He had to be yanked away as she stepped back, her palm suddenly like scuffed ice, moving quick now, past the beggars on the stoops, the hirelings emptying vats of slop, through the market – men hawking garlic, hucksters promising elixirs – brogue like scales, Teutonic edges brittle as glass, waves from the Orient, each one sounding as fast as telegrams themselves.

His mother was marching in silence now, cheeks burnt red, and he noticed the ever-tightening of her grip, an ever-quickening of her pace, so that while he never remarked upon it, it was here, now, amid the sparkling June sun and the beating heart of New York, that Samuel Billings, not yet five, began to apprehend. It came as he caught sight of other little boys too, women tugging them also, winded by shallow breaths that seemed to catch like broken wheels, some hardly moving at all, their children left to hover at their sides instead, while their shoulders shook, heads bowed to their knees, sogging silhouettes dotting the streets like fresh flags of mourning.

When they arrived home, she finally let go, and began to shudder herself, crumpling to the floor, and Sam saw that she was weeping, this woman who'd held him up and guided him forward, turning into a ghost before his eyes.

So that with each new instant, he felt something else, boiling deep in his chest, a child's rage at seeing the world for what it really is, at the silent farewell from the man he'd assumed to be a god.

He walked to her after that, and placed his little hand on her cheek – stood at the edge of the chaise where he'd been with his father, and opened his mouth too. And for the first and final time, he cried over all that was never to be.

CHAPTER 51

Richmond, Virginia
March 1861

The wheelchair's rubber casings were supposed to make it more mobile, and Ulysses found that if he used the wall to push off – his ancient muscles straining – he was able to reach the cell's corner. He could catch a sliver of sun through the bars, and watch as the bats slept in the eaves outside, like a giant beast pulsating, while a few wings flapped at the edges like sentries.

It had been weeks since his letter. Weeks since he'd huddled beneath his wool, scratching away on the pad against his knee, scarcely able to keep his hands from shaking, knowing it was time. That the gamble he'd so long put off had become urgent, the risk of taking action grown worse than doing nothing at all. That the secrets he'd protected all his life would be in jeopardy the instant he was gone.

He'd tracked down the street address as if by Providence, in one of the Yankee journals the guards had let him borrow, coming upon a notice for an old furniture shop, eager to sell its wares at half-rate. He'd gone dizzy seeing the name in print, clutching his brow, reading it over and over again just to be sure. And lifting his pencil, he'd forced the words to come, describing life as he'd come to know it – the way his memories would wrap him up in an embrace – images of Boxwood Grove, soft and green in summers, hard as stone in winters, the way he shook beneath thoughts of Cato, and Rebecca, and his family too.

He wrote of long-ago days then, of watching the horizon while whittling a pole of pine, tracing clouds in the mud, and how at last he'd notice something shimmer. He described squinting toward the mist, to just where the soft hills ended, and the hazy sky began – how the postman would come into view, limping heavily, linen shirt billowing, and getting closer, would wave, loose and eager, so that Ulysses would know everything was alright. "Mr. Clarke!" he'd shout over, narrow knees hopping, wet soil kicking out from behind him. "What word?"

"Take care now, lest you catch the heat!"

"What word?!" Ulysses always repeated.

"And heartily glad to see you too!" would come the reply, though the postman would be chuckling, and he'd reach into his satchel for the latest stack of letters, sealed in the Continentals' red wax. From the top, he'd hand over a folded card of hemp. There was never any mistaking that scribble – bold and slanted and hurried – and now Ulysses' hairs stood on edge just to remember it.

On the move, the first line always proclaimed. *Not to fret: Redcoats running scared.* A few notes about troop movements after that – something about finances.

Then, at the bottom: *Ever yours – And love to all.*

Ulysses would sound it out three times, then once more, relishing the way the ink bled straight through the parchment, picturing his father's fingertips touching the same spots just days before.

"I trust all's well at home?" the postman liked to ask.

"Quite well, sir, now you've come."

"You're a fine boy for saying so." Clarke would strap shut his bag. "Though I'm the token of tidings, mind you, not the Creator that drives them."

In those days, of course, Boxwood Grove had been all Ulysses had ever known: its brick walls towering at the estate's center, fanned by the valley, ringed by orange lilies as bright as the sun; his mother on the portico, hosting the ladies from down the hill, pouring them lemon juice and grog, voices like melodies on the breeze, dresses of pastel, so that Ulysses had known his interruptions better be quick. Quietly, he'd pass up the day's note through the railing.

His mother's eyes would flit neutral at first, but when she'd see what was in his hand, she'd soften indeed. Kissing the card gently, she'd clutch it near her chest, and Ulysses would beam with pride, as if he personally had been responsible for father's safekeeping. Finally, sensing he was in danger of being called up for tea, he'd deliver a bow, letting them gush over his manners as he scurried down the hill.

Cato's cabin had been deep at the property's corner. It'd been part of the slave quarters that lay like a maze – one-room boxes and hardly much more, covered in moss, crowded with the old and the very young – and whenever Ulysses would pass through, they'd stop their work, standing at attention, bowing their heads, as if he were a general inspecting his troops, and not just a boy, flushed beneath his collar.

But then he'd spot Cato!

Invariably his friend would be tending snap beans. A yellow frock always smeared thick with soil. Across the whole of the property, he was the only other boy – slave or no – and he'd spin to see Ulysses, dimpled cheeks puffed out in a grin, brown eyes turned golden in the sun.

"Permission to help, sir?" Ulysses would whisper.

"You've got the devil in you, Master Brooke!"

"Then the devil must fancy chomping beans," and biting into one, Ulysses would stick the other up his nose.

"You're gonna get me sold, Ulysses, I swear."

"I'd buy you back with one of my trusts."

"Don't joke." He'd always beckon his companion to the cabin's rear. "Come, it's safer."

Traipsing alongside the walls, they'd be met with a sour blast of okra, simmering over a dancing white flame, and Cato would kneel by the stones, tilting the kettle atop it coals, hoisting an enormous wooden ladle.

"You first," Ulysses had remarked that very first time – and he wasn't just being kind. There were watchful eyes boring into him, he'd been sure – from the slave women nearby, hair the color of cotton, creases carved deep – and somewhere, deep in his chest, a sensation he couldn't quite distinguish.

"Serving my own self before you? I can't, Ulysses. If your pa were ever to hear…"

So that all at once, the whole place had seemed silent as midnight. The laundry clips had stopped snapping. Half the elders had even looked to be holding their breath. "You cooked it," Ulysses had answered. "You sup with it."

From there, they'd head off down the road, to the wealthiest property in the county – even larger than Boxwood Grove, its half-dozen chimneys piercing the heavens; it'd boasted a copper roof dusted green; a wraparound porch had creaked with the breeze. Its slave quarters had numbered twice as many as back home. The smell of drying tobacco would be dense. Behind the work-wagons, a line-up of pony chaises always circled the main drive. And it was there, beside the lake, they'd find Thaddeus, skipping pebbles softly.

He'd always look up and smile.

Younger than either of them, yet somehow always at ease. Nothing had ever seemed to faze young Tad: neither schoolwork nor the 'pox, not belles, not even chores. For the truth was, he'd long known the path to mischief, without ever finding the one toward trouble: making faces in chapel, then flashing his grin so the governesses wouldn't notice. Ulysses recalled the way his bright blonde hair had waved across his forehead, his green eyes alive, as he'd beckon them over as soon as he saw them arrive.

They'd play into nightfall then, squinting toward the Blue Ridge to the west, swiping invisible swords through the air, as if they were heroes of the Revolution, shouting over the late summer breezes for their infantrymen to follow, imagining themselves grown men, strapping and unbowed, symbols of a new nation. Until eventually, Cato would point to the sun – tucked behind the mountains, its glow no longer attached to any glare – and start to turn away. "Bells already tolled. Field hands are headed to quarters." He'd hold out his hand, leading the other two boys onward, so that as the violet sky darkened, they'd make the walk together.

It was that, then, all of it, which Ulysses preferred writing of now – recalling every bit, as if it'd all only just occurred – as if somehow it were even yet to come. He just wondered if anyone would care. If they even remembered he was here.

He rubbed his eyes, trying to make headway of the memories, to distinguish them from his surroundings now. One of the guards was jiggling an oversized ring of keys behind him, a nasty little man with a pinched nose and a yellow beard, his partner, soft-bellied and slow, staying ever silent. "Time for the warden, Brooke," the guard yipped suddenly, twisting the locks, making a point of binding Ulysses' legs to the chair before wheeling him out.

The room was down the hall, crammed between empty neighboring cells, Ulysses still kept alone, after all this time, lest he warp the minds of any other convicts. There was a desk of cheap pine waiting, and a clock by the window with its coils loose; at its side, a single kerosene lamp had burnt low. Then too, the odor – the fishy, salted fumes of the warden's rotting teeth.

He went by "Love" – short for Lovell – and was constantly tucking in his pudgy chin. He moved with a shuffle that might once have been a strut, had thick arms that might once have been strong, stringy hair that might once have been thick, and when he stood up, he nearly stumbled, forgetting to push back his chair. "'Afternoon, Brooke," he declared too loud.

"Warden."

"Give answer to our queries, and we'd put a halt to harassing you."

Ulysses sighed. The man was less noxious than the guards at least, and by now anyway, these meetings felt more like rehearsing a too-familiar play than suffering through an actual interrogation. "The cash is gone, warden. I spent it as I stole it. The rest of my property remains protected. I've kept up my tax remittance through my attorneys."

"Boxwood slips into disrepair."

Ulysses worked to keep his words nimble, as he'd once done so naturally. "I freed the slaves when my mother passed, sir. As you know."

"I only thank the Lord your poor family was already in Heaven."

Ulysses nodded. It was at this point he'd usually be dismissed. Yet as the seconds passed, neither of the guards approached. His eyes wandered, skimming past the glass paperweight, the telegram papers, the smudged inkwell, all glimpses into a life he could hardly recall. "Well?"

"You've got a visitor," and Ulysses blinked in surprise. "You didn't know?"

"I hoped."

Another moment passed. The warden turned. "He's telling the truth." The guards took hold the chair once more. "We had to make certain there was no plan, you understand."

"How gratifying to know you still fret." But already, Ulysses was being pulled away.

And when the cell door swung open this time, he simply stared.

For how could it be?

The old buckskin breeches were gone, replaced by striped suspenders and checkered gray trousers below. The ribbons had vanished too – how they'd once grabbed the gaze of every gal passing by! – yet there was no mistaking the face: high-flung cheekbones, and easy green eyes. If anything, his hair was even livelier than before, and Ulysses tried to push up from the chair, his own shoulders like rusted-out hinges. "Thaddeus? Not aged a minute?" For once, he felt just as muddled as his age would have him be.

"No, Mr. Brooke," the visitor answered softly. "Tad Billings was my father. My name is James." He leaned over to shake hands. "It's a fine thing to meet you, sir. An honor to be sure."

Ulysses gaped, absorbing the brusque northern accent, plucking at the language like strings on a banjo, sounding as foreign as an Englishman's. "But where then's your father?" he murmured. "Why hasn't he come?"

"He's passed, sir. Just this month." James' eyes shifted downward. "Though he lived to see your letter. It was on his bedside when he left us."

"Ah." Ulysses was winded. "Yes." And he smiled to cover the pain.

No doubt Cato was gone by now too, he thought. After all, there'd been no word from him either: not when Boxwood's slaves had been freed – not any time since. Ulysses refused to ponder the alternative, that his old friend had been trapped inside some new prison instead, cursing him all the while for not taking care of it sooner.

"Sir?"

He looked again. The young man was nearer now, clasping his arm.

"Aren't you alright?"

Ulysses could see the guards growing bored behind them, leaning against the wall, turning away. Sensing his opportunity, he motioned the young man nearer still.

James Billings seemed to understand, and he reached over as if he were lifting the blanket, rearranging it for warmth. Then, in a whisper as near to silent as he could make it, Ulysses gave the instructions he'd planned: the address of the Richmond townhouse, a description of the floorboard at the back, a word about the book of maps underneath. "I've told everyone I squandered it all," he said when he was done. "Yet I never touched a cent."

The young man backed up, eyes rimmed with tears.

The guards still hadn't moved. "Keep it safe," Ulysses said then. "I beseech you. Don't let these Virginians get their hands on it."

The young Billings nodded.

"Go on, then."

Though still, the young man didn't budge. "My father ne'er forgot you, you know." He stood straighter, seeming not to mind if the guards began listening in. "He spoke of you as a prophet, sir. Said that when John Brown was but a babe in the wilderness, it was you who knew what was required." He paused. "I'll be sure my newborn son shall know of you too."

Ulysses sighed. "I'm a dying man. My prophecy none the nearer."

"What prophecy's that, Ulysses?" came the thinner guard's shout.

Except at that, the young Billings turned round for both of them. "The one that's coming hence, sir. No matter your guns." And while they snickered, he stepped from the old man's cell, and right back toward the light.

THE END

ABOUT THE AUTHOR

Matthew Speiser has written numerous pieces grappling with American history, in publications ranging from the Tennessee Historical Quarterly to McSweeney's. His doctoral dissertation examined battles over our national memory of the Civil War, which were waged long after the actual battlefields had quieted. As Chair of the History department at the Marymount School in Manhattan, and trustee on the Garrison Board of Education in Garrison, New York, Dr. Speiser engages with the legacy of America's past every day. He holds a PhD in U.S. History from the University of Virginia. In this, his debut novel, he crafts a riveting tale with historical accuracy and a crackling, vivid style that keeps his audience engaged throughout.

NOTE FROM THE AUTHOR

Word-of-mouth is crucial for any author to succeed. If you enjoyed *Sons of Liberty*, please leave a review online—anywhere you are able. Even if it's just a sentence or two. It would make all the difference and would be very much appreciated.

Thanks!
Matthew Speiser

We hope you enjoyed reading this title from:

BLACK ROSE
writing™

www.blackrosewriting.com

Subscribe to our mailing list – *The Rosevine* – and receive **FREE** books, daily deals, and stay current with news about upcoming releases and our hottest authors.
Scan the QR code below to sign up.

Already a subscriber? Please accept a sincere thank you for being a fan of Black Rose Writing authors.

View other Black Rose Writing titles at
www.blackrosewriting.com/books and use promo code
PRINT to receive a **20% discount** when purchasing.

Made in United States
Orlando, FL
09 February 2023

29734957R00238